The Island

By D.A. McIntosh

The Island

By D.A.McIntosh

ISBN: 13-978-0-0856276-6-9

A special thanks to my friends and family for help with this work of fiction. To my good friends Tony, the Donkey, (Cynthia) Susana the white Peacock and many others, I wish to thank them for their support and the use of their make believe personas for my books. A special thanks to my wife and Cynthia for proofreading my books.

I have always been told that books of fiction are written to help the reader get into another world, a fantasy world you might say, a world to take the reader away from their life and transport them into a world of make believe. I hope this work of fiction is one of those that you enjoy and will read over and over. It is my pleasure to provide you with the transporter to take you to another world.

This book is a work of fiction and it takes place in the future, in the year 2031 to be exact. Technology has progressed to a point of unbelievable, but not as far as the movie 'Terminator'. The things I talk about in this book are a possibility in the future, and possibly sooner than we think.

We, as a technological world, believe that if you can dream it, then it can be created. This work of fiction has our heroes dealing with things that seem real, but which are not. It may seem confusing at first, but read on and you will understand that fact can be fiction and fiction can be fact; it is only a matter of time. Enjoy life, because the future has not been written yet. We don't know what it holds.

The story takes place in part on Ducie Island. The island is real although it is much smaller than depicted in this book. Ducie Island is located in the Pitcairn Island chain in the South Pacific and is the property of Peru. It is a bird sanctuary with many rare, tropical birds. The island does not have airports or any structures; it is uninhabited except for birds. I chose this island because of its structure and location and hope that when the movie is made of this book that the island is only used as a back drop and no human steps on it.

This book is dedicated to the men and women who have served their country as soldiers, sailors, police, firemen, border patrol, CIA, FBI and all the others providing protection to our great nation. They cannot foresee the future any more than you or I so treat them with respect and cooperate when you are asked; they are here to protect you and your family and may be limited in resources.

Some sacrificed a little and others sacrificed everything; their service and dedication will never be forgotten.

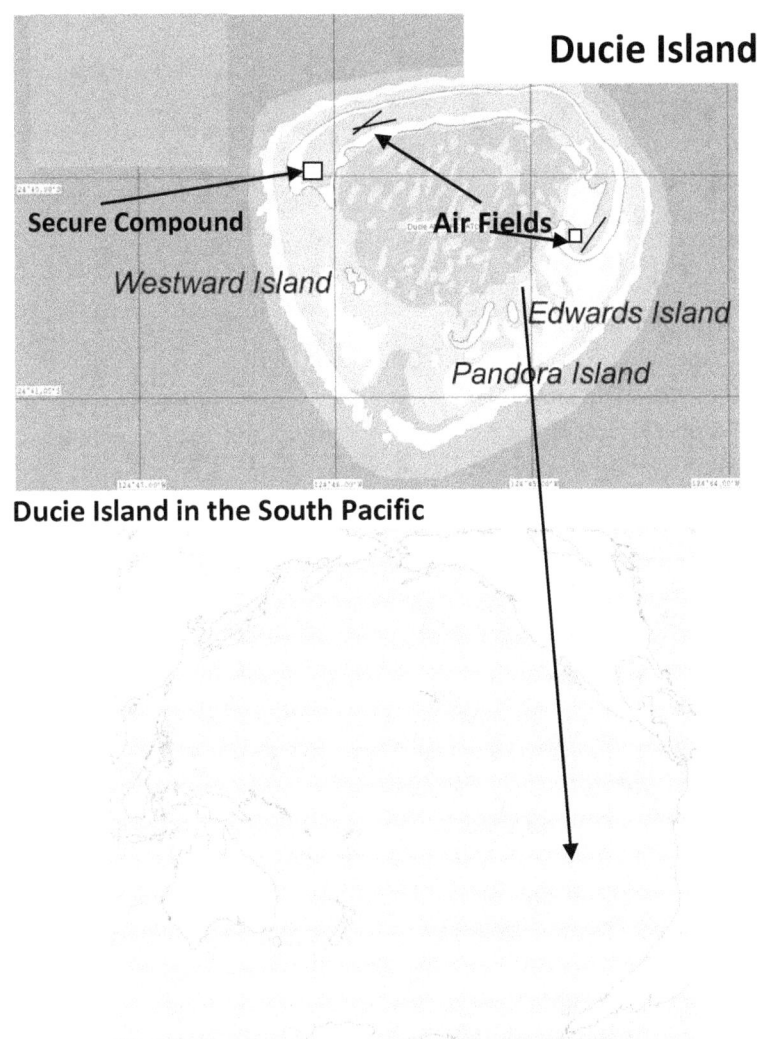

Ducie Island

Secure Compound **Air Fields**

Westward Island

Edwards Island

Pandora Island

Ducie Island in the South Pacific

Location of Ducie Island in the South Pacific

Contents

Characters

Vince Landers – University Professor
Morgan Fields – Female student
Diane Norris – Female student
Frederick 'Freddy' Carlson – Male student
Bryce McClelland – Male student
Edwin Kelsey – Archeologist
Amelia Earhart – Pilot
Fred Noonan – Aviation Navigator
Robert Heinz – Scientist and researcher
Susan Wright – Student from UCLA
Captain Bryan Redmond – USAF F-4 Fighter Pilot
Fran Snow – Commercial pilot
Rhonda Lowery – Biologist
Detective Pamela Becks – Albuquerque Police
Detective Lucy Grayson – Albuquerque Police
Davin Pierce –CIA Field Operative/retired US Army
Connie Pierce – Retired FBI agent and wife of Davin
Josh Randal – Director CIA
Stephanie Randal – Wife of Josh, ex FBI agent, ex-Miami Police officer
Josh Pierce – Son of Davin and Connie, student
Amber Pierce – Twin sister of Josh
Adam Cruz - Assistant Director of Operations CIA
Rocky Soto – Ex Director of R&D, CIA
Tony Sanford –President of the United States
Captain Visalia – All around bad guy

Supporting Characters

Horatio Soto – Japanese Soldier
Frank Sherman – Captain US Army Reserve
David Henderson – Commander US Navy
Todd 'Bear' Henderson – Admiral US Navy
Joanne Morgan – Retired CIA Field Operative
John Polson – Retired Secret Service Agent
Ashley Peterson – Retired Director CIA
Darrell Mitchell – Past President of the United States
Marvin Sanchez – Commander USN Fighter Pilot
Julie Deeks – Captain US Navy Fighter Pilot
Tony – Donkey
Susana – White Peacock
Madeline Graves – FBI Agent
Helen Owens – Director CIA R&D
Hamilton 'Ham' Carver – Police Detective
Max 'Gundog' Hunter – Annapolis Police Officer
Danny Baker – Annapolis Police Sergeant
Raymond Dawg, 'Bloodhound' Captain USN
Michelle Morrison – Nurse at Annapolis Hospital
Robert Holt – White House Doctor
Charles 'Charlie' Brown – Detective Arlington Police
Arlene Ramsey – Detective Arlington Police
Jenkins – Arlington Police officer
Melodie Morris – CIA analyst
Millie – White House secretary
Frank Sorenson - Secretary of Defense
Daniel Robertson - Admiral, Atlantic Fleet Commander
Manny Reagan – General, 82nd Airborne Commander

Where did the years go?

Time always seems to fly when you are working or having fun. Where does that time go? Time travels like a mighty river flowing down stream, only diverting when hitting an immovable object such as a rock or bend in the terrain. It continues flowing and is gone from sight within seconds never stopping. Like the river, time flows forward, never turning back, not knowing what will happen at the next turn in its quest.

Life on this earth also has a beginning and an end, flowing like a river with control; but do we really have a lot of control in how things turn out? The river has a beginning and an end also; but where it flows, it has no or little control. Life throws curves at us all through our lives and we make decisions based on those curves; hopefully, we make the right decisions.

The twins were born and things around the world were not stable, but calm for a while. Davin and Connie endured the terrible twos with the twins and then it was on to kindergarten, elementary school and eventually high school. Both kids loved school and excelled in their studies. They were very competitive, both in sports and academics, but most of the time just between each other. Both were promoted ahead of their peers and soon graduated early from high school and immediately went to college, but not just any college; they were both accepted at MIT, Massachusetts Institute of Technology. This made both Davin and Connie extremely happy and they provided lots of support to their children's pursuit of higher education.

Meanwhile, Davin continued to work with the CIA as Assistant Director of Covert Operations under the command of his best friend, Josh Randal, as CIA Director. Connie worked as liaison to Homeland Security out of the Washington office of the FBI as liaison to Homeland Security in the continuing fight against terrorism and was point on the war against Industrial Espionage. Stephanie Randal no longer was a Field Operative with the company, but instead was working as an analyst.

Life was good overall for everyone; and then the day finally came, when Davin and Connie walked out of their offices for the last time. At least they thought they had. Retiring from the largest Intelligence organization and the FBI did not always guarantee you were fully retired. Like the military, you were subject to call back in case of a crisis which you had special interest in or had needed knowledge or training. But for now, retirement meant a relaxing trip to Kauai and drinks on the beach.

A longtime friend and National Security Advisor, Anthony Sanford, had been elected President of the United States. There had not been any attacks on the country by terrorists in years, mostly because of better intelligence gathering leading in the arrest of suspected ISIS members and other terrorist groups before they could cause trouble.

The economy and safety of the country were two of the promises that Sanford spoke of during his campaign and he was following through with his promise. The country was safe, the economy was growing, and his national support could not have been better. He brought jobs back to the country by imposing high taxes on companies that sent work overseas which forced them to bring their manufacturing facilities back home. He made it cheaper to employ Americans than to send their jobs overseas. But even he made enemies in his climb to the most powerful office on the planet and a few more after getting there.

Technology normally grows exponentially during a military conflict or war, but times had changed. There was a war going on, however, this war was not one of conflict or of killing in the sense of people dying, but a war to see who was able to make the next great product before their competitors did. The first to market would win the market share and controlling interest. Industrial espionage was one of the ways the big businesses gained the upper hand.

It wasn't only big business looking to get the upper hand, it was the government too. They needed new and better means to gather intelligence, which led all the "alphabet organizations" to establish their own Research and Development departments and hire the scientists and technicians to develop gadgets to help gather intelligence. The CIA wasn't one to be left behind. They hired and paid top dollar to have some of the brightest scientists on their payroll. Unfortunately, being paid top dollar did not promise loyalty.

Chapter 1 Study The Past To Learn About The Future

The University of New Mexico (UNM) was founded in 1889 and is presently located on about eight hundred acres just off Route 66 near the heart of Albuquerque. UNM offers more than two hundred degree and certificate programs, ranging from baccalaureate, master, and doctoral degrees to specialized certifications. Among the university's programs is a graduate program in Archeology. This program has both in classroom and field studies at various archeological sites around New Mexico, Arizona and Texas. Upon graduating with a master's degree, the student can opt for one of two programs for their doctoral degree. Program one includes three digs in the Southwest and program two includes two sites: one in Greece and the other in South America.

The weather was typical of New Mexico, warm verging on hot, humidity at an all-time low of ten percent. Today was the first day of class for Archeology 301 in the master's program and Doctor Vincent Landers had a full class of eighteen students. The normal class size was ten, as this was not a skate course like some students in the past thought it was.

"Good afternoon everyone; today is Tuesday March 11, 2031 and I am Vincent Landers, director of antiquities here at the University of New Mexico. I am also your instructor for the next nine weeks. If you are not signed up for Archeology 301, then you are not in the right class. Professor Henry York teaches Arch 101 and 102 and is located down the hall in room C201. You also need to have satisfactorily completed both of his classes, before you can take my class. So, having said all that, if you are in the right place open your books to the first chapter. Oh, one other thing, when we go to our digs, you will need to have clothes that you do not mind getting dirty in, as you will get dirty."

Vince Landers was six-foot-tall, tipped the scales at one hundred ninety-five pounds, had graying hair, and wore a sport jacket and black slacks. He began his lecture starting with "In the beginning there was nothing; man has created everything you see around you and everything that has yet to be dug up. We in archeology, study the past by locating and examining what has been lost over time."

"Sir," Bryce McClelland said as he raised his hand.

"Please introduce yourself and then ask your question," Vince stated when he recognized Bryce.

"Sir, I am Bryce McClelland and was wondering if you have discovered any real artifacts?" To look at Bryce, you would see a high school jock, standing six foot three. He had played football in high school where he preferred to be a running back instead of the quarterback; he was fast on his feet, quick minded, had short brown hair, brown eyes, and usually dressed in jeans with a polo shirt.

"Yes, you are asking about my background and why I am uniquely qualified to teach this class," Vince stated and then paused for a few seconds before recounting his resume. He started with his early adventures in the discovery of an lost Inca city in South America up to his latest discovery which he promised he would discuss at length before the end of class along with a little show and tell. He had been a professor with UNM, Albuquerque, for the past twelve years; he took time off each year to hunt for lost treasures, just like the fictional character Indiana Jones did in his movies of the same name.

After he went through his qualifications, he stopped and finally said, "Any more questions as to my qualifications?"

"Yes, I am Morgan Fields; it sounds like you are an older Indiana Jones. Not that I am questioning your qualifications, but when have you had time to do all that you said you did?" Morgan was five foot five inches tall, blonde and blue eyed, with the figure of a model; she was more of a tomboy than a model, always in jeans, tennis shoes and a nice blouse. Since she was a little self-conscious about her looks, she tended to dress to not attract attention.

"I only teach this class twice a year which gives me time to research and plan my trips. Keep in mind archeology is eighty percent research and only twenty percent actual field work. It all starts with nothing but an idea or a clue of some sort and a lot of research," Vince replied. "Now can we get started, we have three and a half hours to cover a lot of material, starting with a find by Edwin Kelsey in 1915. After extensive research and a lot of clues that led nowhere, he and his team headed for the desert in New Mexico. The state was still very primitive and did not have a lot of roads, but he persisted and was able to locate his target. It took weeks of walking around in the desert, but his persistence paid off. However, it cost him his life. Two weeks after he found his target, he disappeared while chasing another clue."

"Sir, Diane Norris, what did he find?" asked a short five-foot three-inch brunette with hazel eyes and a perky disposition. She was dressed conservatively in a green skirt, white blouse and green sport jacket.

"Good timing, Miss Norris. I have, in this box, the object for which he searched. Edwin was an instructor here at the university and he left it in the care of the museum. We keep this locked up, because we don't know the extent of its power or what it does. We estimate that it is over five million years old. Several of the scientists who have studied it have disappeared after working with it."

"Is it dangerous?" Bryce asked.

"What's so funny, young man?" Landers asked a tall red haired student sitting next to Bryce. "Would you care to say something, Mister?"

"Ah, no sir, I am Freddy Carlson, I am sorry about the chuckle but Bryce is never afraid of anything, that I know of." Freddy said quietly.

"Okay Mister Carlson, to answer Mister McClelland's question. No, it has not killed anyone that we know of; they just disappear without a trace. At the end of the class, I want you, Miss Morgan, Miss Diane and Mister Carlson to come up and I will show you the item. So can we get on with the lecture and then show and tell." Assuming the class was ready to continue, Professor Landers proceeded with his lecture. At fifteen minutes before the end of class, he called up his four students.

"Please, you four, come up here," Vince said and then pointed to Bryce, Morgan, Diane, and Freddy, who was trying his best to look like he belonged here. Freddy was a bit shy, and brilliant; he did not want to attract attention because he was self-conscious about his height, six foot four inches, and his bright red hair, which he inherited from his mother's side of the family. Reluctantly the four stood, walked up front and looked at the box on the table in front of them. Vince reached over and picked up a pair of heavy work gloves, and then opened the box to expose an orb measuring about six inches across. It glowed from an unknown power source. "Please, do not touch the orb."

"Why?" Bryce asked.

"It has a low level radioactive signature, and it may burn you if touched; that's why I am wearing these gloves. Every time a human hand has touched it, it flashes and then starts to glow brighter. Other than that, we have not discovered what it does. Its temperature does not change much, remaining at a constant one hundred and four degrees," Vince said, and then took his eyes off the orb for a moment to address the class. "It was found in the New Mexico desert in September 1915 by Edwin Kelsey, who mysteriously disappeared two weeks later while on a second expedition to the same area. No trace of him or his team was ever found; his camp site was found intact along with his notes and equipment. I have his notes here if any of you wish to read them."

"Wow, cool," Freddy Carlson said as he stared at the orb. Freddy was the geek of the group. He wore horn rimmed glasses over his hazel eyes, and was always in slacks with a dress shirt that had several pens in the breast pocket. Freddy looked more like a jock, weighing in at two hundred ten pounds. He could play football, but instead chose to play chess and go to the gym to workout.

"Yeah, cool," Morgan agreed just as her right hand reached out and touched the orb, going against the rules. The orb flashed brightly and blinded everyone in the classroom for a few minutes; Morgan stepped backward and fell to the floor.

Bryce, Freddy and Diane were also knocked to the floor. Vince fell backward and ended up in his chair, blinded by the flash.

"What did you do?" Vince finally said after regaining his composure.

"I touched it, sorry," Morgan replied and started to cry. "It is glowing brighter, what's going to happen?"

Chapter 2 What Did You See?

Seconds after the flash when everyone's eyes could see again, the students were standing and looking at the orb as if nothing had happened.

"What happened?" Morgan asked to anyone who would answer; the orb was back in its box and not glowing. The five of them were just looking at the orb, wondering what had happened; they appeared to be dazed and confused.

Vince looked up and the classroom was empty, except for himself and the four students looking at the orb. "I don't know," he said as he turned back to the four students standing in front of him. He looked up at the clock on the wall and saw that over four hours had passed since the start of his lecture, and the class was long over.

"I don't know what happened, but we need to get to our next class; we are already late," Bryce commented, "See you tomorrow, sir." The four students quickly left the classroom leaving Vince standing there wondering what happened in the past four hours and coming up with a total blank.

At six that evening, Vince was sitting in a small bistro eating a pastrami on rye and sipping on a cold beer when his four students walked in and approached his table.

"Are you thinking the same thing we are, sir?" Morgan asked as she sat down across from Vince.

"What are you guys thinking?" Vince asked as they sat down. He looked at his four students: Morgan was wearing a short denim skirt with a tee shirt with UCLA stenciled on the front; Bryce wore jeans, sneakers, and a tee shirt boasting Harley Davidson; Freddy was in his normal slacks and dress shirt; and Diane had on green shorts and a tee with flowers on it.

"What happened to the four hours in class? Did we transport somewhere, freeze, or did the class continue with you giving a lecture? We are scared, Mr. Landers," Diane said looking very frightened as she took a seat across from Landers.

"What is that thing you brought into class? Are we going to die or disappear like everyone else you told us about?" Bryce asked looking a little worried and scared.

"I don't know, but what I do know is that anyone that touched it with their bare hands disappeared within several days. The five of us were very close to it when you touched it, Morgan. So I don't know what will happen, if anything," Vince said quietly to his students.

"We don't want to die, Mr. Landers," Diane belted out, a little too loud, getting a few stares from the other people in the bistro.

"Do you want anything to eat or drink?" Vince asked, and after getting a no from each of them, said "Okay, let me finish my sandwich and then we can go."

"Where are we going to go, Mr. Landers?" Bryce asked.

"Not sure, but we need to go to the museum and look at Edwin's notes again; maybe they can tell us something. Something I may have missed when I reviewed them before class."

"Where are we going, Mr. Landers?" Freddy asked. "The museum is not this way."

"I don't know, Freddy. Just going this way for now," Vince said as he drove. "I just have this feeling that we need to go this way. Don't know why, but it feels right."

"Yeah, out to the desert and then what?" Diane said from the back seat. "Don't the rest of you feel it?"

"Yes I do! There is a spot in the desert that we need to go to; it may have the answer we are looking for," Bryce commented from the passenger side of the car.

Two days later, a hikers reported to the local police that they found an abandoned car two miles off the highway with no sign of the driver. When the police arrived, they secured the area and started their investigation. They found a large burned spot a hundred feet from the car with foot prints leading to the burned spot but none leading away from it. In the middle of the burn spot was a small pile of clothes and shoes. They could find no trace of human remains anywhere within four miles of the car.

"I think we need to call in the FBI on this one, Sarge," one of the officers commented as he looked over the scene.

"I have to agree, this has kidnapping written all over it," his sergeant replied. "Get on the horn and call the station, tell them what we have found and request the FBI to pay us a visit and have CSI come out too, maybe they can find something we can't see."

Life around the University did not change much. It was almost like Vince and the four students never existed.

"The Director from the University just called, Captain," the desk sergeant reported. "He says one of his professors and four students have not been in class for the past few days. They are concerned. He says they have attempted to call them and have not received an answer from any of them; they have not notified the parents or next of kin and have requested that we see if we can find the missing professor and students."

"Okay, Sam, who is between cases right now?" the captain asked.

"Detective Becks and Grayson are available; they just wrapped up a case and are sitting around without much to do. It has been kind of quiet lately."

"Good, give it to them and have them report to me on progress. Anything else?"

"No, like I said, it's been pretty quiet in the city."

Two hours later, Becks and Grayson walked into the office of the University director.

"Director, Detective Becks and my partner Detective Grayson, we need to ask you a few questions." Detective Sergeant Pamela Becks introduced themselves and showed their credentials to the director. Becks was five foot eight inches tall, had brown wavy hair, intense green eyes, and a born again cops attitude; she took no bull from potential criminals, but had a way of getting information from suspects without raising her voice.

"Sure, come in and have a seat."

"When was the last time you saw, Professor Landers and the students?" Becks asked.

"Landers had a scheduled class on Tuesday; he was there. The students were in his class; they were also last seen in the class."

"Did they leave together?" Lucy Grayson asked. Lucy was five foot four inches tall, had straight brown hair, brown eyes, and was physically fit. She was a marathon runner and a crack shot with a rifle and pistol. Her track record with the force was impressive, but she walked around with a chip on her shoulder that prevented her from moving up in the ranks as fast as her partner, Becks. But she and Becks were best friends; and she did not hold a grudge when Becks got promoted to Detective Sergeant over her. However, she did hold a grudge with herself. Both were excellent detectives and did not rest until they solved the cases they were assigned. The Captain knew this very well and wanted to reward both of them as often as he could, but politics prevented some of his wants.

"No, I personally did not see Landers or the students; we were told that the class went its entire length and that Landers had the students come up and look at this orb thing near the end of class and then the class was dismissed."

"We need a list of students in that class and the ones you interviewed identified; we would like to talk to them," Detective Pamela Becks requested.

"I will have my secretary provide that information to you as you leave."

"Did anyone have a grudge against those students and Landers?" Becks inquired.

"No, Landers was well respected in the university and among his peers. I know of no one who would want to harm him. As for the students, they were all 'A' students, with great futures in their chosen field."

"Is there anything you can tell us to help us locate them?" Grayson asked.

"Landers usually stopped for a late snack at a small bistro downtown on Main Street. They may be able to help. It was well known around the university that if a student needed to talk to him, they could find him there every evening after his last class. I really think he owned part interest in the bistro."

"We will check it out, thank you," Becks said as she and Grayson stood up to leave. "If you hear anything else, call us. Oh, one other question, is Professor Landers married?" she said and handed the director her card.

"No, his wife is his work; being a professional treasure hunter and archeologist was his passion and did not leave him with any time for a love life as far as we know. No girlfriend, just his work."

Driving to the bistro would take about a half hour.

"Check in with the office, Lucy," Pamela Becks told Lucy as they drove.

Lucy called the precinct while Pamela drove, and listened intently as she was told of a new lead on the case they were working on.

"Pam, the Sarge just got a report of an abandoned car on a side road north of the city off of Interstate 25. "CSI is on their way." Lucy said when she hung up the cell phone.

"Let's check out the car first and then the bistro," Pamela Becks said as she turned the car around and headed toward Interstate 25. Forty minutes later, they drove down a dirt road, and stopped beside a patrol car that was a hundred feet from the abandoned car.

"Hi, Becks, a couple of hikers found the car and investigated but did not touch anything. They are standing over beside the van with my partner. When they got here, they looked around and were spooked when they, ah, well, I think you need to see what they saw; come with me," the patrolman said and turned and walked toward the abandoned car. "The ignition key is on, battery is dead, and the gas tank is empty. When they left the car, it was still running."

"They, you mean there was more than one occupant," Grayson asked.

"Yes, five."

"Damn, what the hell?" Grayson and Becks said in unison as they looked at the large circular ring with five pairs of clothes neatly arranged in the middle, laid as if there were five people asleep around a camp fire.

"Did you check the registration?" Becks asked.

"Yes, belongs to a Professor Vincent Landers."

"Holy Batman, what the hell is going on?" Detective Lucy Grayson commented as she studied the circle and the surrounding area. "What, who did this?"

"That my faithful partner is the question," Detective Pamela Becks stated.

After searching the area, they could find no clues to the location or how the circle and clothes got there. There were foot prints up to the circle but none leaving.

As they were looking around, they noticed a small convoy of Army Humvees racing down the dirt road toward them. The convoy stopped a short distance from the abandoned car. Soldiers piled out of the vehicles and took up positions securing the area.

"Secure the area Sergeant; I need to talk to the police," Captain Frank Sherman ordered and walked over to the police Sergeant Peters. "Are you the officer in charge?"

"Yes, Sergeant Henry Peters, Detective Becks and Grayson over there just arrived and were about to take charge of the investigation. I was just about to call in the FBI. What can I do for you, Captain? How did you know about this and what has the military have to do with an abandoned car?"

"First, Sergeant Peters, we are taking over with the investigation and need you to round up your boys and bring them over to my Humvees; I need to ask everyone some questions. And to answer your question, you don't have the need to know."

"As you wish," Sergeant Peters said and then yelled at his four officers. "Hey, guys, the Army is here to take over, head on over to the first Humvee; they have some questions. Everyone, now! Detectives, they want to see you too."

"Thank you for cooperating. The Army is going to take over here; we have been informed that you were told this is a possible abduction. I will tell you right now, it is not an abduction of the normal kidnapping kind. Our information indicates this abduction was by terrorist forces. We need all your evidence, and I need your sergeant to call me if any more evidence turns up. Detectives, I know you have been tasked to investigate this, and I only ask that you coordinate your investigation through me and keep me informed."

"Okay, who is your evidence collector?" the Police Sergeant Peters asked.

"Sir, this is New Mexico and our jurisdiction; are you telling me that the federal government is over-riding our jurisdiction?" asked Detective Becks.

"Yes, I am, Detective Becks. We will work together on this; but as I was about to say to the good sergeant, nothing is to be released to the press without my okay. Is that understood? This is not your ordinary kidnapping; it goes much deeper, and we can't let out any information before we have all the facts."

"Okay, we will work together; here is my card. How can I reach you?" Becks handed him her card and took his card.

"Sergeant Peters, see LT Burgess; he is logging the evidence. Burgess, come over here," Captain Sherman said, and then yelled for Burgess.

"Sir," Lieutenant Burgess said as he approached.

"Gather all the evidence these fine gentlemen and detectives have and catalog it."

"Yes sir," Burgess responded and then turned toward the police officers. "Have your men stop any further traffic from coming down this road until my forensic team gets here, which should not be too long from now. Once they arrive and my additional security gets here, you can go; and don't tell anyone what you saw here. We will release information to your commander as soon as we have the results of our forensic investigation; and then, and only then, can you notify next of kin and the university as to what happened. Understood, Sergeant and detectives?"

"Yes, sir," Sergeant Peters agreed and then took his men and positioned them at the end of the road to stop the press and anybody else that had no business down here.

"Captain Sherman, have a good day," Becks said as she and Grayson headed for their car.

Chapter 4 Things Are Not What They Appear

"Hello and welcome," a young, tall, lanky bearded man said when the five travelers woke up lying on the beach of a tropical island. A warm tropical breeze had brushed gently over their bodies while they had been sleeping on the white sand under the tall palm trees.

"What? Who are you?" Vincent Landers asked as he looked around and saw where they were and that all five of them were together. His four travelers started to stir and one by one they sat up and brushed off the sand from their backs and sides.

"Where are we?" Diane asked to no one in particular. "Where are my clothes?" she yelled noticing that she and everyone else except the bearded man were naked. She attempted to cover her exposed body with her hands just as Morgan was sitting up and pulling her legs in tight to her breast to keep the guys from seeing her naked; but they had already seen both girls.

"Here, young lady," the bearded man said as he handed her a tan beach robe and then handed everyone else a similar robe. "My name is Edwin Kelsey and I will explain everything when we get back to the compound. Please come with me; it is a short walk. We have been expecting you."

"Edwin Kelsey, you can't be Edwin, he is long dead. Wait, did the orb bring you here?" Landers asked quickly.

"As I said, I will explain when we get to the compound," Edwin commented as he turned and started to walk up the beach.

After donning the robes, they stood and followed Edwin into the thick jungle on a well worn path. Upon reaching a clearing, or rather an abandoned airfield, they saw several aircraft parked in the grass beside the cracked and obviously neglected runway.

"Is that a Lockheed Electra over there beside the F-4 Phantom?" Bryce asked as they crossed the runway. "Wow, there is a Corsair and a P-38 there too; this is so cool. Can I go over there and look at them?"

"Yes, but not right now; I will explain when we get you settled in. Follow me for now. You will have time to explore soon," Edwin insisted as he led them across the runway and up to a dilapidated Quonset hut, like the ones you would see in old war movies. Above the door was a faded sign saying it was Flight Operations. Close by was an old airfield control tower with windows broken but still standing. Behind the operations building, they saw several more buildings which looked like living quarters with old chairs outside the front doors. They could picture pilots and crews sitting in front of the buildings telling stories.

"Please help yourself to drinks and food over there on the table, and take a seat; we have a lot to explain," Edwin said pointing to the food on the table and then indicated that they should take a seat around the table. The chairs looked very old; they were made of wood with no arms and no cushions.

Morgan and Diane took a couple of sandwiches and sat at the table attempting to keep the short beach robes closed so the boys would not see them naked again.

"Okay, Mr. Kelsey what the hell is going on? Where are we, and how the hell did we get here?" Vince asked as he sat across from Morgan at the table watching as Kelsey walked to the front of the room and the head of the table. "Was it the orb?"

"Eat and relax for a moment, and then I will explain," Kelsey replied as he pulled back the chair and sat looking intently at his new arrivals. "You are going to find what I say hard to believe but it will be the truth as I know it."

"Mr. Kelsey, you look very familiar, have we met somewhere?" Freddy said as he dove into his stacked ham sandwich and handful of very tasty potato chips as if he hadn't eaten in days. They would soon find out that they actually had not eaten in days.

"I don't believe so, young man. That would have been impossible," Kelsey replied and then paused for a moment before continuing. "Okay, let me tell you a little story, which started before recorded time and long before men and women started to walk this beautiful planet we call Earth."

"Go on, we have nowhere to go that we know of and all day to get there," Vince replied and then took another bite from his turkey sandwich.

"Before time, there was nothing but a black hole in space, a hole that gathered bits and pieces of space dust to form this planet."

"We know the Big Bang Theory; what does that have to do with us?" Vince asked interrupting Kelsey.

"You will understand in a minute. Please just listen to me," Kelsey said holding up his hand to stop other interruptions. "After many thousands of years, men and women showed up and started to populate the planet, developing, inventing and growing in every aspect of life as you know it. What you don't know is how men and women got here, was it just magic, divine intervention, or something else. Well, we don't really know, but what we do know is men and women developed into the intelligent human that populates the Earth. Now the really hard part to understand is what came next. Freddy, you probably saw my picture in your text books; and remember me as the man who found the orb that sent you here." He paused for a moment to let that set in. "So yes, Vince, the orb did send you here; and it sent me and many others. Some are still here; others, well, they have moved on. Where they went, we are not sure; but they are gone, none the less."

"That would make you over a hundred years old and you don't look a day over thirty. How is that possible?" Freddy responded before anyone else could say anything.

"True, Freddy, I have been on the island for a while, but not a hundred years. I arrived here just about two years ago. As you can see by the food and drink you are eating, we have lots of tasty food. The food, as well as everything else we have, comes from a small, well-stocked warehouse that somehow is never low on anything we need."

"You keep saying 'We'. Who are the 'We' you keep referring to?" Bryce interrupted, looking a bit confused.

"The others will be here in a few minutes. Be patient and let me finish," Kelsey said and then continued, "As I said, I got here about two years ago; don't know how or why, but as you can see I am healthy and comfortable. We have been trying to figure out the 'why we are here' and how to get back to our homes, but have failed completely. At one point, there were two hundred fifty of us here; but now, prior to your arrival, only eight. Before you ask what happened to the others, it is simple; some just disappeared as quickly as they had appeared. Some of the others did what they were told not to do and that was to not go into the jungle but stay here around the airfield and the beach. If we did that, everything we needed would be provided to us as long as we did not go into the jungle beyond the parameter of the airfield."

"So we are prisoners?" Morgan stated. "Can we go home now? I have had enough fun for one day!"

"You are not prisoners, but guests of someone that has the power over life and death," Kelsey said and then looked up at the door as it opened allowing the other seven to enter. "Let me introduce you to our other guests."

"First is Amelia Earhart; she disappeared July 2, 1937 while flying her Lockheed Electra 10E in an attempt to fly around the world. Her plane sits on the air field near the camp where she landed six and a half months ago. Her navigator, Fred Noonan is on her right. Then we have Robert Heinz, a scientist and researcher who disappeared while working on the Manhattan Project in March 1940. Next to him is Ms. Susan Wright, a student from Berkeley who disappeared June 5, 1967 when a gunman opened fire on students; she was one of the students shot by the gunman, but she stands here alive and well. Next is Fran Snow, a commercial pilot who was flying from West Palm Beach, Florida to the Bahamas to pick up a client. She never made it, disappeared November 19, 2009. Her twin engine Piper Navaho is on the field, in perfect condition, yet it will not start. Then there is Rhonda Lowery, a marine biologist who disappeared April 2, 2010 when the boat she was working on ran into a storm and she was washed overboard. And finally, last but not least, is Captain Bryan

Redmond, an F-4 Fighter pilot who was shot down over Viet Nam May 12, 1969; his fighter sits next to Earhart's plane; it is shot full of holes and not flyable anymore. He was lucky to have been able to land in spite of being low on fuel and having one engine out. His Electronic Warfare operator was dead in the back seat of the jet; we buried him with full military, well, as best we could, full military honors. There have been other arrivals that are no longer here that came throughout the years," Kelsey reported. And then he looked around the room at the new arrivals and his old friends.

"Where are they now?" Diane asked.

"Some showed up injured and died before we could provide medical help. Others did what we asked them not to do, and that is they went into the jungle and never came back," Kelsey replied, and waited for his other survivors to sit, but not before they picked up some food and drink.

"Wait a minute, you are telling us that you have been here for two years, but disappeared over a hundred years ago, no way," Vince questioned, shaking his head in disbelief.

"Yes, we have been here a while," Robert Heinz remarked, "And it looks like we will be here a long time. Except for Edwin Kelsey, Amelia and Fred Noonan have been here the longest, arriving about six months ago, and then the rest of us over time since then."

"Yes and no, as Robert said, I guess that is what I am saying. We have been brought here for a reason; that reason is unknown to us," Kelsey said. "Where we were up until we arrived here is unknown to us. But as I said earlier, and like Robert said, we have only been here between six months and two years. We may have been missing for up to a hundred years, but we haven't been here that long. It is like we were transported into the future and ended up here. Vince, what year was it when you left your home and disappeared?"

"Twenty thirty-one," Landers answered quickly.

"I guess it has been over a hundred years since I disappeared then. We don't have any idea as to what date it really is. We have developed a crude calendar, but it may be off by years," Kelsey said and smiled. "There is more to tell, but I think we need to get you some clothes and show you where you can sleep. Dinner is in a couple of hours; we will meet in the mess hall, and after dinner, we will tell you more. You can bring your food and drink; please come with me," Kelsey said as he looked around the room at the new arrivals and his long time companions. "I understand what you are going through. We all experienced it when we arrived, but there is nothing we can do about it. This is an island and we are here because of someone with a lot of power, be it an alien power or whatever. We have talked and talked about it; and have not come up with an answer, at least not yet. Let's get you settled in and meet for dinner, and we will give you more information. A short tour on the way to the barracks is in order."

"So we really don't know what day it is or where we are on Earth!" Diane stated as she stood to follow Edwin.

"What was the exact day and time you disappeared from wherever you came from?" Edwin asked as he stopped at the door and looked intently at each of the new arrivals.

"It was August second, two thousand thirty-one at about 8 p.m. in the evening," Freddy said in answer to the question.

"Well, it was August second, two thousand and thirty-one then; it is now August third, fourth or whatever, two thousand thirty-one, maybe," Edwin said and turned to exit the building.

"Maybe?" Morgan questioned.

"Yes, maybe; remember the dates each of us disappeared. Take Amelia and Fred, July 2, 1937. By our calculations, they arrived here just over six months ago. Which means, if today is August third, which I do not believe it is, then they arrived here around January or February. Understand?"

"Yeah, confusing," Bryce said for everyone.

Chapter 5 The Island

After getting settled into separate rooms in one of the barracks behind the operations building, they were told to come down to dinner at five o'clock. Each room had a wall clock which looked like it had been in the room since 1940.

At a few minutes before five, Vince and his students met in the hallway and silently walked to the building they were told was the dining facility. The weather was warm, about eighty degrees, with a few scattered clouds and a light breeze. Each was wearing some old military clothing that was already in the room when they arrived. The clothes were clean and hanging in a small closet. They were told they would be able to get some more clothes from the supply building in the morning, clothes that would fit better.

"Good afternoon, welcome to our dinner, please help yourself," Amelia Earhart said when she heard the five new islanders enter the dining facility. Without stopping to look up, she dished up some food on her plate.

"Thank you! We have a lot of questions. Are you the one that can answer them?" Vince asked as he walked up beside Amelia, picked up a plate and scooped up some mashed potatoes and what looked like meatloaf. "Is that meatloaf?"

"No, I am not the one to ask; you need to talk to Edwin. And yes, that is meatloaf, enjoy," Amelia replied and then turned to find a chair.

"I don't see him, is he coming down to dinner," Vince asked, wearing a large baby blue shirt over baggy tan pants and very tight military dress shoes which he found in the closet of his room.

"He will be here shortly," Fred Noonan answered between bites. "It looks like we need to find you some better fitting clothes in the morning."

Vince and his four students got their food and sat at a table by themselves.

"What do you think is going on, Mr. Landers?" Diane asked. She had found a pair of dark blue denim shorts, a brown tee shirt like the ones issued to US Army soldiers in the 70s, and flip flops which were too big for her. "You look like a scarecrow, Bryce."

"Yeah, found these in the room, not my size or first choice of colors," Bryce said sitting down beside Morgan in his green overalls and combat boots, several sizes too big for him. "But it is better than running around naked. Although seeing you two naked was kinda nice."

"Kinda nice, is that all, kinda nice?" Morgan said punching him in the shoulder.

"Actually it was very nice," Bryce teased.

"That's more like it," Morgan countered.

"Enough you too, we have bigger problems," Vince said stopping the little teenage playfulness. "Here comes Edwin," he continued and signaled for Edwin to sit with them. After Edwin got his food, he walked over and sat across from Vince.

"Good evening, ladies and gentlemen," Edwin said as he sat and looked intently at Vince and then to his four students. "Guess we need to look for some better clothing for you, those don't look very comfortable. As I said earlier, tomorrow morning we can go over to the supply building and find sizes that fit better."

"That would be nice," Diane said looking down at her ragged tee shirt and baggy pants with the legs rolled up because they were too long, and her bare feet.

"After you eat I, ah, we have a lot of questions," Vince commented waiting for Edwin to eat a little.

"No, go ahead; ask away," Edwin replied and then took a bite of meatloaf, "Damn, this is good meatloaf."

"Okay, you said you would fill us in on more, so please tell us what the hell is going on here. Time seems to have stopped; you are over a hundred years old, but look like you have not aged a day past thirty. We have people, including you, that have been here for at most two years; yet the buildings, rooms and clothes are from around the 1940s. Things just don't feel right, can you explain?"

"It may sound strange, but you are correct in your statement. It doesn't look right and it isn't right," Edwin remarked.

"How can that be?" Bryce asked.

"We don't know. Let me tell a story and it should fill in some of the questions," Edwin started and then paused to take a breath. "I was working in northern New Mexico in September 1915 when I fell into an abandoned mine; the mine was very deep but I never hit the bottom, or rather I never felt that I hit the bottom. I saw a flash just as I got close to the bottom and woke up on the beach about the same place I found you."

"When you got here, what did you find?" Diane asked.

"I found the same as you, the buildings, airfield without some of the planes, they arrived over time. I did find a warehouse full of supplies and everything as you have found it. Over time we have had many visitors; several ships are in the cove on the south side of the island, and we have gotten a lot more airplanes at our airfield. It's a shame that none fly anymore. But even if they did, we don't have fuel to fly them anywhere; and we don't know where we are or which direction to fly."

"Ships?" Morgan asked, "Can't we take one and sail away from here?"

"We tried, but the ships, although fully functional, did not get us out of the cove. There is a barrier reef blocking the way through. The ships got in somehow, but we don't know how. They just appeared one day and the crews were here awhile and then disappeared, leaving their ships here."

"Interesting to say the least," Bryce commented between bites of his meal. He stopped to pick up a can of Coke with a pop top. "How did this get here? Pop tops were not invented until around the mid-eighties and this can is not that old."

"I will get to that and much more about our supplies. Let me start from the beginning. As I previously stated, I disappeared in 1915 and I arrived here about two years ago. Where I was since 1915 I have no idea. The other members felt no time passage from the time of their disappearance from the real world and when they arrived. But time has no meaning here. It was 1937 when Amelia and Fred disappeared, but by our calendar, they arrived here about six months ago. I use the term real world because this doesn't seem to be real. Living here has not been a problem; we have everything we need supplied to us, but we don't know by whom. We are living on an island, which is about twenty square miles, give or take a bit. The interior is mostly jungle. The island has a beautiful beach around most of it, and a large cove which has four ships anchored in it presently. Before you ask, there is a one hundred twenty foot private yacht named *'Freedom'*, a three hundred foot freighter, a larger freighter, Liberty Ship I believe, and a United States submarine, Gato Class. None of the crews are here anymore. We have gone out and searched each ship; did not remove anything that wasn't useful to us at the time, so they are time capsules of when they arrived. You may want to explore them at some time. But I must warn you, we have had a lot of our guests go into the jungle and they never came back out."

"What? You mean that everyone from those ships died in the jungle?" Morgan asked looking very worried.

"No, not exactly, we don't know if they died; they just never returned. And, yes, we did go a little way into the jungle looking for them and did not find any trace of them. We decided that it was best that we did not continue our search deeper into the jungle, fearing we would experience the same fate," Edwin stated. "So do not go into the jungle alone, or together; we cannot promise you will return."

"Noted Ed, we will take that as a warning," Vince replied, "Okay, back to the time difference; you are over a hundred years old and arrived here and found an airfield with buildings from the 40s, like they were built for the military during the Second World War."

"Yes, these buildings were old when I got here; Earhart and Noonan arrived much later; the crew of the US submarine arrived before Earhart. They had settled in, but were restless; the crew kept searching for clues and how to get off the island, and their boat was stuck in the cove. After a while, they headed inland and disappeared. Time does not move here. You said it was 2031 when you arrived; actually it was 2031 when you disappeared. It may be much later here, or even earlier; we just don't know."

"What is your theory as to what happened to them?" Diane asked.

"We don't have a theory except they were overcome by forces unknown to us and died, or well, just disappeared," Edwin replied.

"Where do you get the power for electric and to keep the refrigeration running?" Freddy asked.

"We have generators, something we didn't have in my time, and plenty of fuel to run them."

"Why not take some of that fuel and fly out of here?" Diane asked quietly.

"As I said earlier, we don't know where we are and just to fly off in a direction to parts unknown would be suicidal; we could be only a hundred miles from another island, but which direction is it? We have looked with binoculars we took from one of the boats and cannot see any island or other land anywhere. Earhart and Noonan were flying across the Pacific and reported they were heading east and were unable to locate the island where they were supposed to land. Suddenly they saw a flash and ended up landing here, thinking this was their destination, only to subsequently discover it wasn't. They have no idea where we are, not for the lack of trying. And besides, the generators run on diesel and the planes use Avgas and they don't mix well."

"So we are stuck here for all time and eternity," Morgan commented, "I want to go home, I am tired of this. When can I go home?"

"Ms. Morgan, I cannot answer that. Anymore questions?" Edwin asked.

Getting no more questions, Edwin stood and walked to the back of the mess hall where he placed his dirty plate and utensils in the open window to the kitchen. He stopped at the table on his way out of the mess hall, and said, "Get a good night's sleep; and in the morning, we will find you some better clothing and shoes."

Amelia Earhart, Fred Noonan and several others had left the mess hall, leaving only Captain Redmond drinking coffee across the room.

"Captain, maybe you can provide us with some information?" Bryce asked, not satisfied with what he heard from Edwin.

"Sure, as best I can," he replied and walked over to the coffee pot, refilled his cup and then took a seat across from Vince.

"Captain Redmond, from what we have heard so far, you were an F-4 pilot flying a mission over Viet Nam when you were shot down," Bryce stated.

"Not exactly shot down. I was in a flight of six Phantoms on a bombing mission when out of the sun came several Migs, firing missiles and their cannons. We took evasive action and went ballistic, meaning we lit our afterburners and pulled back hard on the stick to avoid the missiles. I was successful for a while and able to fire a couple of my missiles. In fact, I even took down one of the Migs. We, meaning my electronic warfare (EW) operator in the backseat and I did not know at the time that they were not the real threat. They stayed a little out of gun range and pushed us to the west. Our team fell for it; and as soon as they got us where they wanted, they exited the area as quickly as they came. They wanted us over a highly concentrated area of SAMs which were already heading our way. Evasion of a SAM is difficult at best and since we were low on fuel and had suffered some wing damage, we were almost sitting ducks. Three of my wingmen were able to go low and fast out of the area; two others were hit and we saw parachutes from their birds. My luck wasn't so good; we evaded for a while, but one exploded close to my tail. The explosion damaged my stabilizer and killed my EW operator. I dived down to avoid being hit again; I saw a flash, and the next thing I knew I was on approach to the airfield on this island. How the hell that happened I don't know, but here I am and have been since that day."

"Wow," Bryce commented.

"I thought I was dead; but instead, I am here and wondering how the hell I got here." He paused for a moment and then continued, "May 12th, 1969, and now, staying again in barracks that were built during the Second World War, and wondering how the hell I get home. It is also frustrating to not know what year it is, since time seems to have stopped for us here. You say it is 2031. I haven't gotten older, just bolder. I assume they listed me as killed in action over Viet Nam. The sad part is they will never find my body or my F-4."

"It looks like when you are killed or die suddenly, you are brought here instead, or it could mean you are dead and this is heaven," Freddy hypothesized.

"I don't know about being dead; my back seat operator was dead when we arrived, yet he is not here. Why not?" Redmond queried.

"Good question. And why did the others disappear when they went into the jungle?" Morgan interjected.

"That, my dear, is a good question for sure. So we may not be dead, by your scenario. But that still doesn't tell us why we are here," Vince said. "We have noted people from history, like Earhart and Noonan, along with people that have no historical importance that we know of. So why us, why those on the boats, and the others that have come and now are gone."

"I think we need to find out more information about everyone else that is here," Morgan stated and then continued, "Captain, will they talk to us?"

"They will talk, I will see to that," Redmond stated smiling.

"Tell us a little more about yourself, Captain," Bryce asked.

"Not much to tell, I grew up in a military family, graduated high school and was accepted to the Air Force academy. Finished there just about the time we really got going in Viet Nam. I trained as a fighter pilot. Was sent to Nam, and flew seventy-five missions before ending up here. I was scheduled to rotate out in three months. Obviously I didn't rotate out like planned," Redmond explained.

"What about your family? Is there anything in their past that may have bearing on your arrival here?" Diane asked picking up on the line of questioning that Bryce had started, looking for something that would trigger this event. The four were honor students and candidates for Mensa, the high IQ society, which provided a forum for intellectual exchange among its members from more than one hundred countries.

Redmond went through his family history with a few holes in it that he did not know. His family had migrated to the United States in the early 1700s and established a small business in New York. Eventually they moved west to Texas after the Civil War. There they built a small but profitable cattle business and during World War I, they started to become pilots fighting for the democracy and their beloved country. Redmond came from a long line of pilots and war heroes.

"Okay, let's talk to some of the others," Morgan suggested.

"I will get a couple of them, wait here," Vince suggested, "Captain, would you be so kind as to wait also."

"Sure. Have no place to be right now; and I have read all the books we found here," Redmond stated as he leaned back in his chair.

Chapter 7 The Others

After talking with each of the others, the only common denominator was that each one saw a flash just before they arrived on the island. In the case of Earhart and Noonan, according to history, they were off course during an attempt to circumnavigate the world in 1937 in a Lockheed Model 10 Electra. They disappeared somewhere over the central Pacific Ocean near Howland Island. Amelia told us that she was funded by Purdue University and had high hopes of making a successful flight. They were low on fuel, unsure of their location and more importantly unsure of which way to go to reach Howland Island. First, the right engine started to cough and sputter, due to lack of fuel. They started to descend only to see nothing but ocean below them; seconds later, the left engine quit. Amelia looked over at her navigator and quietly said, 'Sorry Fred.'

"Just before we impacted the water, there was a flash; and we were then on final approach to this island. The runway was lined up below our nose and the landing gear was down. All we had to do was pull the power back on our now running engines and land. Which we did without a problem; we taxied over to the side of the field and shut down the engines when we saw another pilot walking toward us from across the field. We have been here ever since, living comfortably in those rundown barracks, but alive or at least we think we are. Before you ask, that pilot introduced himself as Major Robert French, from the 332nd Fighter Group, a member of the Tuskegee Airmen. At the time, we did not understand who the 332nd Fighter Group or the Tuskegee Airman were, until Redmond arrived and filled in the history of that gallant group of pilots. The pilot said he had arrived just weeks before and is now gone. Where he went, we don't know; he just disappeared one day."

"Thank you, Amelia. Is there anything else you want to relate? Your family history is well known so we don't have to get into that," Vince said, getting no response from her, he decided to pursue it later.

After interviewing everyone, they came to the same conclusion. A large flash happened just as they were supposed to die and the flash brought them to the island.

Sitting around the table, they noticed the sun going down outside. Diane stood and walked over to the light switch, and hesitated for a second not knowing if it would work or not. Finally, she reached out, flipped the switch, and was surprised to see the dusty light bulbs flicker on, casting a dull artificial light around the room.

"What do we do now, Mr. Landers?" Diane asked.

"I don't know; do I look like Indiana Jones or MacGyver. I am just an archeologist and not a very good one at that."

"Don't cut yourself short, sir. You are a good archeologist and great teacher," Morgan said.

"Thanks, but we have a big problem to solve and I don't believe we can solve it sitting here. We need more information and information is something we can get, but we need to spend time on those ships, planes, and I hate to say it, but we need to go into the jungle and soon."

"I agree, sir," Bryce stated and then looked at the others at the table.

"Count me in," Freddy said and each of the girls agreed and then looked at Captain Redmond.

"Of course, I will help as best I can," Redmond agreed, "And I am sure some of the others would help too. This is an island and even though everything is provided, it would be nice to know by whom and how they do it. I have been looking for answers ever since I arrived and have not been successful; but with your help, maybe we can find out what the hell is going on."

"Edwin said he and others searched the ships. Were you involved in that?" Bryce asked.

"No, they did that before I got here," Redmond responded.

"We should go out there tomorrow," Bryce said. Everyone agreed without hesitation, but only after they found some clothes that fit.

"I don't know, Bryce; I think you look pretty good as a scarecrow and I look pretty good in these tight shorts and faded brown t-shirt," Morgan joked, as she stood and acted like a model to show off her clothes.

"Get outta here, Morg," Bryce shot back. "These are faded, scratchy and too big."

"They have clothes in the warehouse; we should be able to find some clothes to fit you," Redmond stated.

"Can we go to the warehouse now?" Diane asked quietly.

"Sure, it's a short walk; come on. Edwin said in the morning, but we can go now if you like," Redmond said as he stood up and started walking toward the door. "This is one of the best stocked warehouses I have seen, we didn't have this much stuff in Nam."

"Really?" Vince commented. "This I have to see; so far everything seems to be so impossible. Everything provided to you, food, fuel, clothes, well everything, where does it come from, how does it get here? It's a mystery of all mysteries. Sounds like a challenge to discover. And we are the ones to discover the answer, or at least give it a good try."

"I would love to go home, now. But finding out how and why we are here would be a good start," Redmond commented. "Let's head over to supply," he said, leaving his coffee cup on the table.

"One final question Captain," Bryce said as he stood and glanced down at the cup and back at the kitchen.

"Sure, ask," Redmond stated, as he stopped at the door and looked back at Bryce.

"Who does the cooking and cleaning in here?"

"We share the cooking most of the time; and when we cook, we do the cleanup. Tonight is my night for both, but some nights it is kind of weird."

"How so?" Morgan responded before Bryce could.

"Well, this may sound really strange."

"Everything sounds strange on this island. Go on," Vince said.

"Well, at least once a week when we show up for dinner, the food is all prepared. It is hot and there is plenty of it, usually steak, baked potato, and veggies of some kind. The weird part is that all of us were sitting in the dining room and none of us prepared the food and we just place our plates and flatware in the little window over there and never see anyone in the kitchen. We leave, and in the morning, the place is all clean and breakfast is waiting for us. No one admits to fixing dinner and cleaning the building. It just happens." Redmond commented as he opened the door.

"No way! Are you saying someone else is on the island and doing things for you without you knowing who they are?" Bryce questioned.

"We have seen a shadow leaving the building late at night, but have not been able to track him or her; it just disappears into the jungle." Redmond replied casually.

"Another mystery we have to solve my young honor students," Vince commented as they followed Redmond out the door and over to supply.

Chapter 8 First Night

During their visit at the supply warehouse, they found appropriate clothing, well almost, the clothing was old but clean. The guys found some Army fatigues and boots to fit and the girls searched long and hard to locate some clothes that would fit them, finally settling on army fatigues and boots to match. The girls took several pairs once they decided they could cut the legs off for shorts and the sleeves to make them more comfortable.

During their walk back to the barracks, Redmond explained that the jungle was pretty noisy at night. He thought it was mostly birds but possibly some predators. He didn't know if that was true, but suggested they stay in the compound, which consisted of the areas around the barracks, airfield and operations building.

"So we are relegated to living our lives in these old buildings without any contact with our family or friends?" Bryce commented as they walked.

"Son, I have only been here for about four months or maybe as long as since 1969 when I was shot down; and for some reason, I haven't aged a day since I got here. Time seems like it has stopped, and we are not moving ahead at all or maybe at a very slow pace. Can you explain that, or why we have been brought here in the first place?" Captain Bryan Redmond questioned. He stopped just outside the front door, placed his hands on his hips, and shook his head.

"I wish I could tell you, Captain, but I don't know. With your help and my young friends here, we will get to the bottom of this, even if we have to break some rules and go into the jungle. I am not going to spend the rest of my life being a beach bum, not yet anyway," Vince said and then paused for a second. "Captain Redmond will you help us?"

"If it gets me off this rock and home to my family, I am in. But if we get off, what or when will it be, 1969, 2031 or some other time?"

"That is a good question for which I hope to find the answer too. Let's go inside and make some plans; we have a lot to do," Vince stated and opened the door to let everyone in just as Edwin, Robert Heinz and Amelia Earhart were coming out.

"Good evening. We are heading over to the operations room for some coffee; care to join us? I see you have some more clothes; guess we don't have to go there in the morning," Edwin said when he saw the six of them entering the barracks, carrying a stack of clothes.

"I would love a good cup of coffee," Freddy said after getting a nod from Vince.

"Morgan why not go with them to keep Freddy company," Vince suggested, winking at Morgan as a sign to gather more information.

"Sure, a cup of coffee would be nice after a day like this. Let me throw my new clothes in my room and I will be right there," Morgan replied and entered the building followed by Freddy. Seconds later, after depositing their clothes in their new rooms, they came out smiling.

They walked off with Edwin, Robert and Amelia with hopes of gathering more information about the island and why they were here. It was a long shot but they had hopes.

"Let's make some plans," Vince said and entered the building. He turned right to enter the barracks day room which was dark, reached over to locate the light switch, and flipped it on. Seconds later, the room was bright with light. "That is amazing."

"Yeah, those generators have been here since the early 1940s and are still running. That says a lot for our Detroit generator manufacturers," Redmond commented, and took a seat at a table near the window; he wanted to be sure they could see when Edwin and the others returned.

"Amazing, yeah! Do you provide them with any service, or is that taken care of too?" Bryce asked as he sat across from Redmond.

"I personally have not done a thing to them. Maybe Noonan or one of the others does. I have seen them, two large 100 KW generators located behind the warehouse; one is running all the time, as far as I can tell."

"We could barely hear them when we got here, they must be muffled pretty well," Bryce interjected.

"I looked at them shortly after I arrived, and they do have a pretty wild exhaust system; they are actually exhausted into water. I guess to keep the noise down," Redmond explained.

"Can we look at them in the morning? I'm just curious about how they are set up," Bryce asked.

"Sure. Right after breakfast," Redmond agreed.

"Okay, we are getting off track. So, after breakfast, we see the generators; after that I think we need to look at the boats to see if there is anything on them that will give us a clue about this place," Vince said and then looked out the window at the setting sun. "I also believe we need to go around the island looking for anything that may help, and then regroup back here tomorrow night. Depending on what we come up with, I think we need to go inland and see where everybody has gone and why they never returned. We may not survive, but I, for one, don't want to live on this island for the rest of my life, even if I never grow old. Immortality is great if you can enjoy the good life with friends, family and everything that life has to offer."

"Mr. Landers, I have to agree. I have been here trying to find a way off and until you got here I had no hope. Everyone else seems to be content on just living their lives out on this rock."

"But you could have left with the others," Diane stated.

"No dear, they were gone when I got here, Fran and Rhonda are the only two that arrived after me, and they are too scared to enter the jungle. And I did not want to wander in alone, even though I thought about it many times," Redmond shot back. "Yes, I am trained to survive and to navigate through a jungle, but I only have one little pistol and fourteen bullets, not much protection. And yeah, I guess I was a bit intimidated when I got here. I was alive, and this place is not that bad once you get used to it, especially considering the alternative," Redmond explained.

"You don't have to defend your decision; we understand. But we also want to go home; and with your help, I believe we can get home or at least off this island," Vince countered.

"Okay, sorry."

"I hope Morgan and Freddy are able to get some more information," Diane said quietly. She tended to speak softly all the time, almost too quiet for anyone to hear.

Across the small field in the operations building, Morgan and Freddy were talking to Amelia about her flight around the world. Freddy had studied the loss of Amelia Earhart while attending flight school a couple of years ago. Freddy had acquired his private pilot's license and built up a couple of hundred hours in Cessna and Piper aircraft. He had plans on getting his commercial license after finishing his Master's degree, figuring the commercial license might help him in his archeological pursuits. Part of his fascination was with Amelia Earhart and her life, so he knew almost everything about her. He asked very pointed questions of her, which she answered correctly every time. She was either the real Amelia Earhart or a very good fake. Morgan turned her attention to Edwin and his archeological exploits; she did not know much about his life but was looking for something that sounded made up.

Chapter 9 Another Time On Another Island

Davin and Connie Pierce were enjoying a relaxing day on the beach in Kauai sipping a couple of foo-foo drinks, the ones with little umbrellas and fruit stuck on the side. They were watching a beautiful sunset, and just doing what everyone does when in the islands; relax, watch sunsets, and drink.

"Connie, honey, don't you think we should call the kids and see how they are doing?" Davin asked between sips, slurring his words a bit mocking intoxication. He had retired from the CIA just four months earlier; and he and Connie were enjoying a long overdue vacation, alone, without the kids, or the CIA.

"Naw, I talked to Stephanie this morning and she saw Amber on campus. She told her that Josh was working on a project at their apartment and would be along shortly, but she had a meeting with the dean about next year's classes. You do remember you helped Stephanie get that teaching position at the university, don't you?" Connie said and then took a sip of her drink.

"Oh yeah; I forgot about that, teaching advanced something or other in the criminal justice department. I guess we don't have to worry about them. How about dinner? What would you like tonight?" Davin replied as he scanned the ocean if front of them, admiring the view and the bikini clad young ladies playing in the surf.

"A nice steak would fit right in about now," Connie replied.

"Yeah; a steak and cold beer, just what I need." Davin agreed quickly.

"Ok, sounds good, but I thought all you needed was me," Connie replied. She paused for a moment as she scanned the ocean and saw a disturbance in the water. "What is that?" she asked as she pointed to the disturbance off shore.

"Don't know," Davin answered as he stood to get a better look. "What the hell?"

"A submarine surfacing? Why the hell are they coming up out there? The base is over at Pearl. Looks like a U.S. Nuke boat," she said as they watched the boat break the surface. Within minutes, the hatch opened and out poured several sailors and a bright orange inflatable raft. The men boarded the raft after it inflated, hooked up an electric motor and battery, turned on the electric motor, and headed directly for shore.

Ten minutes after the nuclear submarine had broken the surface, the raft was beached directly in front of Davin and Connie. A tall sandy haired Lieutenant Commander jumped out of the boat and walked right up to Davin and saluted.

"Mr. Pierce, Mrs. Pierce, I am Commander David Henderson. You know my dad, the Admiral. I have been sent to get you. We have a situation and need you to come with us, now," the commander stated as he watched a small crowd form around him and his team. Two of the other sailors from the boat herded the crowd away from the commander.

"Damn, you are all grown up; haven't seen you since you finished high school. Now look at you, a Lieutenant Commander on a nuke boat. What's so important that they sent you out here to see us?" Davin asked, as he looked closely at David Henderson, "You do have your dad's eyes. How are he and your mom doing?"

"They are doing well, but sir, we haven't much time. You need to pack anything you may need. You will be gone for at least a week or two. I will brief you as much as I can without getting into the classified stuff until we get back on the boat."

"I retired from the agency months ago, David. And Josh is now Director. Did he put you up to this or was it your father?" Davin commented. "And Connie left the FBI shortly after I retired. I am too old for the kind of adventures we had before you were born. And why send a submarine when a plane would be faster?"

"Josh and my father are part of this, but not in the context that you think. Now can we go? You will understand why the boat instead of a plane or faster means. I will explain on the boat," Henderson stated, a sense of urgency in his voice that did not set well with Davin and Connie.

"Okay, let's go! What could be so important that they had to send a million-dollar boat and crew across the ocean to get us?" Davin asked again, as he and Connie picked up their towels. Henderson had difficulty keeping his eyes off Connie, even though she had aged. She had aged gracefully and still turned heads, especially wearing the small white bikini she had on today.

Minutes later, they entered their home on the edge of the beach. "Now will you tell us what is going on?" Connie demanded as she stopped just inside the door and turned toward David Henderson.

"In a nutshell, your children are missing."

"Missing! How? When?"

"Yes, they disappeared around six this evening. That's not all; Josh and Stephanie Randal are also missing,"

Henderson stated, "I will give more details when we are securely on board and have submerged."

"We will be ready in a minute," Connie said, "We just need to lock the house and..."

Ten minutes later, they locked the door and headed toward the little orange boat with two small bags. The seas were calm so boarding the boat was easy. Within twenty minutes, the boat was secured and started to descend into the underwater world once again. Connie and Davin were escorted to the conference room where they were greeted by Admiral 'Bear' Henderson. After exchanging pleasantries, they sat and the Admiral started to brief them.

"Approximately 1830 Eastern Time, your children were walking toward the library on campus when they just disappeared, vanished, into thin air. At the same time, at their own home, Josh and Stephanie Randal, while talking to friends prior to dinner, vanished in front of the other two couples at the house. We have interviewed the couples who are all upstanding citizens and retired members of the CIA. There were only two other students close to the location where your children were walking and they did not see anything useful."

"Who witnessed the disappearance of Josh and Stephanie?" Davin asked.

"Joanne Morgan, John Polson, retired CIA Director Ashley Peterson and retired President Darrell Mitchell along with six Secret Service agents on protection detail for the former President."

"When you say 'disappeared', you mean they left the room and did not return or do you mean they did a Star Trek transporter thing and just disappeared."

"According to the witnesses, they did a Star Trek," Admiral Henderson said. "I don't understand how it happened; we haven't developed that type of technology to the point that we could transport people. Yes, we are working on it, but are years away from making it happen."

"Sounds like someone developed it and is using it to kidnap people, and they are doing it without having to use a transporter room, kind of like the site to site transports that the newer Star Treks did."

"But who and where did they transport to?" Connie asked looking for answers and knowing she would not get any here.

"We don't know; and we also did not want you two to disappear. We believe that by your being down here, you should be safe from transporting; but not one hundred percent sure. We are not taking any chances with your lives."

"What about those that witnessed the disappearances? Are they safe?" Davin asked.

"That we don't know for sure since the technology being used appears to snap up anyone at anytime from most anywhere, at least as far as we know, anyway," Henderson stated and then stood and walked over to the credenza and poured a cup of coffee.

"Where are we going?" Davin asked shifting uncomfortably in his chair.

"We are going to one thousand five hundred feet below the surface as we cruise at flank speed to San Diego. We hope that at this depth you will be safe, at least for now."

"If they do have a transporter like Star Trek, then this will not stop them," Davin said with a sly smile.

"We don't believe that whoever is doing this has a transporter of any type, but we are not taking any chances with your lives," Admiral Henderson stated.

"That doesn't work for us; we need to be on a plane heading home, now," Connie demanded.

"Okay, if you insist; I do not agree but will do as you ask," Admiral Henderson said and picked up the ship board phone, punched in a couple of numbers, and commanded, "Captain, make full speed for Pearl; dock when we arrive. We will be off-loading our passengers. Thank you Captain."

"Thank you Bear," Davin said as he looked at his wife. "Maybe we can catch a flight back to D.C. from Honolulu."

"No, I will make some arrangements for a flight for you." Admiral Henderson said looking a bit worried.

Chapter 10 Time To Explore

Vince and his students took a tour with Edwin, Amelia and Captain Redmond; they were shown the cove with four ships, airfield, generators, and other remains including an old cemetery where those that died were buried along with fifteen other graves with the names and dates of military personnel that died on the island dating back to 1943.

"Let's go to the top; you can see most of the island from there," Edwin said as he pointed toward a path that led up to a small hill behind the barracks.

"Is it safe to go up there?" Morgan asked as she followed Edwin and Vince.

"No, steep climb but perfectly safe, Miss Morgan." Edwin replied.

The climb was not hard and the path wound around but was fairly short. They reached the top and walked over to the edge facing north. They were on the southern end of the island and what they saw was a very thick jungle and a lot of sandy beach surrounding the island.

"Wow, long and narrow. Is that another airfield on the north end?" Morgan asked pointing toward the field which was barely visible from where they stood. Turning around, they saw the runway near the barracks where they had slept. On the field, they could see the eight airplanes, including Amelia's Lockheed Electra, Redmond's F-4 and several more.

"We searched a short way into the jungle and found a half dozen or so crashed planes with the pilots' bodies still in them. We buried them in the cemetery along with their military comrades. Several were Japanese, but we did not care what country they were from. They were warriors and died for their country." replied Redmond.

"Very noble of you," Diane stated. She was from a military family and worshipped her father for his service and her mother for putting up with all his deployments. Including not returning home from his last one to Afghanistan where he had been killed by a car bomb in Kabul.

"Is that another air field over there?" Morgan asked again.

"We would have done more, but did not have the resources," Edwin stated. "And, yes, that is another airfield where there are a few hangers, a couple of Japanese airplanes and a few damaged American planes. Not much of anything is left; we looked at it almost two years ago, shortly after it got here. There is another cemetery there also, with mostly unmarked graves although a few dog tags are hanging on some. Not much else, you can visit it when you want."

"Those that arrived long after you got here; did you see anything of their arrival?" Vince asked.

"Yes, and no, I was outside walking to the operations building one morning with Noonan. We saw a flash in the sky and an airplane came out of it trailing fire and smoke. We could not tell what kind of plane it was because of the distance. We watched it until it crashed on the island. We gathered up a first aid kit and headed in the direction of the crash when we saw a second and third flash and two more airplanes emerged and headed for the island. One of the pilots was able to jump out; his parachute opened and he landed on the edge of the island. We got to him, but he was severely wounded and did not live long. We buried him with the others."

"Do you remember their names?" Bryce asked being more curious than coming up with a theory.

"No, but they are on the headstones we placed over their graves along with their dog tags."

"I would like to go back to the cemetery to get a list of the names there," Bryce said and started down the hill.

"What are you thinking, Bryce?" Vince asked, stopping him before he got too far down.

"Let me make sure of what I am thinking first, sir. It may be nothing," Bryce replied. "When I glanced at the markers earlier, some of the names seemed familiar to me. I want a closer look," he continued and then headed back down the path to the cemetery.

"Miss Earhart, you were about to crash into the sea when there was a flash and you were next on an approach to that runway down there," Diane asked wondering more and more why she was here.

"Yes, we were just about to hit the water. Call me Amelia, we were less than a hundred feet over a calm ocean and then the next thing I knew we were on a straight in approach to that runway. My landing gear was down, so I did a pre-landing check and landed my plane, taxied to the grass on the side, and shut down my engines. There were no other airplanes on the field at the time I landed," Amelia commented.

"Captain Redmond, was that about the same that happened to you?" Bryce asked.

"Yes, as I told you last night, a flash and then on approach to that runway down there," Redmond replied.

"And we were driving and ran into a bit of fog; and the next thing we knew, we were on your beach," Diane replied. "This is all so weird."

"I have to agree, Diane. We need more information," Vince said quietly to Diane and Morgan, hoping that Edwin and Amelia did not hear. "Captain, tomorrow, I want to walk around the island. Will you go with us?"

"Said I would last night and that has not changed. Do you want Ed to come along?"

"I will let you know on that; there is something about him and I am not sure what yet," Vince said quietly to Redmond as they looked at the island before heading back down.

"He is over a hundred years old; and from what I have heard, he has been here the longest and knows more about this weirdness than anyone else." Redmond stated.

"Let's go back down and see what young Bryce has discovered," Edwin said and turned toward the path to go back down.

When they met up with Bryce at the cemetery, they saw he was writing names in a small note pad. Where he got the note pad, they were not sure.

"Bryce, what have you found? Where did you get the paper?" Edwin asked as they approached him at the cemetery.

"I found this pad and pencil in the operations building; hope you don't mind if I use it?" Bryce answered as he continued to write on the pad.

"No, everything here is for us to use. What have you discovered?" Edwin replied quickly.

"Well, the names do look familiar. The last names, look at the last names and the dates that are on the crosses. This may only be a coincidence but I for one do not believe in coincidences," Bryce commented looking up from his pad. "Give me a little time and I will be in a better position to tell you.

"We still have a lot of daylight; do you want to go to the boats?" Redmond asked, ignoring Bryce.

"Let's get some water and head over there," Vince agreed.

Twenty minutes later, the group minus Edwin and Amelia headed down to the beach and then north around the cove. The island actually circled the cove which was more of a lagoon. They could see the other end of the island as soon as they stepped on the beach. Upon seeing the ships in the distance, they started to walk. They were silent as they walked; Bryce trailed behind looking at his list of names and mumbling to himself. Upon reaching the bend in the cove, Vince looked out at the four derelict ships and wondered how they were going to get out to them. "How did you get out there before?"

"We have a small boat over here in the brush. Help me pull it out and down to the water, then we row out. Which one do you want to see first?" Redmond asked.

"The yacht, I want to see the yacht first," Vince replied without thinking much.

Exploring the yacht turned up nothing of interest; they moved over to the freighters and that also turned up nothing of real interest. They found log books that were incomplete, hand written notes by the crews that indicated they had no idea what was happening with their friends and crewmates. The yacht was cruising around the Bahamas when they were attacked by pirates; two of the crew were shot immediately and then there was a large flash and they found themselves floating in this cove with all crew members, the owner of the yacht and his family. They left the yacht and went to shore and the log ended when the captain showed that the owner and his family decided to go inland to locate the source of a strange light they saw at night coming from a small mountain several miles inland. They did not return within a couple of days. And the captain's last entry shows that he and his crew went searching for them. Nothing was entered after that, we assume they got lost or died looking for them." Redmond answered.

"Interesting log entries, but what is most interesting is how the log got back on the boat after the crew went inland," Morgan commented as she examined the log book carefully.

"That is interesting, Morgan. How did the log get back on the yacht?" Vince asked not to anyone in particular.

"I can answer that, Morgan," Redmond started to say, "Not long after I arrived, I found the log in one of the rooms in the barracks and gave it to Edwin. He must have brought it back to the yacht. But I can't be a hundred percent sure he did."

"Why don't we camp out on this boat; it seems to be fully stocked with food and drink?" Diane asked.

"Maybe later, but right now we need to get more information and find a way off this rock," Bryce stated.

The indication from the logs on the freighters only state that they were sailing from New York to England during World War II when they were torpedoed, only to see a flash just as the torpedo hit and they found themselves in this cove beside another Liberty ship from the convoy they were in. The crews entered the island and disappeared inland over the next couple of months. Entries in the log books stopped with the Captains stating they were leaving the boats and going inland with hopes of finding a way off the island. The last entry from both freighters was June 4, 1944.

Chapter 11 Day 3 On The Island

"We have been here for three days and still have no more information than what we had when we arrived. Those three boats didn't turn up much; we still need to get on the sub," Vince commented as the five of them sat in the mess hall eating a breakfast of eggs, bacon and fried potatoes. They had to cook their own breakfast this morning. Everything they needed was in the well-stocked pantry and refrigerator.

"Well, not exactly, sir," Bryce piped in while sipping a cup of coffee; his look turned serious and then suddenly he smiled. "I reviewed the headstones for familiar names and there are several which just don't make much sense."

"Yeah, what do you mean?" Diane asked between bites of her eggs.

"Well, there are some names that, well, let me put it this way. Our hosts are buried in that cemetery, yet they walk among us."

"What?" Freddy asked looking more confused.

"Okay, Edwin Kelsey, according to the headstone, died September 2, 1937. The same year that Amelia Earhart and Fred Noonan disappeared, and they have head stones in there also, dated July 2, 1937. There are also several unmarked graves right next to each of theirs."

"They need to explain themselves. What about the others?" Vince asked becoming more worried about their situation.

"Robert Heinz has a marker with dates of his death. It seems as though our hosts are lying," Bryce commented as he looked intently at his friends.

"Yes, seems as though, but what about the good Captain?" Morgan commented nervously.

"No marker, he may or may not be who he says he is," Bryce acknowledged.

"As of right now, we do not go anywhere alone and do not trust any of our hosts," Vince ordered. "Everything seems so real and I have no idea why they would want to deceive us." He looked up and saw Captain Redmond walk into the room. "Captain Redmond, please sit down, we have a few questions."

"What's on your mind this beautiful morning?" he replied and sat beside Morgan after getting a fresh cup of coffee.

"Redmond, you have been here awhile and have seen a lot. Yet, you have not figured out why you were not killed like your co-pilot. Why is that?" Bryce asked.

"That is a good question, my young friend; and I wish I had a good answer, yet I don't. I explored around the island, but not the interior. Was tempted several times when the others decided to go, but I guess I was not up to the task and decided to just hang out here. We have everything we need to survive; I have no family to go back to, and most of my friends are in the military. Some will never go home; others, well, I just don't know about them."

"We have been told a lot, but there are still a lot of unknowns; and being the inquisitive types that we are, we just can't let it ride and need to find answers," Diane said and then looked at Vince and back to Redmond and said, "Sorry."

"No need to be sorry, Miss Morgan."

"Okay, can we trust you?" Bryce asked.

"Sure, I am an American fighter pilot and am here in the same situation as you. Why would you believe you couldn't trust me?" Redmond asked.

"To start with, all our other hosts have grave markers in the cemetery and you don't. Why?" Bryce asked.

"That is easy. They are dead and I am not," Redmond commented cracking a small smile.

"Will you explain what you mean?" Vince asked.

"That is the simple part. Long before I got here those graves were empty. When Edwin Kelsey arrived he was not doing well, his health was poor. From what I was told, he had a broken leg, multiple bruises and cuts on his body. There is a written log of all the people who arrived before and after Ed got here. He lived here until 1937 when Amelia and Fred arrived. Then he died when he was sixty-seven years old; and according to the log, he slipped and fell, hit his head on a rock, was in a coma for a while and just died. They buried him and within a week another Edwin Kelsey showed up; looked exactly like him and knew everything about the Edwin that was buried in the cemetery. The Edwin you met three days ago and is walking around the compound is the third Edwin we have seen. He is one hundred percent Edwin Kelsey as far as I can tell, but he arrived around two years ago and only knows he has been here for the past two years, nothing about the other Kelsey."

"Wow, are you saying that when one Edwin dies another takes his place?" Vince questioned. "That defies the laws of physics."

"Yeah, it does, and I don't know much about physics; but what I know is what I have seen. They come, live, die and another shows up. Not all of them, Susan, Fran, Rhonda and I have not died yet; the rest have died and returned. Spooky."

"Okay, that sort of explains why Edwin looks like a thirty-year-old, but what about the others?" Diane asked.

"The same thing happens to the others. They live and when they die of old age or from an accident, they are buried; and within a few days, a replacement shows up. And they don't grow old fast. I was shot down in 1969 and don't know what the date is now, but you guys disappeared in 2031. If that is what today is, then I have not aged much, at least my body has not aged. Do you want to see the log book?"

"Yes, where is it?" Bryce asked before anyone else could reply. "Do the others read the log and find out they are number whatever?

"Yes, they do; but, well, they just seem to forget about it. I will be right back. It is kept in the operations building; guess we should have shown it to you when you got here," Redmond stated and then stood and walked out of the mess hall. He returned a few minutes later with a green nine inch by fourteen-inch book with a faded red ribbon sticking out of the top marking a page. He handed the book to Vince, and returned to his seat beside Morgan. "You have been pretty quiet, Miss Morgan. Do you have any questions that I can possibly answer?"

"No, just taking all this in; it is so weird," Morgan commented and then took a sip of orange juice.

"Redmond, this is a very interesting list of guests to this resort," Vince commented as he scanned through the book. "Look here, the entire crew of a United States submarine from World War I and another from WW II. But there is only one submarine out there. Where is the other one? This book was started in 1910 by a fellow with the name of Wilbur T. Heinz from Charlotte, North Carolina. Is he any relation to Robert Heinz?"

"Not sure, but possible. You will have to ask him," Redmond replied. "You will see a lot of familiar names in that book; it is like a lot of people in that book were either related to or were important people in history. There are a couple of kids listed also. Two come to mind right away. Boris Karloff and Sonja Henie showed up here and were around for a while before, ah, well they just disappeared shortly after I got here. As for the other submarine, it either sank in the cove or, well, it just isn't here anymore."

"That is pretty strange, for sure. Both of them died in 1969. They show up here as teens in 1969 and that is the same year they died." Vince stated.

"How old were they when they got here?" Bryce asked trying to put all this together in a logical sequence.

"Early teens probably, maybe as old as twenty; I had just arrived myself, and they were already here. I was introduced and several months later they were gone. I recognized the names and loved Karloff's movies and did get a chance to see Sonja skate during reruns of the 1932 and 36 Olympics. Weird, but from what I read in that book, there is a lot of weirdness going on around here." Redmond answered.

"I will drink to that, Captain," Vince said and continued to scan the book. "I want to spend some time with this book and have Morgan and Bryce review it also. Morgan is a history buff; and Bryce, well, he is just plain smart."

"No problem, put it back in the ops building when done," Redmond stated. "What is your plan for today, after reading that book?"

"I want to finish going through the boats today, especially the sub. That should have some interesting information we could use," Vince said and then continued, "Those other boats just did not tell us enough; the submarine should have some interesting stories."

"Okay, let's go over to the beach and visit our submarine," Redmond agreed, "And then what?"

"And then we need to go into the jungle and see what we find. The yacht logbook mentioned that one of the guests saw a light on a hill in the northern part of the island; maybe we should look for the light," Bryce stated confidently.

"When the crew of the sub came ashore, they brought weapons with them; and they left some when they went into the jungle. They are stored up in the arms room in the back of this building. We can grab a few of them for protection. I also have my pistol and my back seat operator's pistol, both are Colt 1911 forty-five caliber pistols; and I have about fourteen rounds of ammo. There may be more ammo in the arms room. Plus, I have a couple of survival knives. Do any of you know anything about weapons?" Redmond asked.

"Yes, kind of a hobby with me," Bryce stated and then looked over at Morgan. "Thought you said that you only had your pistol; you didn't mention an arms room."

"I said I only had my pistol for protection. I haven't been in the arms room but once since I got here. Sorry, forgot about it," Redmond apologized.

"My father is a hunter and has taught me a lot about guns; why are you asking?" Morgan inquired.

"Those weapons may not have been cleaned in years. I will need some help cleaning them, and then making sure they function before we go tramping through the jungle," Redmond replied.

"Let's get them cleaned and then head for the sub. After that, we go into the jungle. So, pack light, but bring clean water and food," Vince stated and then stood to get more coffee.

"I know of a trail, about a mile up the beach that leads into the jungle; not sure where it goes. I have only been down it for a couple of hundred yards before turning around."

"Sounds like a good place to start; let's get to work on those weapons," Vince stated between sips of his coffee.

"I also suggest we let Edwin know where we are going; he will protest, but not stop us," Redmond suggested.

Chapter 12 Undersea Sailing Club Boat

"It's amazing; the batteries still have enough power to run the lights," Freddy Carlson stated as he climbed down the ladder into the submarine's sail hatch. Entering the cramped sail seemed, well, not seemed, it was like stepping back over seventy years. Freddy had a hard time getting down because of his size and immediately banged his head on the bulkhead in the sail.

"Yeah, pretty cool, Freddy," Morgan replied sarcastically as she brushed her hand across a layer of dust on the top of a piece of equipment in the sail. "It does look like it has been here for seventy years; look at the dust. Wait, where did the dust come from? This is a sealed, air tight piece of machinery."

"Good question, Morgan," Freddy stated as he started down the ladder to the main deck.

"Okay, I will go to the Captain's cabin and the control room. Bryce, you and Morgan take the forward area, Freddy and Diane the rear torpedo room, and Redmond come with me," Vince ordered his team when they reached the main control room below the sail. They were to split up and head for their assigned areas.

"Check your flashlights, in case the lights go out; meet back here in twenty minutes. And stay together." Redmond added.

"Captain, have you been on the sub before?" Vince asked as they snaked their way to the Captain's quarters, hoping to find some clues.

"I came out shortly after I arrived, but didn't search much. The power was off, and my flashlight did not have much battery power left to supply light; so, I didn't stay long," Redmond replied just as they reached the captain's quarters. "Can't understand why there was no power back then and there is power now."

"Everything on this island is pretty weird; and I think, well, right now I don't know what to think," Vince commented as they entered the cramped room. He saw only a small bunk, fold down desk, several photos on the wall, and a safe. When Vince opened the closet, he saw several uniforms and a pair of black shoes.

"What are we looking for?" Redmond asked as he examined the contents of the Captain's desk where he found only a few pencils, a blank pad, envelopes, and a bunch of dust.

"The ship's log and any personal notes the Captain or crew may have left, anything that will help us to understand the why and where we are." Vince responded.

"Here is the logbook," Redmond said as he sat behind the small desk and started to flip through the pages. "Wow, this boat has had a pretty interesting cruise history. She is the SS-402 *USS Bluefin,* keel laid down July 5 1939, commissioned August 15, 1940, in New Haven, Connecticut and originally commanded by Lieutenant Commander Howard "Higgy" Higgins. She headed for Hawaii shortly after her shakedown cruise, and took up station in the South Pacific. She had a crew of six officers and fifty-four enlisted."

"That is interesting, but is there anything in there that can help us," Vince asked.

"Just a sec, Vince," Redmond said; for the first time he called Vince Landers by his first name.

"Look at this," Vince said as he picked up a sheet of very faded paper. "Why didn't he put this in the log?"

"What is it, Vince?"

Forward Torpedo Room

Meanwhile, up in the forward torpedo room, Bryce and Morgan were reading the torpedo room log book and finding a completely weird story.

"Bryce, look at this. It says here on March 15, 1943 they fired two torpedoes at a Japanese destroyer. One hit and severely damaged the destroyer; and the other circled and tracked at them. The entry ends with the torpedo striking the *Bluefin*. How can that be?" Morgan said as she read the logbook.

"It says it hit, but did it explode?" Bryce asked.

"It only says they felt it hit, and then there was a bright flash, and then nothing." Morgan replied as she read the log.

"Bring that with you, we need to talk to Dr. Landers."

"Wait, what is this?" Morgan said as she saw something in the corner below one of the torpedoes.

Engine Room

Back in the engine room, Diane and Freddy were looking high and low for the log book; or any other thing that would shed some light on why they were there.

"Diane, what is this?" Freddy asked as he reached behind a small door and pulled out an old Smith and Wesson thirty-eight caliber pistol. "Cool, this is so cool. Wait, here is the log book." He handed the log to Diane and continued to look around the engine room. He also slid the revolver into his pocket.

"Why don't you check out the rear torpedo room while I scan this log?" Diane suggested.

"Sure, be back in a couple of minutes," he agreed as he turned and started to head further back in the submarine. "No, wait! Vince said not to get separated; you should come with me."

"Just leave the door open, and I will stand by the door; we can keep an eye on each other while I finish this log." Diane said and went back to reading.

"Okay, but why not just sit on the knee knocker and keep an eye on me," Freddy said being a little nervous about going into the rear torpedo room. He was big and strong, but things just didn't seem right on this boat; and he was a bit nervous.

"I am right here; don't be such a wuss." Diane commented.

Diane leaned on the torpedo still in the rack, flipped through the log book and read as fast as she could. Being a speed reader, it did not take her long to finish the book. She just stood there smiling at what she had read. She could not believe the crew on board this boat were younger than she was, some no older than eighteen. These boys trained and went to war before they were of legal age to buy adult beverages in most states. Their dedication and loyalty to the country just amazed her.

"Diane, come in here!" Freddy yelled to her from the far end of the torpedo room. "You have to see this."

Captains Quarters

"Redmond, can I call you Bryan?" Vince asked while still in the Captain's quarters and then continued when he got a nod from Redmond. "This faded yellow page tells me a lot. The captain fired two torpedoes at a destroyer, one hit and the other turned on them, striking just below the sail. There was a flash; and when he looked through the periscope, he saw that they were in this cove with no destroyer in sight. He saw only a nice quiet cove with a Liberty ship anchored about a hundred yards to their port side. The island looked uninhabited through the periscope, so he ordered them to surface. The last entry was not finished, stating most of the crew went ashore to set up a base camp. He assigned three men to remain on board to guard the boat and indicated he would join the crew in an hour. It was signed by Lieutenant Commander Martin Richardson, Commander *USS Bluefin*, March 15, 1943.

Forward Torpedo Room

"That my sweet girl friend is a body. Doesn't look like he has been here long; navy uniform, rank of Seaman 2nd class; I don't see any visible wounds," Bryce commented as he looked over the body that was leaning between the bulkhead and torpedo rack.

"Wow, why is he here?" Morgan questioned.

"Maybe he was the boat guard when everyone went ashore," Bryce replied and then stood up while still looking down at the body.

Aft Torpedo room

"Diane, there is a dead body back here," Freddy said as Diane ducked and entered the torpedo room.

"A WHAT?" Diane yelled.

"A body, a dead body!"

Captain's Quarters

"Let's check the Exec's quarters," Vince said as he and Redmond headed down the narrow hall to the next room. As he pulled the curtain back, Vince stopped in his tracks at what he saw.

"I think we have a serious problem here. What is he doing here?" Vince stated looking at the corpse of the executive officer lying in his bunk, quite dead.

"He looks like he hasn't been dead long. Why didn't I see him when I came on board? Maybe he was, I didn't tour the entire boat. Remember, my flashlight wasn't working very well," Bryan stated as he looked around the small executive officer's quarters.

"Yeah, that is a very good question, Bryan, very good."

"Let's get back to the control room and regroup; find out what the rest of the team has found," Vince said as he stepped back into the narrow hall and turned toward the control room. Redmond was right behind him.

Chapter 13 Exploration

"Time to go," Vince said to Bryan and immediately turned and headed out of the small room. He stopped in the control room below the sail, looked around, and found what he was looking for. While picking up the microphone, he paused and looked at Redmond. "Do you know which switch to flip to make this work?"

"No, but maybe that one marked intercom," Bryan stated not knowing the correct answer.

"There isn't one marked intercom; let me try these," Vince said flipping all the switches to on and then depressed the microphone button and spoke into it. "Bryce, Diane, Freddy, and Morgan, please report to the control room immediately," he said and heard his voice resonating throughout the boat.

Five minutes later, the four students entered the control room frowning. After relating what they had found, everyone expressed concern about the three bodies.

"It's time we dug deeper my young friends," Vince commented. "This is getting weirder and weirder by the minute. Either this is the most elaborate hoax ever conceived; or we have truly stepped into the Twilight Zone."

"It is hard to believe that someone would go to this much trouble just as a joke," Freddy commented.

"We are archeologists and digging is what we do best; so, it is time to dig, let's go," Bryce said and received agreement from everyone.

"Where, sir?" Morgan asked.

"Inland to the place the logbook said they saw a light," Vince stated seriously, "Into the jungle."

"Roger that," Bryan Redmond said quickly. "Before we go, let's go back and get some of those weapons we cleaned this morning, stock up on food and water, and get an early start."

"Good idea, Bryce and Bryan, grab a few weapons and make sure you get some ammo to go with whatever you get," Vince ordered. He then turned to the rest and pointed to the ladder.

After climbing out of the boat to the top of the sail, they immediately got down to the deck and slid down to their small wooden boat tied to the sub. The row back to shore took about fifteen minutes, and once there, they walked quietly back to the barracks. Arriving about forty minutes after leaving the sub, they were confronted by Edwin and Amelia.

"Gather water and food, I don't know how long we will be gone," Vince ordered just as they entered the building.

"I know what you are planning and I advise against it," Edwin stated as he looked Vince in the eye.

"I agree; it is dangerous, and you won't find the answers you are looking for," Amelia stated.

"Edwin, there is a lot of weird stuff going on around here; and we need to find out what it is. And we are sorry you don't approve, but we have to do this." Vince stated.

"You may not like what you find. I know what you found on the *Bluefin,* and it may seem weird; but it is what it is. Live with it." Edwin stated.

"How do explain the three dead sailors on board?" Bryan Redmond challenged.

"Dead sailors? The last time I was out there, there were no dead sailors. Where were they?" Edwin questioned looking even more concerned.

"Forward and aft torpedo rooms, and the Executive Officer was in his cabin," Vince replied looking more confused than before.

"Interesting, the Executive Officer along with two of the crew were left on the boat to guard it. They used to stay in the barracks after getting tired of guarding a boat that would not move. After a while, they took some food and several weapons and left. We looked for them, but could find no trace of them. How long ago do you think they died?" Edwin explained and asked, shaking his head in disbelief and pacing back and forth.

"A few days, maybe a week; they have not been dead long," Bryan Redmond commented. "I have seen a lot of dead in my time over in Nam and they haven't been dead long. No obvious wounds, but we did not inspect the bodies. Maybe we should go back; and, well, get them off the boat and bury them."

"I think you are right; let's get some blankets and go back. Edwin, can you and a couple of others help us?" Vince agreed.

"Sure, there are body bags in the supply room. I will get some and meet you back here in ten minutes," Edwin said and then turned and headed to the supply room.

Forty minutes later, a team of nine was standing on the beach looking out at the *Bluefin* and wondering how the three dead sailors got back on board. There was no dingy tied up to the boat and no indication that they had one stored anywhere on board. But they had not looked too close in all the lockers; they missed the rubber boat in the deck locker. As they rowed out to the boat, Vince, Bryan, Bryce, Edwin and Morgan eyed the boat with concern. What was happening on this island?

Diane, Fred Noonan, Robert Heinz and Fran Snow were paddling out to the boat in a second small boat.

Edwin, Bryan and Vince climbed up the side of the sail and opened the hatch to enter the *Bluefin*.

"Bryan, why don't you go first; then Ed and the rest of us will follow. Bryan, take Ed to the Executive Officer's cabin, I will take Bryce to the forward torpedo room, and Fred Noonan can take Fran to the aft torpedo room. Let's get this done as quickly as we can. The sun is going down and I want to be back on the beach before it gets dark out here," Vince ordered.

"Wait a second, who made you boss?" Edwin questioned as he looked down the open hatch.

"I made me boss, at least for now. You can contest it when we get back to the beach," Vince stated seriously.

"Okay, okay, I will comply for now, but we need to have a serious discussion when we get back to the barracks," Edwin agreed reluctantly and then started down the ladder into the sail behind Bryan.

"This way, Ed," Bryan said as soon as he stepped off the ladder.

As they walked down the narrow hall toward the Executive Officer's cabin, they heard Bryce and Morgan drop into the control room. Footsteps were heard coming up behind them as Bryce and Morgan started toward the forward torpedo room.

"Bryce, be as quick as possible," Vince said. He stopped outside the Exec's cabin and turned toward Bryce as they came up behind him.

"For sure, Mr. Landers," Bryce commented as they passed Landers, Edwin and Bryan.

Edwin opened the door and turned on the light only to find the cabin empty. "Where is the body?" he said as he looked into the small cabin.

"What?" Vince yelled looking over Edwin's shoulder as Bryan muscled his way into the cabin to see that the Executive Officer was not in his cabin. "Check the other cabins," he said and turned toward the Captain's cabin as Bryan turned and headed to the next cabin.

"Where the hell did he go?" Edwin asked looking confused.

"How the hell do I know; he was there two hours ago," Vince replied as he stepped out of the Captain's cabin.

"Nobody in any of the cabins," Bryan commented when they regrouped at the exec's cabin.

"Attention everyone, please report back to me when you get to your assigned area. Let me know if you have a body or not," Vince said into the ship board intercom.

"Mr. Landers, this is Bryce up in the forward torpedo room. The body is gone. We are looking everywhere, but he is gone," Bryce reported and then clicked off.

"Vince, this is Noonan in the Aft Torpedo room; there are no bodies back here."

"Okay, please search every possible place where a body could be as you return to the control room, look everywhere. They were here two hours ago, dead. They did not get up and walk off this boat; they have to be here," Vince said and looked at Edwin and started to speak, but stopped and finally asked, "What the hell is going on here, Edwin? You have been here the longest; and we need answers, now."

"Ah, the truth, as Jack Nicholson said in a movie that aired not long ago. You can't handle the truth!" Edwin stated, turned and walked toward the control room.

Back at the Mess Hall

It took an hour to get back to the beach and return to the compound. When they met in the Mess Hall, the silence was almost unbearable. Nobody spoke; you could have heard a pin drop. All eyes were on Edwin, and he wasn't ready to talk. Sitting alone in the corner, he slowly ate his dinner of pork chops, potato and corn; in between bites, he would look up and take a sip from his glass of tea.

Vince, Bryce, Morgan, Freddy, and Diane sat quietly across the mess hall and watched Edwin eat. Bryan Redmond came into the mess hall, picked up a tray, and dished out some food from the steam table. He looked around, saw an empty seat across from Vince, and with his eyes, he asked if he could sit with them. After getting an affirmative nod, he sat and looked at Vince and then across the room at Edwin.

"He is not talking?" Bryan Redmond asked, questioning the obvious.

"No, he knows stuff and he isn't saying," Vince stated "But he will."

"Where are the others?" Bryce asked Bryan.

"They told me they would be over shortly. Amelia and Noonan were in the library looking at some old books; the others were still in their rooms, I guess. I didn't see them," Redmond replied and then took a bite of his pork chop. "Who cooked tonight, this is pretty good."

"Fran cooked. She is still in the kitchen," Morgan commented, "Yes, they are pretty good. Better than I could do."

"I've had enough of this silence. I'm going over there and make him tell us," Bryce said as he stood and started to move away from the table when Morgan grabbed his arm.

"Don't, wait!" Morgan said as she looked up at Bryce, "He will talk; give him a few more minutes."

As he looked up from Morgan, he saw Edwin walk toward the window to place his tray there to get it cleaned. He stopped, set it down, and then turned toward Vince, Redmond, and the students. After walking over, he stopped, looked Bryce in the eye, and said, "Please sit and I will tell you something that you won't want to hear."

"It's about time, Edwin," Redmond said as he leaned back and turned to look up at Edwin.

Chapter 14 On The Beach

Vince, Redmond, and the students headed to the beach and started in a clockwise direction around the island to reach the cove where the wrecked boats were. Upon reaching the cove, they noticed that one of the Liberty ships was listing to port and the other was gone.

"Now that is weird; where did the other ship go?" Freddy commented as they all looked out over the cove.

"There it is, on the other side of the closest one; looks like she sunk. Just the top of the mast is visible, see it?" Bryce said as he pointed out over the bay. "She went down overnight. But she seemed fine when we were on her a couple of days ago."

"We can't be concerned about her now; we have bigger fish to fry, as they say," Vince replied, "What Edwin said last night just doesn't seem real, we need more answers. Remember what he said, all our answers are at the source of the light; we just need to find the light."

Walking in the soft sand was difficult, but not impossible. They did not make a lot of headway; but by late afternoon, they had reached the northern tip of the island and decided to make camp on the beach and then to penetrate the jungle in the morning.

"Fred, will you gather some firewood while we set up camp?" Bryan requested.

"Sure," he replied and dropped his backpack on the ground. He looked at Diane and asked, "Care to help?"

"Okay, no problem, right behind you," Diane agreed and dropped her pack also.

Their camp would consist of a few old tents they had found in the supply room which were easy to carry and would provide some protection from the elements in case it rained. Bryan and the remaining three people would look for a stretch of hard soil close to the jungle's edge to erect the tents, and build a fire pit. A half hour later, the tents were almost up. They had some problems with the old canvas; but finally after some trial and error, they had all six tents up and the sleeping bags opened and airing out. They were very musty from being rolled up for the past sixty or seventy years.

As they sat around the campfire, they munched on very tasty, very old 'K' rations they had found in the supply room.

"Wow, these are pretty good; what do you think Bryce?" Morgan asked.

"Yeah, tasty. I have had better food at; well, I won't say which fast food joint," Bryce replied at the comment.

"Hey, quit complaining; at least we have food and don't have to go out and hunt for it," Vince commented as he bit down on a very dry cracker.

As the sun set in the west, they all sat quietly around the campfire contemplating tomorrow. What would they find? Would they survive, or was this just a trip into a friendly jungle with nothing to fear except fear itself.

"What do you think we will find in there?" Bryce asked.

"Not really sure, Bryce; there were reports of lights on that hill over there, and I think that is the first place we should visit. At least based on what Edwin said, that is our first destination," Vince replied between bites of what was supposed to be beef stew.

"Beautiful sunset," Morgan commented as she studied the setting sun.

"Yes it is; hope it isn't our last," Freddy acknowledged.

The night was cool, but not unpleasant; the campfire burned well with all the driftwood that Freddy and Diane had gathered. They discussed what they had found on the submarine, and Freddy mentioned he found the old pistol which he showed everyone.

"That little pea shooter is a museum piece; do you think it will fire or explode?" Bryan asked as he examined the old pistol.

"I don't know, and am not going to fire it unless it is my last resort. You gave me this nice Colt to use and I will use it if need be," Freddy commented as he patted the Army Colt Model 1911 forty-five pistol he wore on his hip similar to the ones that everyone else carried.

"Look, it's getting late; and I think we should get some sleep. I will take first watch. Rotate every two hours until dawn. Who wants second watch?" Vince ordered and got a hand raised by Morgan and then Bryce, Bryan, and Diane with Vince pulling the last watch just before dawn. "Now get some sleep; tomorrow will be a long day, and we have no idea what we will find."

"I wish we could just continue around the beach, but those rocks look pretty tough to get past and into the jungle," Redmond stated as he eyed the coastline.

"Yeah, we need to get to the other side anyway; that is where Edwin said the light came from," Vince stated and then crawled into his tent. "Good night."

Chapter 15 The Jungle

Vince was now armed with a Thompson machine gun and a Colt model 1911 forty-five. Captain Redmond was also armed with a machine gun and his own Colt 1911. All four students were given instruction on the use of a Colt and were also armed with a Colt. Morgan and Diane also carried a light aviation model M-2 Carbine with folding stock, while Freddy and Bryce carried the heavier M-1 Garand 30-06 rifles. They broke camp and started up the beach to a path that had been carved into the jungle many years before they got there.

"This path looks well worn; look at those foot prints, almost like they were made yesterday," Bryce commented as he looked at the fresh shoe print. After following the foot prints, they came to a small clearing with a wrecked Japanese Zero. The plane was empty; no pilot or sign of the pilot could be found. Bryce climbed up on the wing and looked inside only to find cobwebs and dust. He brushed off some dust on the cracked seat and found a small Japanese flag. Upon closer inspection, he discovered it wasn't just a flag but a bandana, the kind that the Kamikaze pilots wore into combat.

"It isn't possible that those footprints are from the pilot of this Zero, is it?" Morgan asked.

"No way, man. He would be over one hundred years old. Living out here alone for eighty years, impossible," Bryce replied looking at the old plane, seeing that it had bullet holes near the engine which most likely caused it to crash. "There was no trace of blood in the cockpit and the canopy was open. He must have survived the crash, but where is he now?"

"Good observation, Bryce. See if there is anything in there we could use," Bryan asked.

"Just a faded map, still somewhat readable," Bryce said as he pulled a map from the cockpit. "It's a map of the Philippines showing the Coral Sea. It was one of the greatest American victories in the Pacific war zone. It looks like he was one of the pilots from a Japanese aircraft carrier before he was shot down."

"Let's keep moving; we are burning daylight," Vince said, and followed with, "I've always wanted to say that."

"Cool! What's that?" Morgan said as she pointed to the jungle on the other side of the field. "Something is moving over there."

"What did you see?" Bryan asked as he pulled his machine gun off his shoulder and pulled back on the charging knob to put a round in the chamber. Vince did the same with his machine gun, and watched as the students pulled their weapons from their shoulders.

"Let's go see what spooked you, shall we," Vince said and started to walk around the front of the plane.

"Looked like a man," Morgan said and followed behind Bryce.

"A man? He has to be over a hundred years old, if he is the pilot of this plane."

"He headed down that path; should we follow?" Morgan asked.

"We stay together; and follow," Vince said and got agreement from everyone. Bryan took the lead and the rest followed closely behind. Because they saw footprints in the soft dirt, the man was easy to follow; and the path only went one direction, deeper into the jungle. Minutes passed, and they still had not caught up with the man. When they stopped at a small stream, they saw him enter the brush about a hundred feet ahead of them.

"Let's go; he is going toward the hill on the north side," Bryan said and took off in a trot with his weapon ready for anything. He stopped briefly before he ducked under a tree limb and went into the jungle again. They all proceeded deeper into the unknown. "Whoa!" Bryce held up his hand to stop. "What the hell?"

They all stopped and looked past Redmond where they saw a small primitive cabin sitting in a small clearing. There was a man sitting on a stump in front of the cabin dressed in what could have been a uniform at one time, but now it was just rags clinging to an underfed man. The man raised his hand to signal for Bryan and his followers to come over. They hesitated for a few seconds, before deciding it was safe to proceed. They walked cautiously, entered the clearing, and approached the man.

"What took you so long?" the man said after eyeing his guests.

"What took us so long; how long have you been here?" Bryan asked without relaxing his hold on his weapon.

"Let me introduce myself, I am Lieutenant Commander Martin Richardson, past Commander of the *USS Bluefin*."

"You can't be Richardson; that would make you over a hundred years old," Bryan commented.

"Well, believe it or not, I am Richardson; and no, I don't look my age, a bit thinner and grey, but this island seems to make time go a bit slower."

"Where is your crew?" Vince asked.

"My crew, well, a lot of them are buried right over there," Richardson said pointing to an area about fifty yards from the cabin.

"And the rest?" Bryce asked.

"Don't know. They headed off toward the light a long time ago and never came back. Please pull up a bit of ground and have a seat. I will tell you everything I know about the island; some of it you may already know, but I will attempt to fill in the gaps. Would you care for some lemonade?"

"Sure," Morgan answered.

"Be right back; sorry, I don't have any ice. My ice machine is not working too well; it broke a few days ago," Richardson said as he stood and entered the small cabin. He returned a few minutes later with a tall bamboo container and six bamboo cups on a homemade tray. "Help yourself," he said as he placed the tray on a stump next to him. "I grow lemons in a field down by the creek. I have oranges, grapefruit, and mangos too."

"Industrious, Commander; especially if you have lived out here since 1943 when your boat arrived and you survived. Edwin Kelsey warned us not to come into the jungle; are you the reason for the warning?" Vince asked.

"No, I am not. He has his reasons, but it isn't me; I tend to not go much deeper into the jungle. I could have moved back down to the airfield with Kelsey, but felt safer with my crew. There are six more cabins just inside the jungle within a few feet of this clearing. This one is really our mess hall, my cabin is over there," he said pointing the opposite way from the cemetery.

"You have been here a long time; can you tell us what we can expect to see or run into between here and the light?" Bryce asked and took a sip of lemonade. "Good lemonade."

"Thank you. If I tell you what to expect you would think I am crazy and maybe, I am. But there are things out there that defy reality. Things that shouldn't be, but are there, none the less."

"Enlighten us," Bryan stated.

Twenty minutes later, they sat there stunned at what they had heard from this old sailor.

"Do you think I am crazy?"

"Not sure..." Vince started to say stopping short when he saw a wild burro come out of the jungle and walk toward the group.

"Here comes Tony now," Richardson said. He stood, walked over to Tony the donkey, rubbed his nose, and spoke quietly to him. They both walked back over to the group; stopping short Richardson said, "Tony, this is Bryan, Vince, Bryce, Morgan, and Diane."

"Pleasure to meet you. When did you get here?" Tony said in a gravelly voice.

"Whoa, how, Tony, you speak," Bryan said as he stood and backed up a bit.

"Yes, is there a problem with that?"

"Well, yeah, donkeys don't talk," Bryan said holding up his hand to keep Tony from approaching.

"Sorry to disappoint you, but I have been talking since I was able to walk."

"I think it is cool," Morgan added to the conversation.

"Me too," Diane agreed.

"Tony, how long have you been on the island?" Vince asked.

"I was on one of the Liberty ships headed for England in 1943, when we took a torpedo and started to sink. There was a large flash of light; and the next thing we knew; we were in that cove down there. And yes, I am almost a hundred years old too; but don't look a day over fifteen," Tony commented.

"Wow, a talking donkey, and a submarine captain, both almost a hundred years old, on an island somewhere on mother earth. Where exactly, we don't know; and everyone here arrived after a flash of light. This is getting weirder and weirder the more we hear," Bryce commented. "What happened to the Japanese pilot in the wreck we passed coming here?"

"He is buried over there too."

"What do we do next, Mr. Landers?" Morgan asked.

"We rest, and then continue to the light," he replied.

Chapter 16 Into The Mist

Richardson stood and walked toward the cemetery with Tony at his side. Vince watched him as he approached the cemetery. He only diverted his eyes to answer Morgan's question.

"Mr. Landers are we going to get to go home?" Morgan asked.

"I don't know," Vince replied and then looked back to the cemetery. He could not see Richardson or the donkey anywhere, like they just faded into the jungle. "Where did Richardson go?"

"Huh? He went to the cemetery, didn't he?" Bryce said as he looked toward the cemetery and only saw a mist gathering around the crosses. "Where did that mist come from?"

"The temperature is dropping and heat from the ground mixed with the moisture in the air causes mist or ground fog to form," Morgan stated looking at the cemetery.

"But the temp is not dropping; it is getting close to the hottest part of the day," Vince said as he stood and started to walk toward the cemetery. As his four students and Bryan stood and followed, Vince said, "Grab your stuff; we are leaving."

Minutes later, they walked through the cemetery and looked at the crosses as they passed through. "Do you see the dates on the crosses? Mostly 1944 and, wait, what's this?" Morgan said as he stopped in front of a cross. "It says, LT Commander Martin Richardson, died December 7, 1944."

"What? He's dead?" Bryce almost yelled as he stopped to look at the cross. "Look at the one next to him, Chief

Anthony Moore, a real ass but best Chief of the Boat a commander could ask for."

"Interesting, were we just chatting with a ghost and his donkey?" Diane asked quietly.

"That is highly possible, Miss Diane," Vince commented as he scanned around the cemetery. "What we have is an enigma. And we are going to find out what the hell is going on with this island or die trying."

"I am all for the finding out what is going on, but not so keen on the dying part," Morgan said.

"Me too, let's go figure this out," Bryce commented as he kicked a clump of dirt away from a faded wooden cross. He then reached down to pick up a small object that was under the clump. "Hey, look at this, dog tags; these are Richardson's tags, just lying beside his cross." Then he hung the tags over the cross.

"Thank you," a voice said so quietly that he almost didn't hear it.

"Did you hear that?" Bryce asked.

"Hear what?" Morgan responded, "Are you hearing voices again?"

"Never mind, let's go," Bryce said smiling. He knew he had just heard the voice of Commander Richardson.

"Let's go," Bryan said and then turned and started to walk into the gathering mist and the thickening jungle. Using his recently found machete, he cut away some of the brush to make the ancient path a bit more navigable. Following close behind were Freddy, Diane, Morgan, Bryce and then Vince bringing up the rear of the group. They were tense and could not see more than twenty feet down the path. Although the brush was thick, the mist was thicker.

"Doc, this stuff is getting pretty thick. I suggest everyone hold hands or the back of the person in front of you. We don't want to lose anyone," Bryan suggested to his group.

"Good idea," Vince said and reached out to take hold of Bryce's belt; each one did the same in front of him. They could still see each other, but it was becoming more difficult. "Bryan, stop!" Vince yelled as he felt someone grab the back of his pants. He turned and immediately turned white when he found himself looking into the lifeless eyes of a tall man.

Bryan and the rest immediately turned around to see what the problem was and could not believe their eyes.

"Who are you?" Vince asked the impossibly thin man wearing a ragged flight suit that was barely hanging onto his skeletal frame.

"I know who I am; who are you and why are you here on my island?" the man mumbled as he rested his left hand on an old leather holster and slowly started to pull out an equally old Colt Army Model 1911 semi-automatic forty-five caliber pistol.

"No need to pull that out," Bryan yelled as he came back to Vince holding his machine gun up in hip level firing position.

"Okay, I will not. But you should not go any further into the jungle," the man said quietly.

"Why?" Bryce asked.

"Those that have gone in there have not returned. And you will not return." The man replied in a very quiet voice.

"Who are you?" Vince asked again.

"No matter who I am. I know who you are, and you are in danger if you go in there."

"Who are you?" Vince asked again.

"It doesn't matter who I am. I will be dead soon and so will you."

"What will kill us in there?" Bryce asked as he looked around. He was not able to see much because of the mist.

"Okay, say we don't go further; will you tell us what we need to know?" Bryan asked of the old man.

"I can't tell you what I don't know. I only know going in there is a mistake, one you don't want to make," the old man said and then smiled. His smile showed a lot of missing teeth and stained and broken ones for the teeth that were there..

"You need..." Bryan started to say just as the man turned around and faded into the mist. "Where did he go?"

"He just turned and walked off," Freddy said and pointed down the path the old man turned down.

"What do we do, Mr. Landers?" Morgan asked sounding very scared.

"We continue; we have to find out what the hell is going on," Vince responded and turned and took the lead down the path through the heavy mist, "Do not lose sight of the person in front of you; if you have to hold onto their belt then do so. Let's go."

"Vince, I will bring up the rear and keep an eye on everyone," Bryan said as he followed Morgan thinking that she was a beautiful young lady. And when the last time he had been with a lady, he could not remember. But that thought needed to be put on hold for now. He had bigger things to handle; like why they were here. He had waited too long to find out.

The going was slow; the jungle was thick and covered in spider webs which they did not see until they walked into one and then another. Large banana spiders, which are harmless to humans, were all over the jungle and the mist was hampering their vision. After an hour of cutting branches, and ducking under and around spider webs, the mist started to thin; and their forward view increased from ten feet to twenty, and eventually the mist was almost gone giving them a view of a canyon wall. As they looked left and right, they saw that to the right there was a cliff that dropped off several dozen feet, and to the left, the canyon showed a path between two sheer cliff walls that extended up about a hundred feet on each side.

"Well we either drop down to the bottom of that cliff over there or take the path of least resistance. What do you say?" Vince commented.

"We don't have any climbing gear, so it is the path of least resistance, the canyon," Bryce said with a chuckle.

"What's that?" Freddy said pointing to the tree line across the stream that blocked their way.

"That my young friend is a B-25 Mitchell Bomber, a twin engine light bomber. It is the same type used in the Doolittle raid on Japan during the Second World War. What it is doing here is a good question, and she looks like she is in great shape except being stuck in the trees," Bryan said as they all jumped over the small stream and walked over to the plane, seeing it sitting as if it just landed on its tricycle landing gear with the bomb bay doors open.

"Looks like it taxied in here down that wide path on the other side of her. Wonder where the crew is?" Morgan said seeing a wide taxi way on the other side of the plane with the nose of the plane pointing down the wide path.

"Whoa, the crew is still in here," Bryan said as he climbed up into the bomb bay. I don't think you ladies want to see this. He stopped as he heard someone come up behind him. When he turned, he saw Bryce and Vince walking toward the cockpit.

"Yep, looks like they landed, taxied here, shut down the engines, and just died in their seats. Both pilot and copilot have blood stains and bullet holes in their chests and sides. Bryce, check the navigator," Vince suggested.

"Same here; he has multiple bullet holes in him and the top turret gunner, too. What about those guys back there?" Bryce asked as Bryan examined the bodies in the back.

"All shot to hell."

Chapter 17 Pearl Harbor

The cruise at flank speed on a nuclear powered missile boat under the command of Lieutenant Commander David Henderson was like nothing you could imagine. The ride was smooth, and uneventful. It didn't take long to reach Pearl Harbor. After surfacing two miles outside Pearl Harbor and receiving clearance to proceed into the harbor by harbor control, they proceeded to slowly drive toward the entrance. Within an hour and a half after surfacing, they were tying up to the dock.

"Davin and Connie, there is a car waiting over there to take you to the airfield. I have two FA-18 Super Hornets being fueled that will take you to San Diego to refuel and then on to Washington. When you arrive in D.C., there will be a car waiting to take you to Langley. That is the best I can do for you. Good luck, my old friend. If you need anything else call me; here is my card."

"Bear, you are the commander of ComSubPac?" Davin asked looking at his card.

"Yes, they wanted me to stay on for a bit longer to get the Pacific Nuclear Submarine forces organized better. Not saying the past commander did a bad job, but he and I do things a bit differently. We have had some budget cuts, and there are too many boats in dry dock at any one time. They need to be out on patrol, protecting our country, not lounging on shore. My job is to get them back to work as soon as possible, and safely."

"You have a tough job my friend," Davin commented as he and Connie started down the gangway. Henderson followed close behind; he stopped only for a second to salute the boat's flag and crew.

Minutes later, Davin and Connie had entered the waiting car and were speeding toward the airfield to get a very fast ride back to Washington D.C. Arriving at the airfield, they were greeted by two fighter pilots, Commander Marvin Sanchez and Captain Julie Deeks.

"Good morning Mr. and Mrs. Pierce, come with me to get suited up. We will take off within the hour. We should have you back in D.C. before midnight. I hope you are ready for this," Captain Julie Deeks said as she turned and started toward the ready room to get them in the proper flight suits for the ride of their lives.

"Do I have time to make a call?" Connie asked.

"Yes, but make it short," Deeks replied and then turned to Davin, "Sanchez will take you to the men's locker room to get you set. Mrs. Pierce, come with me; I have a spare flight suit that should fit you perfectly."

Fifty-five minutes later, the four walked out to the waiting FA-18s and the crew chiefs standing beside them.

"Mr. Pierce, you will ride with Sanchez; and your wife and I will have a great time telling stories about you for the next couple of hours," Deeks stated as she stopped beside her fighter.

"These birds are armed! Is that standard procedure when taking passengers?" Connie asked.

"Yes, anytime our birds leave the ground, they go up with a full complement of weapons. We also are carrying extra fuel in those drop tanks. More than enough to make it to St. Louis, but we will stop in San Diego to refuel and refresh. Sorry there is not a bathroom on an 18. And then on to D.C.," Deeks replied and then looked at Sanchez and asked, "Are you ready, Wildman?"

"Yes, sir, three bags full, Skeeter," Sanchez replied using Deeks call sign.

"Let's kick the tires, and light the fires; I feel the need for speed," Skeeter said and helped Connie climb up the ladder and into the rear seat.

"I can understand Wildman as a call sign for you Sanchez, but what's with Skeeter?" Davin asked as he settled into the back seat of the FA-18.

"Well, it used to be Moskeeter because she is damn hard to hit during war games. Hell of a damn good pilot both on the range and in combat. It was shortened to Skeeter a few years ago. I will fill you in on all the gory details during our flight. But right now, I need to get us in the air. So strap in, sit back, and relax."

Chapter 18 The Cave

As they walked through a slot canyon, there were times when they could touch both walls of the canyon at the same time; and then the canyon would suddenly widen to almost eighty feet across. After they turned an especially tight corner, they arrived at a small hole in the wall where the canyon ended.

"Well, hell, I guess we have come to the end of the line," Vince commented and looked into the mouth of the small opening that lay about four feet above the canyon floor. "What do you think, Bryan?"

"We have come this far and are still alive. I want to see this through no matter what we find," he answered as he looked at the dark hole in the wall. He stepped up closer to the hole and peered inside. "There are a couple of torches just inside," he said and then reached in and grabbed one, pulled it out, and sniffed the end. "Still moist. Anyone have a match?"

"No, but will a lighter do?" Freddy said as he handed the lighter to Bryan.

"There is a breeze coming out, so it has an exit somewhere in that darkness," Vince commented as he looked in.

"Looks like the hole is larger just past the lip; ladies, who wants to go first?" Bryan asked indicating the height of the hole from the ground would require helping each one up.

"I will," Morgan said as she stepped up to the entrance, and pointed to the now burning torch. She calmly said, "Just hand me that torch as soon as I get inside."

Seconds later, Bryce and Freddy had boosted her into the hole; she took the torch, and then looked inside. "Holy shit!" she exclaimed.

"What's the problem?" Bryce asked as he pulled himself up into the cave. When he stood behind her, he gasped at the sight that the torch presented him.

"Well, what is it?" Vince asked.

"Seems we are not the first visitors to this cave; there are at least six bodies just inside. It looks like they were living here and died here. And not by natural causes," Bryce reported.

Minutes later, everyone was standing inside the cave looking at the dead soldiers. "They were shot at point blank range. See the burn stains around the wounds," Bryan commented as he inspected the bodies. "Japanese soldiers, their weapons are still here too. Look at that Samurai sword; he was an officer."

"We are burning daylight, and I want to be out of this cave before dark," Vince said as he took the torch. He picked up two more, lit them, and handed them to Bryce and Bryan.

As they moved deeper into the cave, they followed the breeze that was coming from the exit somewhere deep in the mountain. The cave was dark, wet and narrow; but each of the six proceeded as best they could. They knocked down cobwebs, stepped and/or climbed over rocks, and navigated toward the source of the light breeze.

"Look at this," Bryan said as the torch passed over some writing on the wall. After placing the torch closer to the writing, he read, "Kilroy was here. Damn! That doesn't help much. Only means that Americans have been in this cave."

"What does that mean?" Diane asked.

"Nothing really, just a saying the Army used to say and they marked it on buildings and walls as they went through an area. Kind of like saying we are here and this area is now ours," Vince stated.

"Oh, cool," Diane said looking at the faded marking on the wall. "What is this?" she said pointing below the Kilroy at a wire bolted to the wall about ankle level.

"Booby trap," Bryan said and kneeled down to inspect the wire and followed it to the bend in the cave which they would have to go around in a few seconds. Stopping at the Kilroy marking saved their lives. The wire ended at a very old World War II hand grenade braced in a small hole in the opposite wall. Pulling on the wire would have pulled the pin, and the grenade would have killed everyone in the party. Bryan reached down and picked up the grenade, detached the wire from the pin, and slipped the grenade in his pocket saying, "We may need this later."

"Good catch, Captain," Vince said as he looked down the dark narrow forbidding cave. "Let's go, but slowly; we don't need to blow ourselves up."

They turned the corner, and walked slowly as they continued down the cave.

"Seems to be getting colder in here," Morgan said as she stepped gingerly behind Diane. "I am not liking this."

"Come on girl, think of this as just another thrill ride at Disney," Bryce commented as he looked over his shoulder at his girlfriend hanging closely behind him.

"Yeah, easy for you to say, my big hero."

"Settle down you two. I see a light up ahead," Bryan said from the front of the pack and stopped abruptly. "Whoa! Hold up!" he said as he looked down at the floor but did not see a floor. After waving the torch back and forth over the hole in front of him a few times, he finally saw there was a small ledge on the left side that would allow them to pass the pit that blocked their path. He knelt down and aimed the torch in the pit. In the dim light, he saw that the bottom was about twenty-five feet below and had a skeleton lying in a contorted pose, neck bent to the left and legs broken. "He must have fallen when he didn't see the pit and broke his neck and looks like a leg too."

"That ledge doesn't look too big, and falling into that pit would certainly break your fall and several bones too," Freddy said trying to be funny.

"We know, smart guy," Diane retorted slapping him on the back of the head.

"Hey, that hurts."

"Grab hands, and don't let loose as we cross the ledge," Vince stated as he watched Bryan inch across the narrow ledge holding onto Diane's hand tightly; she was holding Freddy's, and he was holding Morgan's with Bryce and Vince bringing up the rear.

"That was wild, let's do it again," Bryce stated as they moved forward. He looked back behind him at the pit which disappeared in the darkness. "Without any light, you would never have seen that pit."

Vince turned just as the pit completely disappeared. "Is any of this real?" he asked and then banged on the rock wall.

"That sounds pretty solid to me," Bryan commented as he and the others looked behind them at the pit which was completely hidden in the darkness. "Stand still for a moment," he said and then walked back to where the pit was and got down on his knees and felt around for the pit. "It is still there; just the lack of light and the way it was constructed makes it invisible unless you are looking at it from the correct angle."

"This place gives me the creeps," Morgan said to nobody in particular.

"What, you would think I would have gotten a lot of dirt on my hands feeling around like that, but I didn't," Bryan said looking at the team in front of him. "Let's get out of this cave. There is a light about a hundred yards ahead. At least there was one a moment ago," he stated as he stared down the cave and saw that the light was gone.

"We need to move on, the light was there a moment ago, and there is no other way to go but that way," Vince said, "Take the lead, Captain."

Forty minutes later, they rounded another corner and saw the light at the end of the tunnel. "There is the exit, my young friends," Bryan said as he pointed toward the light. Within minutes, Bryan was standing in the sunshine with four of his companions standing beside him. "Where's Vince?" he asked looking around at his companions; he did not see Vince.

"He was just behind me," Bryce said as he also looked around for Vince and did not see him. He walked back into the cave to see if he had tripped or was still inside, but found nothing except Lander's extinguished torch.

Chapter 19 Canyon Land

Calling out for Vince and looking around the cave entrance produced no Vince. "We need to move on," Bryan said after a twenty-five-minute search which only frustrated the team more. Where did he go? Was he still alive, and many more questions came to mind as they regrouped at the exit to the cave.

"Okay, let's go; we can't help him if we can't find him," Bryce said, "I will bring up the rear."

"The path goes this way; the jungle is too thick to go through," Bryan commented as he started down the path swinging the machete to cut the thick branches that blocked their path. He stopped abruptly and threw up his hand to indicate that everyone should immediately stop.

"Beautiful," Morgan said as she glanced over Bryan's shoulder at a white peacock that had just come out of the brush and was starting across the small clearing. The peacock stopped and looked at her as if she heard Morgan speak.

"Thank you," the white peacock said, and turned toward the team.

"A talking peacock," Diane commented, "Cool."

"Don't all peacocks talk? They do here," the peacock said and walked toward the team. "My name is Susana. What brings you here?"

"We are looking for answers; maybe you can help," Bryan said kneeling down to look eye to eye with Susana.

"I will tell you what I know."

"Does this path lead to the light in the hills?" Morgan asked.

"Yes, but the path is tricky and dangerous, which you may have already noticed getting this far," she said in her sultry sexy voice.

"How far is it to the light?" Bryan asked looking at the talking bird. "This is pretty weird, talking to a talking peacock."

"I heard that, Captain Redmond," Susana said.

"How do you know my name?" Bryan asked as he looked intently at Susana.

"I know all your names. I also can lead you to your next test," Susana commented.

"Next test?" Freddy questioned.

"You haven't figured it out yet, have you? Everything you do is a test, and this island will test your wits, brains and strength before it will answer your questions. Now, follow me, I will take you to your next test," Susana said and then turned to head down the path at a very slow gait.

"Can you tell us what happened to Mr. Landers?" Morgan asked before starting to follow.

"No, I cannot. Is he gone?" Susana replied.

"Yes, he disappeared in the cave," Bryce commented.

"Oh, the cave, you passed the test of the cave; and in doing so, one of your team was rewarded."

"Rewarded?" Bryan questioned.

"Yes, he is safe; you will catch up to him soon. Now come with me," Susana said as she turned and started down the path.

"What do we do, Captain?" Bryce asked as he brought up the rear of the team; he was following Bryan and the others down the path.

"We follow, Bryce, we follow," Bryan said and followed the peacock down the path. "This is getting extremely weird, my young friend."

As they walked down the path behind Susana, the bushes on the left up ahead started to part and out came Tony the talking donkey.

"Hi, Tony, how are you doing today?" Susana said as Tony entered the path and stopped.

"Doing well, Susana, are you taking them to the bridge?"

"Yes, would you give me a ride? We will get there quicker. My legs are so short," Susana asked.

"Sure, hop on," Tony replied and then turned around and allowed Susana to fly up and land on his back.

"Come on, you don't have much time."

"Not much time, wait a minute Susana. What the hell do you mean, we don't have much time?" Bryan asked as he stopped in the middle of the path.

"Yes, you don't have much time, Captain. You need to be at the end of the canyon and at the bridge before sunset. And that is in an hour. You need to be camped with a fire and eating your dinner or it won't happen."

"What won't happen?" Bryce questioned as he walked up behind Tony the donkey and looked Susana directly in her tiny eyes as she cocked her head to the left to return the stare.

"I can't tell you, but it won't happen unless you are there at the bridge. You must not cross the bridge until morning," she stated. "Now let's go; move it, Tony!" she shouted.

"Okay let's continue this game," Bryan said and started to follow Tony and Susana down the path. The brush was growing thicker; but as Tony approached the thick brush, it parted just enough for the group to walk through and closed up behind them as they passed.

"This is as far as we go, Captain. The bridge is just ahead. Be careful and do not attempt to cross the bridge at night," Susana said and then looked at Tony and said "Let's go home." They turned off the path as the brushes opened up for them and faded into the jungle.

"Where did they go?" Morgan asked as she saw them start to fade into the jungle.

"That is a very good question," Bryan said looking very puzzled at the events as they unfolded. "The bridge is supposed to be right around these trees... Whoa!" he said as he almost stepped off the edge of a very deep cliff.

"Where's the bridge?" Diane yelled as she reached out and grabbed Bryan's arm, keeping him from falling over the edge.

"I guess we camp. There is a pile of firewood over there; let's make a fire and set up camp, can't cross a bridge that isn't there." Bryce said looking around the small clearing. "There is plenty of room to be comfortable."

"Okay, but I am getting tired of all the weird stuff going on," Morgan commented as she removed her backpack and walked over to a level spot to set her tent and bed roll down.

"I'll get the fire started," Freddy said and dropped his pack and started to put together a campfire.

The sun was setting in the west; and as the fire started to blaze, they settled down to a hopefully quiet night of rest. It was a moonless night; the stars were shining extremely bright and a few wispy clouds floated by in the dark sky.

"What do we do now, Captain?" Morgan asked as they sat around a small campfire.

"Well, so far we have a talking donkey, a talking peacock, a missing doctor, a missing bridge, a hell of a lot of weird stuff happening and we still don't know why. Oh, let us not forget the dead people that are not really dead, or are they? What do you suggest we do, Miss Morgan?" Bryan asked being a bit sarcastic.

"I am worried about Mr. Landers, where did he go, what happened to him, is he all right?" Diane added.

"That too, are good questions; but I don't have the answers. Maybe, if we somehow get across that canyon over there and make it to the light, we can find out some answers, or maybe not. There is no guarantee that the answers are there; maybe there are no answers. I have been here for months and have not been able to find anything to explain why I am here, why you are here and what the hell is going on," Bryan commented as he chewed on a piece of dry cracker from his cold Meal Ready to Eat, (MRE).

"Hello," a voice in the darkness said quietly. All five looked up from their meals and saw a figure walk into the light of the campfire. He was dressed in a ragged army uniform wearing the rank of Major and sporting an old army holster with a Colt Model 1911 forty-five caliber pistol with a lanyard connected to his belt.

"And who are you, old fellow?" Bryan asked as he looked up at the old man.

"I am Major Peter Story, executive officer of the garrison placed here to protect the airfield from the Japanese. What brings you and your kids here?" the old man stated, acting as if he had not seen or talked to another human in years.

"Hello Major, I am Captain Bryan Redmond, United States Air Force," he replied.

"Don't you mean the Army Air Corps?" the old man asked.

"No, the U.S. Air Force was formed as a step child of the Army Air Corps and has become a viable asset to the United States in the defense of our great nation. How long have you been here?"

"I don't remember, a long time. May I sit with you?"

"Yes, please; pull up some dirt and take the load off," Bryce cut in.

"Thank you," he said and then sat across the campfire from Bryan. "You are wondering why I am here and why you are here, aren't you? I will tell you in a minute, but first you were told there was a bridge. Well, there is, but you just can't see it yet. It will be there in the morning. You just can't see it in the evening light, but it is there; and as the sun comes up and the light is just right, you will see it."

"As for why are we here, that is simple; the same reason you are here. We are seeking answers and the questions are piling up," Bryan answered. "Will you or can you answer some of them?"

"I will try," the major said and then continued, "Before you say another word, I must warn you; what you have experienced so far is nothing compared to what you will encounter."

"What are you saying, Major? The peacock said it was a test. Is this all a test or something out of an Indiana Jones movie?" Bryce asked.

"Who is this Indiana Jones? No, don't answer that; I don't care. As I said, the bridge will be there for you in the morning; but cross carefully. It is older than I am. Once across, you need to take the path on the left. Do not go down the other ones. They will not lead you to where you want to go. And yes, there will be some tests, testing your intelligence, your skill and cunning, and generally designed to screw with your heads."

"Why?"

"That is for you to figure out," the major said and then stood and walked into the jungle, fading from view within a few feet after entering the bush.

"What happened to Mister Landers?" Morgan yelled at the fading figure.

"You will find out soon... he is safe," he said in a fading voice that matched his fading body. In a moment he was gone.

Chapter 20 Another Airfield

Morning came with a bang. The sun was up before they could roll out of their sleeping bags, all except Bryan who had been up a half hour before the sun appeared. He was pacing at the edge of the canyon looking for the bridge which he had not yet found.

"What's up doc?" Bryce asked as he walked over to Bryan.

"Where is the damn bridge?" he complained just as he turned and saw Bryce pointing to the bridge twenty feet from him. "Oh, there it is? It wasn't there a minute ago."

"I know. I just saw it too," Bryce replied and walked over to the start of the bridge, if you want to call it a bridge. It was very old, made of wood planks interlaced in between with rope, and swayed in the slightest breeze. "That doesn't look very safe."

"Yeah, I have seen better construction by a three-year-old," Bryan commented as he looked at the bridge swinging over the very deep canyon. When he peered down, he saw a river of rapids that in the states would be classified as category five, the most dangerous in white water rafting.

"How an island of this size can have a canyon like that doesn't seem right," Diane said as she and Freddy walked up behind them.

"Very good question, just no good answer," Bryan replied from behind them.

"Do you expect us to cross that?" Morgan said as she, Diane and Freddy walked up to them and looked at the bridge. "That thing must be a hundred years old."

"Yep, we have to cross that and do as the old major said," Bryan said without taking his eyes off the wooden suspension bridge. "We need to find some rope or something we can hang onto if that thing should break as we cross. We cross one at a time. I will go first, then the girls, followed by Freddy and then Bryce. Understood? Now find us some rope or something to hang onto."

"Spread out, but don't go into the bush; you may not come out," Bryce added.

After a quick search of the area, they were able to locate a vine that looked as if it had enough strength to hold them and was long enough to almost reach the other side.

"Okay, are you guys ready?" Bryan asked as he looked at the vine and the bridge.

"Maybe I should go first, I am the lightest," Diane said.

"No, if there is trouble over there, then I want someone that can handle it themselves," Bryan said, not thinking his comment completely through.

"I will have you know, Mr. Tuff guy, I am a Lieutenant in the United States Army Reserve and shot expert on the rifle and pistol range. I was deployed to Afghanistan last year and received a Purple Heart and Silver Star for performance above and beyond the call of duty when I saved my commander's life in a fire fight. Need I say more, tough guy?"

"I stand corrected; you may lead, Lieutenant Diane," Bryan agreed bowing slightly and waving his arm toward the bridge. Bryce and Morgan knew about Diane's service and chuckled a bit when she slammed Bryan down.

"When did you do that, Diane?" Freddy asked.

"Before I started school and met you. I am still in the guard and proud of it," she responded, as she looked seriously at the bridge.

"Let's get a move on, love birds... Grab the end of this vine, wrap it around your waist and move slowly across. Let us know if you encounter any weak boards," Bryan said and picked up the vine about ten feet behind Diane. "We will hang onto this as you cross. If the bridge fails, well, just hang on and we will pull you up."

"Yeah, you better do that; I am not ready to be splattered on a bunch of rocks," she said and started across the bridge. She took each step lightly with one hand tightly holding the vine and the other on the frayed rope holding up the bridge. Each step caused the bridge to creak and sway. She had gone about a quarter of the way, when the board she stepped on broke and part of it fell down into the raging river below. "Shit! I am okay," she called out as she lifted her foot out of the hole that was left when the board broke.

"Be careful," Bryan yelled.

"I am; I am..." she yelled.

Although she carefully stepped across the remaining portion of the bridge, she broke six more boards, but made it safely to the other side. "I made it, who is next?"

It took forty minutes for all of them to safely make it across the bridge. Freddy stepped on a board that looked sturdy and was okay for the others, but it broke when he stepped on it, mostly because he tipped the scales around two hundred ten pounds, at least fifty pounds heavier than anyone else on the team. He fell through the hole and hung there for five minutes before he was able to pull himself up and continue to cross.

"Okay, wow, that was a thrill that I don't want to repeat," Morgan commented. "You okay, big guy?" She received a nod and a little smile from Freddy.

"Let's go, it is still early; and we should be able, barring any interruptions, to make good time," Bryan said as he started down the left path. He swung his machete to widen the path since the brush was thick and wet. It was almost like a tropical rain forest but without the rain.

"Whoa!" Morgan yelled as she tripped over a root.

"Be careful where you step; these roots are thick and slippery," Bryan stated as he slipped and fell. His Thompson machine gun fell off his shoulder and landed beside him. "Damn!" burst out of his mouth. As he attempted to stand up, he almost slipped again. He had to use the machine gun as a crutch to push up enough to grab a limb, and with a lot of heavy breathing, he was finally sturdily standing.

"What happened, Captain?" Morgan asked as she slowly and carefully walked up to him.

"Mud," was all he said.

"Yeah, mud. That is not mud," Bryce agreed looking down at the jungle floor and then pointed at Bryan's feet and the vine coiled around his foot.

"Damn vine!" Bryan asked looking down and not seeing any mud on his clothes. "Where's my Thompson?"

"It's right there, Captain," Freddy said as he looked around where Bryan fell, and pointed to the machine gun lying just under the brush.

"We need to move. Let's go," Bryan said and then turned and started down the path again, watching closely where he placed his feet. Twenty minutes later, they burst through the jungle onto the other abandoned air field.

"This must be the airfield we could see from the top of the hill back at the other airfield," Bryan commented.

"Look, there are a couple of hangers and a few buildings over there," Morgan said as she pointed across the field.

"Yep, one is open. Let's check it out," Freddy said as he started toward the open hanger. When he was about fifty feet from the door, he skidded to a stop, turned and started to run back to his friends yelling, "Run! Run!"

The others just stood and watched as Freddy ran toward them while being chased by a Japanese soldier waving a Samurai sword. The soldier stopped chasing when he saw the other four standing at the edge of the jungle.

"Stop Fred, he isn't chasing you anymore," Bryan yelled at Freddy.

"What?" he said as he stopped and turned to look at the soldier. The soldier was leaning on his sword with the blade slowly sinking into the soil. The soldier was staring at the group, but was not moving much.

"Okay, this has gone far enough; now we have to deal with a mad Japanese soldier that wants to kill us," Bryan said. He handed his Thompson to Bryce and started to walk toward the soldier with his hands out to show he did not have a weapon.

"Right behind you, Captain," Bryce said as he and the others followed.

As he stood in front of the soldier, Bryan eyed him up and down. He saw a young Japanese soldier in an officer's uniform.

"Do you speak English?" Bryan asked quickly.

"Si," the officer replied in Spanish.

"English, not Spanish," Bryan repeated.

"Da," was his reply in Russian.

"English!"

"Yes, I speak English, educated at Harvard as a lawyer. Do you speak English?" the Japanese officer replied in perfect English.

"What are you doing here in a Japanese officer's uniform if you are a lawyer?"

"I was stationed here with my platoon to guard this airfield; our intelligence did not know the Americans were already on the other side of the island and the battle that followed was long and bloody. Most of my platoon died and are buried over there," he reported and pointed to the other side of the field.

"How long have you been here?" Bryce asked.

"I don't really know; it seems like the battle was just yesterday. And this hole in my side still hurts." He moved his right hand away from his side to show a dark red stain on his shirt just above his waist; it was still wet. "You are my enemy; I should shoot you where you stand but I haven't the strength."

"You are hurt," Morgan stated and ran over to the soldier, helped him to the ground, and ripped open his shirt to reveal a nasty cut on his side. "And sir, the war ended over eighty years ago."

"Sir, I believe you think you did arrive just yesterday," Bryan commented.

"What do you mean? The year is 1944 and Japan and the United States are at war," the Japanese officer insisted.

"Can you patch him up?" Bryce asked as he looked over Morgan's shoulder and then looked at the officer and said. "Sir, the year is 2031; we were not even born when you were fighting the war. It is long over and Japan is now a major supplier of electronic gadgets and is a financial super power."

"Yes," Morgan replied as she opened up her pack and removed an ancient first aid pack.

"It can't be; my men and I were being pushed back by American troops when I was hit and fell; the next thing I remember is waking up on a cot in that hanger." And then he noticed that everyone was dressed in old army uniforms; he pulled his pistol from his holster and pointed it at Freddy, "You tell me the truth, soldier."

"I am no soldier; I am a student and am trapped here on this island just like you. Now put that gun down and let Morgan finish patching you up," Freddy said not shying away from the gun pointed at him.

"Now when she is finished, would you like to join us in finding out what the hell is going on or just hang out here and die of old age?" Bryan asked, looking more confused than he was earlier.

"I will come with you."

"Good, we will fill you in on everything we know, since you just got here. It all may seem very confusing, but it will only get more confusing as we move toward that hill over there."

"Why go there?" the officer asked. "Thank you for patching me up young lady."

"No problem, we can't have you bleeding all over the airfield, now can we," Morgan said as she finished cleaning and patching his wound. "You will need a real doctor soon; we are limited in antibiotics and I am not sure if there are any back at the compound."

"I will be fine; there are some medical supplies in the first building over there," he said as he pointed toward the three buildings on the edge of the runway.

"Let's move, Bryce, why don't you fill our new friend in on what we know; and by the way, I am Bryan Redmond, this is Bryce, Morgan, Diane and Freddy. And you are?"

"Horatio Soto, of the Imperial Japanese Army, I guess permanently retired now. Maybe I can start my law practice on this island," he said with a smile.

"We may need a good lawyer to sue whoever is behind this," Bryce replied with a chuckle.

When he reached the first building, Freddy entered and looked around. He came out within a minute shaking his head.

"What's in there?" Bryan asked.

"Unbelievable, take a look," Freddy said and then sat on an old wooden chair that was leaning against the wall near the door.

"Holy crap batman; look at this stuff," Bryan yelled, "Come in here."

Bryce, Diane, Horatio and Morgan walked into the building and stood shocked at what they saw.

"Horatio, you said you were fighting to defend the airfield, did you not see this here. Look at that flat screen television over there. That was built by a company called Sony in Japan. The stereo over there was made in Germany; and this, wow, this is a laptop computer made by Sony in Japan also. This stuff was all developed and manufactured long after the war. In fact, the television was built in 2014, according to the label on the back," explained Bryce as he pointed to each item.

"This is impossible!" Horatio and Bryan both said together.

"Yes, impossible for the both of you, but not us; we came from 2031 remember and this stuff is common in most homes and businesses around the world. And from the looks of it, even here on this island," Freddy stated as he walked back into the building, reached over and flicked the light switch, throwing light on everything in the room. It looked very much like a day room or recreation room for the military stationed here. "We have power, turn on the TV."

Chapter 21 Washington D.C.

After a very long flight, a short fuel stop in San Diego and then back in the air, Davin and Connie finally touched down at Joint Base Andrews, located near Camp Springs, Prince George's County, Maryland. Andrews Air Force Base and the Naval Air Facility Washington merged in 2009 to become Joint Base Andrews. Minutes after parking the two FA-18 Super Hornets outside on the wet tarmac, the ground crew immediately tied down the jets and assisted the passengers out of the back seats and back onto firm ground. The light rain and wind did not cause anyone any problems as they climbed down from the fighters.

"Wow! That was awesome. What do you think, Connie?" Davin said as he rejoined her on the tarmac.

"That was a wild ride, for sure; but I couldn't help thinking about our kids. We need to find them," Connie replied as Skeeter walked up behind her.

"Connie, I enjoyed our conversation and did not realize what your husband and you had done; I was just a kid when you guys disarmed that Soviet boat. And now, I had the pleasure of flying the two of you; and well, it is an honor. Now I know you need to go; here is my card. If you need anything, just call. Admiral Henderson and his wife are good friends, and I will do whatever I can for their friends," Skeeter said smiling.

Sanchez walked up and spoke quietly with Skeeter and then turned to leave, but not before he shook Davin's hand and said "Thank you for what you do."

"Wildman, I will meet you in the ready room; go ahead and secure a couple of rooms for us and call for a car so we can get some dinner."

"Roger, Skeeter," he replied and then walked over to the ground crew to give instructions and then to flight operations.

"Thank you for the flight, and it was a pleasure chatting with you, Skeeter. I will call when we get this done for a proper thank you," Connie stated; then she and Davin walked to flight operations to return the flight suits and leave. There was a car waiting for them in the parking lot to take them to Langley, CIA Headquarters.

CIA Headquarters, Midnight

Davin and Connie walked in the front door of CIA Headquarters and were greeted by the new Assistant Director Adam Cruz.

"Good evening, Mr. and Mrs. Pierce; let's go upstairs, and I will bring you up to date on what we know."

"Adam, what the hell is going on? Have you heard from the kidnappers?" Connie asked as they walked through the metal detectors and followed Adam to the first elevator where he pushed the up button. Ten minutes after arriving in the building, they were being escorted into the main conference room on the third floor. Inside the room were six other agents going over reports, chatting on a secure phone, or studying photographs.

"Please take a seat; just put your bags over in the corner," Adam instructed and then walked to the front of the room and asked everyone to be quiet. "Quiet please. Most of you know Davin Pierce, the gentleman I replaced when he retired four months ago; by the way, you have been missed. And this is his beautiful wife Connie, ex-FBI and co-

conspirator. We welcome you back to the pit, but wish it were not under these circumstances."

"Adam, before we start, I really need to freshen up. It was a long flight; and for some reason, they did not install a bathroom in a Super Hornet," Connie said after she set her bag down.

"Oh, hell, sorry; bad manners on my part. You know where the rest rooms are; we will wait for you," Adam said apologetically.

"Be right back," she said and left the room.

"Is this coffee fresh?" Davin asked when he saw a pot and cups on the side table.

"About an hour old," one of the agents commented.

"That's fresh enough," Davin replied and poured a cup and then walked over to the conference table and sat down. "You know an FA-18 Super Hornet is one hell of a plane, but the seats could use a little more padding."

Minutes later, Connie entered the conference room looking completely refreshed and smiling for the first time since she heard about the kidnappings.

"Okay, tell us what you know?" she demanded as she took a can of soda from the small refrigerator located in the corner. She sat beside Davin, opened the can, and took a long pull on it.

"What we know is not much; but what we do know for sure is that it wasn't a transporter device that snatched them. We haven't nailed it down completely with your kids; but with the Randal's, it is a sure slam dunk. That is, when we compare everyone's recounting of the kidnapping, there is one minor flaw in the timing. What I mean is that we cannot account for five minutes. The investigators showed up at 1935 after being called by Ashley Peterson. They showed the time they were called as 1905 and Ashley and the rest stated they called at 1900 by their watches and clocks in the house. Double checking with their smart phones, it showed that the time mechanism had been tampered with resulting in resetting the time to 1900. How they did that, we are not sure; but it was done. Also everyone that wore a watch compared it with the investigators and all were five minutes slow. Now is five minutes enough time to kidnap two people from their own home, the answer is yes. Is it possible to distract or induce a drug that would cause highly trained people to forget or not see something happening right in front of them? Yes, we have used a similar drug to induce a momentary hypnotic state to remove an item or items from right in front of the person we are talking to. Davin, you know that is true because in some of the cases you worked you used it on your target. Is that not true?" Adam paused and looked intently at Davin and Connie.

"Yes, I know of what you are talking about. It does work, but that is a closely guarded secret. It is a drug that was developed by our R&D section and not shared with any other agency. We did not want that secret to get out. Are you telling me this was an inside job, or that one of our best kept secrets is no longer a secret?" Davin questioned.

"Well, both; we believe that someone in, or who was formerly with the agency, either used or collaborated with someone outside the agency. Or even sold them the formula; we are not sure right now, and only those in this room right now know that we are investigating the internal workings as well as anyone that has recently left the agency."

"Does that mean you are investigating us?" Davin asked.

"No, you two have been cleared, obviously," Adam stated.

"Well, thank you, Adam. Now who the hell used our own drug on our people to do this?" Connie said a bit louder than she had planned.

"We have narrowed it down to six people, two have left the agency for careers with the private sector, one of them is Rocky Soto, who used to be the head of R&D and three of his lab techs. We are about to bring in, Helen Owens, our current CIA R&D director who may be able to provide us with additional information. Meanwhile, the two that are in the private sector are being held at the 14th Precinct. They were told there was a threat on their lives and are being held in protective custody. Soto and the other lab techs are in the wind," Adam continued.

"Okay, do we have any idea where the Randals' and our kids are?" Connie questioned.

"No, we don't."

"And you are still trying to locate Soto and his missing lab techs?" Davin asked.

"Yes," Adam replied.

Chapter 22 Reality Check

After a full day of busting through the jungle by himself, Vince Landers came upon a clearing with four buildings, surrounded by a fence with sharp concertina wire around the top. After walking around the fence, he reached a gate with a camera which tracked him. He saw a speaker box with a button and pushed the button.

Within a few seconds, a female voice broke the silence.

"Welcome Mr. Landers, please come in. Go to the door on building number one on your left. We have been waiting for you," she said and the gate slowly opened.

As he approached, the door opened just before he reached it. Standing in front of the door was a tall man wearing a white shirt and tan shorts; he sported a full beard that was starting to show signs of grey, and his full head of hair had already turned to grey. He reached out to shake hands with Vince. "Welcome, Mr. Landers, please come in; we have a lot to talk about. Glad you found the exit door in the cave; we were worried that you would miss it."

As he turned, he indicated for Vince to follow. They walked down a long hallway to a pair of double doors with the sign that only said, 'Laboratory.'

"Welcome to Central Control or what we like to call the Game Room. I am Rocky Soto. I guess you could say I am in charge of this facility. To answer some of your more pressing questions, as to what is going on, I will get into that soon. Sorry for the theatrics; but as I explained earlier, this is an experiment, and your kids are the guinea pigs, as it were. Your students are fine, and will remain so for now. Captain Redmond is well trained and will not let anything happen to them. They should arrive here in about four hours, give or take a bit. What you see in here are my nine assistants in this elaborate game. Everyone and everything in this room is real; what you experienced out there, well, was not completely real."

"What the hell is going on? Why did you bring us here? Is this some kind of joke?"

"No sir, this is not a joke. And we brought you and your students here to test our new holographic equipment and to demonstrate that we can do anything we want at any time," Rocky commented quickly.

"An experiment?"

"Yes, an experiment, and so far it has proven to be a huge success," Soto continued smiling the whole time.

"Why these kids? They have done nothing to you; and what about that damn orb you sent me with the crazy story about Edwin Kelsey?"

"Please have a seat, ah, where are my manners, you have been walking around that jungle without food or water. Would you like to freshen up, get something to eat or drink before I explain the rest of what is going on?"

"As a matter of fact, yes; I could use the restroom and I'd like a nice steak and beer," Vince commented not really expecting to get what he asked for.

"Barney, get Mr. Landers a cold beer and have the kitchen rustle up a nice steak for him, with a baked potato and a salad; have them deliver it to the conference room when ready," Rocky ordered.

"Sure Rocky," Barney replied, picked up a phone on his desk, and ordered the meal.

"The restroom is right there," Rocky said as he pointed toward two doors, one marked 'Men', and the other, 'Women'.

Minutes later, Vince Landers returned to the control room and was directed to the conference room.

"Have a seat. Your steak should be here in a few minutes," Rocky said as they entered the room. "I would like you to meet some of our other guests. This young man is Josh Randal, current Director of CIA and his lovely wife Stephanie. They just arrived last night; beside them are Amber and Josh Pierce, the daughter and son of Davin and Connie Pierce, the past Assistant Director of CIA. They also arrived late yesterday."

"Mr. Randal are you responsible for this?" Vince questioned as he entered the room.

"Yes, and no, as they say, the buck stops here; these people used to work for me, but now are working on their own. We are here, just like you, against our wishes. Mr. Soto used to work for me at the CIA; he was the head of Research and Development until he was dismissed or rather fired for a multitude of reasons, which I cannot discuss here."

"Be that as it may, let me explain and when the rest of your party arrives you can explain everything to them. I don't want to repeat myself. So, all of you have seen the control room with the monitors and my crew who run the simulations. They also introduce the various holograms when and where we want them to show up. To be honest, the only real person you have been interfacing with is Captain Redmond. He is a fighter pilot, but not from Viet Nam as he said. He was shot down in Iran, during that little shoot out. He was banged up pretty bad which gave us the opportunity to reprogram him and bring him here."

"But Amelia Earhart's and Redmond's F-4 is out there on the ramp," Vince questioned.

"It is true; that is a similar plane of Earhart's, but not the real one; and the F-4 is a real one from Viet Nam which we purchased and brought here. Earhart's Lockheed is lost somewhere in the ocean out there; we don't know where. Most of the other aircraft were here when we arrived with a few other exceptions."

"Holograms, but why?" Josh Pierce asked before anyone else could speak.

"An experiment and a kidnapping, of course. We are about to embark on a quest that will change the world as we know it. The use of my holograms and other tricks we have invented will make it happen, and soon. Mr. Randal, you are one of the most powerful men in the intelligence community and the children are off-springs of the second most powerful man, even though he is retired, or at least he thinks he is. With you and him out of the way, our quest will not fail," Rocky stated and then turned as the door opened and a young woman dressed in kitchen whites entered and stopped holding a tray with a question on her face.

"Oh, Mr. Landers ordered the steak; that's him right there, Michelle."

"Thank you Rocky; I would have figured it out in a few minutes, but your help is appreciated," Michelle said. She set the tray down in front of Vince. "Would anyone else like anything?"

"Yeah, a couple of cold beers would be nice too," Josh Randal stated.

"Be back in a minute, any particular brand?"

"No, just cold and wet."

"So what is the next step in your plan, Mr. Soto?" Randal questioned as he closely looked at the others in the room.

"That, you will find out soon enough, Mr. Randal. Until such time, you are our guest; you will be watched twenty-four hours a day until you leave; any attempt to leave this compound will result in the immediate deaths of everyone that is left. Only I can determine when and how you will leave, get my meaning. The fence is electrified and will deliver a fatal shock if touched."

"Guess we are your guests for now; but rest assured Mr. Soto, there are a lot of people already looking for us, and I would not want to get on the bad side of Davin Pierce."

"Oh, I know about Mr. Pierce and am not worried," he said smiling.

"You should be," Amber piped in.

"What kind of experiment requires kidnapping?" Stephanie asked to no one in particular.

"We needed your DNA and minds to complete the next phase. The four students with you Mr. Landers are among the brightest in the country. We need their brains too, along with yours."

"The orb, what was it with that damn thing?" Vince asked again.

"That thing is a Hollywood prop; picked it up in a small curio shop outside of Los Angeles a couple of years ago. It does nothing but glow and flash a bright light."

"But it was used to kidnap us?"

"Yes, but what you saw wasn't real; my holographic impersonators replaced you in the classroom and we picked you up right after you and the kids left the cafe. The students in your class only thought you were giving a lecture; they only saw a holographic projection of you and your four young friends. The class went on as planned; and after the class, we implanted the memory of the flash and time lapse to confuse you and the kids. That scared them enough to see you at the café where we could remove all of you quickly, and also create a little mystery for the cops and military. It worked rather well, I would say; they are still trying to figure out what happened to you," Soto said as he smiled the whole time. "I must leave you now; please enjoy the refreshments, and ask Michelle for anything you want. She will get it for you."

Chapter 23 CIA vs. FBI

"Okay, what has the FBI got on any of this?" Davin asked.

"We haven't brought them in yet," Adam Cruz stated as he looked very concerned.

"Why the hell not?" Connie questioned and slammed her fist down on the table.

"Well, we wanted you to be briefed first; do you want them brought in?"

"Yes, call them; and get them in here now. If we don't cooperate with the FBI, the boss will come down on us like a sledge hammer," Davin ordered. "Connie, let's go down to the café and grab a cold drink and a snack while we wait for the FBI to show up. Adam, come get us when they get here."

"Yes, sir," Adam said quietly as Davin and Connie exited the conference room.

"Connie, we need to get this under control and fast. There is something bigger behind this, and I want to know what it is. We need all the help we can get; call your friends at the bureau and see what they have learned, if anything," Davin said as they walked down the hall toward the elevators.

"As soon as we get to the Café, I will call. Remember, this part of the building is shielded, and cell phones don't work."

"Right. Forgot!"

"And you were the boss! Are you getting forgetful in your old age?" Connie teased as they rode the elevator down to the ground floor. "The Café is over here, old man."

"Yeah, I remember now; it is strange how fast a fellow can forget things when he is away from it for a short time."

"Let's get our drinks and sit outside; I will be able to call from there," Connie said as she picked up an orange juice and bear claw. Davin poured himself a cup of coffee and also took a bear claw. After paying for their refreshments, they walked out to the patio and sat about twenty feet from the door. Connie pulled out her phone and placed a call to her old boss at the FBI. It was nearing two in the morning, but the phone only rang three times before it was picked up. She asked him to come over to Langley immediately and bring two of his best agents. He commented that one of his best agents was already there, and she was asking for help. After a short four-minute conversation, he agreed to be there within the hour with his two second best agents. He also acknowledged that he had just gotten a call from the night desk asking for him to report to Langley. He had been asked by Adam Cruz, the assistant director.

"Good, see you shortly," Connie acknowledged and hung up. She looked at Davin and started to cry.

"Honey, we will find them; and whoever took them will pay," Davin assured her.

Forty-five minutes later, Adam Cruz came out to the patio and told Davin and Connie that the FBI had arrived and were waiting in the conference room.

"Okay, now that we have the whole team here, let's get down to business. FBI, what do you know about these four kidnappings?" Davin asked taking charge of the meeting when they returned to the conference room.

"Four, don't you mean nine," the lead FBI agent, Connie's ex-boss asked.

"Nine, you have others?" Adam interjected.

"Yes, besides the Randal's and Pierces' children, we have five from the University of New Mexico missing with strange circumstances, similar to yours. They went missing five days ago, in the desert north of Albuquerque."

"Who are they?"

"A university professor, Vince Landers, and four of his brightest students, all with IQs of over one hundred sixty," FBI Agent Madeline Graves replied.

"What does their IQ have to do with this?" Connie questioned.

"We are not sure, but that is the only thing they had in common with each other, except that they were in Landers archeology class together," Madeline answered.

"Okay, FBI, legally we can't work on U.S. soil, so you have lead here; but it will be controlled from this office, is that understood," Adam stated looking at the FBI agents.

"Wait a damn minute, Adam. You are correct in that you are legally not allowed to work an operation on US soil, so why should the FBI follow your direction at all," Madeline complained.

"Because Mr. Randal is our director," Adam countered.

"No! The FBI will work closely with your office, but we will not take direction from the CIA."

"Wait a damn minute both of you! I may have retired a few months ago, and Adam took my place; but no offense, Adam, I have over forty years' experience with this organization. I am in charge of this operation and all of you will follow my directions," Davin stated as he stood and confronted both the FBI and CIA leaders.

"Davin you are retired, and have no authority here," Adam stated.

"That is true to a point. My retirement was voluntary and recall to service is at my discretion; and I officially recall myself to active duty as Acting Director CIA," Davin stated and laid a folded paper on the conference table and slid it toward Adam and Madeline. "That is my recall letter signed by the President, stating that in the case of national emergency, I can recall myself to duty."

"Wow, how did you get this, Mr. Pierce?" Adam questioned.

"Easy, the President did not want me to retire and issued that letter as a way to call me back in case of an emergency. This situation has 'Emergency' flashing all over it. Now, let's get down to business, any questions?"

"I guess the FBI is bowing down to the CIA once again," Madeline stated in a very unfriendly manner.

"Not bowing down, Maddie, working in cooperation with," Connie stated.

"You are too close to this one Mr. Pierce, so Cruz should take the lead, not you," Maddie suggested.

"Not going to happen; Adam is a good agent and friend, but the President put me in charge and that is final," Davin stated and did not get anymore protests. "Now let's get to work and find them; this is not how I planned on spending my retirement."

Chapter 24 What's Next

"Good morning, my new family," Rocky Soto said as he walked into the cafeteria and greeted his captives the following morning. "You will be happy to hear that your missing geniuses are almost here; they have crossed the canyon, met my father Horatio, and discovered the high tech stuff we left for them. They even turned on the television and got a little news off of CNN. There was no news about them being kidnapped which means that the government has hushed up the report. I have some men out waiting for them as we speak; they should be here shortly. In the meantime, I hope you have had a nice breakfast."

"Your father?" Josh Randal asked.

"Oh, I didn't mention that last night; yeah, he is helping with this charade. And I must say, he is loving it. But he really isn't my father, but rather my son. Smart kid, following in his father's footsteps."

"Okay, you have us on this island and locked up in this compound, but with free access to wander around everywhere except that control room of yours. Don't you think we all may escape sometime?" Amber said and then looked at Rocky with very serious eyes.

"True, I have allowed you free movement, almost like a POW camp from the war. We have guards, electrified fences, guns, and of course, the most important part, we are on an island somewhere in the ocean. Which ocean, well, you can figure that out on your own," Rocky stated and then paused for a second. "I will give you one clue; your spy satellites do not cover the part of the world where this island is located. Does that help you, Mr. Randal? Oh, when the rest of your party gets here, the fun will begin." Rocky Soto did not always tell the truth; and the truth was that the spy satellites that were in service did cover every inch of the earth, but not all the time. The satellite that passed over this island only passed over once every twenty-four hours and only snapped a picture of the island once every month. The island was not an area of interest for anyone other than the country of Peru which owned and maintained it as a bird sanctuary.

"Can't wait," Randal stated and went back to his breakfast, knowing that satellites did not take pictures of the entire earths surface so this island could be almost anywhere. "Before you go, can you tell us how you did it?"

"Oh, sure, it was so easy."

"Easy, I know you used a drug to put our guests into a short sleep so you could grab my wife and me. But how did you get Amber and Josh? We were briefed that they just disappeared right in front of several students and professors at the university," Randal questioned and looked over at Josh and Amber.

"Easy, we grabbed them an hour before they were to go to class. Then we projected holograms on the sidewalk walking toward their class and when we had witnesses we turned the holograms off. Simple."

"Your technology is that good?" Stephanie asked.

"Yes, even better than that. We have been having fun with Dr. Landers' four geniuses and Captain Redmond for the past couple of days. It may look like a duck, walk like a duck; but hell it is only a bunch of light that acts and looks like a duck. Get the picture?"

"Yeah, so what's next?" Landers asked still maintaining his cover of working with Soto, but starting to become unsure of his choice.

"Next, well, next is happening today in a few minutes as a matter of fact, but you are not directly involved, Mr. Landers. In time, you and the rest of you will know all, but not just yet," Rocky said and then left the cafeteria.

CIA, Langley, Virginia

"Okay, gentlemen and ladies, we have been here all night and are not much further along than we were last night," Davin stated as he sipped his coffee.

"Do you want to recap any of this?" one of the agents asked.

"No, I want answers, and I want to know where they are. We are not getting the answers we need from anywhere. We need answers," Davin replied being a little disgusted in himself and the people in the room. They were getting nowhere; and there had not been a ransom call or message. They had nothing, no clues, nothing.

A knock on the door broke the tension in the conference room.

"Enter," Davin yelled.

The door did not open, but the handle turned several times. "I said enter," Davin yelled again. This time the door flew open and two armed soldiers stood with weapons drawn and pointing into the room.

"Who the hell are you? Put those weapons away." Adam Cruz yelled.

"Excuse us sir; we just received a call from the front desk that there was an armed gunman in here with hostages," the front soldier said as they lowered their weapons.

"An armed gunman with hostages in a secure conference room inside a secure building, doesn't sound very, well, doesn't sound possible," Adam Cruz commented as he looked at the soldiers. "And busting into the conference room where there are possible hostages is not a good idea either. Who gave the order?"

"You did, Director." The soldier said.

"Impossible, I haven't left this room in hours. When and where was I supposed to have been when I gave that order?" Director Adam Cruz asked.

"Two minutes ago, right there," he replied and pointed down the hall at a spot where he had seen Director Adam Cruz a couple of minutes ago. "You were right over there; but now you are in here. What the hell is going on?"

"Okay, I am in here; and Director Davin Pierce is in charge, now. Do us a favor; look around the room and see who is here. If you see anyone of us out there and we did not come through that door, then shoot them. I want the two of you to stand guard on that door. Mr. Jacobs here will be your interface, and nobody will leave this room without checking with him," Adam Cruz ordered.

"Don't shoot them, but before you take an order from them, please check with me or Mr. Cruz," Davin corrected, "Now does anyone need to use the head before we continue?"

Twenty minutes later, all the members of the team had gone and returned to the conference room without incident.

The two soldiers stood guard on the only door to get into the room and all seemed quiet, at least for the moment.

"Halt!" the guard ordered as he saw a woman approach them. She continued right up to within ten feet of the door and then stopped.

"Mr. Pierce has asked me to join them. May I approach without getting shot?" she asked.

"Please identify yourself, Miss," the guard ordered.

"I am Helen Owens, from the Research and Development Department, down in the basement. Do you want to see my credentials?" Helen stated but did not move to pull her badge or credentials out. She stood five foot six inches tall, had blue eyes, was thin but not too thin, with a well-proportioned, not swimsuit but athletic, body because she worked out four times a week. Her job kept her in the lab a lot and mostly at a desk or table working on projects; she did not want to get the typical big bottom that a lot of women get because of taking jobs that did not allow them to get exercise. Helen was rapidly getting close to forty and single because of her passion for her job. But she dated when she could. She had never wanted to be a field agent because her passion was to be the gadget maker like 'Q' in the James Bond series; and while working with the CIA, she fulfilled her wish and got to play with and develop new high tech gadgets for the field agents.

"Yes, please, slowly," he replied and then to his partner, "Check with Mr. Pierce to ensure he did call for her."

Slowly Helen Owens reached into the pocket of her lab coat and removed her credentials. She stepped closer to the guard, and handed him her credentials. His partner turned back and said. "He called for her."

"Good, we just have to be careful, Ms Owens."

"Rather be careful than dead," she replied and then brushed past both guards and entered the conference room.

"Welcome to our little mystery, Helen. Can you brief us on the use of the sleeper drug that was developed last year?" Davin said as she entered the room and the door closed behind her. She walked over to the table with the coffee pot and poured herself a cup before starting to talk.

"Well, that is interesting. The use of the sleeper drug has not been widely used because of some pretty nasty side effects. I remember you using it on one of the last ops you did, Mr. Pierce. Since then, we have been working on getting it better."

"Side effects?" Adam asked.

"Yes, side effects. Because the drug is designed to create a very short sleep effect, our field agents can accomplish a mission without being detected. The duration of the sleep is from five to thirty minutes, depending on the amount of dosage given. It was designed to be administered in a liquid, in the air as an aerosol, or even by contact to the skin. Although contact to the skin takes a little longer to work, we have been successful in using it on occasion. It is a controlled substance and it is only issued with approval from the Director or Assistant Director and for specific operations. Has there been an incident?" Helen questioned.

"Well, we are not a hundred percent sure, but believe the sleeper drug was used on several high level officials to make it possible to kidnap Director Randal and his wife."

"Oh, no! I need to verify that all of our supplies are still here," Helen said and started for the door.

"No wait. We have more questions and you did not tell us about the side effects and if they are life threatening," Davin said.

"Yeah, the side effects; not life threatening as far as we know; no one has died that it has been used on, yet, anyway. The only side effect that we know is that the target will have a hard time sleeping for a week or two afterwards. And, well, we have had several targets go to sleep after a while and ended up in a coma, which only lasted a few days until they popped out of it."

"Whoa, is there an antidote to prevent the side effects?" Cruz asked.

"Yes and no; we are working on an antidote, but haven't gotten it to work completely. What else do you need to know about?"

"Holographs," Davin answered.

"Oh, yeah our holograph program is state of the art. It was developed by Dr. Rocky Soto's team; and if released to the gaming public, we could make billions. You remember the movie and TV series called Star Trek, the Next Generation with the Holo-deck, which simulated almost anything you wanted. Well, that had to operate within a room and used force fields to make the holograph more solid. That was real Hollywood magic, but now it is CIA magic."

"Are you saying your research department has a working holographic projector?" Connie asked, finally sitting up straight when she heard the holograph description.

"Yes, we haven't gotten past the problem of making them solid, but are very close. Our projections can show up anywhere; and as long as you don't touch them, they look real. Give us another couple of weeks, and we will have the solid part finished. The only way we have been able to make them solid is to project them around a living person, basically changing someone into someone else."

"Damn, that explains how Adam was in two places at one time," Davin said shaking his head in disbelief.

"What do you mean, Mr. Pierce?" Helen asked.

"A holographic Adam Cruz ordered those two guards out there to bust into this conference room and be prepared to shoot an intruder," Davin stated.

"Holy shit! Oops, didn't mean that, sorry," Helen replied quickly.

"No problem, Miss Owens. But yes, it happened just before we called you up here."

"How does it work without a projector?" Adam asked.

"That is complicated, but our system doesn't need a projector; it only requires a small transmitter which can be carried in your pocket or used as a lapel pin. The transmitter will transmit an image around another person taking on whatever person they want to be, such as me becoming Marilyn Monroe for a party; it will project the person and whatever outfit you want to wear. Just takes a couple of minutes to program. You have to remember there are a couple of things that need to take place so it works properly. The first thing is the person you want to project a holograph over has to have the same basic body shape. In other words, a fat person can't project a slim body over himself or herself.

But a slim person can simulate an overweight person; of course, there could be some complications with touch and feel. Also, the person needs to wear the proper footwear to simulate the proper height of the person being projected. There are a few other requirements but in a nut shell that's it. Would you like to see it work?"

"Sure. Have you got a transmitter with you?"

"Yes," Helen said, as she pulled a small black box about the size of a smart phone and just as thin out of her lab coat pocket. She removed her lab coat, exposing high boots and an almost skin tight body suit. "I have a few people programmed in this. Oh, yeah, the other thing is you need to wear an almost skin tight body suit so the clothes that are projected can cover you properly. Let's see, how about Pauley Perrette? You may know her as Abby Sciuto from NCIS," she said as she pushed a couple of touch sensitive keys; and a second later, Pauley Perrette was standing in from of them, complete with visible tattoos and high boots.

"Wow, that is awesome; where do I get one of those? It would be great at Halloween," Connie said as she stood and looked at her. She reached out and touched Helen's hand and then her jacket. "Wow, my hand goes right through."

"It takes a lot of power to do this and it will only last about six hours before the simulation falls apart; we are working on that. As I said, touch and feel needs force fields which we haven't perfected yet. It is best to have the real clothing to put over the holographic projection if you need the touchy feely stuff. Also, years ago, Soto's team developed fingerprint tips to change a person's fingerprints to that of the one they are impersonating. We also have mini projectors we can set up quickly, and they will project indefinitely."

"You said it was initially developed by Dr. Rocky Soto; didn't we fire him last year for misappropriation, and well, some other charges which should have put him in jail, but he made a deal and just got fired," Adam Cruz commented looking over at Davin. "I believe Mr. Randal handled that himself."

"Yes, that is when I took over the lab; he left along with his team of two lab techs and a scientist," Helen responded and then turned off the holographic generator and picked up her lab coat, slipped it back on and then said, "Anything else? I need to get back to the lab; I left some chemistry cooking and a young lab tech watching; not sure if she will remember to turn it off in time."

"Yeah, you can go; if we need anything else, we will call," Davin said and then opened the door for Helen. "Thank you. And I may want to borrow that little black box sometime."

Chapter 25 Reunion

"Good evening, gentlemen; I heard they are holding a secret meeting in there. May I pass?" Director Josh Randal said to the guards as he approached the door to the conference room.

"Director Randal, just a second sir," the guard said and then turned and knocked on the door, which opened a second later.

"Yes," Adam Cruz said and saw Josh Randal standing about ten feet from the door. "Director Randal, come in, we have been looking for you." And then Adam commanded the guard, "Let him in."

"Adam, I know you guys are looking for me and Stephanie, but we are fine," Randal said as he entered the room and got a lot of stares from everyone in there.

"Josh, old buddy, what the hell happened; how did you get away?" Davin asked as he walked up and shook his hand and then gave him a big bear hug.

"Didn't escape, they just let us go. Damnest thing! Grabbed us, took us to the harbor, put us on a boat, and motored us out to a larger boat. They kept us there until a few hours ago when they drove us back to the harbor and let us go; we grabbed a cab and had them drop us off here. Stephanie is down in the café getting something to drink," Randal spoke as if reciting a script as an actor being unsure of his lines, no emotion and monotone.

"Why didn't you call us?"

"They took our cell phones and all our cash, so we could not even use a pay phone. I figured it was best just to come directly here," Randal stated with a very serious look on his face. He then walked over to help himself to a cup of coffee and picked up a donut, one with sprinkles.

"Okay, good, but we still have a problem?" Davin said looking closely at Randal.

"What is it, Davin?" Randal asked and then took a sip of coffee.

"My kids are still missing. Amber and Josh were kidnapped off of the university campus two days ago. Were they with you on that boat?"

"No, just Stephanie and me; and we did not see the kidnappers, or the boat. We did not hear their voices; they did not talk around us, and we were blindfolded and had ear muffs, so any sounds we heard were muffled. Sorry that we can't be of any help with Amber and Josh."

"Okay, is Stephanie coming up or just going to hang around down there until you go?" Adam Cruz asked.

"I asked her to stay there; we both need to go home, shower and change. This has been a bit upsetting to her and we haven't slept in two days. They kept us awake and did not feed us much. After a good meal and shower, I will be back. My car is still at home, I hope. So we need a ride to the house. Oh, is everyone else okay that was at our house when we were kidnapped?" Randal asked

"Yes, a bit shook up, but fine," Cruz replied and reached over and picked up the inter-office phone, waited for someone to pick up and then said, "We need a car, driver and escort for Mr. Randal and his wife. Take them home and post security around the home until further notice." After a pause, he replied, "Good, they will be down in ten minutes."

"Thanks, I will come back in a few hours; let me get some sleep and food," Randal said and bit into the donut. "Good donut."

"See you in few hours, Josh," Davin said as his friend walked out of the room and closed the door behind him. "Something isn't right, Adam."

"What do you mean, Davin?"

"I have known Josh for over thirty years and he never eats donuts," Davin replied.

"He was hungry, hasn't eaten in days and maybe he couldn't resist," Adam responded.

"Yeah, maybe you are right, but in the light of what we saw with Miss Owens and that holographic device. He could have been a fake."

"No way, you know you have to go through multiple bio scans before getting in the building including a DNA and Iris Scan. It is nearly impossible to fool every one of the checks, maybe one but not all."

"Guess you are right, just a bit on edge here," Davin replied and then set his coffee down on the table.

The Island later the same day

"What the hell is this?" Bryce said as they came up to a chain link fence with concertina wire running across the top. Inside the wire were several buildings, but no sign of life anywhere, even though they could see lights in several windows. As they approached the fence, the door in one of the buildings opened and a young woman came out and waved to them. She was tall, brunette, wearing jeans and a white lab coat and a pair of red sneakers.

"Hello, what is this place?" Redmond yelled over to her and watched as she walked toward the fence but did not answer.

"Don't touch the fence, it is electrified," she finally said when she got within fifteen feet of the fence, stopped and looked intently at the six ragged strangers standing about five feet from the fence.

"What is this place?" Redmond repeated as he and the others scanned the compound and the surrounding jungle, and spoke quietly to the rest of his team. "Something's not right, stay sharp."

"Roger that, Captain," Bryce and Freddy said quietly together; and both turned as they heard rustling in the jungle behind them. "Oops, too late, Cap," Bryce said as he saw a team of ten heavily armed men walk out of the jungle behind them.

Redmond turned and saw the men emerge from the jungle. Each one was dressed in jungle camouflage and carried a variety of weapons ranging from MP-5s to M-16s.

"Please place your weapons on the ground, and step toward the gate on your right," the leader of the team ordered and then tilted his head back and yelled to the woman inside the fence. "Donna, open the gate, please."

"Sure, Lou," she replied as she walked over to the guard shed and entered. She threw a switch which turned off the electric fence, pushed a button to open the gate, and said, "Come on in, we have been expecting you."

Redmond, Bryce, Freddy, Diane, Morgan and Horatio laid their weapons on the ground and walked through the gate. Bryce turned to see five of the jungle team disappear in thin air.

"What the hell, did you see that?" Bryce asked Freddy as he hit him on the arm and pointed toward where the soldiers were standing. Where there were ten, there were now only five who were in the process of picking up the dropped weapons.

"What, no, I see five soldiers. There were at least ten a second ago," Freddy commented and shook his head in disbelief.

"Yeah, this is getting stranger by the minute," Redmond commented as he stopped in front of Donna the gate girl.

"Strange, yes, but I feel we haven't seen the last of it," Morgan said as she looked around the compound taking in as much of the place as she could, looking for escape routes, weaknesses and people. She did not see any people except the soldiers and Donna.

The gate swung closed behind them and the five soldiers. "Take the weapons to the arms room and report to Rocky in an hour," Donna ordered and then looked at the new arrivals and said, "Come with me, you have friends waiting for you."

She turned and walked toward the middle building's front door, only stopping to open it, and motioned for them to enter. "First door on the left, please."

"Okay, whatever you say, miss," Redmond acknowledged and walked into the building and then opened the door on the left and looked in.

"Holy crap! Redmond, are you and the kids okay," Vince said as he stood and walked over to the door that Redmond and the students had just walked in.

"We are fine; how are you and what the hell is going on?" Redmond answered and walked up to Vince and shook his outstretched hand.

"Come in, get something to eat; this is the mess hall, sort of anyway. I would like you to meet a few other guests of this facility. But get some food first; it is really pretty good stuff," Vince said and then turned and greeted each of his students. After getting some food, they walked over to the table that most were sitting at and sat down.

"Captain Redmond, Bryce, Morgan, Freddy and Diane, this is CIA Director Josh Randal and his wife Stephanie; beside them is Amber and Josh Pierce. We are all captives of a Rocky Soto, former member of the CIA. His plan is still unknown to us. Eat first and we will fill you in on what we do know." Vince introduced them and then started to tell them what they knew. He started with the kidnappings of the Pierce twins and the Randal's, and moved onto the drug and holograph projections that were used to help with the kidnappings.

"Where did Horatio go?" Morgan asked.

"He was right behind us a minute ago," Bryce stated as he looked around the room. Upon not seeing Horatio in the room, he looked even more confused.

Chapter 26 Randal House

"That went fairly well for a first run," Randal said to Stephanie after they were alone in their home.

"Is that agent going to stay outside all night?" she asked and then looked out the window at the car they had been brought home in. The agent sat behind the wheel typing a message on his smart phone. "We have to be careful," she continued and then reached into her pocket and removed a device that looked like a cell phone and tapped a couple of touch sensitive keys. Suddenly she was no longer Stephanie Randal, but a red-headed woman built almost exactly like Stephanie wearing latex pants and blouse and comfortable walking shoes.

"Stay away from the window, baby," Josh Randal said and then he pulled a similar device from his pocket and pressed a couple of touch sensitive keys. He suddenly transformed into a man built like Josh, also wearing form fitting clothes and dress shoes.

"Jeff, I need a shower; let's go upstairs and get naked," she said and started to pull her blouse over her head.

"I will be right up, Sonia, need to get into the safe and see what secrets we can gather," Jeff said and then turned toward the door to the basement.

"Don't be too long lover. I will be waiting," she said and then sprinted up the steps.

Jeff turned on the light and walked down the steps, not being real familiar with the house he didn't want to trip on anything. "Wow, Randal is a junk dealer," he said seeing all the stuff that had accumulated in the basement. "Now where is the safe, I know it is down here, at least that is what Rocky told me." He looked around and finally spotted the safe. After he walked over to the large gun safe, he said to himself, "Now if I can only crack it." He paused when he heard the water running through the pipes going to the shower on the second floor. "Guess I really need to get up there," he said to himself, but continued with, "Got to quit talking to myself; people are going to wonder about me."

After a couple of attempts to open the safe, he gave up and started up the stairs. He thought there would be more time later to crack into the safe. Minutes later, he walked into the master bedroom and started to remove his clothes. "I will be right in babe," he yelled to her as he removed his shirt and pants.

The Island

"Rocky, our other guests have arrived; but before you meet them, I need to update you on the operation in Virginia," Mike Johns said as Rocky entered the private conference room located on the second floor of the control room building.

"What is the status?" Rocky questioned as he reached for a donut and cup of coffee.

"Jeff and Sonia successfully infiltrated the CIA and are now in the shower at the Randal house. Jeff will return to Langley in about an hour or so where he will take charge of the CIA."

"And what about New Mexico?"

"We haven't gotten a report back as yet, but are expecting our agent to send us a message in about forty minutes, at his scheduled check in time."

"Good, hope their story flies well," Rocky Soto said and then stood and started for the door. "I have some guests to greet."

University of New Mexico

"Professor Landers, let me get this straight. You and your four students went on a field trip and did not inform the school as to where you were going and when you were to return?" Detective Becks questioned, sitting across from Professor Landers in his classroom.

"No not exactly. I informed my student aide as to our plan; and he, as I understand it, was killed in a car crash just hours after we departed. He was a smart kid, had a great future, but accidents happen; and I also left notes on my desk, which are right here as to what we were doing," Vince said to Becks from behind his desk and picked up a piece of paper that outlined the field trip. "And as I said before when I got back, I discovered my car had been stolen and learned that the police found it in the desert north of town. I cannot explain any more than that; we were at an archeological dig down near the Mexican border."

"I guess that explains it, Doctor Landers. If we have any more questions, we will call you," Becks replied and then she and Lucy Grayson stood to leave just as Bryce and Morgan entered the classroom.

"Sorry are we interrupting?" Bryce asked as he stepped into the room.

"No, we were just finishing, how did you enjoy the dig, Ms. Fields?" Detective Grayson asked.

"It was pretty cool, actually dated back several thousand years. It was a good find; and we were able to bring several pieces back with us. Would you care to see them?" Morgan Fields replied.

"Not right now, maybe later. You have a good day," Becks answered for her partner and walked out of the classroom. Neither said a word until they reached their car, when Becks finally spoke up, "Do you believe what they said?"

"Sounds too much like a bedtime story to me," Lucy replied. "So coincidental, everything happened perfectly, almost as if it were planned. And each one said the same thing, like it was rehearsed. I think we need to dig a bit deeper into the accident that killed the teacher's aide, what was his name, again, oh, Timothy Kushman."

"I agree; let's get back to the station and pull that report. And then it's such a beautiful day why not take a drive down to that dig; he told us exactly where it is, should not be hard to find."

"I am up for a little digging; we can check that accident report when we get back. Let's just head south now," Lucy agreed and smiled for the first time today. She really enjoyed a good mystery, and this one was shaping up to be a real winner.

The Island Control Center

"Rocky will be happy; we just received confirmation that Landers and his team have made contact and passed the first test," a Control Center operator said to the center operations manager.

"Good, good. I will inform him in a minute. Have we got anything on the delivery?" the operation's manager asked.

"No, nothing as yet, but the boat should be here before nightfall," the operator stated, returned to his computer, typed in a few commands, and then read what he was given, "The Captain said they would be here by six tonight and to have the dock up and some men to help unload."

"When is the next satellite passage?"

"Satellite will do a north to south fly over at nine tonight; we are safe to bring up the dock and the Captain will be long gone before the satellite gets here."

"Good, tell the good captain to come on in; we will be waiting."

"Roger that, sir," the operator responded and then typed in the new command.

Chapter 27 History Lesson

"Wow, now we have everyone here and I can lay out your part in our game," Rocky Soto said as he entered the secured room where all his captives were being held. "Why the long faces; you have everything you could ever want, except your freedom of course, but everything else. Free satellite TV, hot showers, clean beds in private rooms, and all the food you could ever want. What else do you need; and don't say freedom, you will get that soon enough."

"So why are we here?" Josh Randal asked when he looked up and saw Rocky Soto enter the room followed by his son, Horatio Soto.

"History has taught us that to make a change, sometimes drastic changes have to happen, such as the Revolutionary War to get away from British rule, the Civil War to stop slavery, at least that is what the text books say, World War I and II to stop world take over by dictators; and of course we cannot forget, Viet Nam to stop communist oppression and then Desert Storm/Shield to stop Saddam Hussein and his sadistic ideas. There were many revolutions and mini wars or police actions; and, oh, yeah, Korea, that was a real winner which is still being contested."

"Okay, drastic measures have been used for years to make change. What has that got to do with us?" Randal insisted.

"Well, if you really need to know, I will tell you; there is nothing you can do to stop me now, anyway." Soto reached into his pocket, pulled out a small cell phone, pressed a couple of touch sensitive buttons, and instantly transformed into a five foot six-inch-tall Marilyn Monroe. "Oops, wrong button, let's try this one." Instantly he transformed into Josh Randal; and when he spoke he sounded just like Randal. He looked like Randal and walked like Randal, but he wasn't Randal, because Randal was sitting at the end of the table with his jaw firmly planted on the table.

"What the hell?" Randal said as he stood and looked at Soto. "I had heard we were working on holographic technology, but thought we were years away."

"No, Mr. Randal, we have jumped years ahead. We have even made some major improvements that even my replacement doesn't have," Soto said and then pushed a button and transformed back into himself. "Oh, my manners, this is my son. I believe Mr. Landers' geniuses met him out in the jungle. He will, well, I will tell you his part in all this. Just so you know everything Mr. Landers' group experienced out on the island was a hoax, mostly holographic projections. There were some exceptions; the boats in the cove and the airplanes on the field were real, the crews were long dead. Captain Redmond, you are really the only real person that they encountered out there. And Redmond, I have some bad news for you, too."

"What do you mean, Mr. Soto?"

"Well, history has a way of being bent or manipulated as it were. I don't want to take the time right now to explain it to you. Just keep this in mind; you are not what you think you are. And just like a talking donkey and peacock, things are not what they seem."

"I, ah, I don't understand," Redmond commented looking very confused.

"I will have one of my crew take you aside and explain it to you when we finish here."

"As for my plans, we needed to remove you from your places of pleasure and work to complete our mission. A mission that needed you here and our people living and breathing as you out there; they are there to complete a mission that will turn the United States government up-side-down. And while you slept during the trip here, we were able to get some blood samples and your DNA. Both of which were needed to complete our mission."

"How do you propose to do that, Soto?" the young Josh Pierce asked before Randal could get the words out of his mouth.

"Randal is going to kidnap the President of the United States and a few others just to get things started.

"Kidnap the President; been tried before and failed, the man is not reachable," Randal said as he slowly walked around to the end of the table and stopped within ten feet of Soto and his son.

"That is where you and the rest come in to play; with you, Mr. Randal, you can get close to the President. You, or rather your replacement, will kidnap the current president and then take his place. We will keep the president at a secure place until the right time to release him. Exactly how we do that, I will not tell you; but rest assured that the operation is well under way and there is no way for you or your government to stop it."

"You will never get away with it!" Stephanie commented and then looked around the room at the other captives, wondering how the hell they were going to be able to stop them.

"My dear, I already have; you are here, and my teams are already out there being you and nobody knows the difference. Your DNA has been infused into my people, your fingerprints, voice prints and habits are all in place; in essence, my people are you, top to bottom. Even you could not tell the difference. They will be examined by doctors, and they will not be able to distinguish between you or my replacements. They are perfect in every way, now that we have your DNA and a way to clone you. The holograph tricks are good for a short period to infiltrate and confuse, but my clones are perfect."

"Clones, you don't really mean that; cloning was an experiment years ago. Don't tell me you are now cloning people," Randal yelled as he became angrier by the minute.

"Not exactly, not exactly, but our method does work and it is perfect," Soto concluded. "With the use of our holographic projection, we can be anyone at any time or place we want to be. I guess you could say 'Checkmate', Mr. Randal."

The room sat silent as they watched this man tell them of what he had put into motion, and wondered how they could stop him.

Chapter 28 Eggs Over Easy

"What have we found out?" Davin Pierce asked the room full of CIA agents and technicians.

"Nothing, sir," Adam Cruz stated as Davin entered the room.

"Nothing! We are the best and largest intelligence gathering organization in the world and we have nothing to show for it."

"Afraid so, boss," Adam commented, feeling that he had let down his boss, which he had, but not because he hadn't tried. His men and women had been working all night, but still came up with nothing.

"That's okay, Adam," Davin said just as the door opened again and Josh Randal walked in, looking fresh and ready.

"How do you feel, Josh?" Adam asked when he saw his boss enter the room.

"Fine, Adam. What have we got?"

"As I just told Davin, we have nothing. Our intel has just dried up," Adam said and then turned to Davin. "What's your thought, Davin?"

"My thoughts, I do believe Josh and I need to go downstairs and get some breakfast. When we get back up here, we should have a plan," Davin said and looked over at Josh and said, "Ready?"

"Sure, I could use a big breakfast; haven't eaten much lately," Randal said and followed Davin out the door.

"What is your real story, Josh?" Davin asked as they waited for the elevator.

"What do you mean; I told you last night," Josh replied.

"You left out some of the important stuff. Anytime you leave out things, you have to work hard to keep a straight face; and from what I could see, you were having a hard time keeping a straight face last night. Or was it my imagination?" Davin queried as they entered the elevator and pressed the first floor button.

"Davin, my old friend, we have known each other for over thirty years and you know I can't reveal everything that I know to a room of agents that may not have a need to know everything."

"Yeah, yeah, I know. But Josh, we have a problem and you need to at least fill in Adam and me on everything," Davin said as they exited the elevator and walked toward the café.

"And I will, as soon as I get a couple of eggs, pancakes and bacon. And don't start; I know I said no more bacon, but after what I just went through, I think a couple of strips of bacon won't kill me."

"Okay, let's eat," Davin agreed and entered the café to find it almost empty. At seven in the morning, it was usually very busy, but today it wasn't. "We are so early the day shift hasn't gotten here yet. You don't normally show up till nine."

"When we get back upstairs, you, Adam, and I will go to my office and I will fill you in on the things that everyone does not need to know."

Davin and Josh looked outside at the patio to view a beautiful sunrise; the sun had just crested over the edge of the building and cast sunrays and shadows in all the right places. It created a surreal scene, one that could be used in a horror movie just before the Zombies attacked. The view immediately sent a chill through Davin as he viewed the scene. "I need coffee, how about you?"

"Yeah, coffee, you know how I like it; I will get us a breakfast, same for you, eggs over easy, couple pancakes and bacon?" Randal asked and walked over to the grill and ordered.

Thirty-five minutes later, they had derived a possible plan that they almost completely agreed on, but needed concurrence with Adam and a few of the forensic scientists. They needed a bit more information, and the forensic team would be able to provide what they needed.

"Adam would you come with us," Davin asked as he entered the conference room a few minutes later.

"Sure, right behind you," Adam said and then stood and followed Davin back out the door. He turned to the guards and said, "We will be back shortly; breakfast was ordered for everyone and should be here in a few minutes. Check the cart and then have Barney take it in, the cooks or delivery person does not go in."

"Yes, sir," the lead guard said.

"Oh, yeah, I ordered some for you too. Your relief is not going to be here for a couple more hours and I thought you might want some coffee and food," Adam said before he jogged down the hall to catch up with Davin and Randal.

"Thank you sir," the guard replied, looked at his partner, and smiled.

Randal's Office

"Please have a seat, gentlemen," Randal suggested and then walked around to behind his desk and sat. "Davin wanted to know what I held back last night; and yes, I did hold back some information, but guess you two really need to know. Since most of the agents in the conference room do not have a need to know, I couldn't and would not say what I am about to tell you.

"Okay, Mr. Randal we are all ears," Adam said as he sat across from Randal in an overstuffed leather chair identical to the one Davin sat in.

"When we came in last night, my first goal was to let you know we were okay; and that is what everyone needed to know. What I did not tell you is that once they got us on the boat, they took us to a room, undid the blindfolds, and locked us in. We heard nothing for hours; the room had no windows and a double lock on the door. We assumed and found out later that there was an armed guard standing outside our door. After several hours of searching the room and finding nothing to help us, we grew tired and laid down on the bed. We fell asleep within minutes. It was weird; we should not have been tired, but felt exhausted, almost like we were drugged. Without having a watch to know what time it was or how long we slept, we woke up later feeling tired and noticed the needle marks on our arms," Randal said and then pulled up his sleeve and showed them the needle marks. "We don't know what they did to us or how long we slept. Shortly after, they took us back to shore and let us go. As we worked our way back here, we tried to figure out what they wanted; and the only thing we could figure is that they wanted some of our blood for something."

"Okay, maybe the forensic team can tell us what they could use your blood for," Adam suggested.

"We can ask them without telling them why we want to know," Davin said and then asked. "Is there anything else you want to tell us?"

"Nothing that affects the case at hand," Randal stated and then rolled down his sleeve and pulled open the top right hand drawer of his desk from which he pulled out a small bottle of scotch and three glasses. "It is a little early, but a short drink among friends would be great. It's five o'clock somewhere, isn't it?"

"None for me, Josh," Davin said.

"Me neither, we have too much work to do," Adam agreed shaking his head.

"Okay, guess I will pass too. Really too early anyway," Randal said as he finally decided to not have one.

"I will talk to the forensic team and see what they can tell me," Adam said, stood and started for the door, just as Davin stood and turned.

"Davin, please sit; we have some other things to talk about," Randal said watching as Adam got to the door. "Thanks, Adam."

"What is it Josh?" Davin asked as he sat back down and leaned back into the chair.

"I'm worried. They took Stephanie and me, violated us by taking our blood and I have no idea what else. I have asked Stephanie to come by at ten today to pick me up. We are going to meet with our doctor to see if anything else happened to us. And no, we don't want to see the company doc, because he might make a big stink over it. I will report to you, and only you, as to what he says."

"Okay, deal," Davin agreed, "Now we need to get back into the conference room and outline our plan."

"I will be right there; go ahead and start without me," Randal said and watched as Davin left the office. After the door closed, Randal pulled out a cell phone, typed in a short message, and hit send. The message had two words, "Eliminate Pierce." The message was received almost instantly at the control room on the island and handed to Soto. He looked at it and agreed, and then sent a text back with one word, "Cruz."

Chapter 29 Arlington, Virginia

"Central, this is Delta fourteen," Officer Danny Baker said into his personal radio as he looked over at the two bodies lying on the fifty-yard line of the Naval Academy Football Stadium. The night was cool and turning colder as it got later in the evening. It was by pure luck that they found the two lying there; their normal route around the campus did not bring them to the stadium unless they had a call of a disturbance or possible vandals. Vandalism around the Naval Football stadium was minimal, since this was a Navy town; and the neighbors kept a good open eye on the area. The only reason they were there was that they got an anonymous call about a dark van cruising the neighborhood.

Danny Baker had been with the Annapolis Police Department since he graduated from college, moving up in ranks to Sergeant. He was six-foot-tall, had a bald head and unshaven face; his uniform was always perfect. His goal was to make Captain before retiring, but he had time to wait; he was in no hurry.

"Go ahead Delta Fourteen," cracked the radio.

"Send a bus down to the stadium, two victims, unconscious teens on the fifty-yard line. Unknown cause, we will stay on site until they arrive," Baker said and then looked at the two lying on the ground at his feet. They were dressed only in jeans and tee shirts, no shoes or socks, looked a bit roughed up, but breathing. Both appeared to be twins, but had no identification and without doing a complete pat down Baker could not be sure other than that they were alive, without possibly causing additional harm.

"Bus on the way, Delta Fourteen," replied control. "ETA fifteen."

"Roger, control."

"Any idea how they got here, Danny?" his partner Max 'Gundog' Hunter asked. He was five foot eight, and had a passion for weapons; he had picked up his nickname while serving as a gunner on an Army attack helicopter known as a Super Blackhawk. He operated a 30mm mini-gun on the side of the helo; and when the barrels got too hot to continue using, he would lift up an old model M-60 machine gun and continue to protect his side of the chopper by laying down a concentrated fire on the enemy. He had received two Bronze Stars, three Purple Hearts for wounds, a Silver Star, and three air medals before finally leaving the Army and joining the Annapolis Police department. Since joining, he became the senior weapons trainer and the man to go to when weapons were involved.

"Don't know, but if we hadn't come by to check out that dark van which is nowhere to be seen, these two might have frozen to death," Baker stated and then thought for a moment before asking, "Do you think the driver of the van called it in?"

"No way! Why would they do that?"

"Maybe they wanted us to find them," Hunter suggested as they looked around for evidence such as tracks or anything else that could lead them to the van or how the two kids got here.

"Delta Fourteen, detectives will be there in about twenty. Stay on site until they arrive."

"Ten Four, Central," Baker responded. "Hey, look at this," he said and pointed toward a pair of tire tracks.

"Could be our van dropping off these two," Hunter commented, "Detectives probably should bring forensics with them."

"I'll call it in."

Twenty minutes later, the bus with a couple of EMTs on board stopped at the edge of the field and walked over to where Baker and Hunter were waiting.

"Can we get the lights on, Officer?" Detective Hamilton 'Ham' Carver asked as he and his partner pulled up at the edge of the field behind the EMT vehicle.

"Sure, we called the field caretaker and he should be here in a minute," Baker said and then turned around to look at the two teens just as the field lights popped on and threw light all over the field turning the dark into day.

"Wow, you are good; I ask, you supply," Carver said with a chuckle.

"Your wish is our command ole' great one," Baker responded and shook Carver's outstretched hand. They had attended the academy together and ended up being lifelong friends. They were always joking with each other over the years, spending time with each other's families and sometimes even going on vacation together.

"Yeah, at least you remember your place, my loyal subject."

"Watch it; remember a sergeant outranks a detective in this department," Baker reminded his friend.

"Oh, yeah, I guess you are right again, Danny. So what do we have?"

"Received a call about a dark van cruising the neighborhood, especially around the stadium. We came over. And as we drove down the road, over there, we saw a van parked on the other end of the stadium and came over to investigate. But when we got there, it had already left. We got out, walked around the stadium, and came across those two lying there. We checked to see if they were still alive and thankfully for them they are. Called for EMT. We found tire tracks near the kids but no van."

"Hey doc, how are they?" Carver asked as he and Baker walked over to where the EMTs were working on the twins.

"Multiple contusions, possible concussions; they are still out, possible coma. We won't know until we get them to the hospital. Both have needle marks on their arms; could be drug related. We will have the hospital run a complete Tox run on both of them. We need to get them moved now, may we?"

"Sure, get them out of here," Carver said and then turned back to Baker and Hunter. "What else can you tell me?"

"Nothing really, just the tire tracks and that the van we saw was a Chevy panel van, no windows, dark color; it was too far away to get the license plate; and even so, the one we saw may not have been involved at all. It was at the stop sign and when we turned to go around the block it moved on. There was no writing on the side so it wasn't commercial."

"Maybe when they wake up, we can find out what was going on," Carver commented, "You two get back on patrol; we are going to follow the EMTs to the hospital. Catch you later Danny."

"Take care, Chuck, Dinner Sunday?"

"Sure. Five?"

"Five is good; bring Maggie and a salad. I will have plenty of beer and Sue is fixing a turkey."

"Sounds good; see you Sunday."

Chapter 30 Captivity Is Forever or Not

Josh Randal got up and slowly walked around the café looking in every corner, under every table and chair until he finally returned to his chair.

"What were you looking for, Randal?" Morgan asked.

"Bugs," Randal stated and then smiled and looked over at Vince Landers.

"Mr. Landers, you and your crew were out there on the other side of that fence; you saw things, are we on an island?" Josh Randal asked as they sat around the small café having a cold drink.

"Did you find any bugs? And yes, we are on an island; and there are several ships and a submarine in a cove on the east side. There are also at least ten airplanes located on two different airfields. Six are on the field close to where we arrived; the rest are on an airfield close to this compound," Vince stated and then turned to Bryce and asked. "Can you tell Randal the type and condition of the planes?"

"No bugs that I could find, but these people are pretty tricky. What about the planes?" Randal asked as he looked at Bryce.

"Sure, sir. The airfield on the south end has Captain Redmond's F-4, damaged and probably not flyable; there is Amelia Earhart's Lockheed, not sure of the condition but looks flyable. There is a P-51, a Corsair, a P-38 Lightning, a Japanese Zero and a B-17 bomber, all in various conditions but not visibly flyable. The north field had four very badly damaged Japanese Zeros, a couple of wrecked Corsairs and a few large hangers; doors were closed so we could not see what was inside."

"What about fuel?" Randal asked.

"I saw several fuel trucks behind the Operations building, but did not check them for fuel. There was also a fuel storage tank near the end of the runway, contents unknown," Bryce replied and then asked, "What is on your mind, Mr. Randal?"

"I am not sure yet. We have some boats or ships in a cove out there; we are still inside the fence, and they have guns and we don't. It will be difficult to get out, but I am working on it." Randal said quietly.

"Electrified fence, armed guards, holographs that look real, we really don't know how many are here," Diane piped in, questioning any decision to try and escape.

"I don't plan on staying here for the rest of my life," Randal shot back. "Soto did say that he would determine when and where we would be released. Do we wait until he decides, or go on our own?"

"Sir, we don't even know how much time we have to live. They have replaced us back home; they may not need us anymore," Morgan stated and looked around the room.

"You are correct young lady, but I am not waiting to find out. There has to be a way out of here and off this island, whether it be on one of those boats or we fly out. But one thing for sure is we need to find out where on the earth we are. And looking at the sky tonight may help with that," Randal commented and then looked at his wife, Stephanie. "Honey, you have studied the stars for years; do you think you can narrow down our location?"

"Get me outside tonight; and I will do my best, as long as I can see the stars. I will fabricate a simple Sexton to shoot the stars," Stephanie commented.

"I will get you out tonight. Go make your sexton," Randal said to her.

"Okay, we don't have any maps?" Morgan said.

"Yes, we do," Freddy said and pulled a faded chart from his back pocket. "I took this from the sub; and here is one from the Japanese Zero that we found crashed just off the beach."

"Good job, Freddy. Pass that over to Stephanie, please; she will keep it under wraps."

"To get everyone out of here, we need to take the Lockheed or the B-17; both are pretty old and are a long way from here. But first, we need to get out of here. I can fly either one, but will need a co-pilot, especially on the 17," Captain Redmond spoke up.

"I will be your co-pilot," Randal said, "I don't have time in big birds but do fly when I can."

"What's your plan on getting us out of here?" Vince asked.

"Not sure yet, and for now I know they will do whatever they need to do to stop us including separating us or slipping in a clone or holographic replacement." Randal paused for a second, thinking about how to distinguish the people in this room from any possible clone or holographic impostor. "Okay we need to revert back to the old days by using a sign and counter sign to identify that you are the real person you say you are. We will change it daily until we are flying or sailing away from this island."

"Okay, from here until eight in the morning, if you challenge anyone in this room with the word 'Viper' you will respond with 'Banana'. And then you will say 'Lamplight' and then the response is 'Robot'. If all the challenges and responses are correct, you will know you are speaking to the real person, hopefully."

"Sounds easy enough," Morgan said and then stood and walked over to the cooler and pulled a cold orange soda that was buried in the ice.

"Still need to figure out how we get past that fence and away from these crazy people. And then to the airfield, fuel an airplane, pre-flight it and take off without being caught. Impossible," Freddy stated looking confused for the first time since arriving here. "I have a couple of hundred hours in Cessna's and can help, but I will not be much help flying one of those big birds."

"Okay, may not be the best plan. The only way to do all that is to make sure all these crazy people are incapacitated. We need to break into the lab and get some drug or something to put them to sleep, all of them," Randal stated seriously.

Chapter 31 Fifty Yard Line

"Greg, have we got all our teams in place?" Rocky asked his head controller.

"Rocky, my old friend, the kids were dropped last night and have been picked up and taken to the local Annapolis hospital; they are still in the induced coma we left them in, but should wake up in a couple of hours. They will not remember a thing, just as planned."

"Good, we will keep Mr. and Mrs. Pierce in the dark for a while. Let them worry about their kids. Jane and John Doe will keep them guessing. And by the time the fingerprints get back to the hospital identifying them, they will have left the hospital," Rocky stated.

"Yeah, should work just fine. It usually takes a couple of hours to run the prints and with that they can make their escape. The only problem is if they use one of those fancy new portable fingerprint identifiers."

"What are the odds of that?" Rocky questioned "And why didn't you tell me about this earlier. We could get screwed if they find out who they are before they wake."

"Didn't think of it at the time," Greg said and stepped back expecting to be slammed.

"You had better hope they don't use one of those gadgets," Rocky said seriously and then looked into Greg's eyes. "If they identify them before they wake, your body will never be found."

"Yes sir. I will make sure they awaken in the next few minutes," Greg responded and then immediately walked over to the control board and pressed a couple of keys which immediately sent a signal to the transplants in the two kids.

The transplanted receiver activated their nervous system and started to pump more oxygen to their brains which caused each of them to start to wake.

At the same time, a young police detective had entered the hospital with his lieutenant and asked at the desk where they could find the two Does. After being given the room number and directions, they proceeded to walk over to the elevator and pressed the button for the third floor. As they quietly waited, they looked around the hospital lobby and noticed a man sitting in the corner who seemed to be familiar to the lieutenant.

"Hold the elevator; I need to check out that old man in the corner, he looks familiar," Detective Hamilton Carver stated and started to walk toward the man. The man seeing that he had attracted attention stood and started to walk toward the door.

"Just a second sir," Hamilton said as he approached him. The man bolted and ran out the door. "Gundog, stop the old man coming out the front door, now," he ordered into the handheld radio to his officer waiting outside at the car.

Hamilton exited the hospital a second later, and found his officer holding the man on the ground and working on putting handcuffs on him.

"Hold on Gundog, I just want to talk to him, not arrest him, at least not yet," Hamilton said as he walked up, "Please stand up and don't run; you are not in trouble, at least as far as I know. Why did you run out?"

"I, ah, I saw all you cops last night and didn't want any trouble; and then when you started to come over to me inside, I panicked. I was hoping you didn't see me last night;

guess you did. I didn't do anything wrong," the man said nervously and almost too quiet to hear.

"Look, I did see you hanging around the football stadium last night and wanted to talk to you then, but you disappeared. I just want to ask if you saw anything, like who may have dropped two kids off on the fifty-yard line."

"I did see the men who did it, sir, ah, but not much; I was just sitting there minding my own business when this van sped up and stopped near the gate. I ducked behind the bleachers and watched. I ah, wasn't doing anything wrong. I sometimes go there and imagine the old days," the man mumbled.

"The old days, what do you mean? Did you play there?"

"A long time ago, I was a student at the academy; spent twenty-two years serving our great country and then retired. I played on that field during my time at the academy. Beat Army in every game I played in from 2001 to when I graduated in 2004 and then I was off to flight school."

"Thank you for your service. When did you retire, sir?" Hamilton asked.

"After twenty-two years of service, that would have made the year two thousand twenty-two when I retired. I have been living in a little house down the street from the stadium since then," the old retired sailor stated.

"What else can you tell me about last night?" Hamilton asked just as Officer Danny Baker walked up.

"Not much, sir; there were two dressed in black. I could see they had guns and I just watched. It was dark and I couldn't see their faces. I used my cell and called your office to report it; and then I left when I saw your officers show up," the old man responded.

"Please my name is Hamilton Carver, most call me Ham. I should be calling you, sir. By the way, what is your name? I may need to contact you to help identify the people that we are looking for." Hamilton said and pulled out his pad.

"Retired Captain Raymond Dawg, call sign 'Bloodhound' US Navy," Captain Dawg stated proudly. "Flew F/A-18 Super Hornets until I got too old and then drove C-130s and C-141s until they benched me."

"I remember you; my dad used to take me to the games before I joined the force. I saw you play. You were one hell of a quarterback. Often wondered what happened to you," Hamilton said acknowledging Captain Dawg.

"Served my country, got old and got retired, now fighting cancer and a whole bunch of other problems, some caused by being in the Navy, others just because I got old."

"If you remember anything about what you saw last night, please call me or Detective Baker," Hamilton said as he handed him his card and indicated for Baker to give him his card too.

Chapter 32 If They Only Knew

Detectives Hamilton Carver and Sergeant Danny Baker stepped off the elevator on the third floor and approached the nurse's desk.

"Where can we find the two unknown kids?" Carver asked the nurse on duty.

She looked up and then back to her computer, typed in a couple of commands and then without looking up, she said, "They are gone, officer."

"Gone, they can't be; they were in a coma when we called an hour ago. How could they just be gone?" Baker questioned and looked down the long hallway.

"Yes sir, they woke up, got dressed and walked out of here. We could not stop them; they said they had to go and left," the head nurse said as she walked up behind the two officers. "The officer that was supposed to be guarding them is also gone. He walked away a few minutes before the kids woke up, and we haven't seen him since."

"Who was on duty here, Danny?" Carver questioned.

"We didn't assign anyone; they were in a coma and the doctor said they probably would not awaken for days, if ever. There was no need to guard them," Danny replied quickly. "I think we screwed up, boss."

"No, I think they planned this. We don't know who they are, where they went, and hell, we have nothing. Did we at least get pictures of their faces?"

"No we didn't; nurse, did your staff take pictures?" Danny asked the head nurse.

"Sorry," she replied holding up a digital camera. "I was heading in there to do just that when I found out they had left."

"Did anyone see them leave?" Carver asked.

"Yes, Nurse Morrison did; she was on duty and in there when they awakened."

"May we speak with her?" Danny asked and turned to look back down the long hallway.

"Sure, I will have her come to the waiting lounge to meet with you in a few minutes; she is in room 397 right now and that is all the way down at the end of the hallway. I will call her and have her come to you."

"Where is the waiting room?"

"Second door on the left, down that way. Please wait there; she will be right in," the head nurse said and then pulled her handheld radio from her pocket and called for Nurse Morrison to report to the waiting room.

They did not have to wait long when a tall, blond hair, blue-eyed nurse walked into the room; she looked more like a Victoria Secret model than a nurse, but as they say, looks don't tell the whole story. Nurse Morrison was a dedicated nurse with years of experience both in the emergency room and intensive care.

"How can I help you, gentlemen?" Nurse Morrison asked as she entered. She did not take a seat because she had to get back to work.

"Just one question, Miss Morrison. Did you see those two kids leave the building?"

"Yes, I was walking down the hall, when I heard noise coming from their room. I opened the door to find both of them getting dressed; and before I had a chance to stop them, they pushed past me and out the door, ran down the hall, and exited down the stairs fast. They almost knocked me to the floor pushing past me and that isn't easy."

"Can you remember anything else that may help us find them?" Danny asked as he stood and looked at Nurse Morrison.

"Nothing, sorry."

"Thank you; here is my card; if you remember anything please call. Oh, if we sent a sketch artist down here, would you be able to describe them for him so we can have a sketch of the two kids," Danny said handing her his card.

"Sure, I get off duty at midnight."

"Thank you," Carver responded as he watched Nurse Morrison leave the room and admired her figure from behind.

"You can stop drooling, Ham. She is a beautiful woman and I wouldn't mind having her take care of my needs," Danny said as he also admired the beauty as she left.

"Yea, I have to agree. Are we just two dirty old men or what?"

"I think we are the 'or what'," Danny agreed, "Let's get out of here and call in for the artist to come by. Maybe we should ask Jennifer to come by; she is the best artist we have."

"You call it in; I need to stop by the rest room before we leave," Ham responded.

Many miles away on a secluded island

"Phase two is in full swing, Rocky," Greg, his head controller, said as he saw his boss walk into the control room.

"Great, how long before Randal has his meeting with the president?" Rocky asked.

"He will make the appointment at eleven this morning local time for a private meeting this afternoon. He will be accompanied by our holographic projection of Davin Pierce," Greg stated with a smile. "Your plan is coming together."

"Good, I know what happens next, what about the kids?"

"They escaped from the hospital, our inside nurse said that no pictures, fingerprints or DNA tests were run. She was put in charge of them and made sure they were not disturbed. She has talked to the police and they are sending a sketch artist over to see her. She plans on given them some good pictures of kids that look nothing like our two."

"Does she have a way out when the time comes?"

"Yes, but will only use it if threatened."

Chapter 33 Who's On First

"Josh and Davin, how are you two doing?" asked President Tony Sanford a man who came up through the ranks, starting his career as an FBI undercover agent and working his way up to Congressman, National Security Advisor and then presidential candidate. When he ran for President, by a stroke of luck, he won the election in 2030 by a slim margin beating out the Democratic front runner.

"Doing fine, sir but we have a problem which we need to discuss and hopefully come up with a solution quickly," Randal stated and then sat across from Sanford on the large sofa.

"What seems to be the problem that brought both of you down to the big house this late in the day?" Sanford questioned sitting with his legs crossed while he sipped a cup of coffee. He drank coffee day and night; the caffeine kept him sharp. Davin strolled around the room looking at the pictures on the wall as if he had never been in this room before. This was his first time, but Sanford did not know that. "Davin, you seem nervous, what's the problem?"

"Someone has kidnapped my kids. They were taken five days ago and we have not heard anything. Also, there were four students and a professor from the University of New Mexico that disappeared and suddenly showed up three days later," Davin stated as he walked back around in front of President Sanford. "Something is happening over which we have no control and don't even understand yet. We just needed to let you know that the country may be in grave danger, including you, sir."

While Davin was talking, Randal leaned over, picked up the President's cup, and carried both his and the empty president's cup over to the coffee bar. He returned full cups back to the coffee table in front of each of them.

Within a few minutes, President Sanford was asleep on the sofa. Randal stood, walked over and checked for a pulse. After getting a strong reading, he pulled a cell phone from his pocket, tapped in a couple of numbers, and then placed the cell in the President's pocket instantly projecting a holographic image of Davin Pierce around President Sanford.

Davin Pierce reached into his pocket, tapped a couple of buttons and instantly turned into President Sanford. Randal took a blood sample from Sanford and placed it in a capsule and shook it up. Getting the result, he was hoping for, he then inserted a hypodermic needle and injected it into the new president. "Now they will not be able to tell the difference. Call the doctor!"

Minutes later, the White House senior nurse came to the door and found Davin Pierce lying sick on the sofa.

"Where's Doctor Holt?" President Sanford asked.

"He is on his way, but was off campus when you called, so I rushed here," she replied as she was examining Davin. "We need to get him to the hospital, now. He has had a heart attack," she said and then pointed to the phone on the president's desk. After getting a nod to use it, she called for an emergency cart and ambulance.

Twenty minutes later, they had placed Davin on a gurney and wheeled him out to a waiting ambulance.

Minutes later, Randal, the nurse and the holographic Davin were heading down Pennsylvania Avenue in an ambulance with the lights flashing and siren blaring. As the ambulance ran down the street, it turned off its siren and flashing lights, slowed and turned north of Pennsylvania Avenue, disappearing into the traffic.

Back at the White House, Doctor Robert Holt walked down the hall toward the Oval Office; he was stopped by a Secret Service agent before reaching the office.

"Good afternoon, Doctor Holt. Did you hear what happened this afternoon?" the agent asked.

"No, what happened?" Holt replied.

"Davin Pierce and Josh Randal were here from the CIA and Pierce had a heart attack; they rushed him to the hospital," the agent replied.

"Oh, I just got a call that someone was sick in the Oval Office, I was off campus and raced over here as fast as I could. Took me longer than I expected, traffic is terrible out there."

"Come with me Doc," the agent said and then turned and raced to the Oval Office, stopping at the President's private secretary's desk asking, "Is President Sanford in?"

"Just a second, I will see if he is busy," she responded. "Sir, I have the doctor and Agent Hershey out here, may they come in?" After getting a response of yes over the phone, she looked up at the two waiting, and said, "Yes, go on in," while she pressed the button to unlock the door.

"Sorry to disturb you, sir, but we seem to have a bit of confusion. Doctor Holt just arrived to assist a sick person in your office. Are you okay?" Agent Hershey asked.

"I am fine Hershey. Mr. Pierce was here and developed a problem; he was wheeled out by your nurse."

"Okay, I will check in with the hospital and my assistant and let you know how he is," Doctor Holt replied, "Sorry to bother you, sir."

"No problem, Doc."

Chapter 34 The Great Escape

They had been on the island for four days and hadn't located any means of escape. The treatment they received would be classified as four stars if it were a resort. They had access to most of the compound with the only restriction being the electrified fence.

Morning, on the fifth day on the island, broke with a bang, literally. The explosion of light and fire shook the entire compound; plaster fell from the walls, and the bulbs from the lights blew out. Every captive bounced out of bed, grabbed some clothes, and immediately ran outside to see what was happening. Some were standing there in their underwear, while Morgan and Diane were only in a loose tee shirt and holding their pants and shoes.

"What the hell is happened?" Morgan asked over the noise of the explosions and fire.

When they regrouped outside the building, what they saw was like a scene from a horror movie. Several buildings were on fire, two had collapsed in on themselves. Two guards were lying on the ground outside the control center building which had smoke billowing out of several windows and the roof.

"I don't know, but it looks like a war zone," Redmond commented looking around at the buildings. "We need to get to some kind of cover!"

Morgan slipped on her pants, ran over to the two guards, and immediately checked to see if they were alive. At the same time, Redmond and Bryce ran over to the gate which was hanging loose on its hinges.

"Wait, it may still be electrified," Randal yelled and then looked at Morgan, "Are they alive?"

"Yes, they are," Morgan yelled back.

"Is the fence hot?" Randal yelled to Redmond. Redmond grabbed a piece of wood, threw it at the fence, and watched it bounce off without causing any sparks.

"It is cold; let's go," Redmond yelled back over the roar of the fire and more small explosions. He reached out, pulled the gate open, and ran out followed by Freddy, Diane, Amber, and Josh Pierce.

"Stephanie, GO!" Randal yelled at them. "Morgan, get their weapons and go!" Bryce turned back and ran over to help retrieve the weapons, and then both ran to the gate.

"Got them, coming!" Morgan called back as she stood up after retrieving two rifles and two pistols along with a couple of ammo belts.

"Let's get out of here, Morg," Bryce said as they headed for the gate. Just before they reached it, several shots were fired at them that struck the ground near their feet, but that did not stop them. They ran through the gate, threw the pistols to Randal and Redmond, and then stopped and returned fire at the guard that had fired at them. They ran into the jungle at full speed with bullets flying past them as they headed deeper into the jungle. Luckily, nobody was hit; they escaped into the jungle, and did not stop running until they were about a half mile deep.

"Wow, what the hell happened back there?" Vince asked as they all stopped to catch their breath.

"They let us go," Randal stated. "It was too easy."

"What do you mean? They made a mistake and over loaded something and blew themselves up," Redmond stated as he looked around the small clearing they were in. "We need to move on; they are probably getting a party together to follow us."

"That is a true statement, but I do believe they staged that escape. We don't have the luxury to discuss it now. I vote to go for one of the ships and sail it out of here," Randal said, "At least when we run out of fuel, we will not crash."

"I agree," Bryce said and then stood and started down the path they had traveled six days earlier.

"Let's go," Randal said as he checked the load in the pistol he carried, "Morgan did you get the extra clips for this Beretta?"

"Yes, here," Morgan said and handed Randal four more clips as they followed Bryce and Redmond down the path.

Two hours after escaping from the compound, they broke out onto a white sandy beach on the northwest side of the island.

"Take a break, but stay close to the jungle. Redmond and I will stand guard," Randal said as he stepped onto the beach, "Wow, this is a beautiful island. Where is the resort?"

"I believe we just left the resort, honey," Stephanie said smiling.

"Vince, Redmond, how far to the boats?" Randal asked as he looked around at the sandy beach and tropical jungle. "This would make a nice resort island; when we find out where we are, maybe I will retire and build a resort here."

"No way, baby! I have had enough of this island," Stephanie commented as she sat on a shaded patch of sand.

"The cove is a couple of miles down the beach on the south side. Do you think they are following us?" Vince asked.

"Not sure, but my guess is that they are, or at least will be, once they put out the fires and contain the explosions. If, in fact, they were real," Randal said.

"Not real?" Vince asked being a little confused.

"We did see a lot of holographic displays while there; they may have put on that display to let us escape," Randal stated. "I don't know why they would let us go; we are on an island and they know we may not be able to get off it. So why let us go? They will not have to feed us or worry about us taking over the control center and stopping what they are doing. And they know it would be crazy for us to come back and stop them."

"Maybe we should go back and stop them," Bryce suggested looking around at the group.

"Not sure if that is a good idea; assuming they did stage this escape, they will expect us to go for one of the airplanes or boats and leave the island. If we did go back, they have us out gunned. They also have those holograms that will confuse the whole situation; because we will not know who is real and who isn't, we will waste the few bullets we do have. If we were to go back and attack, we need a very well organized plan. But keep in mind my new friends, the best well designed plan of attack usually goes to hell as soon as the shooting starts. So, if we could get back in without firing a shot, we could possibly have a fifty percent chance of success."

"The big question is, do we go back, or not?" Bryce asked to everyone.

"Their plan is to destroy some lives, possibly kill some people including us and the President of the United States. I think we owe it to the world to stop them," Randal said.

Chapter 35 Fact or Fiction

"Are they gone?" Rocky asked as he walked into the control room, waving his hand to clear the smoke in the room which did not move at all and he thought to himself, *'Hell, holographic smoke is so real.'*

"Yes, they escaped just as planned. We have turned off the holographs and all is well again. No guards were injured and they got away with two Berretta 9mm pistols and eight fully loaded magazines and two M-16 rifles with also eight fully loaded magazines holding twenty rounds each. The weapons are functional, but the bullets are blanks; they look real, but when fired, the projectile is made to cause no harm to anyone they shoot at; so they are virtually harmless. Just as you ordered, they are defenseless," Greg responded with the correct answer.

"Great! Do you think they will come back and try to take over the control center?"

"That is a very good question, Rocky. I don't know what they will try. Should we send out the team?"

"Yes, send them out, but tell them just to watch and report. I want to find out how brave our captives are, and if they will turn back to try and take over the compound, or will just try to sail one of those derelict boats out of here. I know they won't go for an airplane, even though they could fly out easier. But not knowing where we are, that would be suicidal. If they go for a boat, then tell Captain Visalia to kill all of them."

"With pleasure."

"Switching gears, does our Randal have the President at the safe house?"

"Yes, they arrived and checked in about an hour ago. President Tony Sanford is resting comfortably, he is sedated and sleeping. Randal and Stephanie, aka Doctor Holt's nurse are guarding and waiting for instructions. What should I tell them?"

"Tell them, ah, tell them that their relief will arrive shortly and to stay awake. We are about to start phase three; it's time to destroy Davin Pierce's life," Rocky ordered. After a short pause to think through some alternative options, he continued, "Let's move up the schedule a bit. Have our two kids steal a car, ah, a fast car, something flashy. Tell them to drive south toward Florida, dump the car as planned, and find another. Make sure they leave finger prints on the car; we want them to know who is turning bad."

"What if they get caught?"

"All the better; they will then have a criminal record, and Mr. and Mrs. Pierce will know their spoiled kids are becoming criminals," Rocky said quietly. "When the relief team gets there to guard the president, have our Randal and wife change to Mr. and Mrs. Pierce and have him kill someone. Ah, maybe he should show up at Adam Cruz's house and kill him, yeah, kill Adam Cruz."

"Your wish is my command, my master," Greg said with a laugh.

"Just do it," Rocky said and then stormed out of the control room. He abruptly stopped, turned around, looked at Greg, and asked, "Where the hell is my son?"

"Last I saw of him; he was heading toward the arms room."

"Holy shit, what the hell is he doing going down there?"

"That is a good question, boss."

On the Beach

The heat and humidity were having a race to see which would get to the top of the thermometer first. By ten in the morning, it was already hitting ninety degrees and the humidity was right behind it at eighty-five percent. Clouds were forming on the horizon; and it was beginning to look like a tropical storm was brewing.

"Hope that storm holds until we can get to some cover," Morgan commented to no one in particular as she kept glancing toward the storm.

"We should be to the cove across from the boats in about an hour," Redmond said over the roar of the pounding surf.

"Good, that storm looks like it will be here by late this afternoon," Vince replied as she looked at the storm.

"I think we should take the yacht. It would be the most comfortable and I am not sure I would trust the World War II submarine or freighters," Bryce commented and stopped for a second to look behind them. "I think we are being followed."

"What makes you say that, Bryce?" Randal asked.

"Well, I just saw a soldier duck back into the jungle when I turned around."

"What took you so long to see them?" Redmond said as he stopped and turned to face Bryce.

"We have been watching them watch us for the past hour," Randal stated as he stopped to wipe the sweat off his face. "They are just following for now, and we are watching them."

"Time to take a break anyway. Let's grab some of that shade over there, and I will keep an eye on our friends back there," Redmond suggested and got a nod from Randal in agreement.

"Yeah, take twenty. That storm is still way off and we are almost to the cove. In another hour, we should be resting quietly on a luxury yacht. Hopefully, she has some edible food and drink on board," Randal said and then sat on a palm tree that had fallen down.

"Captain Redmond, you have been here the longest; do you have any idea where on this big earth this island is?" Diane asked.

"No, sorry I don't. I have been trying to figure that out since I arrived," Redmond replied shaking his head.

"I did a couple of sightings over the past few nights and have a reasonable idea as to where we might be," Stephanie commented and then paused for a second. "With the help of the chart that we have, I am able to narrow it down to the South Pacific, most likely in the Philippines or east of them. There are hundreds of islands in the chain and most are not inhabited. If we sail west from this island, we should hit another island just over the horizon."

"I really hope you are correct and that the compass on the yacht works; well, I also hope the engines will actually work too," Randal said. He looked back the way they had come, and saw a lone soldier standing about half way between the jungle and the surf. "Our friends are getting bold back there; look," he said as he pointed down the beach.

"I think it is time to move on. They are getting too bold, and they probably out number and out gun us. And there is no good cover here, let's move," Randal said as he stood and started to walk down the beach toward the cove.

Chapter 36 Sands In An Hour Glass

"Where the hell am I?" President Tony Sanford asked to the blank wall he was forced to look at all the time. He was bound tightly to the rough bed he was lying on and could only see the ceiling and two walls. Attempting to loosen his binds was useless; they were too tight, and all he had accomplished was to make them tighter and cut into his bare skin. *'Damn it! I am the President of the United States, and am being held captive by a bunch of fanatics.'* He laid there and thought of how easy it had been to take him out. And he wondered why Davin and Randal were doing this; they were friends.

"Good afternoon, Tony. I can still call you Tony, can't I?" Josh Randal said as he entered the room. "I guess you are wondering why you are here; well, I am not going to tell you just yet. But rest peacefully, the only reason you are still alive is because we need you alive. Your part in this is not over yet, but will be in a few days, so just rest."

After he paused to take a breath, he walked around the room, and then spoke again quietly, "We will release your bindings if you promise to behave yourself. You can't escape; the walls are a foot thick, made of pre-stressed concrete. You may have noticed that there are no windows in this room and only one door, which is locked and bolted from the outside. It is made of steel; the hinges are on the outside, and there is no door handle on the inside. So you see this cell, as it were, is not escapable."

"Why are you doing this, Josh? We have been friends for years, been through a lot of shit together; you were the best man at my wedding. Why?" Sanford asked.

"Simple, my old friend, money; lots and lots of money, and truly I am just tired of the same old BS from the government. It is time to shake it up a bit, starting with you going down," Randal stated and then walked over to Sanford and leaned over him, pulled out a knife and cut the bindings.

Sanford attempted to get off the bed, but found his legs still bound and only proceeded to almost fall on his face when he landed on the floor. Randal stood back, watched, and then threw the knife straight down into the wood floor. "Cut your own bindings, Tony. I have a lunch date with Stephanie. Your lunch will be delivered soon. I took the liberty to order for you; I hope you like it."

As he looked up from his position on the floor, hanging partially off the bed, Sanford said quietly, "You will never get away with this Josh. There are hundreds of Secret Service and police looking for me already."

"Oh, that is where you are wrong my old friend; your replacement has been sitting at your desk since you left, and they have no idea he is a clone."

"Clone, cloning is illegal," Sanford said and reached for the knife. He found it just beyond his reach, and said, "A little help, Josh."

"Get it yourself," Randal said as he quickly turned and knocked on the door which immediately opened for him. He exited and the door slammed shut. Sanford heard the bolts slide into place and felt completely isolated for the first time in years.

He slid further off the bed, but still could not reach the knife. After a long struggle, resulting in pulling the bed partially across the room, he finally reached the knife. With a little extra force, Sanford was able to get the knife free from the floor; and within a few seconds, he was free of the leg bindings and sat on the floor leaning on the wall.

'A clone, who the hell developed a clone of me? And how did they get me out of the White House without being seen?' Sanford quietly commented as he sat and contemplated his seemingly hopeless situation.

Chapter 37 Changing Places

Adam Cruz left Langley at seven in the evening and drove home, stopping once at a Wendy's to grab a couple of burgers and fries for dinner. It had been a long day and nothing was coming together on Davin's missing kids. When he reached his home in Arlington a little past eight, he pulled in the garage and started to close the door, but not before he noticed a car pulling into his driveway and thought. *'That looks like Davin's car. What the hell does he want? I just left him at the office.'*

Cruz watched as Davin's car stopped and the door opened. "What's up Davin?"

"Just needed to talk to you off campus; have you got a second?" Davin replied and started to walk over to Cruz just as the door to the house opened and Cruz's wife Jessica stepped out.

Davin looked over at her and then back to Cruz and continued to walk toward him and waved at Jessica. Reaching behind his back, Davin pulled a large caliber Colt Python revolver out of his belt and pointed it at Cruz.

"What the hell are you doing, Davin?" Cruz yelled when he saw the gun being pointed at him. Before he had a chance to dive for cover, Davin fired the weapon three times striking Cruz in the chest with all three bullets. Cruz was thrown backwards, his body hit the automatic garage door closer, and the door started to close.

Jessica screamed and ran back into the house, praying that Davin would not follow her. When she reached the hallway credenza, she pulled out a Smith and Wesson 357 magnum pistol; and hurried further into the house. She slammed the door behind her, reached for the phone, and punched in 911. Davin turned and started to walk toward the door but changed his mind and returned to his car, opened the door, tossed the forty-four magnum on the passenger seat and climbed in. He needed a witness and she just saw everything; no reason to kill the only witness around. He climbed in and started the car, slipped it into reverse and slowly backed out of the driveway. A smile crossed his face as he drove off.

Minutes after Davin shot Adam Cruz, a police cruiser pulled up with lights and siren blaring. Davin was long gone by the time they arrived. Each officer jumped out of the cruiser with weapons drawn, carefully approaching the house. One officer spoke into his radio, "Where is Mrs. Cruz?"

"She is in the house," the radio responded, the officers approached the front door and knocked.

"Who is it?" Jessica yelled from deep in the house.

"Police, you called about a shooting," the officer responded.

The front door opened slowly and Jessica looked out at the two officers; tears streamed down her face. Obviously shaken, she had her pistol in her right hand, cocked and ready to fire.

"Mrs. Cruz, are you all right? Please put the weapon down."

"No, a friend of ours just shot my husband," she blurted out sobbing uncontrollably, placing the pistol on the credenza.

"Where is your husband?"

"In the garage," she said and pointed toward the door to the garage door.

Two more officers came to the door and entered behind the first two.

"You two stay with Mrs. Cruz; Tom and I will check out the garage," Officer Denise Zuckerman ordered and they entered the garage.

"Damn, what the hell was he shot with?" she asked her partner. "Call for the M.E. and detectives." leaning over Cruz, checked for a pulse, but, unfortunately, did not find one.

Twenty minutes later, the medical examiner and detectives arrived; and after a few minutes, the M.E declared Adam Cruz dead from multiple gun shots to the chest. He had died instantly.

"Mrs. Cruz did you see anything?" the detective asked as they sat quietly in the living room.

"Yes, I did; I saw it all. Adam came home and had just parked his car in the garage when another car pulled in the driveway. Davin Pierce stepped out of the car and shot Adam in cold blood. They were friends; they worked together. Pierce retired a few months ago, and Adam was his replacement. Davin's kids were recently kidnapped which may have caused him to snap, but I don't know why he would do this."

"Are you sure it was Davin Pierce?"

"Yes, we have known each other for years. Why would he do this, why?" she cried uncontrollably.

"We don't know why, but we will find out," the detective said and then pulled out his cell phone and called in to find out where Davin Pierce was right now.

CIA Headquarters, Langley, VA

It was almost midnight, and most of the team had gone home or to the company supplied barracks located in the basement. Suddenly a light knock on the conference room door got the attention of the remainder of the men and women in the room.

"I'll get it, don't get up," stated Davin who was already standing as he looked at the information on one of the big screen monitors; he walked over to the door and opened it. He saw the guard standing there with a very concerned look on his face.

"What can I do for you?" Davin asked the guard.

"Sir, we just got a call to detain you until the police get here," the guard stated.

"Detain me, why?"

"They didn't say; just told us to keep you here until they arrive and then take you down to the lobby. That's all we know, sir."

"Okay, come get me when they get here; I will be working right here," Davin replied and then closed the door. *'What the hell is going on now?'*

Forty minutes after the guard informed Davin that the police wanted to talk to him, the guard knocked on the conference room door again. Davin answered the knock and was told the police were in the lobby.

"Mr. Pierce, I am Detective Charles Brown and this is my partner Detective Arlene Ramsey with the Arlington Police, is there a place we can talk privately?" he asked as he showed Davin their credentials.

"Yeah, we have a conference room right over here. What is this all about?" Davin asked as he escorted the two detectives to the conference room just off the lobby.

"Sir, you have an Adam Cruz working here?"

"Yes, he is the Deputy Director of Operations, working directly for the Director, ah, Josh Randal. Why do you ask? He went home a couple of hours ago," Davin replied as he sat down across from the two detectives.

"Mr. Pierce, Adam Cruz was gunned down at his home shortly after he arrived home. The details are still sketchy at the moment. Where were you at eight this evening?" Brown asked.

"Gunned down, by whom? Is Jessica all right?" Davin questioned the officer.

"Mrs. Cruz is fine; shook up, but fine. We have moved her to a safe house in case the killer comes back," Brown stated and then asked again. "Where were you at eight this evening?"

"I was in my office going over some reports, trying to locate my missing children. Why, am I a suspect?"

"Quite frankly, yes you are. Mrs. Cruz identified you as the shooter. I need to ask you a few questions." Brown said and waited for a reply.

"Sure, I have nothing to hide, except the tons of secrets in this building." Davin replied sarcastically.

"Was there anyone with you in your office?" Brown replied and pressed on with his questions.

"No, I was alone. But the agents in the conference room upstairs knew where I was; I told them I did not want to be disturbed. The guards at the front door would know if I left at any time; there is only one way in and out of this building without setting off massive alarms." Davin replied.

"Do you have a forty-four Magnum revolver?" Brown asked.

"And, yes, I own several weapons; two are forty-four magnum revolvers."

"Where are your revolvers? Detective Ramsey asked looking at Davin closely.

"My revolvers are at my home, locked up." Davin answered getting a bit disturbed with the accusations.

"Where is your wife?" Brown asked quickly.

"She is at home, worried about our kids. They have been missing for days; and we recently received a report that two kids were found unconscious in Annapolis, but they disappeared." Davin paused and took a deep breath.

"Sorry about your children, how old are they?" Ramsey asked concerned. "We need to pick up the weapons; does Mrs. Pierce have access to them?"

"They are twins and twenty years old. And, ah, yeah, she has the combination to the safe. Am I being accused of killing Adam Cruz?" Davin asked.

"Not at this time but I suggest you do not leave town or for that matter not to leave this building without me knowing where you are going." Brown stated.

"Okay I understand you are basically putting me under house arrest, I will stay here, if you insist." Davin agreed.

"I know you are concerned and worried about them, but right now you have a bigger problem. Mrs. Cruz identified you as the gunman that killed Adam Cruz. I trust a man of your caliber and position with the CIA will not attempt to leave the country."

"I am innocent; I have not left this building since I arrived six days ago. It goes without saying that I will cooperate with you in every way. Adam Cruz was a friend and co-worker. You can find me right here; my office has a suite attached. If I need to leave the building, I will call you first and you can escort me; or would you like to leave an officer here."

"That will not be necessary, Mr. Pierce. I will suggest that if you have to leave the building that you do call me or Ramsey and then have two of your armed security guards go with you. For your protection, sir; we don't believe you killed Adam Cruz, but until we are sure you and your wife are not a target, we will be putting twenty-four-hour security protection at your home."

"Who would do this, and make themselves look like me to kill a friend?" Davin questioned and then stood and paced around the room. He looked tired and very worried. "I know there are ways to change your features to look like someone else; they do it all the time in Hollywood, but why kill Adam?"

"Mr. Pierce we will get to the bottom of this; just be patient," Ramsey stated, "Before we go, would you call your wife to let her know what is going on and that we will be stopping by to pick up your weapons. We have to go now; you be careful, and we will be in touch."

"Thank you, detectives. Keep me informed. And I will not leave the building," Davin said and then called for an escort to take both detectives out of the building.

"What are your thoughts, Arlene?" Charlie Brown asked as they walked to their car.

"I think we have a serious problem; Pierce is a highly respected member of the CIA and the guards did verify that he did not leave the building. But there has to be a way in and out of this building without setting off alarms. And guards can be bribed and there is loyalty, protect their own as it were," Arlene Ramsey stated and then paused to think, "I heard that there is an underground railroad that links this building with several others in Washington, including the White House."

"Yeah, I have heard that too, but is it real? And if Pierce did leave on an underground railroad and kill his assistant, why would he do it? Why would he kill him, what is the motive?"

"That is what we have to figure out, the why; what would his motive?" Arlene said looking confused and concerned.

Chapter 38 Are They That Stupid?

Twenty minutes' rest and contemplation was all Randal needed to make a decision that could quite possibly end everyone's life or make it easier to get off this island. As they say in war, the best laid plans go to hell when the shooting starts and Randal was about to start the shooting.

"Here's the deal, ladies and gentlemen. We are going to split up, some of you are going to head for the yacht and the rest of us are going to shake up the competition," Randal stated quietly and kept looking over his shoulder at the team that was waiting down the beach. He had no idea what they planned on doing, but he hated not knowing; and he usually made things happen instead of waiting.

"We are going to do what?" Morgan asked looking very concerned.

"There are eight of us, and I have no idea how many are behind us; but a small team can overpower a larger one with the right plan," Randal started explaining, but then paused for a moment to catch his breath. "So, Redmond, Bryce, Josh, Diane and I are going to back track and stop those fools back there. The rest of you are going to the cove, get on the yacht and get her ready for a cruise. You may have to get fuel from the airfield but make sure it is ready to go when we get there. You may only have a couple of hours, but I have confidence in you. Slip over to the sub and retrieve any weapons that are still there and take as much ammunition as you can carry."

"Sounds like fun. Maybe we should take the sub; it has a deck gun and torpedoes," Morgan suggested.

"Well, I don't know about that, do any of you know how to run a submarine and fire a deck gun without blowing yourself up?" Redmond asked, cutting in on Randal's plan.

"That could be a problem, maybe the yacht is the better choice," Morgan agreed.

"Redmond and I will handle the M-16s, Josh and Bryce the pistols. Diane, I need you to do something that is a bit risky, but you are the key to the success of my plan."

"I am ready for most anything, what do you want me to do?" Diane asked.

Randal took Diane a little way down the beach and sat her down on a fallen tree and explained his plan to her.

"Okay, I'll do it," Diane agreed smiling for the first time in a long time.

"Good, I need to brief the others and in an hour we go; I will give you time to get ready. Let's go back to the rest of the team," Randal said as he and Diane stood and walked back to the rest of the team.

Two hundred yards down the beach

"Captain, they are just sitting there; what should we do?" a young soldier asked his commander as they watched the escapees.

"They know we are watching them and that will make them stupid. They will try something, possibly circle back and attack us, which they will lose pretty quick. They only have four weapons that are loaded with blanks. They don't know that, do they?" Captain Visalia commented as he looked down the beach through a pair of ten by fifty binoculars. "They seem restless and should start to move soon."

"Do we follow, then?" the young soldier asked.

"Yes we follow, our orders are to follow and not kill yet. We will kill them soon, but Rocky wants to play with them a while. I am not sure why, but he is the boss and we follow his orders, no killing, yet," Captain Visalia said sounding not real happy about his orders.

Waiting was the hardest thing a soldier had to do. Hurry up and wait was the military way. Sometimes you waited and then returned to base, while other times you waited for days and days before going into action. During that long wait time, soldiers would get bored and start to drop their guard, paying less attention to what needed to be done. Visalia's men were getting restless; two of them had already fallen asleep under the shade of the palm trees. With the light breeze blowing off the ocean, it had been very easy to fall asleep.

Visalia only had six heavily armed men with him; that's all he felt he needed to take care of a group consisting of one soldier, an aging CIA officer, three women and six kids. It sounded too easy for even two of his highly trained mercenaries. Especially since they were virtually unarmed and defenseless, he could eliminate all of them in minutes by himself.

"What the hell? Are they that stupid?" Visalia commented as he saw a nearly naked woman walking toward him on the beach. Diane was wearing a button down shirt with no buttons buttoned, no pants except her panties and a smile.

"Wow, she is beautiful and looking for trouble," the young soldier commented keeping his eyes on her as she slowly strolled down the beach.

Chapter 39 Shots In the Dark

Detectives Brown and Ramsey arrived at the home of Davin and Connie Pierce to retrieve Davin's forty-four magnum pistols at ten fifteen in the morning. They needed to run ballistic tests on them with hopes that neither one was the weapon that killed Adam Cruz. After ringing the door bell, they waited for someone to answer the door. They waited and waited, and no one answered. Ringing the doorbell again resulted in the same quiet response; they also tried knocking loudly with no response.

"We were told she was here; go check the back. I will call for back-up," Brown ordered, as he picked up his cell phone, and called the precinct to ask for back-up.

"Charlie, you need to come see this," Detective Arlene Ramsey called from around back.

Charlie stepped off the front porch, walked around to the back yard, and then suddenly stopped as he rounded the corner of the house. "Holy shit, what the hell is going on with this family?" he said as he eyed the scene in front of him. He pulled out his cell phone again, called dispatch, and requested the medical examiner and forensics to report to the Pierce house. Lying in a pool of blood was a woman that was obviously dead; that was easy to tell because of the large holes in her back.

"Do you know what Mrs. Pierce looks like? Is that her? Detective Ramsey asked as he looked at the body, "Quite pretty, but also quite dead; hope it isn't Mrs. Pierce."

"No, I don't know what she looks like; go into the house and see if you can find a photo or purse," Charlie ordered.

Ramsey walked over to the back door and checked. It was unlocked; she entered and said "Wow! What the hell happened here?" After looking around in each room, she finally located a picture of Davin and Connie on the dresser in the master bedroom. The glass was broken and the room was a mess, someone was looking for something. As she looked at the picture, she almost smiled and yelled out, "Not Mrs. Pierce."

After exiting the back door, Arlene Ramsey walked over to Detective Charles Brown and handed him the picture, "Looks like it is not Mrs. Pierce. But who is she, and why is she in the Pierce's backyard, dead?"

"Very good question," Detective Brown commented and then turned when he heard the gate swing open and saw the Medical Examiner and assistant walk in.

"What have we got?" the M.E. asked as she walked over to the body, "Whoa, three GSWs to the back, large caliber, death was instant. After pausing for a second to quickly assess the body, she looked at her assistant and said, "Bring the gurney."

"Time of death?" Brown asked the Medical Examiner (M.E.)

"Just a second," replied the M.E. and slipped her liver probe into the body and read the meter. "I would say between eight and ten last night."

"Thank you," Brown replied and then turned and started for the back door. "We need to find those weapons and get them to forensics. They may have been used to kill that woman back there. She may have been mistaken for Mrs.

Pierce. Same build, same hair color and in the dark it would have been easy to make a mistake like that."

"Charlie that will be easy, I saw a large caliber pistol lying on the kitchen counter when I went in; that may be one of them. How many did he say he had?" Ramsey asked as they entered the back door which opened up to the kitchen. There was a stainless steel Colt Python forty-four magnum lying on the counter just like Ramsey had said. She leaned down and sniffed the barrel, "It has been fired." She slipped on a pair of rubber gloves, carefully picked up the weapon to keep from disturbing any finger prints, slipped the cylinder open, and removed six empty cartridges. "Three in Cruz, three in the woman out back; this just gets better by the minute."

"Yeah, it is looking more and more like Mr. Pierce is our killer or this is one heck of a framing," Brown stated. "We need to take this one down to forensics and check the serial number to see if he is the registered owner."

"Let's get the forensic team in here to see what they can turn up," Ramsey suggested. When she looked out the back door, she saw that the forensic team had arrived and stepped out the back and said, "Sam, we need your guys to check out the house too, it has been turned upside down."

"Let me get my team started here, and I will be right in," Sam said.

"Okay, Arlene we need to go. Sam, you have this; let us know what you find. We are heading to your office, anyone there that can check this weapon?" Brown asked and started to walk out the gate.

"Yeah, Tim is there; he can run ballistics on that hand cannon," Sam replied as he pointed to the pistol that Ramsey held. He then looked inside the house and stated the obvious, "Wow, what a mess." He paused and then said, "Go, we have this."

"Thanks, Sam," Ramsey said with a sly wink.

Chapter 40 Once A Night, All Night Long

It was a cold and rainy night in Northern Virginia; the roads were wet and slippery, but young Josh drove the stolen 2025 fire-engine red Corvette as if he were a seasoned NASCAR driver. The car performed as the marketing hype predicted. At speeds exceeding one hundred and forty miles per hour, the car clung to the road as if it were glued to Interstate 95.

"This is fun, little lady," Josh said as he passed car after car and watched in the rear view mirror as several pairs of police cruisers pulled out and accelerated rapidly behind them, lights and sirens blaring. "We have company, finally."

"It's about time; we have been racing for an hour without seeing a cop anywhere," Amber commented, looking over at the speedometer. "Push the pedal down, babe."

They were only look alike of Amber and Josh Pierce; they were not brother and sister, but actually boyfriend and girlfriend. They had been dating for years before being recruited by Rocky for this undercover operation to destroy Davin and Connie Pierce's life. Life had been good for them as aspiring actors; for this assignment, they were told to have fun and break the law as often as possible and to not get caught too soon, but leave finger prints everywhere they went.

"Pedal to the metal, Miss Amber," Josh said as he pushed down on the pedal increasing the speed to one hundred ninety-three miles per hour. As they headed south on Interstate 95, they easily outran the police cruisers which could only reach speeds of just over a hundred forty miles per hour. As the cruisers faded behind them, they slowed briefly and took an exit to Richmond. "We need to change cars, look for a good candidate."

"How about a nice Ferrari or Lamborghini?" Amber questioned as she looked around for a nice car to steal.

"Would be great, but this is Richmond, Virginia, not Hollywood," Josh said as he turned off the freeway and headed east toward the city at the speed limit. "There is a gas station; we need fuel, and maybe there is a nice car we can take."

CIA Headquarters, Langley, VA

The sky to the east of the building started to project a multitude of colors over the trees. A new day was slowly making an appearance. Low clouds to the north and west were promising that the humidity was going to be high and that rain was a foregone conclusion. Life in northern Virginia was starting to come awake. The agents at CIA Headquarters were waking, getting dressed, grabbing mugs of coffee and slowly working their way down to the café.

Davin had slept in his private quarters just off his old office, if you want to call what he had sleep. He had tossed and turned most of the night. It had been a restless night full of worry and concern. At precisely eight that morning, Davin walked into the conference room to find two intelligent operatives working on some files. "Good morning, sir," one of the operatives said without looking up to see who had walked in.

"Morning, lady and gentleman, anything new?" Davin asked and then set his breakfast of an egg muffin and orange juice on the end of the table before he sat down.

"That smells good; did you get that from the café?" the young female analyst asked as she started to stand. After getting an affirmative nod from Davin, she said, "Think I will run down and get some food; could use a break after being here all night." After a pause, she answered his question, "Got a report of the two Does that escaped from the hospital, possible sighting outside of Alexandria. No identification as yet, but they lifted some finger prints from a car they were attempting to steal. We'll have results shortly."

"Let me know what they find, one way or the other," Davin replied and then picked up his muffin and took a bite. "Hmm, not bad."

A knock at the door broke the silence in the conference room. Davin being the closest to the door, rolled his chair backwards toward the door, stopped just short of slamming into the wall, and opened the door. "Yesssss?" Davin said dragging out his words.

"There are two detectives down in the lobby; they want to speak to you," the guard said when he saw that it was Davin who answered the door.

"Okay, tell them I will be right down," Davin responded to the guard.

"Yes, sir."

Ten minutes later, Davin had taken the elevator down to the lobby and stepped out to see Detective Charlie Brown and Arlene Ramsey waiting for him.

"Mr. Pierce we need you to come with us," Brown stated as Davin walked up to meet them.

"I have things to do here, like locate my children; and when we do, I need to get them," Davin stated.

"Look, Mr. Pierce, we did not want to arrest you at your place of work; but if you resist, we will have to cuff you and that may get ugly, if you get my meaning," Ramsey stated bluntly.

"Are you arresting me?"

"We have sufficient evidence, and an eye witness to arrest you; but we understand by your statement and the verification by your guards, that you never left the building," Brown said. "Can we talk privately somewhere?"

"Yes, come with me; the conference room over here is as secure as you are going to get without going upstairs." Davin lead them to the conference room off the side of the lobby. "Now what the hell do you mean by 'you have evidence'?"

"Mr. Pierce, we went by your house yesterday and found a woman dead in your backyard; your house was a mess and your wife wasn't there. Besides that, we have run ballistics on a Colt Python forty-four magnum of yours, and it is the weapon that killed Adam Cruz. Mrs. Cruz also confirmed that you were the shooter; and will testify in court to that. So, without causing a scene Mr. Pierce, please cooperate and come with us."

"But I have been here for the past seven days. I have not left the building; and you verified that with the guards, didn't you?"

"Yes, but we know that there may be other ways to exit the building and return without going out the front door. Is that a true statement, sir?" Ramsey stated as he sternly looked at Davin across the table.

"If there is another way out of this building without going out the front door, please tell me where that exit is?" Davin asked.

"Rumor has it that there is an underground railroad that is used by your high officials to move from this building to the White House and other federal buildings and facilities around the country. Is that true, Mr. Pierce?"

"No, it is not true. We have a lot of secrets which we cannot let the people know about, but an underground railroad is pretty good. I would love to have one; driving in D.C. traffic to visit the White House or other Federal buildings is a royal pain in the ass," Davin said. In an attempt to keep the railroad a secret, he even laughed at the comment.

"Do you need to let anyone know that you will be leaving with us, and do not know when you will return?" Brown asked.

"Yes, I would like to call my wife; and also, I need to let Randal know what is going on."

"Is Randal on site?" Brown asked.

"No, haven't seen him since lunch yesterday; he said he had an appointment with the President at one o'clock. He did not return after the meeting."

"Leave a message for him with his secretary and let's go," Ramsey said.

"Okay, but hurry," Brown ordered becoming impatient. "We will wait here for you."

Chapter 41 Distract and Conquer

Diane strolled down the beach as if she had not a care in the world; she walked close to the water, leaned down and touched the surf. It felt warm and inviting. She slipped off her shirt, dropped it to the sandy beach, and slowly walked into the surf and up to her neck in the warm water. It felt very good against her nearly naked body. She didn't want to get out, but her job was to distract the soldiers which she was doing extremely well; they could not get their eyes off her body.

Meanwhile Redmond, Randal, Bryce and Josh slowly moved through the jungle being as quiet as church mice. Within a few minutes, they were behind the soldiers and ready to strike like cobras. Diane was soaking up the sun and the eyes of most of the soldiers were watching; the other three were asleep. The Captain did not want to wake them for fear of them running down the beach and attacking the young lady, a desire which he had. They had been on this island for almost a year without the company of a woman. There were six women here, but they were the wives or girlfriends of others in the camp. One of his soldiers attempted to rape one of them several months earlier, and he had not been seen since.

Redmond, Randal and Josh were within two feet of the three sleeping soldiers; and on Randal's signal, they each stood up and grabbed the soldiers in a choke hold from which the soldiers could not break or make a sound. Within seconds, the three were not just asleep, but unconscious and were dragged deeper into the jungle. Bryce retrieved their weapons and moved behind the others. A minute later, the soldiers were tied and gagged. Randal ordered each to switch weapons, leaving the ones they had been carrying stacked behind some bushes near the captives.

"Okay, we got those; now let's get the other three," Randal ordered, "Check your weapons, those others were loaded with blanks."

"How did you know?" Bryce asked.

"Experience my young friend, experience," Randal commented as he checked his new weapons; each had retrieved an M-16 with six magazines, a Berretta 9mm pistol and combat knives.

"What's the plan?" Redmond asked.

"Easy one, you and I walk up behind them with our weapons aimed at them and tell them to drop their weapons; if they fail to do so, thinking we have the non-functioning weapons, I will fire two shots into the sand at their officer's feet to get their attention. Bryce and Josh will move down the beach through the jungle until you are parallel to them. Stay hidden in case they bolt, at which time you will defend your position."

"Sounds good to me," Redmond agreed. "Let's do it."

They walked out of the jungle about ten yards behind the three soldiers and stopped with their weapons trained on the three. Randal clicked off the safety on his M-16 and yelled to the soldiers lying on the sand watching Diane, "Hey, are you enjoying the show?"

Captain Visalia turned. As he jumped up, he simultaneously began bringing his weapon up with him, but stopped when he saw two men with M-16s pointed at him and his men. Quickly sizing up the situation, he yelled back to

Randal as he brought up his weapon. "Those weapons don't have real bullets in them, but mine does."

"Stop right there, Captain. These are not the same weapons we left the compound with," Randal said and pulled the trigger sending two bullets into the sand between Captain Visalia's feet.

Visalia's other two soldiers looked up at him hoping to get a command to either lay down their weapon or turn and fire. Visalia looked down at his men and over to where his other men were supposed to be sleeping and swallowed hard, seeing that he and the two men with him were in trouble, but it was two against three.

"We don't want to kill you, but will if we have to; so please, lay down your weapons and walk over to the water. NOW!" Randal ordered.

"It looks like we have no choice, but you will never get off this island. We have more men, and you will be found and killed next time," Visalia yelled back as he laid his M-16 on the sand and then removed his pistol belt and let it fall. As he looked at his men, he ordered. "Leave your rifle on the ground, and remove your combat gear. Follow me to the water's edge as they command; we have lost this one."

"Captain, not the edge of the water; get in the water, completely underwater. I want your heads wet, now do it," Randal ordered.

"Are you going to kill unarmed men if we don't?" Visalia asked as he stood ankle deep in the surf.

"The thought had crossed my mind," Randal said and then yelled a little louder, "Josh, Bryce come on out." Seconds later, the two men stepped onto the beach from their hiding place not more than twenty feet from where Visalia and his men were watching Diane. Each of them glanced down the beach to where Diane was playing in the surf and smiled.

She looked down the beach and saw the soldiers standing in the surf. She walked up the beach, picked up her shirt, and slipped it on, smiling at the boys. She waved, and then headed toward where she had left her pants to wait there for Randal and the rest.

"Get their weapons, Bryce," Randal ordered and then with three M-16s pointed at Visalia and his men, Randal walked up and looked the Captain in the eye, and commanded, "I said get in the water." Then he pushed Visalia into the surf; his two men walked in on their own.

"Now, one at a time starting with you, Captain, come here," Randal proceeded to tie him and then each of the others. After completing tying each of the soldier's arms behind their backs, he escorted them to the edge of the jungle where they were secured to trees and gagged.

"Why the dunking in the surf?" Josh asked of Randal when they were sure their captives were securely bound, gagged and out of hearing range.

"Bugs, Josh; he may have had an earwig to communicate with their base or some other type of communication device. The water hopefully would short them."

"Oh, cool," Josh commented as they started down the beach toward Diane.

Chapter 42 Escape From CIA Headquarters

Arlene Ramsey and Charles Brown, detectives from the Arlington police department, waited in the lobby of CIA Headquarters for Davin Pierce to return from his office. He needed to notify his team that he was going to Arlington with the detectives and should return soon. Besides there was no other way for Davin to leave the building without the guards knowing it, or was there? He must have had to leave via the front door lobby.

Ten minutes went by, then fifteen; Brown walked over to the guard desk and asked for him to check on the location of Pierce.

"This is not like those Silicon Valley high tech places; we don't have locators on each of our people, sorry," the guard replied with a smile.

"Thank you," Brown commented and walked back toward Ramsey who was sitting quietly in a visitor chair on the south wall. Just before he reached her, he heard the elevator doors open. He looked toward the doors and saw a shapely young woman walk out; he smiled at her and she returned the smile. Turning, she walked past the guard smiling and opened the door behind him and left the lobby, headed for the café.

"Where the hell is he?" he asked Ramsey, not expecting an answer, but Ramsey stood and pointed behind him.

"He's here," Ramsey said as she pointed.

"Sorry I took so long; there were a million questions by my team which I could not answer easily," Davin said as he walked up to Brown. It also took him a while to decide whether to run, hide and search for his kids, or just cooperate.

Running via the Underground Railroad which he had access to would only prove to Ramsey and Brown that there was a hidden way to leave the building, a secret he did not want to share with the cops.

"Glad you made it back; we were getting worried," Brown commented, "We have a car out front; do you mind riding with us?"

"No, I am with you," Davin said as he followed Brown out the door with Ramsey close behind. "Where are we going, if I may ask?"

"The station of course; we have some questions and there are a couple of other people that would like to talk to you," Ramsey piped in as she climbed into the passenger seat with Brown behind the wheel.

"Do you have any questions that you want me to answer right now?" Davin added, "I have nothing to hide."

"Oh, we have questions, and so do our forensic experts. We will discuss it when we get to the station."

"If you insist, I will just sit here and be quiet," Davin responded and sat thinking until he asked, "Am I under arrest?"

"Not at this time, Mr. Pierce, but only because we don't really believe you would kill Adam Cruz," Brown commented as he drove toward Arlington.

"Why not? I have killed before, in the name of our country, during wars and while working as a field op for the company. Killing is easy," Davin stated.

"Are you confessing to killing Adam Cruz?" Brown asked as he almost ran a stop sign.

"Oh, no way, José! I have no reason to kill Adam; and I hadn't left that building in seven days, up till now of course."

"We just need some answers," Ramsey commented.

Chapter 43 The Cove

Vince and his team arrived at the cove about an hour after splitting up from Randal and his team.

"Wow, the yacht is still here," Morgan commented as they approached the water. "The dingy is over there," she said as she pointed toward the bush.

Freddy and Vince walked over and started to drag the dingy to the surf. "Okay ladies, let's get this tub in the water." With the help of all five of them, they were able to get the dingy in the water and climbed aboard; rowing out to the yacht took another fifteen minutes.

"Nice boat, guys. Do you think she will get us to anywhere away from this island?" Amber said as she eyed the luxury of over a hundred feet of private yacht with the name *Freedom* painted on its transom.

"I will check out the engine room," Freddy volunteered and started to head for the door to the engine room.

"Do you need any help?" Morgan offered, "I am pretty good around engines."

"Bet you are," Freddy replied and waved her to follow.

"Amber and Stephanie, do you know much about navigation and steering a boat?" Vince asked.

"Yes, been sailing a lot with Connie and Davin. I think between the two of us we can get us somewhere more comfortable than that prison back there, if Freddy and Morgan can get those engines started," Stephanie stated and headed for the bridge with Amber in tow.

"I will check the food and drink stocks, and fix some lunch for us," Vince said as he walked into the galley with no one listening. "Wow, this boat has it all; we shall eat like royalty," he said when he opened the pantry and then turned and looked at the bar which was equally well stocked. There was even a fridge filled with ice and beer. He reached in, grabbed a beer, twisted off the top, and took a long swig. "Damn that is good."

"Vince are there anymore beers up here," Randal asked as he and his team walked into the galley, and saw that he had a beer in his hand.

"Hell yes, in the fridge, it is full," Vince said as he pointed toward the fridge. Randal opened the fridge, pulled out a couple of beers, and started to pass them around.

"I would prefer a Jack and coke," Diane said as she took a beer and passed it over to Josh.

"The bar is fully stocked, help yourself," Vince said as he returned to his cooking.

"What's for lunch? I am starving," Bryce said as he took sips of his beer and then leaned over the stove for a peek at what was cooking.

"I found some cans of Beef Stew and am just heating it up for us. Guess I need to open a few more cans," Vince said and opened the pantry and retrieved a few larger cans of stew. "What did you do with those soldiers, kill them I hope."

"No they are tied up on the beach, but we have their weapons and radios. So we will hear if more start this way, which they hopefully will not anytime soon," Redmond replied.

"Should have killed them," Vince said under his breath but loud enough for some to hear.

"Maybe we should have, but didn't," Redmond returned and then concentrated on his beer.

"Ken, ah, I mean Josh," Amber started to say, "Ah, I am getting hungry and we have been running for hours and I need to pee and get something to eat; can we stop at the next fast food place?"

"Sure, sweetie, the next exit is about four miles and we should be able to find something there. This is a pretty nice set of wheels," Ken aka Josh said, and pushed down on the gas pedal of the 2029 Ford Mustang Shelby Cobra they had borrowed from a car lot in Richmond. They felt it was a fair trade; they left the stolen Corvette, with an empty fuel tank and lots of finger prints. The police should have a field day with that car. After pulling off the next exit, they saw several fast food places and gas stations lining the road. "Ah, pick one and we can pee and eat."

"The Jack in the Box doesn't look too crowded; let's eat there. Have you got any money?"

"Sure, Rocky made sure we had cash and credit cards. More to incriminate the kids," Josh said as he pulled the hot Mustang into the parking lot. When he saw a Police patrol car down the street, he was a little concerned. He hoped they had not put out an all-points bulletin for a stolen Mustang with two young kids driving it. When the patrol car turned on a side street and disappeared, he quit worrying. After parking the car close to the back, they got out and walked inside; Amber immediately headed for the lady's room while Josh walked up to the counter and studied the menu.

"May I help you?" the girl behind the counter asked.

"In a minute, sister in restroom, but I will start with a Spicy Chicken Combo, enlarge it, please," he ordered and then when Amber walked up he asked her, "What do you want, sis?"

"I'll have a Southwest salad and ice tea," she told the counter girl.

"Thank you; that will be eleven fifteen."

Josh handed her a twenty and got his change; their food arrived seconds later. After walking over to an empty table, they sat and enjoyed a quiet lunch. While they enjoyed their quiet lunch, a police car pulled in and parked beside the Mustang. Two officers got out and eyed the Ford and were talking but Josh could not hear what they were saying. They continued to eat their lunch and watched as the two officers walked in, stopped at the counter, and ordered lunch. The officers got their lunch, walked toward Josh and Amber, and sat at the table across from them.

"Is that your Shelby out there?" one of the officers asked Josh.

"Yes, love it."

"Beautiful car, what's under the hood?" the officer asked between bites of his hamburger.

"Four twenty-eight, seven hundred horse power, six speed standard tranny. You like Mustangs?" Josh replied, attempting to keep the nervousness out of his voice.

"Yeah, I picked up a two thousand fifteen Cobra a few years ago, been working on its restoration; she has a strong engine, also a four twenty-eight, fuel injected of course. Great car, but body was a little rough when I got her. It's going to the paint shop in a few weeks and then I will be almost done," the officer proudly stated.

"Cool, would love to see her sometime."

"Check the car shows in a few months; I plan on showing her. By the way, I am Wayne King, here is my card. Call me sometime; I would love to get a better look at your Shelby."

"Thanks, but my sis and I are heading to Miami for a new job. Not sure when we will be back this way; but if we do, I will call you," Josh said and then looked at his sister. Since he could see that she was finished with her lunch, he asked, "Ready?"

"Sure, long way to go and only a few days to get there," Amber responded.

Chapter 45 Who Done It?

It was late in the afternoon, when Detective Brown pulled his car in the parking lot of the Arlington Police Department. He found a spot to park, parked the car, and then turned in his seat to look at Davin Pierce sleeping in the back seat.

"Time to wake up, Mr. Pierce, we have arrived," Detective Brown said and reached back to shake Davin's leg.

"Ah, okay, are we there?" Davin slurred as he woke up.

"Yeah, let's go; we are running out of daylight," Ramsey commented as she stepped out of the car and opened the door for Davin.

"Wow, nice digs," Davin commented as he got out and looked at the Colonial style office building that was the Arlington Police Headquarters.

"Come on Mr. Pierce, if you like the outside, wait until you see the inside," Charlie Brown stated as they strolled toward the steps leading to the tall double doors. Once inside, Davin was led to a set of stairs that could have been used as a movie set. After climbing the stairs, he felt like he was on the set of *'Gone with the Wind'* and he was Clark Gable telling that young southern bell *'I don't give a damn.'* That is exactly what he felt like doing right now, because he did not give a damn. He was being accused of killing a friend, which he had not done, but the evidence might prove otherwise. After reaching the second floor, he was escorted to a small conference, or rather interrogation, room, and asked to take a seat. Ramsey walked on down the hall while Brown took a seat across from Davin.

"Okay, we are here in your interrogation room which means that now you need to interrogate me about the murder of my friend, Adam Cruz. So go ahead and start your questioning," Davin said.

"Mr. Pierce, you are a respected member of our largest intelligence organization in the world. There have been problems with some of your folks over the years discrediting your company. The Feds put a couple of your people in jail for selling secrets to the Russians; and there was an agent, or ah, operative, arrested for killing a Soviet agent. And now, your organization is having another high official being accused of murder. What have you got to say before we start the questions?" Detective Brown stated as he waited for Ramsey to return. The door opened and Ramsey walked in carrying a large manila envelope.

"Mr. Pierce, we have an eye witness stating that you shot Adam Cruz in cold blood when he returned home from his place of work at CIA Headquarters. Do you deny shooting Adam Cruz?" Ramsey asked as she sat down across from Davin.

"I did not shoot Adam Cruz," Davin responded quietly.

"Mr. Pierce in this envelope is the eye witness statement and a copy of the forensic report on a Colt Python forty-four magnum pistol registered to you, which we picked up at your house yesterday. The weapon is registered to you, has your finger prints on it and on the empty casings still in the cylinder. In a court of law that is enough evidence to put you away for a long time. Can you explain how your weapon, with your finger prints all over it, was used to kill a friend? You were seen firing this pistol by your friend's wife, who has

245

known you for years. And you sit there and tell us that you did not kill Adam Cruz."

"I did not kill Adam. I was in my office when you said he was killed. Until you dragged me down here, I had not left that building in seven days," Davin insisted but not looking too worried.

"You seem very calm for a man facing life in prison," Ramsey stated.

"Do you know where my wife is?"

"We have been looking for her and have not had any luck locating her. If you have any idea as to where she is, we would like to make sure she is safe," Brown stated.

"Wish I knew. My kids and wife are missing, and you are accusing me of murder; the day is just getting better and better," Davin responded to the accusations.

The door opened and a tall African-American man walked in and looked at Ramsey and Brown and then jerked his thumb to have them leave. Ramsey and Brown stood and left the room without saying a word.

"Mr. Pierce, I am Kim W. Pike; I am the Arlington District Attorney. I have two jobs concerning you; one job is to provide you with a lawyer if you can't afford one yourself, which I do not believe that you cannot afford one. The second and more important one in your case is I am the D.A. that is going to put you in jail for the rest of your life. We have the evidence and an eye witness; this is a slam dunk as far as we see it. You are lucky that Virginia does not have the death penalty. If this were being done in Maryland, you would get the death penalty; and I would be smiling when they put you down."

"I will need to call my lawyer now," Davin said quietly to Pike.

Pike turned and opened the door and let Ramsey and Brown back in. "He is all yours, book him."

"Mr. Pierce you are under arrest for the murder of Adam Cruz; you have the right to remain silent, and anything you say may be used in a court of law. You have the right to a lawyer; if you cannot afford a lawyer, one will be appointed for you. Do you have any questions about your rights?" Ramsey stated and indicated for Davin to stand up, "Please empty your pockets."

Chapter 46 Where the Heck Are We?

"Hey everyone, we have a lot of fuel and the engines do start," Freddy announced when he and Morgan returned to the galley. "Wow, lunch! Is there enough for two hungry engineers?"

"Sure, help yourself; we saved the rest for you two," Vince said as he stuck another spoonful in his mouth.

"Any crackers?" Morgan asked as she spooned up a bowlful.

"Is anyone watching the beach?" Randal asked as he shoveled in some more stew and watched as Morgan and Freddy sat at the bar with their stew.

"Yes, Stephanie and Amber are up in the bridge eating and keeping an eye out," Vince commented as he stood to place his bowl and spoon in the dishwasher. "This yacht has almost everything we need: food, fuel, and a way out of here."

"Let's get this tub moving and out of here," Randal suggested.

"The engines are running; all we have to do is turn this that a way and push the throttles forward until we move farther away from here," Bryce indicated candidly.

"By the way, the generator on this tub is one that automatically starts when the batteries get low to keep them charged; it has burned up some fuel, but the main tank is still nearly full," Freddy commented between bites of food.

"That is why we have ice and cold beer. This boat has taken care of itself, while sitting idle in this cove," Vince commented.

"Someone call up to the bridge, and make it so," Randal ordered.

"As you command," Bryce said. He then stood, picked up the ships intercom, and called up to the bridge. "Bridge, this is sailor Bryce, I am going forward to bring up the anchor while Freddy gets the stern anchor; once we are unhooked, please engage the engines and steer us out of here."

"That's a big ten four, little buddy," Stephanie called back almost immediately, "By the way, there seems to be some activity on the beach around where you left those soldiers."

"Got it, we will be on the lookout; going forward now," Bryce acknowledged and then headed forward to bring up the anchor while Freddy headed to the stern. Five minutes later, both anchors were up, the engines were engaged, and the *Freedom* yacht started to move and turn toward what they believed to be a break in the reef around the cove. Bryce stood on the bow, and watched the depth of the water to ensure they did not run into the reef and end their escape before getting started. Using hand signals, he was able to guide Stephanie through a small but navigable hole in the reef.

Twenty minutes after engaging their engines, the *Freedom* yacht burst into the ocean and took a course to the east.

"Hey guys, this boat has a working GPS; I know where the heck we are. According to it, we just left Ducie which is one of the Pitcairn Islands," Stephanie announced over the intercom, pausing for a moment and then reported, "We are over three thousand miles from Fiji to the west and just short of a thousand miles to Easter Island. There is Pitcairn Island which is a closer inhabited island, but it does not have an airport. According to the travel book up here, they have a population of under one hundred and the only way in is by boat. I am turning toward Easter Island unless anyone objects."

"No objection down here; make it so number one," Randal ordered and then added "It's going to be a long trip."

Two miles off the coast of Ducie, the ship headed east at about fifteen knots; the ship rode smoothly on the light chop that the ocean was providing them at the moment.

"Lots of activity on the beach, Josh," Freddy said as he returned to the galley and grabbed a soda from the refrigerator. "Do you think they will come after us?"

"If I were a betting man, and I am, I would say, 'Yes'. They will not stop until we are all dead and at the bottom of the ocean," Randal stated. He stood, picked up his weapon, and walked to the stern to keep an eye on the beach as it faded into the horizon.

They did not have to wait long. A small dot rose from the island; and after reaching an altitude of two thousand feet, it banked toward the east and started to get bigger. The closer it came, the more it resembled a helicopter, a very deadly helicopter armed with a thirty millimeter mini gun also known as a Gatling gun.

"Holy cow! What the hell are they doing with that?" Randal said and then yelled forward. "We have company, get your weapons! Stephanie evasive maneuvers, NOW!"

The *Freedom* yacht started to make sharp turns; Stephanie immediately slammed the throttle to max getting the boat to increase speed to twenty-four knots.

"That's all she's got," Stephanie yelled, "Amber, go below and get some weapons for us."

"Right away, Steph," she replied and ran out of the bridge and down to the galley where the rest were gathering up their weapons and heading out to the deck to protect themselves from the very possible destruction of their escape craft.

The pilot of the helicopter spotted the yacht, dropped down to about fifty feet off the water, and flew directly at the yacht. When he got within a hundred yards of the yacht, he opened fire with his mini gun, not expecting much in the way of return fire. Most of the rounds slammed into the water around the boat with only a couple hitting the stern causing no real damage except to the wood work. Randal dove for cover and then brought the barrel of his M-16 up and rested the barrel on the transom. After he clicked the selector from safe to auto, he carefully aimed as best he could on the approaching helo, and slowly pulled the trigger. More bullets slammed into the yacht and tore up the transom, but missed Randal by inches. Randal continued to slowly pull back on the trigger until he felt and heard his weapon send its deadly hot bullets toward the helicopter. They might still be out of range for the M-16, but he had to try, anyway. At the same time from further up the deck, he heard the report of several more M-16s.

The helicopter pilot started to jerk his chopper left and right to avoid being hit, but he was a few micro seconds late. Six bullets slammed into his windscreen, punching holes and striking the bulkhead behind him, barely missing his head. "Get your weapon ready, back there," the pilot ordered his gunner not knowing that two of the six rounds that punched holes in his windscreen went on to hit his gunner, killing him instantly. Not getting a reply, he turned his head to see the body of his gunner hanging on his safety strap obviously dead. "Damn!"

He pulled hard up, turned his helicopter to the right, climbed to two hundred feet, and reevaluated his situation. The people on that boat had weapons and knew how to use them. He was in this for the money, not to get killed. The money was very, very good; and he was told he would get a big bonus if he were to sink the yacht and kill all on board. He had no problem with killing, but he did have a problem with dying. After circling back, he decided he would make one more pass; and if he survived and did sink the boat, he would be very happy; however, his odds were not good. While accelerating and diving down to water level, he jinked and jiggled as he was taught in combat flight school; and then as he got closer, he opened up with the mini gun sending nearly five hundred 30 mm rounds toward the boat. Many struck and tore up various parts of the yacht; luckily they did not hit anybody, although they came very close to taking out Vince and Freddy who had ducked behind the refrigerator as the large 30mm rounds slammed into the fridge.

"Damn, knock that bird down!" Freddy yelled. "He just killed the beer!"

More M-16 rounds searched for a vulnerable point on the helicopter, and finally several hit some hydraulic lines. The helicopter began to spill fluid into the passenger compartment and down the back of the pilot.

"Damn it!" the pilot yelled and pulled the collective up and twisted his throttle to max; the helicopter climbed rapidly to over three hundred feet. The pilot turned back toward the island, praying that the old bird would make it back to land before exploding or crashing into the ocean.

Randal and his team stood and watched as the helicopter turned away from them smoking and losing altitude.

"Hope he makes it," Amber said as she and Stephanie watched from the bridge. "Damn, look," she said pointing to the control panel.

"Yeah damn, that was the GPS. At least we still have the compass," Stephanie said and looked at the compass which sat on top of the console with a large hole in the side of it. "Damn."

Chapter 47 Gone In Fifteen Seconds

As they approached the South Carolina border on I-95 in a heavy downpour cruising at a moderate speed of eighty-five miles per hour, Josh and Amber were smiling and looking for a place to spend the night. The road was dark, wet and slick, but the tires held firm to the road. Traffic was minimal for the weekday night with few travelers and a bunch of heavy eighteen wheelers.

"It is getting late and I am tired. Don't you think it is time to stop, eat and sleep? I am getting really bored with this job; do you think Rocky would miss us if we just disappeared?" Amber asked and continued to look for an exit.

"I am with you on that my sexy little fake sister," Josh agreed and then saw an exit sign, "Look, just what the doctor ordered, an exit with hotels."

"Good, look, there is a Hilton. Let's go there; they usually have a good restaurant close by," Amber said as she pointed to the Hilton just off the highway.

"Sure, sounds good to me," Josh said as he pulled off the exit and stopped at the stop sign, looked both ways and then pulled out turning left toward the Hilton.

A half hour later, they were walking down the hallway to their rooms. "Let's freshen up and get something to eat before bed; I am starving," Amber said and then slipped her key into the lock. After dropping his bag on the bed, Josh walked into the bathroom, relieved himself, washed his hands, and then stood looking at his face in the mirror, thinking. 'How the hell did we get messed up with this? Time to get out!'

Back in his room, he opened his bag and pulled out a clean shirt, removed the one he was wearing, and put on the clean one. Amber pulled some clean clothes from her bag, went into the bathroom, and turned on the shower.

"Don't take too long, I am hungry."

A few minutes later, he heard the shower stop. Amber opened the door and came out of the bathroom wearing a short light colored summer dress with spaghetti straps and low cut front.

"Whoa, are you trolling tonight?" Josh said being a bit shocked at her outfit.

"No, just wanted to be comfortable. Oh, I don't have on anything under this either," she teased and then took his hand and pulled him into the hall. "Let's go, I am hungry."

They pulled the door closed behind them, started down the hall toward the lobby, and stopped only to get directions to the restaurant. Once seated at their table, Josh started to speak, but was stopped by Amber. "Wait, I have something I need to say."

"Okay, speak."

"I am tired of this; I want out now. We need to get out before we get arrested or killed. There I said it," Amber admitted, picked up her menu, and started to look for something to eat before the waitress showed up.

"I agree. We need to make a plan to disappear tonight," Josh agreed and looked over his menu.

"What can I get for you two tonight?" the waitress asked when she stepped up to the table.

"I will have a Coors Light and a glass of ice water," Amber replied quickly.

"Make that two, please," Josh agreed.

"I will be right back with your drinks; do you know what you would like for dinner?"

"Not yet. Thank you," Josh replied.

Minutes later, they had their drinks; and had ordered dinner. While waiting, they planned their disappearance. Dinner arrived. They enjoyed their steak and lobster dinners; and the decision they had made would be put into play first thing after dinner.

Amber and Josh went back to their room and hugged for a moment. She removed her light summer dress and stood in front of the mirror admiring her naked body, and thought about what they were doing. Intentionally destroying someone else's life went against her morals, and she was glad that she and Josh had decided to end it tonight. Josh sat on the edge of the bed admiring her figure and wanted to take her right now, but knew he did not have the time. They would have plenty of time, once they broke away from Soto.

Josh changed his clothes, set his alarm for eleven o'clock and laid down on the bed; it was eight-thirty, so he would be able to get a couple of hours of sleep before he would have to leave. Amber crawled in beside him and they hugged until they both fell asleep.

Eleven o'clock came too quickly. Josh rolled out of bed and checked his watch; he liked that watch, and it never lost time. After pulling on his shoes and waterproof jacket, he left his room, pulled the door closed, and checked that it locked. It might be hours before he could get back, but he had to do this. When he would get back, Amber and Josh would become Ken and Erin once again, disappearing forever.

After walking over to the Shelby Mustang, he admired its lines and the speed it was possible of; but it was stolen and they would be looking for it, if they were not already. Being a car theft was a felony in most states, and then transporting the stolen car across state lines just increased the penalty. He just needed to move the car and borrow another to get back to the hotel quickly.

Josh got in the Mustang and drove it to the coast and parked it at Holiday Inn near the beach, where he saw a white Nissan sitting in a dark corner of the parking lot. He pulled the Mustang in, and parked four spaces from the Nissan. As he exited the Mustang, he purposely dropped the keys and casually walked to the lobby entrance and entered. At the counter, he asked the attendant the location of the lobby restroom. After getting directions, he walked to the men's room where he removed the latex copies of Josh Pierce's fingerprints from his hands and the latex mask that had covered his face and neck. He slipped on another pair of latex gloves that had fingerprints of a someone he did not know, to prevent leaving his real fingerprints anywhere around this hotel or on the car he was about to steal. Within a few minutes, he came out with a face of a young oriental male with coal black hair, that nobody would remember and a wearing a different looking jacket that was actually the same one, only reversed. Luckily, since it was late at night, there were no other people in the hallway who might have noticed his changed appearance.

Josh walked out the side door as a young oriental male and up to the Nissan. Within fifteen seconds, he had the door opened and began to hot wire the car. After checking the fuel gauge, he was pleased to see it had three quarters of a tank. Two hours later, Josh pulled into the parking lot of a Wal-Mart and before leaving the car, he poured a small amount of gas on the floor and set a fuse that would start the fire a few minutes after he was gone. The car would burn destroying any possible evidence that he had been in the car. Three minutes after setting the fuse of a matchbook and lit match, the car exploded into a small but effective fire ball.

He immediately went back to his room and opened the door. He saw Amber or rather Erin lying nude on the bed; immediately decided they had time, and stripped his clothes off and crawled in bed with her. Two hours later they were getting dressed.

"Have you gotten us some flights?" he asked.

"Yes, we fly at nine to Miami," she replied quietly. "You need to change your face so we can leave as Ken and Barbie instead of Josh and Amber or whoever you are right now."

"Good, we have time for breakfast and did you call for a cab or does the hotel have a shuttle?" Josh said as he closed the door of the bathroom, returning a couple of minutes later as Ken. "Feels good to be myself again and have you with me as my sweet beautiful Erin."

"They have a shuttle. Let's get breakfast. And don't forget I am Erin now, not Amber; and you are Ken. Don't slip up baby," Erin said as she walked to the door and reached for the handle.

"Where is your mask?" Ken asked.

"Cut it up and flushed it in small pieces."

"Wait, I need to do that," he said and pulled out a knife and started to cut up the mask; minutes later, he had a pile of latex on a towel lying on the bed. After cutting it up, he fed pieces in the toilet and flushed several times until it was completely gone and then flushed twice more to make sure.

"Good, let's go; I am hungry," Erin said and opened the door. They walked out and headed for the restaurant. They stopped at the lobby counter to find out when the shuttle would leave for the airport. After dragging their bags to the restaurant, they sat and ate a full breakfast. At eight fifteen, they boarded the shuttle for the airport; and shortly after, disappeared into the crowd of the airport.

Chapter 48 Island Party

"We have lost contact with the Pierce kids. They seem to have fallen off the grid. They're not answering my calls and their location transmitters are no longer functional," the control room operator reported to Rocky.

"Damn, I was hoping they would go a few more days; let them go. We have bigger fish to fry. They have done a very good job and were paid well for it," Rocky ordered as he looked around the room for the head controller, Greg. When he did not see him, he became worried; but then asked the room. "What happened to our helicopter? Does anyone have an answer for me?"

"Sir, the helo was damaged and attempted to make it back to shore, but didn't. She went down about nine hundred yards from shore; we have a boat going out to look for survivors."

"Call the *Bonaventure* and have the captain bring her in; we may have to move our operation," Rocky ordered and after a short pause he added, "Get Greg in here now; we need to talk. And find my damn son."

"Yes, sir," one of the operators said as she stood and ran from the control room.

Twenty-five minutes later, Greg and Horatio walked into the room.

"What's up dad?" Horatio asked as he walked up behind his father.

"Well, if you must know, the prisoners have escaped on the yacht; and they shot down our helicopter. I have ordered the *Bonaventure* to pick us up," Rocky said referring to his ship.

"Okay, sounds serious. What do you want me to do?" Horatio asked.

"Well, this party seems to be over at this location, but I still have a few tricks left. I want you and Greg to take a team out to the sub, get her fired up and go after the yacht; sink her!"

"Really, is that old boat capable of doing that?"

"Yes, we have been doing regular maintenance on her for years. She is fully functional, and the torpedoes are hot and ready too. Greg, you are in charge; you have served on subs in the past and know what to do, and my son will act as your second. So, as they say in the movies, 'Just do it.' No that's not it; ah, never mind. Just go, NOW!"

Horatio and Greg hustled out of the room and headed toward the barracks to gather up some men to help operate the submarine. They only needed the ten men that had been trained on its operation. An hour after the order had been given, a crew of twelve was headed through the jungle for the beach. It would take two hours to reach the cove and get out to the sub, and another couple of hours to get her ready to sail. Meanwhile, the *Freedom* yacht was getting further away from Ducie Island. They knew the yacht was running at nearly max speed to open the distance between them and the island, so the crew of the sub had little chance to catch them since the maximum speed of the sub on the surface was about eighteen knots.

"Why did dad send us on this wild goose chase; that yacht is capable of running faster than we can, so how are we expected to catch her?" Horatio asked as they opened the hatch of the sub and started to climb down.

"That is a good question. My only thought on that is that he wanted us off the island for your safety. The escapees will get to Easter Island long before we will and inform the authorities about what is going on. They would then send the military out to destroy the island or at least attempt to capture and detain whoever is left there. He probably figured you would be safer running now than later," Greg stated as they entered the control room and started turning on systems.

Their team immediately went to their assigned posts and activated the systems required to operate the boat.

"That does sound possible; but why take the chance on being captured?"

"He doesn't plan on being captured; the *Bonaventure* is a fully capable ship with identical systems that have been the back up for everything we have done on the island. He plans on moving the operation to the ship and continue until either captured, sunk or they get clean away," Greg commented and then paused and looked around the small control room. He picked up the intercom, pressed the button for the entire boat, and spoke. "All areas report."

Within a few seconds, he had his answers; all systems were a go except the engine room. There was a problem. Someone had sabotaged the engines, and it would take several hours to get them running again.

"Get to work on it; we need to move this boat as soon as possible," Greg ordered.

"Not going to happen," the reply came.

"What?"

"These engines will not start without a complete rework, they did a good job of busting them," the engineer stated.

Chapter 49 Mr. President

"Wake up Mr. President, time to get up; you have things to do. Your breakfast is here; you don't want to eat it cold, do you?" the voice at the door asked without opening the door. "I am going to slide it through the slot. When you are done, just slide it back out."

A second later, a plastic tray slid through the slot complete with plastic fork, knife, spoon, and two napkins. On the tray were two fried eggs, potatoes, bacon, a carton of orange juice and a Styrofoam cup of coffee with sugar and cream on the side.

"At least they are not going to starve me; that looks pretty good," President Tony Sanford said aloud knowing they were probably listening, but didn't care. He reached over and pulled the tray in front of himself and started to eat, "Good, still hot."

After finishing his breakfast and almost enjoying his coffee, he slid the tray through the slot and then spoke to anyone who might be listening, "Really would be nice to get a shower."

"Soon, Mr. President, but not yet; just sit tight. You will get what you want soon," a voice responded through a hidden speaker. That was what Sanford really wanted to know, were they listening and watching him. He got his answer.

White House Oval Office

"Mr. President, your breakfast is ready, do you want to eat in the office or the dining room?" the president's secretary asked over the intercom.

"Dining room, please, I will be right there," President Tony Sanford responded back to her and then stood, straightened his jacket and walked to the door. Approaching his secretary's desk, he stopped and asked, "When is my first meeting and with whom?"

"Secretary of Defense at nine thirty and you are having lunch with the Prime Minister of Japan."

"Thank you. I'll be in the dining room if you need me," he said and then winked at her causing her to blush.

"You are such a tease Mr. President," she said as he walked away.

Tony Sanford enjoyed a quiet breakfast in the dining room; no one came in to disturb him, which made breakfast even more enjoyable. He finished eating, wiped his mouth on the cotton napkin and then stood and walked back toward the Oval Office, thinking on the way, *'Wonder how the real Tony Sanford is enjoying his breakfast, probably not as well as I did.'*

Halfway back to the Oval Office, he was intercepted by the Secretary of Defense and a General and an Admiral whom he did not recognize.

"Sorry, sir, for being a little early, but we have a lot to discuss and need your input," the Secretary of Defense said as he caught up to the President.

"Come on in; help yourself to some coffee. I need to use the head before we start," President Sanford said as they walked down the hall toward the office.

Sanford took twenty minutes to return to the office; he had to make sure his disguise had not slipped or started to fail. Shortly after getting the real Tony Sanford out of the White House, he had entered the Oval Office private bathroom, turned off his temporary holographic projector, and donned the latex mask that would ensure his disguise would not fail at the wrong moment. The holograph was great, but only for short periods; so Rocky and his team had stolen ideas from movies of the past and created realistic latex masks that could be worn indefinitely. Which would not slip, and felt real to the touch. He had created two masks for each of his fake replacements, Sanford, Josh and Amber Pierce, Davin Pierce, Josh and Stephanie Randal and as a little insurance one for Connie Pierce too.

"Okay gentlemen what have you got for me today?" President Sanford asked as he walked back into the Oval Office.

Chapter 50 Who Are You?

Detectives Ramsey and Brown were sitting at their desks going over the evidence against Davin Pierce. The forensics confirmed the weapon from Davin's home was the murder weapon; and the eye witness was one hundred percent positive that Davin Pierce was the shooter.

"Arlene, this is a slam dunk; Pierce is guilty. There has to be a way he got out of CIA headquarters, and did the hit," Charlie said sitting across from his partner.

"It is pretty solid. But how did he get out of the building. According to everyone we have talked to, there is only one way in and out without setting off alarms and that is the front lobby. How did he do it; and the bigger question is why?" Arlene responded thumbing through the paperwork.

"There has to be a secret underground passage or railroad to move between buildings without being seen. Someone knows and isn't talking."

"We have to find that somebody who will talk to us. It may be a national secret; but without it, the jury will find him innocent because of reasonable doubt. Pierce has an alibi and a lot of people will state that he never left the building. Reasonable doubt and he walks," Arlene countered. "If we can get even an anonymous statement that there is a passage out of there then we have him."

A young officer walked up to their desks and stood there waiting. Finally, Arlene Ramsey looked up and said. "What's up, Officer Payne? Are you new here? Haven't seen you before." Noticing the name on his uniform.

"Yes, Ma'am got placed here right out of the academy, been here a couple of days," Payne replied

"Cool, welcome to Arlington. I am Arlene Ramsey and my quiet partner over there is Charlie Brown; and yeah, he gets a lot of kidding about his name, but he is a damn good detective. What have you got for us?"

"We have a problem," Payne stated not smiling at all.

"A problem you say; what's the problem?" Charlie said smiling.

"You need to come with me detectives; you have to see this," Payne said and then pointed toward the hallway.

"Right behind you," Ramsey said as she and Brown stood and followed Payne down the hall.

After entering into the holding cell section of the precinct, he stopped in front of cell number four and pointed into the cell.

"Who the hell are you?" Ramsey asked the man sitting on the bunk in the cell. After getting no answer from him, she asked again louder, "I said who the hell are you?"

The man didn't say a word, but pointed toward a latex mask laying on the edge of the bunk complete with hair. At closer inspection, the face they saw was of Davin Pierce.

"Holy shit, he did it. That is how he got out." Brown exclaimed looking at the mask and the man in the cell. "That CIA killer just made us into fools."

"Who the hell are you?" Ramsey asked the man sitting on the bed in the cell, again.

"I am Allen Siegel, I am an analyst at CIA in Langley. I admit I took Davin Pierce's place, because it is what we do. Sorry for the confusion," Siegel replied, "And, yes, I know I may be charged for obstructing justice and helping a suspected killer escape. But Mr. Pierce did not kill Adam Cruz;

and he needs time to prove it. So back off a little and let him find the real killer."

"That is not possible Mr. Siegel; and we will leave you in there for now, at least until we get this figured out," Brown stated.

"Put an all points out for the capture and arrest of Davin Pierce, considered armed and dangerous," Ramsey ordered Officer Payne, who turned and ran down the hall toward the Desk Sergeant.

Payne got down to the Desk Sergeant, but didn't stop to tell him about the APB for himself; instead he continued to walk past the desk and right out the front door.

After talking to the man behind the bars that were supposed to hold Davin Pierce, Ramsey and Brown returned to their desks wondering how it happened.

"Sergeant where is that APB on Pierce?" Ramsey asked the Desk ergeant over the phone. "What, didn't Officer Payne tell you we wanted an All Points on Davin Pierce who has broken out of our jail?"

"Officer who?"

"Officer Payne, tall, good looking, young, brown hair," Ramsey stated.

"We don't have an Officer Payne in this precinct," the desk sergeant replied.

"What? Who the hell is Payne? Is he still in the building?"

"No. An officer walked past my desk ten minutes ago that fits his description; he's gone."

"Damn!" Brown said and then looked at Ramsey.

"Pierce gets someone else to pose as him; and then he poses as someone else that is in the building, and walks right out past the guards, commits the murders, and then walks right back in. Nice trick and only the CIA operators can pull it off; they have had years of practice in deception," Arlene deduced.

Chapter 51 South Seas Adventure Ride

The morning of the second day at sea came with a vengeance; the South Seas were kicking up, and dark clouds were moving in from the north. This is going to become an 'E' ride, if you remember those from our favorite Disney parks of the past. 'E' rides were the ones that were the most thrilling and terrifying. After many years, Disney changed the ticket program and you could ride any ride at your own risk if you met the minimum requirement and the 'E' ride ticket disappeared into history.

"It looks like it is going to be a rough ride for a while," Freddy said as he steered the boat on the course that Stephanie had established hours earlier. It was his turn at the wheel; his partner in crime was Diane. She picked up a pair of binoculars and eyed the storm.

"Yeah, that looks real nasty, and it is heading directly toward us," Diane said before putting down the binoculars.

"Better tell the others to buckle up," Freddy said and then thought for a second, "And ask for Mr. Randal to come up."

"Be right back," she said and hurried off the bridge and down the stairs to find Randal.

Minutes later, Randal and Diane entered the bridge. Randal picked up the binoculars and looked at the storm. Under his breath he said, "Holy shit, what next?" He moved the binoculars left and right, and stopped suddenly when he saw something he never expected this far south.

"What is it, Mr. Randal?" Diane asked.

"After all we have been through, you can call me Josh. What I see is another ship, just at the edge of the horizon between us and that storm. Maybe we should see if they have a working radio. What do you think?" Josh stated as he studied the ship. "I can't tell its nationality, but any ship right now might be able to help us. She is headed west; a little detour by us and our paths will cross."

"What heading sir? Oh, maybe just turn in that direction; we don't have a compass," Freddy commented looking a little silly for asking.

"Yeah, turn toward that ship and slow to about ten knots when we get closer. Try to get close, but not cross its path; it may not be able to stop in time before it would ram us," Randal ordered, "I will be right back."

He left the bridge to alert the rest of the team and to retrieve his weapons. He wanted to be prepared, just in case. He did not trust many people, and running into a lone freighter in the South Pacific was suspicious. It might be running drugs, guns, slaves, almost anything. And he wanted to be prepared for anything. He warned the rest who retrieved their weapons and positioned themselves along the port side of the boat.

As they got closer, Randal was able to read the name on the bow of the ship, *Bonaventure,* flying under a Panama flag. "Interesting flying a Panama flag, what are they running?"

The *Freedom* yacht had closed to within five hundred yards, slowed to about ten knots, and turned to run parallel to the *Bonaventure.* The *Freedom* then slowed more to match her speed. Josh watched the *Bonaventure* through his binoculars and was not too pleased with what he saw.

"Maintain this distance for a few minutes; and then slowly move closer, but no closer than ah, fifty yards."

"You got it Captain," Freddy responded and watched the distance between the two ships close slowly.

Freddy steered the *Freedom* yacht to within fifty yards of the freighter and matched her speed. Randal watched the bridge and scanned the deck of the freighter looking for anything weird. He finally got what he was looking for when a sailor on the freighter stood up with an RPG and fired at the *Freedom* yacht.

"Full speed ahead, Freddy!" Josh yelled and Freddy slammed the throttles to full, and the yachts twin fifteen hundred horse power engines immediately lifted the bow and threw everyone to the deck as the twin props bit into the water. The boat immediately jumped to fifteen knots and continued up to twenty-four knots. The RPG missile passed harmlessly behind the yacht. Freddy turned the yacht hard left and started to zig-zag to hopefully keep the gunner from firing another missile up their backside.

"Turn us back to the east and continue on to Easter Island," Josh ordered. "I guess they did not want us to bother them," he said with a chuckle.

"We only wanted to use their radio; do you think they will try to follow us?" Freddy asked.

"No, they have another mission to complete and we are faster. But keep an eye on them," Josh stated and then asked, "What is our estimated arrival at Easter Island?"

"According to your wife, it should be about forty hours from Ducie; and we have been running for twenty eight, so maybe by late this evening," Freddy replied.

"Maintain best speed as long as you can; that storm may slow us down a bit, but do what you can, Freddy."

"Yes, sir."

The storm hit but wasn't as bad as expected; the seas did grow to about six foot swells, and Freddy had to cut speed to twelve knots and ask for more assistance, since he wasn't a seasoned boat driver. Josh stayed on the bridge to assist; he had many more years on the water than Freddy.

Officer Payne walked out of the Arlington Police Department and turned right to head toward the parking lot. After looking around at the parked cars, he decided to take Ramsey's and Brown's car, just for the fun of it. Minutes later, Payne was driving out of the parking lot in a relatively new Chrysler 500.

Twenty-five minutes later, Payne pulled over and parked the Chrysler at the Greyhound Bus station in Alexandria. He went inside, opened locker 44, and removed a small suitcase. Within minutes, he was out of the bus station and back in the car. After driving another ten miles, Payne pulled into a Wal-Mart parking lot, parked and slipped out of the car. Taking the suitcase, he walked across the parking lot to a truck stop and entered the restroom where he changed clothes and removed his Officer Payne mask and uniform; once again, he became Davin Pierce. Then minutes later, Davin Pierce became the unknown face of his new identity, a man named Kelly Donavan. He placed the police uniform in the suitcase, but kept the pistol and ammunition, slipping it in the back of his pants and covering it with his new suit jacket.

Kelly Donavan left the truck stop and walked down the street to a rental car agency. Using his new alternate identification that he had stored with the suitcase, he rented a car.

Driving out of the city, Davin, as Kelly Donavan, had a lot to consider and had no idea where to start. He picked up one of his new burn phones, looked at it, and considered who to call. Connie came to mind first; she must be worried to death. He knew that she had left home and went to a predesignated safe house that they had established years ago. Calling from a burn phone would get her attention, and she would answer it. He would keep this phone to call only Connie.

'Answer the phone, baby,' Davin said quietly listening to the ringing and was about to give up when the call was answered.

"Hello," a female voice said quietly.

"Honey, this is Davin. I can't talk long, are you okay?" he asked.

"Yes, where are you?" Connie asked quickly.

"I can't answer that; and before you ask, I did not kill Adam. And yes, well, I didn't really escape from jail because I never was in jail. One of my analysts took my place. Look, I need you to stay safe, and don't talk to the police; stay where you are; there is enough food there for months. I will contact you soon. Love you," Davin said to his wife.

"I will stay here; you be safe, and let me know what I can do to help you. Don't forget, I still have a lot of contacts with the bureau."

"I do, and will, as soon as I have something to go on. I will call again soon, got to go now," Davin said and then hung up the cell phone.

He continued to drive until he reached McLean, Virginia where he stopped at a Holiday Inn and checked in under his new name of Kelly Donavan. Being this close to headquarters was risky; but as Donavan, he could move freely around the country poking his nose into areas that could possibly produce a trail to who killed Adam. He had a lot to track down and very little time to do so. Only a few people at the company knew him as Kelly Donavan, so he worried less about being discovered.

Sitting in the overstuffed leather chair in his room, Davin was deep in thought; he had to decide on his next course of action. He needed information and contacting his people at headquarters would get some of the information. Also, he still had contacts with the FBI because of Connie's connection. Knowing that his call could be traced he had to be very careful. After making his decision, he picked up a second burn phone, another of the six that he had, all of which were not traceable back to him as a person, but calls could still be traced to his location. After getting out of the chair, he picked up a small bag with the cell phones, weapon and additional disguises, and left the room.

Davin drove south out of town until he saw a Sonic fast food drive in. He pulled into a space and ordered some lunch. While waiting until it arrived, he picked up his cell phone and dialed the number for headquarters.

"Good afternoon; how may I direct your call?" the receptionist said when she answered the phone.

"May I speak to Sean Fox?" Davin said using the code name to be connected to the duty officer of the day.

"Just a moment, sir, I will connect you." Davin waited for several minutes before a voice came online; he knew the number was being traced so the longer he was online the easier it was for them to locate him. He would dispose of this phone after this call.

"Hello Davin, how are you?" Josh Randal said quietly when he picked up the phone.

"Hi Josh," Davin replied, suspecting that a team of CIA, FBI and/or police would rain down on him any second.

"I heard you evaded the police and are on the run. I can't help you, you know that old buddy," Josh commented with no feeling in his voice.

"Who the hell are you?" Davin picked up on the lack of feeling, his friend Josh would never not help him; they were friends for life. He knew when Josh was lying or when something was wrong, and he felt something was drastically wrong with Josh right now.

"You know who I am, Davin; we have been friends for a long time. But the cops are all over this; and you know, we are legally bound to not operate covert missions on U.S. soil."

"So true, but who the hell are you?" Davin asked again, "If you don't tell me, I will hang up and disappear until I find out what the hell is going on."

"Okay, Davin if you must know. My friends call me Rich, that's all I will say for now. Your friend is dead; my boss had him and his lovely wife killed days ago. So you have to deal with me; and I am in charge of the largest intelligence organization in the world. We will find and kill you as a rogue agent even on home soil."

Davin listened and then finally said, "Don't bet on it, Richard. Two can play this game, and I never lose," he said; not waiting for a reply, he hung up the phone.

Leaning back in the seat of his rental, he thought about his next move. Josh may be dead but he wasn't; and he was damn good at his job, finding and eliminating the opposition. Now it was him, alone, against the CIA, FBI, every police department in the country, and whoever was behind all this.

He suddenly lost his appetite and placed his lunch back on the tray and just thought, how did this happen?

Chapter 53 Damage Is Done

It was another beautiful tropical day on Ducie Island; Rocky and his team were rapidly packing up everything they needed to take, and planned on burning the rest. His contact in Langley had just called and informed him that Davin Pierce was on the loose, but he had it under control. Rocky wasn't worried about Washington; he had the President and a man in charge of the CIA. Pierce had been accused of murder and was on the run, while his kids had arrest warrants out for them. Even if the real Josh Randal returned, he would be arrested for kidnapping the President; and if Rocky had the president killed, it would ensure that Randal would be charged for kidnapping. On the other hand, he had another way of running this operation and that was the way he was leaning toward. Rocky planned on releasing the President just before Randal got back to the states; and the fake Randal would disappear. The President would point a finger at Randal; and have him arrested for kidnapping. His other option would be to have his fake president kill the three men presently in the Oval Office. He made his decision and sent the order to his operatives.

Pierce's kids would be arrested for multiple car thefts, and Vince and his four geniuses would be arrested for conspiracy and kidnapping. The fake Randal would make sure Captain Redmond would die suddenly if he made it to the states.

"Get moving ladies and gentlemen, the *Bonaventure* will be here in a few hours," Rocky ordered. "Any word from the sub? Did they start moving yet?"

"Sorry sir, someone sabotaged the sub and the engines will not start," the technician replied between stuffing manuals into a box.

"Order them back here to help with the evacuation," Rocky ordered; then he thought, *'Everything is in place, there is nothing left to do except run for the hills. The damage is done.'*

Two hours later, Horatio, Greg, and the submarine crew walked into the control room.

"Welcome back, it was a shot in the dark anyway. You would have never caught up with that yacht; they are faster and had a head start," Rocky said as his son and crew walked in. "Have your men help set the charges and let's blow this place, literally. Set them for twelve hours from now, we should be well away from here by then, the *Bonaventure* arrives in an hour."

"Yes, sir; got it covered," Greg said as he acknowledged the order and turned and headed out of the room followed by his team. Horatio stayed behind to talk to his father.

"Dad, we need to talk."

"Not now, we need to get off this island before the U.S. military shows up," Rocky stated and then headed for the door.

"What about those on the other side of the island?"

"Expendable, most are holographic projections anyway. But don't worry we are not blowing up that compound, just this one," Rocky said as he exited through the door, leaving Horatio standing in the control room confused.

"Ducie Island, this is the *Bonaventure*, do you copy?" the speaker on the desk crackled.

"We copy, *Bonaventure*. What is your ETA?" the control operator responded quickly.

"Raise the dock; we are two hundred yards off the coast ready to dock," the *Bonaventure* stated.

"Dock is coming up," the operator stated as he flicked a couple of switches that would raise the submerged dock to a level six feet above the water.

"Thank you; we will be docked in about twenty minutes," the *Bonaventure* announced.

"Find your father and tell him the boat is here," the operator suggested to Horatio.

"Yeah, we need to go," he said and hurried out of the control room to locate his father.

Two hours after the *Bonaventure* was docked, a stream of men and women carrying their bags were followed by several small trucks that were off loaded from the ship to move material. It took nearly six hours to load the ship; but once loaded, the ship untied from the dock and pulled away. Using a remote control, Rocky commanded the submersible dock to sink back into the ocean.

"Where to, Rocky?" the Captain asked when Rocky entered the bridge.

"North to the shipping lanes, and then to Fiji; make best speed for Fiji," Rocky ordered as he looked out at the island as it receded into the distance. Then he turned and looked out over the open ocean, thinking he had succeeded in destroying the two people that had destroyed his life and credibility. He had his revenge.

Chapter 54 Looking Deep

"Connie, I need you to contact your friend in the bureau and see if she will meet me today," Davin asked his wife when she answered on the second ring. He was using the cell phone he had previously used to call her; the second was sitting on the bottom of the Potomac River. He had removed the battery and crushed the phone under the tires of his rental car before tossing it into the bay.

"I will call her, where should I tell her to meet you?" Connie asked.

"Can you trust her not to turn me in?" Davin asked.

"You can trust her; if I tell her to help you, she will without questioning. But by doing so, if she gets caught helping you, she could be brought up on charges for helping an accused killer."

"She will not know it's me. No chance of that," Davin stated to calm her down.

"Okay, I will call her and see if she can meet you; who should I tell her she is meeting?" Connie questioned.

"Kelly Donavan, private investigator from Washington. Don't set it up until tomorrow; I need to make sure my backstop is in place," Davin said referring to the information that needed to be in place identifying Kelly Donavan as who he said he was.

"Okay, I will set it up for you. Anything else you need from me, besides a soft shoulder to lean on."

"I sure could use that right about now. Be careful; there are things that just don't seem right," Connie said quietly.

"Yes, I know. Be careful," Davin said and then hung up the phone.

Davin waited for twenty-five minutes before making his next call. His call was to CIA Headquarters; but this time he wanted to speak with his old secretary, who was also a trained analyst.

"Rebecca, how are you doing this lovely afternoon?" Davin said when she answered the phone.

"Doing fine, are you well?" Rebecca, replied, recognizing Davin's voice and using good tradecraft did not mention his name because she knew he was a wanted man, she immediately pressed the scrambler which would prevent any outside wire taps from understanding what was said. Rebecca allowed a few people to call her Becky, close friends mostly and Davin was a very close friend as well as her boss.

"I am doing well, Becky. Need you to do me a favor," Davin replied and then paused to think about how he needed to ask his favor.

"Anything for you, we are secure." Becky stated and then listened.

"Remember, Kelly Donavan? He needs to be revived quickly. Start with the credit cards; I need to buy a computer. Can you do it?" Davin asked

"Yep, Kelly will be alive and well in a couple of hours, credit cards up in twenty. Can you wait that long for the rest?"

"Sure can, thanks Becky. Call me on this number when done."

"Talk to you in a couple of hours," Becky said and then hung up.

"Call me on this number when ready, thanks." Davin said before she hung up.

He planned on asking Becky to do a little research for him when she called him. He walked out of this room, drove down the street to a big box store and purchased a laptop computer paying with cash. He needed to do some research on his own. Two hours later, Becky called and let him know that Kelly Donavan was alive and well. She then asked if there was anything else he needed, and how soon.

"Yes, put together everything you have on Rocky Soto and the people we fired with him, even the classified stuff. When you have it together, call and I will come in to read it."

"That may take a while, I will call you. Be careful Kelly," Becky said and then hung up the phone.

Davin, aka, Kelly Donavan, sat in his hotel room in front of his newly purchased computer and started to search for anything he could find on Rocky Soto and his merry men and women who were on the verge of taking down the CIA and who knows what else.

Three hours and fifteen minutes later, Davin's number three cell phone rang. He stared at it for a minute and considered not answering. But knowing that only one other person had that number, he picked it up and did not say a word.

"Kelly, bad news," Becky said without waiting for him to reply.

"What is it?"

"The President has shot and killed the Secretary of Defense Frank Sorenson, Admiral Daniel Robertson and General Manny Reagan in the Oval Office and then he disappeared. There is a search for the president; but he is in the wind."

"What did you say?"

"I said…"

"No, I heard you, but don't believe it, killed three high officials in the Oval Office and then vanished?"

"Wait, there is a news bulletin." After pausing to watch the newscaster, Becky continued, "The President has been located on the Washington Monument grounds. He was arrested; according to the news, he had a weapon with six bullets missing. They believe it is the murder weapon, but that is speculation."

"Where are you? Are you alone?"

"In my office, and yes, I am alone," Becky responded and then added. "I have what you want, when do you want to come in?"

"I will be there in an hour; meet me in the lobby," Davin stated and then hung up.

Greetings from Easter Island

Forty-three hours after leaving Ducie Island, they were still about ten miles off the coast of Easter Island. The cruise had taken its toll on everyone's nerves and tension was running high. They had gotten this far without too much trouble, except for the run in with that freighter which did not want to be bothered by a simple luxury yacht and fired a warning shot at them. All was going well; the yacht had been running at almost full speed for the past thirty-seven hours without so much as a hiccup. They felt they were home free, but all was about to come splashing down around them.

"Josh we have a high speed boat approaching our port bow," Vince said over the ship board intercom which was finally working, thanks to Bryce and Freddy rewiring the system.

"Are they heading straight for us?" Randal asked considering all the possible scenarios.

"Yes, and they should reach us in about three minutes. What do you want to do?" Vince asked as he steered the yacht on the heading to Easter Island.

"Maintain course; I will be right up," Randal replied; then he ordered everyone to get their weapons and stand by. Upon reaching the bridge of the yacht, he grabbed a pair of high-powered binoculars and looked out at the speeding power boat. "Looks like a forty-foot Cigarette, similar to the one Davin has back home," he said to Vince and then added, turn starboard ten degrees and see if he turns away from our path."

Vince steered the yacht starboard about ten degrees, guessing because the compass was busted and so was the GPS. He lined the bow of the yacht with the bow of the Cigarette boat speeding toward them.

"He is turning to port, looks like he doesn't want to ram us and..." Randal said as he watched the boat close on them and then turned slightly and then abruptly slowed as they got closer. "Maintain your speed, do not slow down."

The cigarette boat stopped and sat drifting and turning as if to go back the way they had come. When the yacht was almost broadside to them, the speed boat accelerated and matched the speed of the yacht. Once they matched their speed, the boat turned toward the yacht closing the distance between them to less than a hundred feet and the pilot waved and smiled. Randal returned the smile and waved, and then yelled "GET DOWN!"

Suddenly four men jumped up from being hidden in the cockpit and opened fire with automatic weapons. A hail of bullets struck the bridge and the side of the yacht. Bullets ripped into the bridge and control panel with no less than six hitting Vince; he was dead before he hit the deck. Three bullets had also struck Randal and thrown him to the deck. It was pure luck that Randal was not killed also. Reaching for his pistol, he crawled to the doorway and fired a couple rounds back at the boat. He found it difficult to aim because of the blood dripping down into his eyes and his left arm in pain where one of the bullets had passed through.

The gunners continued to spray the yacht with heavy fire; bullets slammed into the galley causing a small fire and explosion. Morgan grabbed a fire extinguisher and immediately put out the fire.

Once they expended all their bullets, the gunmen quickly ducked down and changed magazines in their AK-47 assault rifles and were about to open up again when the side of their boat was struck by return fire from the yacht. Fiberglass and wood fragments were flying everywhere; the gunmen attempted to hide behind the boats outer wall, but were unable to as bullets passed right through the thin boat's outer hull.

Bryce in the stern and Redmond on the bow created a cross fire on the Cigarette boat. The concentrated fire on the Cigarette boat forced the driver to push the throttles full forward, but not before he and two of the gunman were hit.

One of the surviving gunmen dove into the cabin hoping not to be hit while the other gunman ducked quickly behind one of the boats fixed seats to keep from being hit. However, the fiberglass side of the boat did not stop the M-16 bullets from reaching him.

When Bryce and Redmond stopped firing to reload, Josh and Freddy, located mid-ship, opened fire with their M-16 rifles. Randal had crawled to the door and opened fire. Knowing that his little nine millimeter pistol would not do much good at this distance, he crawled back to the helm and turned the yacht to close the distance between them and possibly ram the Cigarette boat while keeping his boat at full throttle.

"Aim at the engine compartment!" Randal yelled down to Josh and Freddy, as they closed the distance, and hoped they would hear him over the reports of the M-16s. Seconds later, smoke started to pour out of the engine compartment of the Cigarette boat, and it started to slow down. Either they heard him, or decided to stop the fight by disabling the boat themselves; either way, the Cigarette was slowly falling behind them.

Randal saw a hand reach up from the deck in an attempt to adjust the throttles to maintain speed, and he fired three shots to just below that hand hoping to connect with a target. Immediately, the hand dropped as bits and pieces of the console exploded sending fiberglass and wood flying.

"Damn," is all Randal said when he saw Vince lying on the deck in a pool of blood staring back at him with lifeless eyes.

"Is everyone all right down there?" Randal picked up the intercom and yelled.

When he did not receive a reply, he became very worried, and yelled again; and then noticed that he was not transmitting as the intercom control box was in more than one piece and had several holes in what was left of it. He turned to go to the door just as Stephanie walked into the bridge holding a pistol in her right hand, to check on him and she did not look happy. After rushing over to Vince lying on the deck and realizing that he was dead, she stood and hugged Josh.

"I am glad you are not hurt," she said before she realized that he was bleeding from his left shoulder and blood on his face. "You're hurt."

"I am okay, is everyone all right down there?" he asked.

"No, Redmond is dead; Morgan was hit in the leg, while putting out a galley fire. We have her patched up; and Bryce and Freddy got a few scratches, nothing major. Young Josh and Amber are fine, they have a few cuts from flying glass; and I am fine. Diane did not fare as well; she took a bullet to her left side and is bleeding. We need to get her to a hospital fast. Morgan is watching her and has the bleeding under control for now, but she needs medical attention." Stephanie said sadly.

"Damn. Take the wheel for a second," Randal said and then picked up the binoculars and looked at the boat that had attacked them, it was burning and starting to list to the port side. "They will not be coming after us again."

"Honey, the left engine is starting to overheat," Stephanie stated as she looked at the gauges.

"Don't shut it down; run it as far as we can," he ordered, "We may have to run this last bit on one engine, but not until we really have to."

Three hours later, they pulled into the harbor of Easter Island and proceeded to dock. It took a half hour to convince the customs officer that they were escapees from Ducie Island and Randal needed to contact his office immediately and get help out here. And, of course, they had a lot of explaining to do about their two dead friends and why the yacht looked like Swiss cheese from the hundreds of bullet holes and damage to the bridge.

The local Coast Guard was dispatched to the approximate location to see and recover any survivors of the fire fight. No boat or bodies were found, just some wreckage floating around the big blue ocean.

Diane, Randal and Morgan were rushed to the hospital leaving Bryce, Josh, Amber and Freddy to talk with the local police and customs about the attack. The police immediately concluded it was a random attack from local pirates; they had been having trouble lately with them and were working on getting it under control and failing.

Sitting across the street at a small coffee shop was Captain Visalia, Soto's head assassin. He was sipping on a cup of coffee and eating a cinnamon roll. He saw the ambulance leave with Randal and the girls; all three looked in bad shape, but from his distance he could not be sure. A coroner's vehicle pulled up seconds later, and out jumped a man and a woman; they rushed into the customs building and although he could not see, he assumed they went directly to the damaged yacht. This told him that someone had died in the assault, he had executed. But whom, he did not know; and would not until he got to the morgue to find out. It really didn't matter to him anyway; he had been ordered to kill all but Randal and the Pierce kids and that was what he planned on doing. He did wonder what had happened out there, and where his men were. If they did not return soon, he would assume they were all dead. Visalia might have to hire some local talent to finish the job.

"Holy shit!" yelled one of the technicians.

"What is it?" Horatio asked as he walked over to the technician who was pointing at the radar screen.

"We have company."

"How long before they get here?" Horatio asked.

"They are overhead now; how did they get here so fast?" the technician commented.

"I don't know," Horatio said to the technician.

"They must be fighter jets from a carrier," the technician said looking very worried.

"I need to find my dad," Horatio said and ran out of the radar room heading for where he thought his father would be. Horatio was running across the deck, but stopped when he heard the roar of jet engines. Looking up toward the sound, he saw four F-35s flying about a thousand feet over the water heading straight for the *Bonaventure*.

"Dad, dad," he yelled when he found his father in the galley getting a cup of coffee. Down here, he could not hear the fighter jets flying overhead.

"What is it my son?" Rocky asked looking up to see his son rush into the galley.

"Fighter jets, American fighter jets are overhead," he burst out.

"Nothing to worry about; we are just an old tramp freighter heading from Peru to Fiji. They can't stop us or even board us from up there, and they don't dare fire on us without knowing we are a threat. So relax, they are grabbing at straws and are looking for an island which is well behind us. There is no way they can be sure that we came from there. Get something to drink; and let's go up on deck and watch the air show."

"Okay, if you say so." Horatio grabbed a soda and both of them walked out of the galley and up to the deck to see the fighters.

"They are probably heading to Ducie Island and hope to find someone there. They likely have some kind of transport plane behind them with troops to drop or land there. We are gone; they will not find anything and in another hour the whole place will blow up and destroy any thing we may have left. Don't worry. I have it under control. I sent a team of our commandoes to Easter Island in the C-130 that we had hidden on the island. They are to eliminate everyone except the Randal's and the kids. Their fate is set; and when they arrive back in the states, they will be arrested and thrown in jail. And they are tasked to make it look like Randal killed them," Rocky stated as he pointed to the formation of F-35Cs. "Ah, US Navy, there must be a carrier somewhere out there; tell the Captain to be on the lookout for the carrier and other military ships and aircraft and to keep all weapons cold and out of sight, for now."

"Okay, be right back," Horatio said and then started to run but was stopped by his father.

"Don't run, walk!" Rocky yelled at his son.

CVN 78 *Gerald R Ford* super aircraft carrier
"Skeeter, Home Plate," the Combat Control Officer on the *Enterprise* called over the radio to the lead F-35 flying toward Ducie Island.

"Home Plate, Skeeter, here. We have checked out four freighters north of the Pitcairn Island chain. Nothing out of the ordinary," Skeeter replied, "Heading for the island now, ETA four minutes."

"Roger, Skeeter, report upon arrival."

"What's the ETA of the transports?" Skeeter asked.

"Six hours, minimum."

"We will stay on station as long as fuel allows; see you soon."

"We are heading your way; our ETA is twelve hours," the CCO said and then placed the microphone in its cradle. He stopped and looked at the activity on the flight deck, preparation of three Seahawk helicopters with long range fuel tanks and a team of Marines were being executed on the hanger deck for an assault of the island.

"Commander, what's the status?" Admiral 'Bear' Henderson asked as he entered the flight control tower near the top of the island.

"Admiral, glad to see you made the trip over from your son's boat to our little island," the CCO said seeing the Admiral walking toward him. "We have four F-35s heading to Ducie Island; they have seen several freighters well north of the island but nothing suspicious."

"Sir. Emergency Action Message just came in, Eyes Only," a young yeoman said as she rushed into the control room, stopped and saluted the Admiral and her Commander.

"Thank you." The CCO took the message, opened it and looked very pale when he read it, "Has this been authenticated?"

"Yes sir."

"Thank you," he said and then handed the message to Admiral Henderson.

"Make the order," Henderson stated and then sat in the command chair.

"Exec, order General Quarters, we have just gone to DEFCON Three," the CCO ordered.

There are five levels of the DEFCON Warning system. DEFCON Three is known as Round House, and it increases the force readiness above that required for normal readiness. DEFCON one is an indication that nuclear war is imminent. The message that had arrived on the *Ford* this afternoon ordered DEFCON Three because three high ranking members of the cabinet had been murdered in the Oval Office by the President of the United States. President Tony Sanford was now in custody pending a full investigation. He was being held in a secure location under heavy guard and a suicide watch. This event constituted a violation of national security.

"Captain, where is my son's boat now?" Admiral Henderson asked.

"He is about three hundred yards off our port bow at four hundred feet. Why do you ask? Thinking about going back to the sardine can?"

"No, but I may need to send them on a side mission again."

Chapter 55 Stitches

Josh was lying on the operating table feeling useless; he had failed in protecting the people he had vowed to protect. Now two were dead and another two were injured. The nurse that stood at the head of the operating table raised the mask and placed it over his nose; he was already half asleep because of the drugs they had injected in him so resisting was impossible. He fell into a deep sleep regretting everything that had happen in the past week.

Down the hall, Diane was going through a similar procedure; her wounds were serious and removal of the bullet would be a tricky operation. The bullet that struck her was located next to her liver and very close to her spine. It was a tricky operation and she could end up paralyzed if the bullet was too close or lodged in her spine.

Four hours later, Randal was resting in the recovery room; they had removed two bullets and patched his head where one had grazed his temple. The headache he had slowly gone away because of the drugs they were pumping into him. The curtains were drawn; and the only sound he heard was the steady beeping of the machines he was hooked up to.

A nurse walked in and saw that he was awake and asked, "How are you feeling, sir?"

"I have had better days. How are the two ladies that came in with me?" he asked quietly, finding it difficult to speak.

"The one with the leg wound is in a bed just down the hall from you, recovering," she replied. "The one with the bullet wounds in her back is still in ICU, listed as serious; but we are watching her closely. We have high hopes she will recover fully. But only time will tell."

"Thank you," he quietly said and then fell asleep.

"I am calling about three gunshot wounded patients," Stephanie said to the receptionist when the nurse answered the phone.

"Just a moment, please." After a long pause, the receptionist continued, "I am transferring you to the ER recovery desk."

"Yes, Ma'am are you related to any of the patients?" the nurse asked before transferring her.

"The man that was brought in is my husband; when can I come down to see him?" Stephanie asked.

"Two are in recovery, should be awake in an hour or two so you can visit. The other one is in ICU and under constant watch."

"Thank you," Stephanie said and then was about to hang up the phone.

"Wait, there was a gentleman that called a while ago asking about them, is he with your party?" the nurse asked.

"Did he give a name?"

"No, just asked their condition about which I could not say any more than what I told you. He did say he would stop by soon."

"Thank you, please call the police, and have them put protection on those three; they may be in danger. We will be right down," Stephanie requested before she hung up.

The nurse started to dial the phone, when a tall man walked up to the nurse and said, "I am here to question the three that were involved with the shootings."

"And you are?"

"Sorry, Detective Sergeant Mark Bond." He showed some credentials of the detective sergeant that he had killed just an hour earlier and whose body he had left in a trash container not far from the hospital.

"Just a second sir," she said as she looked at her control board. "They are still in recovery sir and will be awake in a couple of hours," she lied, not believing the detective. "Can you come back in a couple of hours?"

"Sure, hard to talk to anyone if they are still asleep. I will be back soon. Thank you," he said and then walked out the door.

He exited the hospital, but did not leave the area. He walking over to the car he had taken from the dead detective, opened the door, sat behind the wheel, and waited. He suspected that some of the rest would show up soon, and he wanted to be here when they did.

He did not have to wait long. He watched young Amber and Josh Pierce, Stephanie Randal, Bryce McClelland and Freddy Carlson climb out of a couple of cabs and enter the hospital.

Chapter 56 CIA Undercover

Kelly Donavan parked his rental car in the visitor parking area located about one hundred fifty feet from the lobby entrance. He had easily passed through the front gate fooling the gate guard with his fake IDs and pleasant smile. He climbed out of the car, admired the beautiful weather of Northern Virginia, not too hot, a few clouds, no rain today.

This made wearing the mask much easier, so he wouldn't sweat under it. Sweating under the mask was a problem, as it could cause the mask to come loose. On the other side of the coin, if it was too hot outside, most people would sweat and there would be visible sweat on their forehead. The mask did not sweat and might give away the fact that he was wearing a mask.

He loved this old building and what it stood for, having worked for the company for the better part of twenty years before hanging up his shield. And now there was someone trying to destroy everything that he and Josh Randal had successfully accomplished since they took over. The reputation of this building and the people in it was never better. The things the men and women could do, once they received more funding and better equipment, for freedom was beyond real.

"Kelly Donavan, here to see, ah, Rebecca Haynes," Davin stated as he approached the guard station.

"Yes, she is expecting you. Please have a seat over there," the guard said as he pointed to the chairs on Davin's right.

"Mr. Donavan, good afternoon. I am Rebecca Haynes," she said as she entered the lobby. "Let's talk in the conference room, off the lobby." Pointing toward an open door on the far side of the lobby.

After entering the room, she pulled the door closed and pressed the secure button which immediately turned the room into a secure facility that kept any recording devices from working and prevented anyone outside the room from monitoring what was being said. She walked over to Davin and immediately gave him a huge hug.

"Good to see you, Becky," he responded; and when she released him, he pulled a chair out for her to sit and then sat across from her.

"Davin, ah, Mr. Donavan, your backstop is in place as I said earlier and should hold for as long as you need it. Now, as far as Mr. Soto and his displaced team is concerned, he has been a very busy little man. Here are all the files I could get on him and his team. You are not going to be happy with what I found, but most likely you already know most of this."

"First, what's with the President?" Davin asked quickly.

"Like I told you; he shot and killed three people in the Oval Office. From what I found out, he used a Colt Commander forty-five caliber pistol with a silencer, two shots to each, one in the chest, the other in the head. Then he walked out of the office and his secretary said he walked down the hall to the elevator to the residence and that was the last anyone saw of him. She did not know what he had done since the office is completely sound proof. He was found wandering around the Washington Monument with a gun in his hand; he seemed dazed and confused. Two of our analysts are over at FBI talking to him. They reported that he said he had been kidnapped by Josh Randal and you, taken somewhere, and held captive until he woke up on a bench at the monument with the gun in his hand. How he got there, he doesn't remember. That's all they have reported so far. So, you are wanted for kidnapping and murder."

"Wow, they are building a pretty strong case against me and Josh, aren't they," Davin commented.

"Yes, they are; and if they found out that I was talking to you, I would be in jail too. But I am not worried about that, I know you are innocent. You are innocent, aren't you?" she asked.

"I am innocent, and with your help I plan on proving that both Josh and I are innocent," Davin said. He paused for a second and then said, "Now what's this about Soto; does he have someone named Richard working for him?"

"Do you suspect him being behind all this?" Becky asked being very concerned about everything that was going on.

"Yes, very sure. I don't know why; but in light of what is going on, and the use of some of our own technology, it points directly to him. But I have no evidence to prove it, yet."

"May I bring in someone else that might be of help with this?"

"Sure, who do you have in mind?"

"Helen Owens, head of the department that Soto used to run."

"Bring her down," Davin agreed.

"I will be right back," she said and left the room, returning a few seconds later. "She will be right down; she knows Kelly for now. We can brief her later if you wish."

A light knock on the door interrupted them; Becky got up and let Helen in the room, securing the door and setting the control to secure.

"Helen, I would like to introduce you to Kelly Donavan. He is a private investigator working on the Davin Pierce case in cooperation with the Arlington Police. Kelly, this is Helen Owens."

"Pleasure, Miss Owens. Rebecca says you may have some information that may be helpful to the investigation?"

"Yes, we are secure here, correct?" After getting a nod from Becky, she continued, "I received a call from Josh Randal a little while ago; and after verification that he was who he said he was, we talked. He was kidnapped and taken to an island in the South Pacific along with his wife, four students, their professor and the Pierce's twin children. He said they were not supposed to get away, but they did and are now on Easter Island and waiting for transportation back to the states."

'My kids are alive,' Davin almost blurted out, but held his tongue and just smiled a lot. He finally managed to say, "But the president is being held for murder. How could Randal and Pierce have kidnapped him, when he had never left the White House until after the murders? Did you verify that Randal was really out of the country? He may be out of the country right now, but when did he leave to get there; or was the call really from Easter Island?"

"That may be true, but I would believe Mr. Randal or Pierce before the evidence," Becky commented.

"Are you sure the person you talked to was Josh Randal?" Kelly asked.

"Yes, I asked him a couple of questions that only he would know," Helen stated.

"That is very interesting," Kelly said.

"How so?" Helen asked being curious about the statement.

"Not sure, yet. Things are just not adding up or falling into place as they should," Kelly stated and then just sat and looked at the two women across from him.

"If there is anything else you need from me, Mr. Donavan, just call. Do you have a card in case I hear from Mr. Randal again?" Helen said as she stood to leave.

"Thank you, Miss. Owens. Here is my card. Please call when you hear from Mr. Randal; I would like to talk to him. Have him call me at the number on the card," Kelly said as he handed her his card and walked her to the door. Becky walked over and pressed the secure button to unsecure the room before opening the door, and then pressed again once she left to secure it again.

Chapter 57 Convictions

Stephanie and the Pierce kids were sitting in the waiting room when the nurse approached and told them that Josh was being moved to a private room and they could go in and see him in a few minutes.

A few minutes turned into a half hour, but finally they were told they could go into room 324.

"Can we see Diane and Morgan?"

"Who? Oh, you mean the two Janes. One is in room 328; she is awake. You can go in if you wish. The other one is still in ICU; I will let you know when she comes out," the nurse said and then walked away. She stopped just short of the door, turned and continued, "I forgot to mention both rooms have police guards on them; you will have to identify yourselves to them before they will let you in."

"Understood. Thank you," Stephanie said as she headed for the door behind the nurse. "Can we get her moved to this room with Mr. Randal; it would be safer for her."

"I will check and let you know," the nurse said as she left.

"Hello, may I speak to Director Adam Cruz?" Randal asked when he heard a familiar voice answer the phone; he was still in pain and a bit high on morphine, but needed to talk to his office.

"I am sorry sir, but Mr. Cruz is not available. Is there anyone else you would want to speak with?" the receptionist asked, recognizing Josh Randal's voice.

"Is this Laura? This is Josh Randal; I need to speak to whoever is the highest ranking person there," Josh stated.

"Mr. Randal, I know it is you; but you should know that Mr. Cruz is dead, and Mr. Pierce is in jail. You are in charge," Laura stated quietly.

"I know I am in charge, but I am not there right now. Who is the duty officer today?" Josh asked, letting her comment about Cruz and Pierce slide, but wondering what the hell was going on back home.

"Are you all right Mr. Randal? That would be Ms. Helen Owens; she is the duty officer today. Let me connect you. Just a moment, please."

"Not completely, but don't worry; I will be okay shortly. Please connect me to Miss. Owens."

"Good afternoon, Josh, I guess you have heard about Mr. Cruz and Mr. Pierce. How can I help you?" Helen Owens said sounding a little confused about the call from Randal when she had seen him leave the building a few hours ago.

"First I am not in Washington; I am right now in a hospital on Easter Island with Stephanie. We were kidnapped; and, well, I will fill you in later on the rest of that."

"But you can't be on Easter Island; I just talked with you a couple of hours ago. Wait did you say you were in a hospital?" Helen asked.

"Yes, got into a little fight; and well, the other guy is in the morgue. But please, listen to me Helen," Josh stated knowing that she did not believe him.

"Is this some kind of joke? I saw you leaving the building a short bit ago; wait, you are not kidding are you?" Helen seemed very confused.

"Helen Owens, I personally promoted you to head of the R and D when I fired Rocky Soto. Remember what I said to you that day?"

"Yes, I will never forget it."

"I have never repeated that to anyone and whoever is there that looks like me, is not me and would not know what I told you. Would he?"

"No I guess he wouldn't."

Josh repeated the words that he had told her privately and then said "Do you believe me now?"

"Yes, but who is in your office? He looks and talks like you, his finger prints match the system and well, oh hell. He is using a holographic projection of you, just like I showed you; no, like I showed Mr. Pierce and his team. In every way, he is you."

"You have a holographic projection system?" Randal asked and almost laughed, but it hurt too bad to laugh.

"Yes, Soto was working on it when you fired him; and my team and I completed it. It works, but only for a limited time."

"How long?"

"About two hours, give or take a few minutes," Helen replied.

"That's how they did it." After pausing for a second he continued, "Look, don't confront him; he is dangerous. We have to stop this. Do you have any idea where Davin is?"

"Last I saw of him; he was leaving the building with a couple of cops early this morning. And you need to know there is a warrant for the arrest of his kids, Josh and Amber, on multiple charges of Grand Theft Auto and a long list of other charges."

"I need you to do something that isn't in your job description."

"What do you need?"

"We have no money down here. I need the company G-5 to come down here and transport us back to the states. Have them bring cash and credit cards for Stephanie. I will be the only one flying back for now, that's if they release me from this hospital bed. Until we resolve this, the kids need to stay here. I need you to be my eyes on the inside until I get there. And last and most important, connect me to Admiral Henderson."

Chapter 58 Undersea Navy

Lieutenant Commander Henderson was standing in the control room of his nuclear missile boat thinking about dinner. He was hungry and tonight was steak night on board his boat. It only happened once every two weeks, but his boat's mess steward knew how to prepare a great steak even at four hundred feet below the ocean waves. He was worried about his friends; and there was nothing he could do from where he was.

"Duty Officer you have the con. I'm going to dinner," Lieutenant Commander Henderson said as he looked around the control room as he was leaving. The boat's commander was already in the board room waiting for him.

"Sir, Emergency Action Message," the communications officer announced over the shipboard intercom. "I will be right up with it."

"Waiting Smitty," Henderson replied, knowing that the transmission of an EAM over the very low frequency system that the Navy utilized to communicate with submerged submarines was slow in the best of times. He didn't have to wait long, Smitty walked in carrying the message, followed by his communications assistant holding the authentication tablet.

"Decrypt and authenticate," Henderson ordered.

"Authenticated, sir; it is real," Smitty said as he handed the paper to Henderson. After reading the message, Henderson immediately ordered the boat to General Quarters and announced that they were now at DEFCON Three. He picked up the shipboard intercom and asked for the board room. "Captain would you please report to the control room,

ASAP." He had barely finished the request when the captain walked into the control room and looked at Henderson with concern.

"What do we have that put us at DEFCON Three and took me away from a great rib-eye steak?" he asked.

"The president has been arrested for killing the Secretary of Defense, Commander of Atlantic Fleet and a General from the Air Force. That's all the details we have sir," Henderson said and handed him the message.

"Verified?"

"Yes sir."

"Okay, bring us up to periscope depth and raise the antenna. I need to talk with your dad."

"Bring the boat up to six zero feet and raise the antenna," Henderson ordered and watched everyone jump into action.

Twenty-five minutes later, after the commander had a long private discussion with Admiral Henderson on board the *Gerald Ford*, he ordered the antenna retracted, dove to eight hundred feet, and proceeded at flank speed toward Easter Island. This would leave the carrier group with only one nuclear submarine, but he did not think they would need both for a few days; and this had just taken priority.

A nuclear submarine was much faster submerged than it was on the surface and cruising at flank speed they could travel the twelve-hundred-mile distance quicker down under than on the surface and do it without being seen.

"We can do nothing else up here Henderson, let's eat steak; it may be the last good meal we get for a while," his commander said and they both walked out of the control room and headed for the board room one deck below.

Without saying a word, Henderson followed his commander to the board room for dinner and a quiet private discussion with his boss. He was very interested in hearing what his father, the Admiral, had told his commander; and if he stayed in the control room, he was not going to get the answers he needed. Why were they rushing to Easter Island? What was there that had required them to leave the carrier group? Were they going alone?

Chapter 59 Time to Call in the Calvary

Kelly Donavan walked to his car and smiled a little. He knew that he had little to smile about. Although he had learned a lot from the file that Becky had provided, he still did not know where Soto was, or when or how he was going to nail him to a cross. That man had destroyed his life, and the lives of his family and friends.

After starting the car, he slipped it in reverse and backed out of the parking spot. He turned to head out of the hotel lot when he saw three police cars screaming into the hotel lot. He stopped to let them pass and hoped they were not here for him. Moments later, the cops jumped out of their cars and ran toward a room on the first floor passing by Davin. The last officer stopped, looked into the window and then said, "You need to move on, Sir."

"Yes, sir," Donavan responded and drove his car out onto the street and headed toward Washington. It was time to pay and Soto was about to pay big time.

While driving to the Annapolis Navy Yard, he thought about his plan to enlist the help of some old friends. Hopefully he could find them. When he pulled up to the gate at the naval yard, he stopped, produced his identification, and stated that he needed to speak with Admiral Henderson. The guard directed him to the command headquarters building.

After he parked out front, Donavan got out and walked up to the front door, entered and stopped at the front desk where he showed his identification and asked to see Admiral Henderson.

"Sorry sir, the Admiral is not here and hasn't been here for several weeks. Was he expecting you?" the guard asked.

"Actually no; I meant to call ahead, but, well, no excuses. Is his aide in?"

"No, they are both on extended sea duty, by choice, no less. But I was told he would return by the end of the week. Can I make an appointment for you?"

"No, I really have a need to speak to the Admiral as soon as possible. Is there a way to contact him?"

"I suppose so; let me get the Staff Duty Officer and see what we can do," the guard said, as he picked up the desk phone, and dialed a number for the duty officer.

"Sir, we have a Mr. Kelly Donavan down here that needs to speak to the Admiral on an urgent matter." After pausing to listen, he replied, "Yes, sir, I will tell him."

"Mr. Donavan, Commander Drake said to wait here; he will be over in a minute and take you to the communication center. But he needs to know the nature of the emergency."

"No problem," Donavan said and then turned to locate a chair to sit and wait. Upon seeing no chair was available, he just stood there and waited.

"Mr. Donavan, I am Commander Drake, the Staff Duty Officer; I understand you need to talk to the Admiral on an urgent matter. Will you fill me in on this urgent matter?"

"Sure, is there somewhere we can talk privately?" Donavan agreed.

"My office is just across the parking lot; it's pretty secure. We can do there." Commander Drake said.

"Let's go," Donavan said and followed Drake across the parking lot.

"Commander, I am with the company and we have reason to believe that a group of terrorists have kidnapped several high level government officials. I have been tasked to ask for the Navy's help in locating them. There is a good possibility they are on a ship somewhere out there," Donavan stated handing the commander his CIA credentials.

"Okay, I believe we can help with that," Commander Drake agreed. "The Admiral is on the *Gerald Ford* in the South Pacific, so it may take a bit to reach him; but let's try to reach him."

"I assume they have SAT phones out there."

"Yes, of course, this is the modern Navy," Commander Drake said joking around.

After dialing the number, he had for the *Ford*, he waited for a connection.

"You have reached the *Gerald Ford*; how may I direct your call?" a sweet female voice said when the phone was answered.

"This is Commander Drake, Staff Duty Officer, Annapolis Navy Yard. Is Admiral Henderson available?"

"Give me a moment to locate him, sir," she said and then clicked hold.

They waited and waited, four minutes passed and then five, six and seven; and finally she came back online and said, "Sorry for the wait, sir. He will be on in just a minute."

"Admiral Henderson, Commander, how can I help you?" he said after another three minutes passed.

"Admiral, I have a Mr. Kelly Donavan here from the company; he needs your assistance. Here is Mr. Donavan," he stated and handed Kelly the secure phone.

"Thank you Commander; Admiral, Kelly Donavan, we need your assistance..." he started and then told the Admiral all he knew and when finished the Admiral filled him in on what he knew, putting more blocks into place.

"Just so you know, I have a nuclear sub and a fast frigate heading toward Easter Island as we speak. A flight of F-35s are over Ducie Island and a C-5A Super Transport is almost there with a platoon of marines. I believe we have the area under control. As for Mr. Soto, we don't know if he is still on the island or not. That will be answered as soon as the Marines arrive in about, ah, two hours. Stay in contact with the Commander; and when we get confirmation of the capture of Soto, we will call. If he isn't on the island, then what do you suggest."

"Search all the ships going and coming from anywhere near that island," Donavan stated quickly.

Chapter 60 Mouse Trap

"Nice of you to stop by," Randal said as he saw his wife and the Pierce twins walk into his room.

"Who were you talking to when we came in?" Stephanie asked when she saw him all bandaged up and on the phone. "You just got out of surgery and already on the phone. Keep this up and you are going to kill yourself if I don't do it first," she scolded.

"A friend," he said and then added, "There are people out there trying to kill us and you are worried about a few little holes in me. So sweet, give me a kiss," Josh Randal said with a smile when he saw his wife and two of his favorite children and they were not even his. "Hey, Little Josh and Amber, looks like you two have been in a fight," he joked.

"Just a little one, you should see the other guy," Amber teased smiling at her dad's best friend.

"Look, I was just talking to the company and got some good news and some really bad news," Randal stated and then paused, "I need you to stay here on the island for a while; that is the good news. The bad news is there are warrants for your arrest," he said while he pointed to Josh and Amber.

"What did we do?" Josh asked quickly.

"Supposedly you stole several cars and out ran the police in three states," he answered and then looked at Stephanie and smiled again. "You need to be the den mother and keep everyone safe. Do you still have access to the weapons?"

"No we don't; the police confiscated them when we docked. Said they were evidence, and it was illegal to have weapons on the island. But you have a guard outside the door and there is one guarding Morgan and another with Diane," Stephanie replied and then added, "We almost had to be strip searched before he let us in here."

"He would have enjoyed that I bet," Randal replied and started to laugh, "Oh, don't make me laugh; it hurts," he said holding his side, but not too hard because of the bandages. Reaching over, he pressed the morphine drip to reduce the pain a bit.

"Go easy on that, old man, you are not used to being so high all the time," she said and then sat beside her husband on the bed.

A quiet knock on the door interrupted their chat. Randal yelled but not too loud, "Come in."

The door opened and Detective Sergeant Mark Bond entered the room and closed and locked the door behind him.

"Well, well, we meet again, what a nice little reunion we have," Bond said as he pulled his jacket aside to show the pistol in his belt holster.

"What the hell are you doing here? You will never get away with killing the four of us with a guard standing just outside the door," Randal said quietly.

"Oh, you are misinformed Mr. Randal; I am not here to kill you, at least not yet. I don't need to kill you, because you will die soon enough, all of you."

"So you are going to wait outside and kidnap us, take us someplace quiet and kill us, so classic and old school."

"Maybe so, but it works so well in the movies. I am just going to add a little twist to it. In the movies, they fail to kill the good guys; I don't fail," Bond, aka Captain Visalia stated. "I will be leaving now, keep looking over your shoulders. I will be there sometime; and when I strike, you lose. Just remember, I never lose. You all are dead, but your bodies just don't know it yet."

"Your boys failed on the beach, and again off the coast here; what makes you think you will succeed this time," Stephanie stated as she stared down at Visalia.

"I will succeed. I could kill you right now, but as you say I wouldn't get away. So till we meet again, be safe," Visalia said, unlocked the door, and slipped out. Josh and Stephanie started to go after him, but were stopped by Randal.

"Don't, we will get him soon enough," Randal stated. "Get that guard in here; I want to talk to him."

The guard came in as requested. "Do you know who that man was that just left?" Randal asked.

"Yes, he was Detective Sergeant Bond."

"Have you ever met him before today?"

"No, why do you ask?"

"Because he is not Bond; his name is Visalia, and he may have killed the real Detective Bond."

"But he had his credentials," the officer said.

"I know; you had no idea. You need to report this to your superiors immediately. He could have killed us when he was here, but didn't," Randal said and then dismissed the officer.

After the officer left, he walked over to the nurses' station and asked to use the phone. He needed to call his station and report the incident.

"Stephanie, we are safe in here. The officer will report it and they will send more police. But we cannot stay here forever; besides, I need to get on a plane and fly to D.C."

"No way, Josh, you are not leaving us here alone with that maniac," Stephanie protested.

"I will not leave until he is either dead or in jail," Randal promised.

"You better not leave us alone here," Stephanie stated again.

"We need to set a trap for that old boy and then spring it," Randal stated; after thinking for a second, he said, "I need some paper, a pencil and a calculator."

Chapter 61 Run Don't Walk

A thousand miles away on a remote little island in the South Pacific, a United States Air Force C-5A Super Galaxy transport approached the island of Ducie from the northeast and made a low approach, banking to the north, as it descended to one thousand feet. The pilot eyed the small atoll with concern; she had been told there were two airports on it, but could not be promised that they were in good enough condition to land on.

Major Rhonda Olson, aka Hula Girl, had more than six thousand hours flying the beast and had landed in places that were less inviting than this island. To look at her you would think she could handle a large airplane like this one. Standing five foot four, one hundred and forty pounds, dark hair and brown eyed she had everyone fooled.

The runways were long enough, originally built to support fighter aircraft during the World War II, and they looked in relatively good condition from the air. She planned on making one low pass; and if it looked safe enough, she would land her beast. Otherwise, her cargo of Marines would have to bail out and she would just fly home without them, missing out on the fun again.

After passing over the southernmost air field, she banked again over the lagoon and eyed the northern air field, which was closest to their objective. She dropped her flaps and then banked again to line up with the longest runway, dropped the landing gear, and pulled back the throttles.

"We are on final approach to Ducie Island; it is a short runway, so make sure you are buckled in tight. We will be on the ground in three minutes. Get your suntan lotion out and ready," Major Olson announced over the intercom. "Check list, Jim."

"Landing gear, check," Jim started to read down the checklist as Rhonda answered him when the item was complete. Three and a half minutes later, the main gear touched down on the rough runway. When she pulled back on the throttles past the indent to reverse thrusters, the huge aircraft quickly diminished speed to a slow roll.

"Open the hatch," Major Rhonda Olson ordered her crew chief Sergeant Blake and then saw the red indicator light come on as the rear cargo door was lowered.

"All you marines, get off my plane," she yelled over the intercom, and pressed the green light button on her console which signaled them to unbuckle and leave.

"Run, don't walk. Go get that ass," Rhonda continued as she completed her order.

One hundred four marines in full combat gear raced off the cargo ramp and in precision movements divided up and entered the jungle, heading directly for the secure compound.

After a short hike through the bush, Captain Walter Phillips halted his men just outside the compound and surveyed the area before sending in a small team to check it out. The team moved out and entered the compound through the open gate and spread out, looking for anyone or anything that would give them a clue.

"Rambo one this is Rambo four, the compound is empty, but we did find some explosives. Wait until we disarm them," the team leader called to his commander.

"Roger, Rambo four. Advise when clear," Phillips responded and then ordered teams two, three and five to spread out and search all around the compound.

An hour later, all five teams had reported all clear. Captain Phillips called back to his plane and reported all clear.

"Hula Girl, Rambo One. All clear here. Looks like they vacated quickly, this area is secure. I have sent a team back to retrieve our vehicles from your bird." Captain Phillips, aka Rambo One, spoke into the microphone.

"Rambo One, roger, vehicles are fueled and ready." Major Rhonda Olson said.

"Thanks, Hula Girl." Phillips replied and then clicked off the radio.

"Call the Ford and report all clear on the island," Rhonda ordered her co-pilot as she walked to the back of her plane and looked at the jungle around her. From the air, she had thoughts of lying on the white sandy beach on an island somewhere; and now after seeing this little bit of tropical paradise, she imagined it again. "Hey, Jim, did you bring your bathing suit?"

"In my travel bag, why?" he asked.

"Well, we are going to be here for a few days, and I thought why not go over to that beach and catch some rays; the sun will not set for several hours. Get your bag and let's go to the beach. Bring your weapon; we may encounter a sea monster and need to defend ourselves," Rhonda said and then ran back into the plane and grabbed her travel bag. She opened it, retrieved her bikini, a towel and her sidearm, a nine millimeter Berretta. "Let's go." Pausing she looked over at her Crew chief and spoke to him, "Sergeant Blake, stay with the plane, get both Humvees and Helo unloaded and ready for Captain Phillips. We will be back in a couple of hours."

"Do you think that is wise, Major. There may be hostiles out there," Sergeant Blake responded.

"I did not see any hostiles, and we will be armed. Carry on, Sergeant," she ordered with a smile. "Oh, when done, secure the bird and join us; bring the cooler. It has some drinks."

"You got it Major," Sergeant Blake replied,

"Captain Stanis is asleep up on the top deck; you may need to wake him and his co-pilot. If you need me, call on the radio, I have mine on channel six. Also, call so we know you are coming, so I can tell you where we are." Olson said with a wink.

Chapter 62 Lock and Load

"Admiral, we just got a message from Ducie Island," the yeoman reported to the admiral.

"What did they say?" Admiral Henderson asked, "Just read it."

"Captain Phillips reports the compound is empty; they have secured the northern part of the island and have sent a team to the south end to secure it also."

"Thank you, yeoman," Admiral Henderson said and then turned to the captain and asked. "Where is the *Dolphin* and *Baitfish*?" referring to the sub and frigate they had sent to Easter Island.

"They will arrive in about an hour or so," the Captain answered as he studied the chart in front of him. "We are here, Easter Island here, and Ducie here," he said as he pointed to each spot on the chart. Shipping lanes are about here." He drug his finger from Lima, Peru to Fiji and to the U.S. But that is only a couple of the many established shipping lanes. There could be hundreds of ships in the Pacific Ocean at any one time. If Soto and his merry men left by way of boat, they could be anywhere by now; we don't know when they left or which direction they headed. What do you propose we do Admiral?"

"How many birds do we have on board?"

"Are you proposing what I think you are about to propose?" the Captain asked knowing the answer before he asked.

"Yes, launch all but a few to protect the fleet, and send them out looking for that one strange boat that looks like it is escaping from jail," the Admiral stated and then thought for a moment, "No scratch that; it would be a waste of man power and lots of fuel. We need to come up with a better plan."

"I have to agree. But what? We don't have enough information to just go out and search every ship and plane in the area. And we don't have the manpower either," the Captain agreed and studied the chart in front of him, thinking. "Do you think this Soto is responsible for all this; or is it true that the president killed three people in the Oval Office and that the Assistant Director Davin Pierce killed his replacement?"

"I have known Pierce for years; and unless he has completely cracked, he would never kill unless he had a good reason or was ordered to do so. As for Randal being kidnapped and almost killed on Ducie Island, that I believe and trust Randal to be telling the truth. But he only knows part of the story; maybe I should get back to the states and assist in finding out the whole story."

"I will get a crew together and fly you to Panama where you can catch a transport back to D.C."

"Not yet, Cap. Not yet," Admiral Henderson said and looked at the chart that the captain was studying. "What I really want is to lock and load on this ass and blow him to hell and back. But we can't do that because we don't know where he is."

"My feelings exactly, Admiral."

Chapter 63 A Better Mouse Trap

"This fake detective expects us to walk into his trap and die; we need to make sure it doesn't happen that way, kind of like what we did on the island," and Randal started to explain his idea.

"You better have a good plan, because this time we don't have any weapons, any jungle to sneak through, or Diane to walk naked to distract him," little Josh commented; he was getting used to being called Little Josh but it had taken awhile.

"So true, but we do have the US Navy," Randal stated and then pointed out the window to the ocean view that he had from the third story window of his hospital room.

"The Navy, when did they get here?" Stephanie asked looking out the window at the U.S. Navy Frigate *Baitfish*.

"Just a few minutes ago; somehow we need to talk to whoever is in charge on that frigate," Randal stated.

"That should not be hard, look what is coming up beside the frigate," little Josh said as he gazed out the window at the sleek form of a nuclear submarine coming into view.

Two hours after Randal and his team saw the arrival of the submarine and frigate, the guard outside Randal's room knocked and poked his head in and said they had another visitor.

"Sir, do you know a Commander Henderson?" he asked the room.

"Yes, is he a Commander or Admiral?" Stephanie piped in.

"Commander, he insists on talking to you. Should I shoot him or let him in?" the guard joked.

"Shoot him," Randal replied and then quickly said, "No wait, if he is tall and with a buzz haircut then let him in, nobody in their right mind would wear his or her hair like that unless they were in the Navy. Let him in."

The officer swung the door open wider to let LT Commander David Henderson enter. As soon as he was in the room, Stephanie gave him a big hug and a kiss on the check.

"Hey, get your hands off my wife, you cad," Randal yelled at the son of his best friend. "What brings you to our humble little spot on the earth?"

"Orders from dad; of course, he told me that you and Davin got yourself into a bucket of very hot water and needed me and my boys to save your ass again. Sorry. Save your butts again."

"Well, that is putting it mildly. Have you heard the whole story?"

"As much as we can get from the news services and your office; hopefully you can add a bit more to it," Henderson commented.

Randal and Stephanie filled Henderson in on what they knew, from their kidnapping, the island and their escape in an old yacht called *Freedom*. She added the little firefights they had and the loss of Redmond and Vince and the damage that was done to Josh, Diane, Morgan and the others.

"Okay, you say that one of the commandoes is here on this island. And he visited you here, and has threatened to kill all of you." After a short pause, he then said, "What can the Navy do for you?"

"We need to set up the perfect mouse trap and make sure he walks into it," Randal stated confidently.

"Easier said than done, Josh," Henderson replied smiling.

"A true statement, but with your help we can make it work. How many marines do you have on board?"

"A platoon."

"Civilian clothes, hand guns only except for four snipers. We will have to clear the op with the local police and customs. But I believe they will let us run this without complaining too much. You will have to do the talking; if we leave this building too soon, he will do his best to kill us as promised. Exactly when or where would be his decision. We need to change that decision."

Randal outlined his plan and then asked Henderson to grease the skids with the locals and to get his marines briefed and ready for a fight, one they would not lose.

"We do this tomorrow morning at nine. The nurse said they will release me then, if I am ready." He finished and then looked at his wife and the kids. "Dave, can you order some of those marines here to escort my wife and the rest back to the hotel and protect them for the night?"

"Sure, no problem," he said, pulled out his phone, and placed an order for eight marines in civilian clothes and only handguns. "They will be here in less than two hours. Lieutenant Craft will report to you."

"Good. Now Steph, you take everyone back and get some sleep. Have you checked on Morgan and Diane?"

"Yes, they are doing fine. Diane is not able to be moved, just yet; but in a few days, she will be up and teasing all the male doctors around here."

"Good, I was worried about Diane."

Chapter 64 A Much Better Mouse Trap

Two hours later, a team of marines walked into the hospital one or two at a time; they spaced their entrances between six and ten minutes apart. They thought they would seem less obvious entering that way; all were dressed in tropical clothing, some in shorts and a nice shirt, others in summer slacks and sandals. Each marine carried in the small of their backs either a Berretta nine millimeter pistol or a Glock model 30 forty-five caliber pistol with extra magazines.

Two marines stayed in the lobby to see if anyone suspicious followed them in, and three remained near the nurses' station on the third floor, while Lieutenant Craft introduced himself to the officer at the door of room 324 and was then allowed access to the room.

"Good evening, ah, everyone. Lieutenant Robert Craft, USN. I have five more marines waiting to escort you to your hotel, Mrs. Randal."

"I guess it is time to go; see you in the morning," Stephanie said as she stood, walked over to Josh and kiss him hard on the lips and then walked toward the door.

"EL. Tee, did you bring something for me?" Randal asked looking at the young marine.

"Yes, sir." After receiving a paper bag from the marine, Randal quickly glanced inside and smiled.

"What did you bring him, Craft?" Stephanie asked quickly, standing at the door ready to leave.

"A new toy, thanks EL. Tee. I will return it when this is over." Randal said to the young lieutenant.

"Hopefully, you will not need to use it," Craft commented and then looked at Stephanie. She and the kids followed Craft out and met with Bryce and Freddy in the hallway.

Morning came like it always did on a tropical island, with a large splash of sun and rising temperature. The temperature was already warm and climbing to a daily normal of about eighty-five degrees.

Over the night, long before the sun came up, twelve teams of marines left the confines of their frigate and moved on shore. They rented cars and positioned themselves along the route that would be used to bring Randal and his team into harm's way, one more time. Midway between the hospital and the hotel was a small coffee shop; several of the marines positioned themselves there which provided them with an excellent view of the road. Snipers were also positioned along the route on top of buildings that provided complete coverage of the hospital and the hotel.

The plan was for Stephanie, Little Josh, and Bryce to drive to the hospital and get Randal, Morgan and hopefully Diane. Amber and Freddy would wait at the hotel until they received a call to go to the coffee shop to meet with everyone else. The local police did not change their routine, and continued regular patrols as if nothing was going on; they had been told there was a military exercise on urban warfare within their city and to not interfere. They were to fade into the woodwork if any shooting started, and would be told when to come back out.

At nine fifteen, Stephanie met with everyone in the lobby along with LT Craft and three marines in civilian clothes.

"Mrs. Randal, I understand you were Miami PD before marrying and worked closely with your husband and Mr.

Pierce at the company," Craft asked when they came together.

"Yes, why do you ask?" she answered curious as to where this was going.

"Here." He handed her a Glock Model 30 forty-five caliber pistol with a ten round magazine.

"Okay, I can handle this," she agreed taking the pistol and checking the magazine for a full load and then slid the slide back to place a round in the chamber.

"I see you haven't forgotten how one of those works."

"No problem," she responded and then slipped the pistol under her blouse and in the waist band of her slacks. "Let's get this party going."

"Roger that little lady," Craft said and then looked at his men and nodded. They started for the door and walked into the sunshine with everyone else in tow. "Shall we walk or ride?"

"Walk, it may draw that bastard out," she stated and headed for the door.

They walked down the street with two marines about twenty feet ahead. Craft and another marine followed but not too close. They needed to draw Visalia out; give him an opportunity to strike and then take him down. The walk was uneventful; no one was shot, and nobody came out to kill any of them. Reaching the hospital at a few minutes after ten, they entered without incident.

After checking with the floor nurse, they were told that neither Randal nor Diane were going to be released; their condition had not improved enough to safely release them.

Morgan was waiting in Room 324 with Josh; she had already been signed out and was ready to leave.

"Yeah, I have to stay for a while longer; they are telling me that the wound on my side is looking infected and are pumping more antibiotics in me to counteract it. They said if they can't stop it, well, it may kill me." Randal stated.

"Holy crap, what next?" Stephanie yelled.

"Did they say how the infection started?" Craft asked.

"They are not sure; may have been an airborne virus," he said.

"Damn, Visalia was here, he may have introduced an airborne virus while here. We need to be tested, now," Bryce stated quickly.

"Call a nurse or doctor," Morgan ordered, Randal pressed his call button and within a couple of minutes a nurse rushed into the room.

"What's the problem?" she asked as she entered.

"We think we have been infected with a virus and need everyone in this room and possibly the entire hospital immediately checked for possible infection," Randal stated quickly.

"What makes you think you have been infected?" the nurse asked.

"A man was in here yesterday that stated he was going to kill all of us and smiled as he left. We believe he was carrying a virus and infected us. That is why Mr. Randal's wound is not healing."

"Stay where you are. I will be right back. We need to take blood from everyone."

An hour later everyone had given blood and it was in the lab being tested for every imaginable virus they could test for. Everyone waited; Morgan and Freddy walked down to visit Diane as they waited for the results.

"If he did infect us with a killer virus, then he has won. But where did he get a biologic that quick," Stephanie asked her husband.

"He may have brought it with him from the island."

"May I have your attention," a doctor asked when he entered room 324 two hours later and he wasn't smiling.

"What is it, doctor?" Randal asked hoping he was here with good news.

"I have good news and some bad news," he started to say and then paused to take a big breath. "You are infected with a very deadly strain of botulism. If not treated quickly, you will die horribly. Well, not all of you, Mr. Craft is not infected, but the rest of you are."

"Do you have the antidote?" Bryce asked for everyone.

"No, that's the bad news," the doctor said sadly.

"Wait, Morgan and Craft were not here when Visalia paid us a visit; how is she infected and Craft not?" Randal said and then thought for a second, "Damn it, the boat; we were infected on the damn boat. They knew we would take it instead of the submarine. They planned for us to take the boat, and we were infected from the beginning. Craft, call your ship and see if they have the antidote," Randal summarized quickly.

"Yes, sir, already dialing," Craft replied and started to speak into the phone, "Doctor, can you tell my Doctor what you need?"

"Sure."

"I guess our better mouse trap backfired," Morgan stated quietly.

"Not exactly, they just outsmarted us, again," Stephanie replied as she looked around at her friends and family. "Are we contagious?"

"Yes, he did outsmart us," Randal said and then looked over at Craft hoping for a positive answer.

"Sir, they have a small amount on the frigate and on my boat. The doctor is contacting the *Ford* and asking them to rush whatever they have. He said they can synthesize some in a few days," Craft replied and then asked the doctor, "Doc, how much time do they have?"

"No, you are not contagious. That is the good news, it takes seven to ten days to incubate the virus; and you have been here two days. We have some time and will administer what we have to slow down the virus. It is luck that we found it early; as it gets stronger, it is more difficult to stop."

"But we spent three days on the boat, so we really only have two, maybe three days before it will be fully incubated. And then to put it mildly, we are toast," Bryce stated.

"Yeah, I forgot that. We need to do something fast," the doctor stated, "I will be right back with some antibiotics," he said and rushed out of the room.

Chapter 65 Mouse Traps Are Dangerous

"Hello," Randal said into the phone after the second ring.

"Good afternoon, Mr. Randal. I hope you are feeling, well, I really want to say, I hope you are not feeling well today."

"Hello Visalia, how are you doing today? Looks like a great day to die, are you ready?" Randal shot back at Captain Visalia.

"Yes it does, Mr. Randal. By my calculations, you have maybe two to three more days to breathe fresh air and then it will be the confines of a small rectangular box."

"Don't count your chickens before they hatch, we are not done yet."

"Is that Visalia?" Bryce asked from across the room.

"Oh, even if you beat the virus, which I do not believe you will, then my men and I will ensure that you die along with everyone else in that hospital. Do you follow what I am saying, Mr. Randal? I prefer to not destroy that hospital; but if you survive, I will have no choice."

"There are innocent people in here. What gives you the right to kill them?" Randal stated growing extremely angry with this homicidal maniac.

"You give me the right. As long as you live in that hospital, they are a target," Visalia stated with conviction.

"We are coming after you, Captain, and you will not win. I swear to you that I will hunt you down and kill you with my bare hands if need be," Randal said and then slammed the handset down, knocking the phone to the floor.

"Calm down, Josh; we will get him," Craft stated and then pressed speed dial one immediately connecting him to the frigate's communications. Speaking quietly into the phone, he got the information he needed and then pulled his team radio from his pocket and contacted his team leaders.

"We have a location; team 2, check it out," Craft said and then passed the location to his team. "Teams three, four and five, remain in place."

"You got a location?" Randal asked.

"Yes, I had our communications section set up and monitor all incoming calls to your room and trace. We got a location, chances are he is gone already, but we will check it out without tipping our hand. We also now have his cell phone IP address and are tracking his movement. We should have him soon."

"Good work, LT. Keep me posted on any updates."

"We will close the trap shortly; I promise you that."

The doctor had sent in nurses to administer antibiotics to everyone except Craft just before the call came in. Randal asked if the doctor would come in for a minute and talk to him and his group, who were sitting around his private room waiting to be assigned rooms of their own. They could not leave until the virus was under control. Morgan left and walked back down the hall to rejoin Diane, who was still in a lot of pain and waiting alone in her room.

The nurse brought in the doctor and also had rooms ready for everyone. Stephanie would be set up in the room with her husband; Freddy and Bryce were across the hall. Josh and Amber would share a room, since it was the last available room and they were brother and sister.

"Doctor, the *Gerald Ford* has agreed to process and deliver a large amount of the antidote to you by late this evening. Knowing that, when do you think we can get out of here? The longer we stay, the more danger the hospital is in. We can be transported to the *Ford* if you will allow it. Their hospital facilities are equal to yours, possibly better," Randal asked.

"If they can come and get you, I will release all of you tonight. You will be safer on the *Ford* than you will be here," the doctor agreed.

"Good, everyone get ready to move to the biggest damn carrier in the world," Randal ordered and then looked at Craft and nodded.

Craft called the frigate which quickly called the *Gerald Ford* and got confirmation that the C-2H Super Greyhound would lift off within the next twenty minutes and arrive on the island in about two hours. They asked to have all patients transported to the helipad for transport to the carrier. The C2-H was the newest version of an old standard in aircraft design, not requiring a runway or the use of the catapult the earlier models of the Greyhound needed to get off the carrier. The C2-H super Greyhound was a jet powered, vertical takeoff and landing transport aircraft capable of carrying two squads of marines and equipment or up to twenty-four passengers. Moving Randal and his team along with their marine protection would be a piece of cake for this aircraft.

"Rambo one, two," Craft's radio spoke.

"Go ahead, this is one," Craft responded.

"Negative on target."

"Roger, return to the coffee shop."

"Was that your team?" Randal asked.

"Yes, negative contact, but we are getting closer. The C-2 will be here soon; you may want to start getting ready to move."

Two hours and ten minutes later, Randal was being wheeled out to the helipad followed by his wife and team. Craft and his team had a watchful eye on their surroundings.

Stepping out of the shadows, Visalia walked out toward the group with his hands held on the top of his head. Behind him were two of Craft's marines assisting Visalia along.

"Lieutenant look what we found in the bushes," Rambo Three team leader said as they walked toward Randal's group. "What do you want to do with him; kind of skinny, should we throw him back?"

"Cuff him to the landing gear," Craft commented smiling.

"You got it sir," Three said and started to walk over to the landing gear with a protesting Visalia.

"He had two local bad boys with him; we turned them over to the local pros," Three commented and then added, "It was almost like he wanted to be stopped, go figure."

"No wait, the crew chief will not want to clean up the mess he will make to the side of his bird; just cuff him to a seat and keep an eye on him. Call the other teams in. I will call the boat and have another C-2 come and get them. Have them assemble at the Coast Guard helipad."

"Thanks Doc," Randal said to the doctor as they boarded the C-2.

"Let's go home; well, our temporary floating home. I guess when he saw the C-2 landing at the hospital helipad, he decided it was time to do some business, but didn't count on your men waiting for him. Not real bright, but I guess he thought it might be his last chance to complete his mission." Craft stated as he helped Randal on board.

Minutes later, the C-2 lifted off the helipad and banked toward the ocean for its two-hour flight to the *Gerald Ford*. At the same time, a second C-2H lifted off the deck of the aircraft carrier *Gerald Ford* and headed toward Easter Island to pick up the other teams.

Chapter 66 Recovery Isn't Easy

The flight to Howard Air Force Base in Panama was uneventful, but long. Stephanie Randal slept most of the way; and when they finally landed, she was greeted by a very hot, humid day. The temperature was close to one hundred degrees; and the humidity was so thick, the pilot almost had to abort the landing. Rain in Panama usually fell in buckets; heavy thick drops would slam into the earth with the force equal to ten million buckets of water being poured on a small spot of the planet. After fighting the rain and wind, the pilot slipped the C-2 onto the runway with a small chirp of the tires.

Stephanie stepped out of the C-2 and stood for a moment under the wing watching the rain. It was letting up, and she hoped it would stop before the C-2 had to move. The pilot walked up behind her, and watched the rain. "It's coming down pretty heavy, Mrs. Randal. Sorry, I don't have any umbrellas in the bird," he said.

"It is slowing down, should stop soon. It always does down here. Rains heavy for twenty minutes, stops, and starts again in an hour or so."

"Been here before?"

"Yeah, Josh and I spent some time down here a few years ago, enjoying the sites and entertainment," she answered.

"How is Mr. Randal? I thought he was coming."

"His infection has not cleared up like the rest of ours; still, we were stuck on your carrier for three days more than expected. Glad your doctor is top notch, got the antidote and fixed us right up. But he and Diane were not healing as fast, so he would not release him."

"Hey, you were right; it is almost stopped," the pilot commented as they started to walk toward the terminal. They were stopped halfway across by two individuals dressed in dark slacks and white shirts; neither one wore a tie, but wore a dark suit jacket, which obviously hid the sidearms they carried.

"Mrs. Randal, I am FBI Agent Madeline Graves and this is Detective Hamilton Carver from the Arlington Police Department. We were sent here to escort you back to Arlington for your safety; you are not under arrest. With everything that has been happening in the metro area, it was felt by my superiors and the Arlington Police that an escort would be best," Graves said showing her credentials, Carver showed his also.

"That is very nice for your concern. Can I at least make a call before we go?" Connie asked.

"Sure, let's get inside, and you can make your call," Madeline said and led the way into the terminal. Stephanie walked over to the waiting room and sat down to dial the number she had been given.

"Hello, honey. Just landed at Howard Air Force Base and was met by my new escort, FBI agent Graves and Arlington Police Detective Carver. Do you know them?" she asked when Josh answered.

"I met Graves a few months ago on another case. She is about five four, maybe one hundred twenty pounds, nice figure, great smile, when she smiles, and natural red hair. I think it is natural, looked natural to me." Josh continued to describe Graves.

"Yeah that's her, she must have been memorable."

"I called and asked for her to meet you when we decided you would take my place," Josh said, "You may need the extra help anyway."

"I appreciate the confidence you have in me." Connie replied.

"I didn't mean it that way. Having some inside help is not a bad thing. Go with it," Josh pleaded quietly, feeling like he just got slapped.

"It's okay, honey. They may be helpful in the long run; we have a lot to explain and it will be just my word," Stephanie finally agreed. "Look, I have to go; they are getting antsy, and I just heard that the G-5 is ready to leave. The weather is going to get worse down here, and they want to be above it as quickly as possible," she said and then added "I will call when we get to D.C. Bye."

"Good bye, honey and be safe."

The G-5 left the ground fifteen minutes later and immediately disappeared into the clouds. The ride was not smooth. They were bounced around for the next fifteen minutes, until they broke through the clouds to a dark blue sky. The discussion on the corporate jet ranged from the kidnapping of Josh and Stephanie to their escape on board the old *Freedom* yacht. She did not leave anything out and included the escape on the yacht that had been anticipated and was well planned by Soto to include the food being poisoned. She also discussed how the capture of Captain Visalia, Soto's head assassin, was planned and executed.

They touched down at ten minutes after nine that evening, and boarded a waiting SUV which took them to a safe house in Alexandria. Plans were made to go to the Hoover

Building, home of the FBI, and have Stephanie fill out a statement. Once that was done, it would take some time to get the charges dropped on Little Josh and Amber. No charges were ever made for the supposed kidnapping of the President since he was never missing. Getting Tony Sanford out of the charges of murder would be a bit more difficult and might never happen.

"What about Davin Pierce?" she asked Madeline.

"That is another problem. We have an eye witness. His weapon was used in the crime. His finger prints are on the gun, and he was not seen at CIA during the time he was seen supposedly killing Adam Cruz. When we find him, he will be charged with first degree murder along with a list of other charges. Right now, he is a fugitive and will be captured, tried and convicted of murder. Virginia does not have the death penalty, lucky for him; but he is looking at no less than life without parole."

"Damn!" was all Stephanie could say. "And the President?"

"He is being held at a safe house under heavy guard and a suicide watch. He was caught with the murder weapon in his hand outside the White House grounds. He says he didn't do it, that he was kidnapped by your husband and Mr. Pierce. But we have no way of knowing that is true, since he was still in the Oval Office and was seen by everyone until he killed three high ranking members of his staff in the office. He can't explain that away. The jury will find him guilty and he will be sentenced to life without parole also," Madeline stated.

"That is not good. I have known Tony Sanford for more than thirty years; he could not have killed them in cold blood. It is not his nature."

"The stress of the job could have caused him to crack."

"No way, Maddie; who was the last to see him?"

"The White House Secretary as he left his office and walked down the hall was the last to see him. He passed by two Secret Service agents and went through the kitchen and out the back door to the garden. The gardener saw him walking around the property, but paid little attention to him and kept working on the garden. He did say he saw a Secret Service agent coming from the back of the property who had entered the White House," Maddie said sitting in the conference room discussing the different cases.

"I am about to tell you something that may blow this whole thing wide open."

Chapter 67 The Dump

Arlington, Virginia, a very large city, located near Washington, D.C., was not far from Langley, home of CIA Headquarters. The National Security Agency, commonly known as NSA, was also nearby. Many years before Josh Randal and Davin Pierce started working for the company, the two agencies would not share any information collected. And it went even deeper than that; none of the intelligence organizations would share anything directly. The analysis and linking of all the information together fell on one organization, known unofficially as *The Dump*. Inside the Dump was a collection of analysts from each organization: CIA, FBI, Army, Navy, NSA, state and local police and the rest of the alphabet organizations that collected all sorts of intelligence.

Before Josh and Davin became major players at the company, they worked with many of the life time players at some of those organizations. Davin, Josh and Stephanie had hopes of being able to utilize some of the expertise and talents they knew still worked at the Dump.

Davin dressed and disguised as Kelly Donavan had just contacted an old friend that knew him as Kelly. They agreed to meet later that day at a restaurant in Arlington. Prior to that meeting, Kelly Donavan called the Arlington Police station and asked to speak with the officer in charge of the Davin Pierce case.

"Sorry Mr. Donavan, but the officer in charge is not available right now; his partner is here. Would you like to speak with him?" the desk sergeant asked.

"Sure," Kelly agreed and was put on hold.

"This is Sergeant Danny Baker, how can I help you Mr. Donavan?"

"I have been hired to investigate the murder of Adam Cruz and need to talk with you about that case. Can we meet sometime today?"

"Mr. Donavan, I am not at liberty to disclose any information about that case and you should know that. This is an active case. Mr. Pierce is wanted for murder and if you have any information about this case you need to come into the station and give us everything you have," Baker stated. He paused for a second and then added, "If you get any information or discover the location of Mr. Pierce and do not pass that information to us, you will be charged with obstructing justice. Do you understand, Mr. Donavan? Who hired you?"

"Now, Sergeant Baker, I can't tell you that; but I will say, they are highly placed in the government and have tasked me to represent them because they cannot."

"If you know the location of Mrs. Pierce, we need to talk to her as soon as possible," he said and then asked, "Are you working for the CIA, Mr. Donavan?"

"No."

"Then this conversation is done," Baker said and hung up.

"That was rude," Kelly Donavan said quietly as he looked at the receiver. "Guess I need to go a different way to get what I need." He disconnected the call by pressing the END button on the cell phone as he walked out of the restaurant and headed for his car. He dropped the burn phone into the trash can as he passed by knowing full well that the

Arlington police would trace any call that came into the station, just as a 'precaution'; and they had the right to do so because of the newest Patriot Act signed into law less than two years earlier.

Driving around town, proved to be a little tedious and nerve racking. It was only two in the afternoon. His meeting with his Dump friend was not until four, so he just drove, stopping once to fill up the gas tank and get a coffee, but otherwise he just drove.

At three forty-five Kelly drove to "Sammy's BBQ" just off the main street in Arlington. Kelly walked in and took a booth near the back. He waited twenty-five minutes before his friend Melodie Morris walked in and waved. She sat down across from Kelly and smiled. "Been a long time, Kelly, where have you been?"

"You know where I have been, Mel. I really need your help. I should not be asking, but I am in a real mess. I can't turn to the cops for reasons you already know; and I can't go back into the company too many more times without attracting too much attention from the local police."

"I know; and I also know I don't want to go to jail, so I can't give you anything classified. I know your clearance level was much higher than mine, but I can't do jail."

"You will not go to jail; no one will know you helped me, promise," Kelly assured her.

"You are correct that you are in deep; here is all the Dump has on the case, mostly from the FBI but a little from the police; they have been playing nicely the past few months," Melodie said as she slid a large manila envelope across the table. "Are we going to have dinner since we are here; it is the least you could do for all this."

"Sure, order anything you like, Mel," Kelly said and then signaled for the waitress to come over. After the waitress left, Kelly opened the envelope and read the documents and examined the pictures that were included. "Wow, looks like I am toast, they have enough evidence to put me away forever. And what is this? Connie is being charged with conspiracy and accessory to murder. Melodie, you did not see me or know anything about me. For your own safety I have to go, here is enough to cover your meal and a few drinks. Thank you," he said as he stood and put a hundred dollar bill on the table and then leaned down and kissed Melodie on the forehead. Without another word, Kelly left the restaurant and got into his car, driving quickly but not too quick to his motel, gathered his stuff, put the key on the dresser and left. Picking up an unused burn phone, he dialed Connie's number and told her to get ready to leave; he would be there in an hour. After hanging up, he dialed a special number that was untraceable and waited until it was picked up.

"Hello Becky, another and hopefully the last favor," Kelly said quickly.

"What do you need?"

"Backstop for Connie. I will pick it up when it is ready. Call me."

"I'll call shortly," Becky said and then hung up the phone and looked up at the man standing in front of her.

"That was good Becky. When you have it done, tell him to pick it up at the bus station in Alexandria in the usual drop site. He should still have a key; he never turned it in," Josh

348

Randal ordered Becky. "You should have told me when he called the first time, I could have helped; he is my friend."

"Yes, sir," she agreed not letting on that she knew he was a fake. "I didn't know what to do; he said not to tell anyone, even you, and something about plausible deniability."

"That makes sense; he wouldn't want to involve me, for my safety. Okay, you are right, Becky. Go ahead and do the backstop for Connie. Let me know when you are done."

"Yes, sir."

Chapter 68 Reasonable Doubt

"Becky, glad you called. Is it ready?" Kelly Donavan asked when he answered the cell phone.

"Yes, I will have it at the regular drop in an hour," she replied quickly and then added "Tell Connie to take care of you."

"Thank you, Becky, been a pleasure working with you," Kelly said and then clicked off. Standing beside his car he became worried, Becky had used the code they had developed years earlier to let the other person know if they had been compromised. He climbed into his car and pulled his Colt M1911 out of his bag and checked the magazine, ensuring it had a full load. He jacked a round into the chamber and clicked on the safety.

Driving to the bus station would take a half hour, so he decided to avoid the station in Alexandria all together; instead he headed to the alternate drop at a specific Starbucks coffee shop in Arlington. The Starbucks had been used as an agent dead drop ever since Davin and Josh moved into the main offices. Only a few operatives knew about the alternate; Becky was one of those.

Becky's warning pretty much guaranteed that the Josh Randal at the company was the fake and that the real Randal was most likely dead. Becky had to watch herself carefully, first going to Alexandria and placing a package with blank paper in the locker and then she would drive to Arlington and leave a second package with the real backstop information in it for Davin.

Josh Randal followed Becky to the bus station in Alexandria and positioned himself in his car and waited. He had not removed his mask of Josh Randal, but was acting now as Richard Kosh, hired assassin. If seen killing Pierce, he would be seen as Josh Randal which would ensure Randal going to jail for murder. He had his escape route planned and did not anticipate any problems. As he watched Becky go inside, he anticipated killing Davin Pierce just for fun. He wasn't ordered to kill him, but doing so would satisfy his ego. Soto might not be very happy about it, but what the hell; he didn't care. And just for the hell of it, he would kill Becky too. Randal would be charged with two murders.

At ten minutes to three, Richard Kosh, as Josh Randal, climbed out of his car and walked into the bus station. He took a seat across from the lockers, and pretended to read a newspaper which he had purchased at the little paper stand. He waited, knowing Pierce would show up soon. He did not have to wait long, when a tall man, built like Davin Pierce walked up to the lockers and stood there for a moment, looking for the correct locker. Richard stood and started to walk across the lobby toward the lockers, his hand on his nine millimeter Smith and Wesson pistol. Slowly he pulled it part way out of his pocket as he got closer and saw the man insert a key into the correct locker. He pulled out his pistol and leveled it at the man's back and was about to pull the trigger when he heard the words no one wants to hear just before he was about to kill.

"Drop your weapon and put your hands on your head. NOW!" the police officer ordered.

"You may want to do what he said," the tall man at the locker said as he turned around and pointed his own pistol at him with one hand and held up his badge with the other.

The officer behind him reached around and took the pistol from Richard and then proceeded to put on handcuffs and read him his rights.

"How did you know?" Richard asked.

"Little bird told us. Now let's go. You have a lot of explaining to do, Mister Randal, or should I just call you Richard?"

Hoover Building, FBI

Madeline and Stephanie were sitting in the main conference room with the Deputy Director for the FBI, District Attorney for Washington D.C, and the lead Secret Service agent from the White House. They were discussing the three murders that Tony Sanford, the President supposedly committed.

"Deputy Director Smith, I was a Miami Police officer long before you were out of high school and I know a thing or two about investigations. The evidence against the president is overwhelming, but there are some holes in it," Stephanie commented as the discussion and all the evidence was on the table.

"It is a slam dunk; he was the only one in the office. He was seen leaving the White House, and walked around the back yard in a daze. And later, he was found holding the murder weapon outside the fence at the monument. His fingerprints are on the gun and bullets; he doesn't remember leaving the White House or killing anyone. And he insists that he was kidnapped by Josh Randal and Davin Pierce, held captive for over a week and then woke up on a bench in a daze and holding his pistol. What else do we need to convict him? He killed two high ranking officers and the Secretary of the Defense in the Oval Office," Smith recanted feeling they had a case of premeditated murder in the first degree.

"I have to agree with Director Smith," the District Attorney agreed.

"What if I can throw some reasonable doubt on the fire?" Stephanie offered with half a smile.

"What do you know that we don't, Mrs. Randal?"

"First, it was reported that a Secret Service Agent was seen walking around the back forty after Mr. Sanford disappeared. Has anyone identified that agent? The answer is no; he has not come forward and nobody has seen or can identify him. The front gate guard reported that an agent drove out of the White House property shortly after the murders. Is it possible the agent is the killer, and not the president?"

"Those are all true; we have been looking for that agent, but the name he signed when he left is of an agent that was off duty; and when we confronted him, he said he was at a ballgame with his family at the time of the murders. We checked his alibi and it is rock solid; not only his family, but the entire minor league team stood up for him; he is one of the sponsors of the team. So it was an imposter. But that only proves that we had an imposter on the grounds, but not that he killed those men. I agree he could have been the killer, but the eye witness when the president walked out of the Oval Office is solid."

"Are you really going to charge the President of the United States with murder?" Stephanie argued.

"Yes, unless you can convince us otherwise, he will stand trial like any other American for committing murder," the DA stated.

"I have two more feathers to pull, and I need your indulgence on this. What I am about to show you is highly classified and cannot be shown or told to anyone outside this conference room. I only know about it because my husband is the Director of CIA and I hold a clearance level as high as his because of work I have done with the company. Do I have your agreement?"

"Of course, Mrs. Randal, if what you are about to tell us will show beyond reasonable doubt that Mr. Sanford is innocent, your secret will stay with us."

Stephanie stood and walked over to the end of the table so everyone in the room could see what she was doing. She did not speak, but slowly turned around in a complete circle and faced them, watching their faces turn from confused to shock, to amazement. She was standing in front of them, not as Stephanie Randal, but had instantly turned into the singer/actress Madonna. Without saying a word, she spun around again; and this time she was a tall oriental woman. When she spoke, everything she said was in Chinese. After spinning one last time, she stopped and looked directly at the Deputy Director; and he saw his wife. Stephanie spoke and she sounded exactly like his wife. Smiling, she started to spin again.

"How the hell are you doing that?" the director asked as he stood and started to walk around the table, but stopped when Stephanie raised her hand to stop him; she immediately turned herself back into herself and smiled.

"Do I have your attention now? It is highly possible the person that shot and killed those three was using a device similar to the one I am using," she said holding up an item that looked like a smart phone. "This is the latest in smart phone technology; the R&D section at the company has been working on this for several years. They also have technology to back this up with latex masks and fingerprint tips. Helen Owens is the head of the R&D section over there. She met with me this morning and is waiting outside this conference room to answer any of your questions. May I bring her in?" After receiving an affirmative nod from everyone, she walked over to the door, opened it, and signaled for Helen to come in. Seconds later, Helen Owens walked in and answered all their questions without touching too deep into the classified areas.

"Miss Owens, you are saying that by using that device a person could become anyone they want to be for as long as they want?" Madeline asked.

"No, not as long as they want; they will have to use a latex mask after a couple of hours; the battery on this does not last long."

"One thing you need to know. Rocky Soto was the head of CIA R&D up until a year ago, when he was fired for misappropriation and various other criminal acts. Miss Owens took over and completed the project. He may have improved the technology to a level higher than what we just showed you and has used it against us."

"That does throw a shadow over the evidence, but not completely. What else do you have? I am still not convinced. Yes, it is a pretty good trick; but without something a little more solid, we can't just drop the charges," the district attorney stated looking a lot more confused.

"Okay, Maddy, you have been talking to the Fernando Visalia and Richard Van Horn that you have in lock-up. Will you tell these fine gentlemen what they told you?" Stephanie asked.

"Mr. Visalia is actually singing like a canary, trying to save his own ass, as it were. Van Horn is cooperating but not as much; we will convince him shortly. What Visalia told us so far is pretty enlightening. He and his team of mercenaries were hired shortly after Mr. Soto was fired from the company. His job was to protect the island, and it escalated from there. With his assistance, he helped kidnap Mr. and Mrs. Randal, the Pierce kids, and the four students from the university. He also admits that Mr. Vincent Landers was in on the kidnapping. He described the use of a holographic device, Hollywood style latex masks, and something he had previously never seen. That was the use of the captives' DNA and other devices to turn one person into someone else, such as a young lady that could pose as Mrs. Randal and another as the President and so on. He wants a deal and is downstairs with a couple of my agents working out a deal and confessing to his part in the whole affair. With his confession, well, it does throw reasonable doubt on the whole case," Madeline reported.

"Damn, that does change things; I still need more information, but in light of what you have presented I will hold off on filing charges against the President," the D.A. stated.

"I suggest that we research this deeper, and in the meantime, release the President to his regular security service," Madeline suggested and received agreement around the table. "Sounds like Rocky Soto has played us, but good."

"I will put the order out right after we finish here," the Deputy Director of the FBI stated. "Charges on the Pierce kids are also going to be dropped; go ahead and call them, bring them home."

"Is it possible that the same technology was used to frame Davin Pierce?" Stephanie asked.

"Possible, but until we investigate and get more evidence for or against him, he is still considered a fugitive and will be caught," the director stated and was not smiling. "Sorry."

Chapter 69 Running Free

Six o'clock that same evening, Davin, aka, Kelly Donavan pulled into the driveway of a small ranch house forty-six miles outside of Arlington. He was here for one reason, to pick up his wife of over twenty years. He had stopped at the Starbucks and retrieved the package that Becky had left for him, examined it, and then drove straight to the ranch house. Well, almost straight, he made several detours and circled back twice to make sure he wasn't being followed.

He entered the house, walked through, and exited out the back door into the nicely landscaped yard.

"Hello, Kelly. What took you so long?" Connie asked and gave him a big hug and kiss.

"Had some unfinished business in town with the hope that what I did will help us."

"What did you do?" she asked.

"Just a little of 'Who's on first'?'" Davin said with a smile.

"It's that old Laurel and Hardy routine?"

"Yes, but the way I play, I know 'Who's on first'. Now let's get out of here before someone tracks us down."

"Where are we going?"

"To the land of the free, home of the brave."

"We are in the land of the free, home of the brave; quit kidding around. Where are we going?"

"Arizona, maybe, maybe North Dakota, not really sure, but one thing is for sure is we need to leave the east coast tonight. They have a warrant for my arrest, and one on you for aiding a suspected murderer. They will put us in jail for a very long time unless we can prove we are innocent. That is going to be difficult since I believe Josh is dead and possibly the kids and Stephanie too. We have a few allies, but basically we are on our own until we prove we are innocent."

"Okay let's go; I have my bag packed in the bedroom.

Twenty minutes later, they were heading west toward St. Louis. Connie had dyed her hair black and put on a latex mask that changed her looks enough to pass off as Mrs. Brenda Donavan, housewife.

They were running for their lives, not knowing for sure if Josh, Stephanie, and their kids were alive or dead. They had heard on the radio that the charges against the President were being dropped based on new evidence that proved he had not killed anyone. There was no news about the Randal's or his kids.

Four days later, Davin and Connie pulled into Phoenix, found a hotel for the night, and checked in. After showers, dinner, and a couple of stiff drinks, they hit the bed for a much needed rest. They were free for the time being, but would not rest easy until they found out who had killed their family and best friends.

Chapter 70 Coming Home

At twenty-three fifteen hours, Josh Randal was still in his office going over the evidence piled high in the middle of his work table. He was tired and worried about his friend Davin and his wife. The evidence was overwhelming against them; there was an eye witness, and fingerprints on the weapon that belonged to Davin that was used to kill Adam Cruz. He and his team could not talk the District Attorney out of putting a warrant out for him. Davin and Connie were on the run and he felt helpless, because he could not prove their innocence. He picked up his warm cup of coffee, and raised it to his mouth; but stopped before he was able to take a sip, because he was interrupted by his phone ringing. It was his private line, the one that was only used by a select group of field operatives.

"Randal," he said into the receiver hoping that it was good news he was about to hear but knowing it might not be.

"Are you alone?" the familiar voice asked.

"Yes, Davin, alone and very worried. Where are you?"

"Can't tell you right now, Josh."

"They have a rock solid case against you and Connie. What can I do to help you?" Josh questioned expressing his concern.

"First, I want to come in, but not to the police. They will just put us in jail, and that will not solve this." Davin stated quickly. "If I come in, I will stay at the agency until this is cleared up; if we can't figure it out, then I guess I go to jail forever."

"When do you want to come in?" Josh asked. "Before I forget, there is a warrant for you and Connie for the murder of Denise Nickels, a neighbor of yours.

"Denise? Tell me what happened," Davin responded.

"She was found in your backyard shot in the back with your gun. Why was she there?"

"I don't know. Who would kill her?"

"They say you killed her with the same weapon that killed Adam. But why, she doesn't even look like Connie, different color hair, shorter, but very pretty. Why would someone kill her, and why was she in your yard?"

"I don't know, but we will find out."

"We are trying to locate Rocky Soto; we believe he is responsible for a lot of this, but cannot find him," Josh stated.

"Three days and I will come in through the tunnel. I will call before I enter," Davin interjected.

"Okay, Davin, I will continue to work on this until we get you cleared, but I do have to ask. Why did you kill Adam? If you wanted your job back, I would have given it to you if you just asked." Josh said with a chuckle.

"Very funny, I don't want my job back; I am retired and want to live the balance of my life with my family and friends. By the way, are you and the kids completely cleared?"

"Yes, and we are working on the same angle to clear you; but with the evidence, it is very tough."

"Understand, I am innocent except for my escape from the police. I did do that, and hope Allen Siegel has been released from jail. He volunteered to help me."

"Allen was released yesterday with a warning that if he ever did something like that again, he would not see sunshine for a very long time," Josh stated

"I will be in the tunnel in three days. Turn on the air conditioner," Davin said and then disconnected the line.

Josh sat there staring at the receiver hoping that Davin and Connie would make it back to the tunnel without incident.

After looking at his coffee cup, he decided that it was time to get a fresh cup. Josh stood and walked over to the credenza and lifted the coffee pot only to find it empty. He shook his head and set it down, looked over at his desk, and then headed for the door. Ten minutes later, Josh walked into the café on the first floor and looked around at the people that were still at work at this late hour. This building was very much like Las Vegas; it never slept and never closed. As he walked over to the large coffee pots on the side wall, he nodded at a couple of his analysts and received smiles from both of them.

"Mr. Randal," a young female analyst said as he started to fill a cup.

"Good evening Janet. Don't you normally work the day shift?" he asked.

"Yes, but under the circumstances with Mr. Pierce, my team is working overtime to help clear him. I hope we are not out of line, sir."

"No, we appreciate what you are doing and we will clear him. That I am sure of."

Chapter 71 Purgatory or What

Davin and Connie were sitting in their suite at the hotel contemplating their next move. He had already made his plan to return to Virginia and they would leave in the morning, in disguise. Using his fake identification and credit cards, he was able to rent the car in Virginia with plans to drop it off in Arizona; but they changed their mind while driving, and now had made up their minds to go back and hide out in the private secret facility built in the basement of CIA Headquarters.

"Let's get dinner, Davin. I am getting a bit hungry." Connie said as she looked over at her husband, who looked very worried. "I know you are not okay, but get over it. You are innocent, and we will prove it."

"I know we will prove it, but I don't want to give away national secrets to do so. I am not sure what to do. So we go back into purgatory." He paused a second, and then said, "Let's go eat."

Twenty-five minutes later, they walked into a small bistro a few blocks from the hotel, not knowing that the bistro was a local stopping place for a lot of the Maricopa County Sheriff's department. Sitting at a table near the back, Davin and Connie ate slowly and watched as several officers came and went, none paying more attention to them than any other person in the bistro. As each officer came in, they would scan the patrons noting anything out of the ordinary as well as searching for the faces that they had seen in any of the APBs they had received over the past week or two.

"Looks like we are safe, as it were." Connie stated as she watched a couple of uniformed officers come in and order coffee and a pastry. They took seats near the door, watched the street, ate their snacks, and drank coffee, while quietly chatting.

"Yeah, for now. Let's finish and get some sleep, or do you want to leave tonight. It is still early and the sun will be up for about another hour or two."

"No, sleep, get up early, and then head out." Connie insisted and took another bite of her salad.

"You win. Up at six and on the road by seven. Should not be too much traffic since it will be Saturday."

Davin and Connie returned to their hotel room, removed their disguises, took a shower together, and watched a little television.

Nine o'clock came fairly soon, and they headed to bed. Morning would come too early for them, but they had to do this; going back was the only way to solve the problems they had.

They both were completely unsure as to the outcome and their future.

Leaving the hotel in the morning was completely uneventful for Kelly Donavan and his wife. The rental car was a midsized Chevy with a V-6 engine and four doors. After backing out, Davin headed for Interstate 10 and drove south toward Tucson. They were not in a hurry and figured the southern route would offer better weather, as Interstate 40 across the northern part of Arizona tended to get high winds and heavy storms this time of year. They also wanted to be closer to the border in case they had to run for it. The drive, without exceeding the speed limit by much, would take most of the three days they had planned. At highway speeds, it would take about eight hours to reach El Paso, and they planned on stopping on Interstate 10 around Fort Stockton.

Three days later, they pulled into a Best Western hotel. After a night's rest, they would return the car and take a cab to one of the few entrances to the tunnel.

The cab dropped them at Arlington Cemetery; they left their luggage at the Arlington Bus station in a CIA operated locker. They would have Josh get someone to retrieve the luggage and bring it in later in the day.

They walked slowly between the markers at Arlington Cemetery where they checked the dates and names of each of the military markers, reminding themselves that this country was built on their blood, sweat and tears. Davin thought maybe he was one of the lucky ones, or then again, maybe they were. He had served, bled, and nearly died while doing two tours in Viet Nam, one in Panama and his final tour during Desert Storm.

They finally reached a crypt with the names of four Marines, two sailors, and three Army Rangers that had lost their lives in World War II, Viet Nam and Desert Shield. The names were of brothers in arms who were also related by blood. They were the father, grandfather, brother and sons from a long time business man that was not able to serve himself because of a weak heart. The man was Ed Jansen, former Director of CIA, Covert Operations, from 1985 to 1995. Ed was buried with his relatives in this crypt; but besides being the final resting place for nine decorated heroes and one CIA kingpin, this vault housed the entrance to the tunnel. The fact that the tunnel was here was not well known, and the proper code to open the door for entrance was only known to a few key people. Davin Pierce was one of those key people.

"Honey, what I am about to show you is a very tightly kept secret. There are only twelve people on earth that knows about what you are about to see. I know I can trust you not to discuss this with anyone other than me."

"After all these years you have to say that?" she questioned.

"No, just wanted to see your reaction. But seriously, this is a highly classified crypt. Look around and make sure there is not anyone watching us or nearby to see us enter the crypt; we will not be coming out this way again," Davin told her quietly.

"I think we are clear. This crypt was positioned correctly to provide good visual all around. I don't see anyone paying us any attention," Connie stated as she looked around the cemetery.

"So, let's go." Davin said as they stepped up to the door of the crypt.

Davin flipped open a key box and pressed a couple of buttons which activated the electronic lock, opening the bolt. He reached the door handle and pulled it open, and they stepped inside.

Once inside, he pressed a couple of hidden buttons which caused the door to close itself and lock with a very quiet click. The lights came on as the door closed and Davin and Connie walked to the back of the crypt. They glanced at each wall to view the names of the fallen. Upon reaching the back wall, Davin turned slightly to the right and pressed a brick on the wall that was four feet from the floor. The brick turned to expose a key pad with ten numbers, an iris scanner, and a hand print pad. Davin reached forward and pressed six separate keys, leaned in and had his iris scanned, and then placed his hand on the palm reader. They waited. Within seconds, a panel in the back of the crypt slowly slid open exposing a spiral staircase going down into a very dark hole.

"We have to go down there?" Connie asked quietly and then asked, "Why a crypt?"

"Almost as secure as a bank vault; and the only relatives alive for these gentlemen are long dead and buried, just not here," Davin said and smiled, "Let's go; the light will come on as soon as we start down, and the door will automatically close and seal again. Do me a favor. Sweep our footprints away as we enter the stairs," He handed her a broom which was kept at the top of the stairs to be used to hide the escape route.

Connie took the broom and walked back to the front door. She then removed the footprints while she backed toward the stairs, and finally returned the broom to the hanger inside the stairwell.

"Let's go. All dusted," she said and stepped on the top step of the stairs and watched the door slide shut and the lights come on exposing a very deep winding staircase. "Wow, how deep is this?"

"Eleven hundred forty-four steps to the bottom level," Davin stated as he started down.

"That is, ah, about twelve hundred feet. Are we going to climb all the way down?"

"No, we climb down about forty feet, and then take the elevator the rest of the way."

Within fifteen minutes after entering the crypt, they had reached the first level. Davin pushed the button beside the elevator's door and waited.

When the elevator arrived, they stepped in and Davin opened a compartment which had another key pad. He pressed a couple of buttons, leaned in to have his iris scanned again, and pressed his hand against the palm scanner which caused the doors to close. He pressed the button for B-10 and stood back.

"Hang on," he said. The elevator dropped rapidly to level B-10. The ride lasted about forty-five seconds and then rapidly slowed and came to a stop; the doors slid open.

"Welcome to Purgatory," Davin said as they stepped off the elevator into a dimly lit hallway.

"Where are we?"

"The inner sanctum of the most powerful intelligence organization in the world; this is an area that only a few know about, and that number gets smaller every year. Commonly known among those that are in the know as Purgatory."

"Does the President know about it?"

"Yes and no, a few do, but most don't. President Sanford knows, because he has been here," Davin commented as they walked down the hallway.

"We have the executive suite, but let's stop by the kitchen to see if Josh was able to restock it."

"Sounds good, I could use a drink."

"Me, too. This way," he said as she tagged along.

Chapter 72 Trouble in the Orient

Sitting alone in the Oval Office, President Tony Sanford was in deep thought. The FBI and CIA, working together with the District Attorney, were able to shed reasonable doubt on his suspected killing of three members of his cabinet. He was innocent, but couldn't prove it himself. Right now, it was just a wild story about being kidnapped and then released on the mall with the weapon in his hand. But there was no residue on his hands which would have been there if he had fired a weapon.

Tony picked up his phone, dialed the number for Josh Randal over at CIA, and waited until it was picked up.

"Good afternoon, Mr. President. How can the company help?"

"We need to talk. I am sitting here trying to figure out how they were able to fool everyone. Can you be here by four o'clock?"

"Sure, see you at four."

"And bring your wife and that FBI agent Graves." Tony requested.

"Okay, no problem, see you at four," Josh said and then hung up his phone.

Tony went back to reviewing the documents on his desk. He did not like what he was reading. He stopped for a moment, looked at his phone again, and then decided to get his National Security Advisor in his office now. Fifteen minutes later, his NSA knocked on the door and entered.

"Come on in; it looks like we have a situation brewing in the South China Sea, and North Korea is rattling sabers again. What the hell do you know about this that isn't in the report?"

"Sir, that report is about all we have at the moment. Our sources are working on getting more information on both areas. What we don't know is why the North Koreans fired on the Chinese cruiser. The Chinese are being tight lipped about the incident, and the Koreans rarely admit to anything. Our satellites show a burning cruiser listing heavily and lots of oil around the ship."

"Okay, so your guys are watching the area closely; when you get any update, please bring it to me. If they start fighting, they may drag Japan in which will drag us in too. I don't want to go to war again; the terrorists in the Middle East were enough for any one President, and it lasted through four administrations. I am damn glad it was done before I took office."

"I know, it was pretty bad for a while, but finally it is quiet over there; and we haven't had any attacks in, let's see, about seven years now," the NSA stated with a smile.

"North Korea hasn't been causing any problems since 2018, what has them up in arms now?" Sanford asked.

"What little we can pull together is that China actually started it. Not the shooting, but China decided to put restrictions on imports from North Korea. They said the North Korean products were defective and hurting the Chinese market. North Korea says they were not selling defective products, and had been selling the same products to many countries including us as part of our international relations and fair trade with everyone."

"Why now?"

"North Korea is a loose cannon and has been for many years. They tried to reunite with the South a few years ago and failed," the NSA stated.

"Okay, keep me posted. Now go and find out what the hell is going on out there," Tony Sanford said.

"Millie, let me know when Randal and his crew get here," Sanford said to his secretary as he stood in the doorway of the Oval Office.

Later a knock on the door to the Oval Office broke the silence in the room and startled Tony Sanford. He had been looking over the daily Intelligence report again; and again, not liking what he was seeing. The NSA had answered his questions, well almost. There was something missing; and he didn't like not knowing which is why he called his longtime friend to come by. The CIA had ways of finding out about things that were not generally publicized or even passed on to the President without directly being asked. He was about to ask two very pointed questions.

After he got up from his desk, he walked over to the door which had been locked to keep from being disturbed. He glanced for a moment at his watch, and noted it was ten minutes to four. Since it was time for his guests to arrive, he unlocked the door and pulled it open. He found Millie standing there smiling.

"Your visitors are here, sir," she stated quietly.

"Thank you; let them pass, if they know the password," Tony said as a joke.

"I think they do; may I ask what it is today?" she replied as she played along.

"Have you got a beer?" he responded and then added, "The answer should be 'Yes, and it is very cold'."

"Is that a hint?" she asked.

"Yes, please. Show them in." Tony said with a smile and then greeted Josh, Stephanie and Madeline Graves. "I just ordered some refreshments; come on in and have a seat. We have a lot to discuss. Hello again Miss Graves, glad you could make it on such short notice."

"No problem, sir. Anytime the most powerful man on the planet calls I will come running. And please call me Maddie."

"Thank you, nonetheless. I have several questions that I believe you can help me with," he said, and then waited for everyone to take a seat around the coffee table.

"I asked you three here to help me get my head around two, maybe three things that are bothering me and will not stop until I fully understand what the hell happened, and what is being done to fix this and a couple of other national security problems we have."

Chapter 73 Resolutions

Somewhere in the South Pacific, Rocky Soto and his team were cruising along at a nice slow pace of about seven knots in their converted freighter.

"When do we arrive in Tahiti, dad?" Horatio asked as they sat eating some dinner in the galley.

"We should be pulling in tomorrow morning," Rocky Soto commented between bites of food. "But we will not be staying long, just time enough to restock and refuel and then we leave."

"Good, I'm getting tired of this tub," Horatio stated and then asked, "Do you really think the North Koreans will fall for those phony videos you made?"

"Oh, yeah, didn't you see the news this morning? No? The North Koreans almost sunk a Chinese frigate; and I do believe, it is all because of our little video of the Prime Minister and our little girl. We will broadcast the next one later tonight. And by the way, this will be our home for another couple of weeks, so get used to it."

"If it works, won't they start a war?"

"Maybe, but what I really want is the United States to get real nervous and forget about looking for us, at least for a while, anyway," Rocky said smiling at his plan. "If a war starts, so be it. We will be safely tucked away causing as much disruption as we can from afar."

White House

"Josh will you and your lovely wife please explain to me in layman's terms what the hell is going on. How did you clear me? Where is Mr. Pierce and his wife? That would be good to start with; no, first explain to me about your being kidnapped and your escape. I am so confused."

An hour and two beers later, Josh and Stephanie had finished explaining to President Tony Sanford the entire sequence of events and how it was done. They went into detail, with Madeline Graves' input, on how he was kidnapped and set up as a murderer.

"Pretty elaborate hoax. And you think this Rocky Soto is behind it all, developing a super holographic system that works so well that a person could become anyone they wanted, all the way down to finger prints and DNA. Wow, amazing, simply amazing."

"We thought so too," Madeline said.

"I still find it hard to believe, but you have found enough proof to make sure we are cleared from all bad doings?" Tony asked.

"Yes, all is good," Madeline stated.

"One final question about the holographic stuff, do we have technology as good as his?"

"No, ours is good, but not as good as theirs. We are working on it, but are still a long way from being able to turn a person into someone else that is an exact copy of the original. We can change into someone else with a portable holo generator and add fingerprint tips to disguise the fingers, but cannot change the person's DNA, even on a temporary basis."

"Okay, when?"

"We are working on it; can't give you a definitive date, but maybe within a year or less," Josh replied.

"Miss Graves, what are you doing to track down Mr. Soto?" Tony asked.

"Well, that is the rub, Mr. President; we are kind of dead in the water as it were. We know Mr. Soto is possibly behind this and the one person we have in custody is talking, but not giving any names. He is a mercenary with a long rap sheet, so he will be doing time for his involvement but is only talking to save his own butt. He has asked for a deal and we are prepared to give him something for more information. He told us about the holographic kidnappings and the compound on the island, but will not incriminate himself. Even so, what he has admitted to will get him a nice long stay at one of our federal prisons."

"Miss Graves, thanks for coming down; I need to talk to Josh on some other matters. Do you need a ride back to your office or home?"

"No, sir, I have my car out front. If you have any more concerns or questions please call me," Madeline said and stood to leave. She reached out with her hand to take President Sanford's out stretched hand.

"Thank you," Sanford said and walked her over to the door and spoke quietly to her before she exited the room.

"Josh, can we talk openly," Sanford asked indicating that Stephanie was still in the room.

"Yes, Stephanie has a clearance as high as mine and has the 'need to know' to almost everything that goes on down at the company," Josh replied understanding that the President was concerned about having his wife in on this discussion.

"What is the CIA doing to track down Mr. Soto? And before I forget, where is Mr. Pierce?"

"First off, I have field ops around the world looking for anything that will lead us to Soto. If he sets foot on any piece of land, we will find him."

"You have agents on every bit of land around the world? Your budget must be way too high to afford that."

"No, you know we don't have agents all over the place, but we do have informants that have been alerted with photos and descriptions; and they will report to their handler, who may or may not be in the same country."

"I know; remember, I was FBI for many years before turning into a political chump."

"Anything else?"

"The use of satellites is not feasible until we locate what continent he is on and then we can track him."

"Do you think he has anything to do with the Chinese and North Korea incident in the South China Sea?"

"I wouldn't rule out anything with Soto."

"Now, Mr. Pierce, and before you say anything, I know he is in Purgatory and I also know he did not kill Adam Cruz. But I do need him to stay a wanted man and his wife a wanted woman."

"How do you know he is there? I thought I was the only one that knew."

"He called me this morning and told me everything," Tony replied.

"Why do you want him to stay on the run?"

"By the way, Ms Graves also knows that Davin is innocent, and is keeping the case open to help his cover story," Sanford started to explain, "I need Davin and Connie to infiltrate a known militia group located in North Dakota. They are starting to cause some friction between the local authorities, Homeland Security and the FBI. It is a dangerous assignment; and well, I need you to brief them and provide whatever you can in techie stuff that they could use."

"Are you sure they are the best to do this? And why us? Our charter prevents us from running ops on U.S. soil."

"Well that's why they are best for this. They are no longer CIA; they are rogue and wanted by the FBI for a double murder. Evidence is pointing toward Connie as the shooter of the woman found in their backyard."

"Who planted that evidence?"

"I have been working with Ms Graves, and she helped there. Now here is the location of the militants; the name of the head man is Brian Every, or at least that is what he is calling himself."

"Why are you, President of the United States, dolling out assignments?"

"It's personal; and since you will find out sooner or later, I will tell you right now. Brian is my brother, actually my half-brother, from my dad's second marriage. Two years after my mom passed away, I was ten at the time, he remarried and they had Brian. His real name is Brian Sanford. It's a long story; but to make it short, I went off to college, joined the FBI, and you know the rest, because you came into my life while I was with the FBI. To the point, Brian was able to send me a coded message with a warning."

"Your brother? How? We thought you were an only child. A warning?" Stephanie asked.

"Yes, I will explain that part later, but he is my brother; and we have not spoken since he joined this group. He recently told me that the group he is with is getting ready for war and they have developed a plan to attack Washington D.C. and kill me. He doesn't want me dead, and will do anything to prevent that. He also knows I am assigning some undercover agents to join his group to help him stop the attack. He did say they have the equipment and personnel to do the job."

"Do you trust him?" Stephanie asked concerned for her friends.

"Yes, he is not a killer; he joined this militia under orders from me; and to pretend he was against how our government was being run. He did some rallies with them, nothing violent. The group's original head man was arrested for punching a police officer and ended up being convicted and sentenced to three years. He didn't last long, some red blooded American criminals decided that his militia group was anti-American and he was killed. Brian was appointed the new commander of the group; but his lieutenants are pushing to overthrow the government, and are making plans to do so without his assistance. He is playing along so he doesn't get killed. I need Davin and Connie to infiltrate the group, link up with Brian, and stop this plan before it happens."

"Tall order, but we will make it happen," Josh agreed and then asked, "Is he Secret Service?"

"Yes."

The story continues in "Target"

Reference Information

Information from Wikipedia, the free encyclopedia

USS *Triton* **(SS-201)**, a Tambor class submarine, was the first submarine and third ship of the United States Navy to be named for Triton, a mythological Greek god, the messenger of the sea. Her keel was down on 5 July 1939 by the Portsmouth Navy Yard. She was launched on 25 March 1940, sponsored by Mrs. Ernest J. King, wife of Rear Admiral King, and commissioned on 15 August 1940 with Lieutenant Commander Willis A. "Pilly" Lent (Class of 1925)[8] in command.

USS Triton SS-201

Final Patrol

Falling under the strict tactical control of Admiral James Fife, Jr., *Triton* (now in the hands of George K. MacKenzie) on 16 February began her sixth and final war patrol, hoping to destroy enemy shipping between the Shortland Basin and Rabaul. She reported smoke on 22 February and a new Japanese radar at Buka. On 6 March, the submarine attacked a convoy of five destroyer-escorted ships, sinking the cargo ship *Kiriha Maru* and damaging another freighter. One of her torpedoes made a circular run, and *Triton* went deep to evade it. She attacked another convoy on the night of 8 March and claimed that five of the eight torpedoes she had fired scored hits. She could not observe the results or make a follow-up attack because gunfire from the escorts forced her down. On 11 March, *Triton* reported she was chasing two convoys, each made up of five or more ships. She was informed *Trigger* (SS-237) was operating in an adjoining area and ordered to stay south of the equator. On 13 March, *Triton* was warned that three enemy destroyers, including the *Akikaze* were in her area either looking for a convoy or hunting American submarines.

On 15 March, *Trigger* reported she had attacked a convoy and had been depth charged. Even though attacks on her ceased, she could still hear distant depth charging for about an hour. No further messages from *Triton* were ever received. Post-war examination of Japanese records revealed on 15 March 1943, three Japanese destroyers attacked a submarine a little northwest of *Triton's* assigned area and subsequently observed an oil slick, debris, and items with American markings. On 10 April 1943, *Triton* was reported overdue from patrol and presumed lost, one of three lost in a month. This gave her 6,500 tons for the trip to Brisbane.

Amelia Mary Earhart (/ˈɛərhɑːrt/; July 24, 1897 – disappeared July 2, 1937) was an American aviation pioneer and author. Earhart was the first female aviator to fly solo across the Atlantic Ocean. She received the U.S. Distinguished Flying Cross for this record. She set many other records, wrote best-selling books about her flying experiences and was instrumental in the formation of The Ninety-Nines, an organization for female pilots. Earhart joined the faculty of the Purdue University aviation department in 1935 as a visiting faculty member to counsel women on careers and helps inspire others with her love for aviation. She was also a member of the National Woman's Party, and an early supporter of the Equal Rights Amendment.

During an attempt to make a circumnavigation flight of the globe in 1937 in a Purdue-funded Lockheed Model 10 Electra, Earhart disappeared over the central Pacific Ocean near Howland Island. Fascination with her life, career and disappearance continues to this day.

The **Tuskegee Airmen** /tʌsˈkiːgiː/ is the popular name of a group of African-American military pilots (fighter and bomber) who fought in World War II. Officially, they formed the 332nd Fighter Group and the 477th Bombardment Group of the United States Army Air Forces. The name also applies to the navigators, bombardiers, mechanics, instructors, crew chiefs, nurses, cooks and other support personnel for the pilots. The Tuskegee Airmen were the first African-American military aviators in the United States Armed Forces. During World War II, black Americans in many U.S. states were still subject to the Jim Crow laws and the American military was racially segregated, as was much of the federal government. The Tuskegee Airmen were subjected to discrimination, both within and outside the army. All black military pilots who trained in the United States trained at Moton Field, the Tuskegee Army Air Field, and were educated at Tuskegee University, located near Tuskegee, Alabama; the group included five Haitians from the Haitian Air Force (Alix Pasquet, Raymond Cassagnol, Pelissier Nicolas, Ludovic Audant, and Eberle Guilbaud). There was also one pilot from Port of Spain, Trinidad, Eugene Theodore.[3]

Pilots of the 332nd Fighter Group at Ramitelli Airfield, Italy; from left to right, LT Dempsey W. Morgan, LT Carroll S. Woods, LT Robert H. Nelron, Jr., Captain Andrew D. Turner, and LT Clarence P. Lester